W9-AJS-119

My Life and Adventures

Also by Castle Freeman, Jr.

Judgment Hill

Spring Snow: The Seasons of New England from The Old Farmer's Almanac

The Bride of Ambrose and Other Stories

My Life and Adventures

A Novel

Castle Freeman, Jr.

St. Martin's Press
New York

Note: *My Life and Adventures* is a work of fiction. It contains some particulars of the state of Vermont that are fact, and it contains some truthful historical matter on the United States, generally. Everything else in the book is invented and corresponds to the existing condition of things only by chance.

 For information, address St. Martin's Press, 175 Fifth Avenue, New York, N.Y. 10010.

www.stmartins.com

Library of Congress Cataloging-in-Publication Data

Freeman, Castle.
My life and adventures : a novel / Castle Freeman.
p. cm.
ISBN 0-312-28261-3
1. Vermont—Fiction. 2. Latin America—Fiction. 3. Inheritance and succession—Fiction.
I. Title.

PS3556.R3838 M9 2002
813'.54--dc21 2001058859

First Edition August 2002

10 9 8 7 6 5 4 3 2 1

For Alice

Contents

Yes, take it all around, there is quite a good deal of information in the book. I regret this very much, but really it could not be helped: information appears to stew out of me naturally, like the precious ottar of roses out of the otter. Sometimes it has seemed to me that I would give worlds if I could retain my facts; but it cannot be. The more I calk up the sources, and the tighter I get, the more I leak wisdom.

—MARK TWAIN, *Roughing It*

Truly in vain is salvation hoped for from the hills, and from the multitude of mountains.

—KING JAMES BIBLE: *Jeremiah 3:23*

1. Where I Lived and How I Came There

1

Between two and three every summer afternoon on Bible Hill, a railroad train seemed to pass through the sky above the valley to the east. You couldn't see it, but you'd hear it, distinctly, not its whistle but its progress, the unmistakable rattle and bang of cars bumping over switches in a yard. Where? Trains still ran through Brattleboro, but Brattleboro was twenty-five miles away, and it lay south, not east. The sound of the train I heard every day seemed to come over the hill from where the village ought to be. There was no railroad down there. I about made up my mind I was hearing a train that went through Brattleboro, its rattle somehow being reflected back to Bible Hill off the clouds. But you'd hear it on days when there were no clouds, and anyway, the trains in Brattleboro went through at night.

There is a Hawthorne story, "The Celestial Railway." It's a slight thing, not a story at all, really, but a kind of game or sally in the arch, allegorical mode that, with Hawthorne, passes for high spirits. I don't think he ever was a great writer, but he made great titles, and *the celestial railway* gets perfectly the invisible train that ran in the sky above the Dead River in those days. We had all that up here. We had roads that went no place, villages that had disappeared, strange animals and birds, a vanished aristocracy of the mad, trains that weren't there, witty lawyers.

It was that kind of place altogether, Bible Hill. Still is.

Consider the state of Vermont, one of those parts of our enormous country that people in other parts, even distant parts, think they know something about. They think they know good things; green hills, cows, little farms, covered bridges, white-steepled villages, country roads. And they think they know other things: impoverished hollows, failing schools, disintegrating communities, a more and more embittered class consciousness, lazy citizens and zealous magistrates who would make their tiny state large as the last redoubt of a hell-bent and complacent socialism. All these things America thinks it knows about its next-to-smallest state. It doesn't. It knows nothing—or close enough.

For my part, I couldn't have found Vermont on the map, didn't even know its iconography, the hills, cows, and the rest; knew only an obscure president, a beloved old poet, and an importer of Irish woolens who advertised in the copies of the *Saturday Review of Literature* that lay unread on my mother and stepfather's coffee table in Chicago.

But ignorance acknowledged is enlightenment commenced—all the classics agree on that. I was lucky to know nothing of the place. As an old writer has said, where the Green Mountain State was concerned, I was blessed by a happy combination of defects, natural and acquired. We Noons are fortunate in our lacks, fortunate in our failures. And it's a good thing we are, because we lack much and we fail not seldom.

How could it be otherwise, when there is so much to see and

understand—so much history, so much science? The celestial railway is a weather sign, I have lately learned. Distant sounds in the sky, clearly heard—church bells, forges, voices, artillery, bands of music—mean the weather is going to change. It's all perfectly well understood and has to do with the increase in water vapor in the atmosphere that precedes a cyclonic system or an anticyclonic system or whatever you please. Now, if the sounds are made by bells, trains, guns, bands, and so on that *aren't there at all,* will the changing weather be imaginary, too? No: the weather's always real.

The other day, I came home up Bible Hill by the back way and had to stop for twenty, twenty-five wild turkeys that were crossing the road. I sat there in the middle of the woods and watched while they crossed before me like a file of clockwork grenadiers on parade. They can hardly fly. The big toms stand to the height of your waist or higher. Wild turkeys demonstrate better than do less absurd species how nature shaped the birds out of reptilian stuff, for they have a kind of antediluvian look: a class of minor dinosaurs, snake-necked and gaited like a palsied drum major. There are more preposterous birds in Tasmania, perhaps.

On Bible Hill, they are hunted. They are hunted but almost never killed, for they are the sharpest, shiest thing in the woods, and they keep hours that defeat the grimmest hunter. To kill a turkey, you must rise in the middle of the night, cover yourself, your clothes, your shotgun with brown and green paint, enter the woods, pick your spot, hide yourself, and get set, all not less than two hours before first light. Then you must remain utterly motionless, noiseless, scarcely breathing, waiting for the gray hour when the turkeys leave their roosts in the pine and hemlock thickets and go forth. Out there in the humid woods, hugging the soft dark ground, you hold yourself ready, watchful, but entirely still as three-thirty becomes three-thirty-five, becomes three-thirty-seven. . . . Of course the sun wakes you around eight. The mosquitoes have drunk your blood, the ticks have communicated to you every kind of obscure and incurable disease, and the damp earth has fused your joints. The turkeys are long gone. You might as well get to your feet, if you can, and stagger out. Don't forget to unload your gun.

All up and down the state, any summer morning in season between three and four, the woods are full of thousands of turkey hunters curled up on the ground, embracing their Winchesters. They are fast asleep. No, they are in a state deeper than sleep; they are in a state of suspended animation. They might be enormous chrysalids, harmless, unknowing, bewitched, like a hall full of courtiers in a fairy tale, while all around them the turkeys parade among the trees in perfect safety, their heads bobbing to their stilted stride.

DOWN THERE

There was a man called Pablo, a Bolivian (he said), who was a driver for the Unibank grandees and who was supposed to do a little on the side in the pimping line. Well, the driver part was true—we had Pablo driving them all around the capital—and so why not the rest, as well? Certainly drivers, chauffers, taximen, and their like all over the world are the ones who can tell you where to go. It's something everybody knows.

Hitchcock liked it at the time. Pimps are gold because they understand cash, they are fearless, and if you have one of them, then you have his girls, his boys, his sacred objects, whatever they are; and if you have them, then you have their clients—and Bob's your uncle. Hitchcock liked it well enough. We called Pablo "Asset: Peabody." I was his banker.

The week Peabody came up with someone who knew someone who was partners in a certain air charter company that was owned by a salvage outfit out of Panama City, Hitchcock had gone home to his class reunion at St. Paul's or St. Mark's or wherever you please. There were only the two of us down there. I had the watch alone. Peabody wanted to meet. I was authorized to do that. We went to the bar at the airport. Peabody was ready to do business. He needed fifty thousand U.S. right now, or we could forget the whole thing. Peabody had more than a story. He had a sample, in a carry-on bag from Air France. He showed it to me. It wasn't light verse, and it wasn't Kellogg's cornflakes. I held on to it and closed with Peabody. I was authorized to do that, too, at the time.

Hitchcock returned from the dreaming spires and antique towers to the land of the palm and the pit viper, to find no Peabody, no Pablo, no fifty thousand. The sample, we discovered at last, came out of an old B-17. It was practically an antique. Where did he get it? The thing was, I had produced the same kind of result before, more than once, though never so expensively.

"Let me understand," said Hitchcock. "He told you they were moving a lot of these?"

"A container," I said.

"Exactly. And he left this one with you?"

I nodded.

"And on the strength of this, you released how much?"

"Fifty K."

"My God," said Hitchcock. The thing sat on his desk. It looked most like an old-fashioned coffee grinder.

"Mark, Mark," Hitchcock said. "This is not your game, Mark."

I said nothing.

"This is not your game," Hitchcock said again. "You might try the priesthood. It doesn't matter if they believe what their people tell them."

"I'm not a Catholic," I said.

"Well, well," said Hitchcock, "they'll take anybody these days, I'm told."

Hitchcock's telephone rang. He picked it up, listened. Looked at me.

"Who is it that wants him?" he said into the phone. He listened again. "Just a moment. I'll find him."

"For you," he said. "Someone named Appletree. Know him, do you?"

"No."

"It may be someone from the embassy, someone acting for Peabody," said Hitchcock. "Take it at your desk. Record it."

I went to my desk, started the recorder, picked up the phone. I heard the hollow, rasping echo of the long-distance lines. I said, "Hello?"

There you are, son.

Hello?

Is that Noon? Mark Noon?

Yes.

You are a hard young fella to get ahold of, you know that?

Really?

I guess. I been trying to get a hold of you for a week. I thought you lived in Michigan.

I used to. Now I'm here.

They gave me a number in—where was it? Not Detroit.

Ann Arbor.

That was it. College boy, I guess?

Who is this, please?

Ann Arbor. Michigan. University of Michigan. Football school. Big Ten. My name is Orlando Applegate. I'm an attorney at law, son. Up here in Ambrose. I'm an attorney here in Ambrose, Vermont.

Okay.

I'm the attorney for the estate of Hugo Usher. That name mean anything to you?

Yes.

The estate provides for a bequest to Penelope Noon.

I'm not Penelope Noon.

You're her son, ain't you?

That's right.

She's dead, ain't she?

Yes.

You got no brothers or sisters, do you?

No.

Then you'll do.

A bequest, you said?

That's right.

What kind of bequest?

Cash money, son.

That's the way Lawyer Applegate talked. He said *ain't.* He said *don't.* He said *son.* Lawyers hereabouts in Mr. Applegate's day talked that way because they wished to sound like farmers. They wished to sound like farmers for business reasons: At the time, lawyers were few up here, farmers many. Today farmers are few, lawyers many, and so they don't try to talk like farmers anymore. *Cash money, son.*

You're kidding.

So help me. Cash and securities, some pretty good securities, some not so. You got . . . let's see. You got GM here. Here's Texaco. Here's the Royal Typewriter Company. I'd sell that one, I believe.

Right.

Then there's another part of the bequest, too.

What's that?

A house. Old place. A little land. Used to be Claude Littlejohn's place. Of course, Claude's been gone what, seven years?

Where?

Where what, son?

Where's the place?

Where? Where'd you think? It's right up on the hill here. I'd pack my bag and come and get it if I were you.

How much, uh . . . What sums are involved here, did you say, Mr. Applegate? Mr. Applegate, is it?

Orlando Applegate, attorney at law. I didn't. I didn't say, son. I said the bequest was cash and real property.

Exactly. And the amount of cash?

A hundred and fifty thousand dollars.

Say again?

A hundred thousand dollars and a half.

You're joking.

No joke, son. And the real estate. Don't forget the real estate. The house. And the land. Together.

Yes. How's this, Mr. Applegate? Send the hundred and fifty thousand. We'll see about the rest. How's that?

Nope.

Nope?

Can't do it, son. Bequest says cash portion to be paid over when and only when you take up residence on the other portion, put it that way.

Come on. He can't do that. It's like an entail.

A which?

An entail. It's medieval. He can't do that. Can he?

Usher? I guess he can. Hugo can do whatever he wants, son. He's dead. He's gone. Been seven years, nearer eight. It's in his will. Sure he can do it.

Okay. No problem. I'll sell the place.

Well, that might not be the easiest thing.

Why not?

I'll tell you what, son. Your best move might be if you could get on back here and have a look for yourself.

I can't do that, Mr. Applegate. I don't have furlough till next year.

Furlough? What's that you're in there? The army?

No.

Jail?

No.

Well then, if you ain't in the army and you ain't in jail, why, you can quit and come ahead.

I don't know, Mr. Applegate. I'll have to think about it.

Do that. I would.

Where can I reach you?

Right here. Central-seventeen.

What's that?

That's a telephone number, son.

All right, Mr. Applegate. I'll think about what you've told me. I call you.

Call collect.

Sure.

When?

Soon.

2

Years ago, probably a third of the people on Bible Hill, and in the township that contained it, were profoundly, irredeemably peculiar. I'm talking about men and women who were not ill, not psychotic, exactly, but very, very odd and making no effort at all to act otherwise; men and women in a concentration that today would give the town its own page in the *DSM.* There was the lady who collected sticks. There was the veteran of the American Expeditionary Force who had had both his legs shot away in the Argonne forest and who sat in his wheelchair outside the post office in fair weather, challenging those who went in and out to a footrace. There was the gentleman who in all seasons went about his business in the town pushing a big schoolroom clock in a hand barrow. There was the green lady. There was the pickle king. And, mind you, these were in the village. In the surrounding hills were failing farms where the conduct of the farmers and their wives, their dependents, even their livestock won't bear thinking about to this day. On Bible Hill, at the place down the road from this house, the old fellow, after the death of his wife, lived for twenty years on nothing but potatoes. He didn't throw away the peelings. He tossed them into a corner of the kitchen. They piled to the ceiling. One summer day, the potato skins took fire like a rotting haymow and burned the place to the ground, and the owner with it.

Think about it: A third of the town was running at least a quart low. Why? Are we talking about a place like one of those trans-Alpine villages dear to the pioneer ethnologists, where all the men had eight fingers and all the women had twelve toes? Was it medical? Was it genetic? What was the matter with these people?

Well, the short answer is: nothing. There was nothing in the water or in the soil that caused a third of the population to wander into mania. The phenomenon was not medical, it was historical. Mania was then a form of personality, the grand or florid personality that you seldom see at large anymore but that was formerly available to all, and especially to those living in isolated, out-of-the-way places like this, where, from never encountering the healthy, uniform resistance of other minds, men and women were apt to grow in odd ways, as plants artfully confined grow strange limbs and flowers—all testifying to what Marx and Engels called "the idiocy of rural life."

THE BIG BEND

The Big Bend Motel was ten miles out of Presidio as you went north. It was on the old two-lane. The federal highway had evidently passed it by. It smelled of packed dirt and sometimes of diesel and always, slightly, pleasantly, of some kind of cooking or baking, or burning anyway, which I never discovered the source of but which I found all over the border country. Perhaps the smell was the fumes from the fires of the underworld, the hell far to the south that was the capital, fumes much attenuated by distance but still faintly present.

The walls of the Big Bend Motel had at one time been finished and painted pink to look like adobe, but the finish had flaked off, and so had the paint, and it seemed the place was made of concrete blocks. One thing about it was that the doors of the living quarters or units were too short. Every one of them ended three inches from the floor. Clearly, all the doors had been bought in a job lot somewhere else and hung up anyhow, but the business turned out well, because the floor clearance made it easy for low-riding varieties of the local wildlife, which were abundant, to get in and out. My neighbor at one time, a truck driver from Tennessee, found a tarantula had come into his unit from under the door. It was one of the big ones, the size of a dinner plate. It was the color of a fox, and it had twelve eyes. The trucker let it come and go as it pleased. He taught it to drink milk out of a saucer, like a kitten. It was company, he said. The Big Bend was a place where truckers stayed, along with others in need of company. The owner lived over the river, in Chihuahua City. He had been trying to kick me out for two weeks, but not too hard. Nobody was waiting to take my place. The Big Bend was off the highway, as I have explained. And it had an unthrifty look, too, I guess.

Now they were banging on the door again. It was daytime. I seemed to be on the floor. I could see their feet in the gap under the door. Broad brown feet. They were banging and calling my name. In the bed, one of the girls who shared my unit moaned and turned onto her stomach. She put her bottom—also brown, also broad—up in the air and burrowed her head under the pillow. The banging on the door went on. They wanted the rent, perhaps. I hadn't left the unit in three weeks, more than that. I stayed in there with the blinds closed and twenty-seven cases of beer and sometimes with the girl, her sister, her cousin, and her mother. We all piled in together and wriggled around, like earthworms or garter snakes. The girls were nurses. They went in and out. They dealt with the landlord. I have no usable Spanish.

Now the brown feet that had been visible under the door were in front of my nose. I rolled onto my back. The nurse was sitting up in the bed, holding the sheets modestly in front of her body. She was talking to three men who stood over me. From where I lay on the floor, they looked like large trees or office buildings.

"What do they want?" I asked the nurse.

"They want you out," she said.

The biggest of the men held in his hands a baseball bat, one of the newfangled bats made of aluminum. I hate the sound they make when they connect, don't you? I sat up.

"I need a telephone," I said. "Will you ask them if there's a telephone? I have to make a call. It won't cost them. Then I'll go."

The nurse spoke to the men.

"In the office," she said. "They will show you."

I left my unit and crossed the courtyard to the motel's office. The nurse, wrapped in her bedsheet, went before me, and one of the three men walked on either side. The one with the baseball bat stayed behind. In the office, the nurse got on the telephone and began talking, trying to get a connection that would put me through to the north. It took her ten or fifteen minutes, but at last she got there.

Mr. Applegate?

There you are, son. I'd about given up on you. What's it been, a couple of weeks? More?

I have no idea, Mr. Applegate. Mr. Applegate?

Yes, son?

I'll come. I mean, I'm coming up there.

You won't regret it, son.

Where are they now, the rural demented? They're gone. Gone to Thorazine or lithium or whatever you please. The truly odd have become rare. Who knows why? Who cares? Blame TV, the interstate highway system, broadcast news, advertising, the other forces that, as we enter a new century, make us all so much easier to get along with. The pickle king, the farmer burned to death by potato peelings, they lie in hillside graveyards enclosed by stone walls, shaded by old maple trees. They lie beneath soft marble stones, which do not conceal their peculiarities, but, rather, celebrate them. Walking upright on the earth today are men and women less colorful. Still, in this township at least, a few of us even now try to hold up the old standard, however feebly. We Noons are sound Tories; we're traditionalists.

Mr. Applegate?

What is it, son?

I haven't much choice here. I'll come up there. I've got no place else to go. But I'm puzzled.

About what, son?

Did you say your Mr. Usher has been dead for seven years?

I said he'd been gone for seven years.

But you're executing his will.

Trying to.

So he's dead.

In law, he's dead.

But not in fact?

In fact, son, nobody knows. I guess he's dead. It looks like he would be. Makes no difference really. Makes no difference to you. Makes no difference to me.

What happened to him?

He disappeared, son.

Disappeared?

I'd say so. No sign of him, seven years. The law says after seven years, he's dead.

That's when you go to work.

You, too. I'd get myself up here quick as I could if I were you.

I've told you I'm coming. Let up on me, can't you?

Son, all I'm trying to do here is give you a bunch of money. You don't seem to want it too bad. That strikes me as peculiar. I'd thought you'd be keen. You have things going pretty good for you where you are, I guess?

I wouldn't say that.

What do you do there, for work?

Um. You know, one thing and another.

Somebody said you're some kind of professor.

I was. Some kind. No more. They sacked me. I've been doing other things. Right now, I'm planning my next move.

Uh-huh. I had a hell of a time trying to talk to the operator just now. What kind of place is it you got down there?

It's a kind of hotel.

What's that they talk on the phone?

That's Spanish, Mr. Applegate. They're Mexicans.

Mexicans. What in the world are you doing down there with a lot of Mexicans?

Well, let's see. I've been fucking a couple of them. Haven't I? I guess I have.

I'd think you'd know that for sure, son.

You'd think.

Listen, son. Up here, it's eleven in the morning, a little past. What time's it there?

Oh, Mr. Applegate, I don't know. Jesus.

But it ain't anywhere near noon, is it?

I guess not.

Before noon and I'm thinking you ain't a hundred percent sober, are you, son?

Not sober? Certainly I am.

Uh-huh. Tell you what you do, son. Get some sleep. Then get on down to the depot, get yourself a ticket. Go on now. Ambrose. Vermont. It ain't a real big place, but you'll find it all right. Past Brattleboro. Get to Boston and take a left.

I finished talking to him and returned to my unit. I found my things in the courtyard, the nurse gone, my door locked, and there, standing in front of it, the large guy with the metal bat. It looked to me as though I had checked out. So I went back to the office and made a deal with the owner of the Big Bend for the undrunk portion of my beer dump. He forgave my bill and let me have enough to hire a taxi to Presidio. You could get the bus in Presidio.

Well, the years come and go and things change. They go forward, but they also go back. Years ago, when a third of the township were lunatics, there was a real train that carried passengers and freight up the valley from Brattleboro. They ran four trains a day. Now it's hard even to find the old roadbed where it's lost in the woods; the people—apart from an acceptable minority—are as sane as you or I; and the train is invisible, it's immaterial, and it runs through the sky. On the other hand, back in those days, there weren't any turkeys in the woods of Bible Hill. In fact, there weren't any woods at all. The woods had been cut down to clear for farms. Vermont was a farm state then, a grain state: a kind of semivertical Illinois. Then the farms went down, the woods came back, and somebody decided turkeys were wanted. They brought the turkeys in from New York. No kidding. Turkeys weren't born on Bible Hill; they didn't plan to be here. But one way or another, here they are. They were brought in from someplace else and turned loose. They seem to like it. Now they are here with the rest of us, waiting to see what comes next.

2. Brute Neighbors

1

In a place like Bible Hill, they will tell you, you don't have neighbors. Or, yes, you have deer, raccoon, bears, and the like for neighbors. But other people, if they are to be found at all so far back in the hills, are never close enough to be anybody's neighbor. You are on your own. Of course it isn't true. You are not on your own. You may wish to be, but you are not. Everybody has neighbors. Who are yours? is the question, and What are you going to do about them; they about you?

Mine were four. Beginning at the bottom of the hill, where the Bible Hill road left the road to the village, and continuing for three miles or a little less to the point near the top where it dwindled away in the woods, you came first to the Bracketts, then Miss Drumheller, then me, then Calabrese. From any one of our places to any of the others was a bit of a hike, it's true, but that doesn't matter. It's not nearness that makes neighbors; it's not space at all. What is it?

Mr. and Mrs. Brackett lived in what had been the old district schoolhouse down at the corner. When I arrived, Arthur Brackett must have been about fifty. Most people called him "Tubby." He was a quiet, collected fellow who acted as though he might be a little deaf. He wore khaki shirts and trousers, kept carefully mended, washed, and ironed by Mrs. Brackett. Tubby had the RFD route out of the Ambrose post office. His wife stayed home. She liked birds, and their house was hung about with bird feeders, birdhouses, and birdbaths—too many of them.

Miss Drumheller's place was another mile up the hill. She had been a schoolteacher in the town, had taught in the schoolhouse that was now Bracketts', until the old school districts had been combined and the little schoolhouses shut down. That had happened sometime around 1940, so Miss Drumheller must have been eighty, eighty-five. She still lived alone, with the help of a visiting nurse. Mrs. Brackett helped her, too, some. So in time did I.

Calabrese was another kind of deal.

Carlo? Keeps to himself, don't he? Sure, I sold him his place, Littlejohn's sugarhouse it was, part of your place years ago. Ten acres, was it? Divided out of Usher's. Carlo's put a lot of work into it, I hear. I haven't seen it. Carlo don't want people to come around. It seems like he had trouble, somehow, before. In New York, was it? Philadelphia? I don't recall. More like twenty acres, now I think of it. Why not? Man wants privacy and's willing to pay for it, let him have it, what I say.

What kind of trouble?

I don't know, son. I never heard. Some trouble. He had plenty of cash, I know that. Walked into this office on a Tuesday morning, said he was looking for something like a camp, lots of privacy. No neighbors. I had Usher's estate. I thought of that sugarhouse. Took Carlo up there. Shook hands that afternoon, started the paperwork. Carlo drove up there that night, slept in his car, he said. Next day, passed papers, he went back to Philadelphia owning it, and I wish it was always one half that easy. I do. Real estate's a hard grind, son.

Gee, here I always thought real estate's easy bucks.

You earn every penny, son. People spend that kind of money, they think they have to be smart even when they ain't. That puts a terrible strain on them. They don't act for the best. They put you right through it.

They do? I'm sorry to hear it. I was thinking about going for my license, you know?

Don't do it, son.

He seems like a nice enough guy, though.

Who does?

Calabrese. He seems all right to me.

What Calabrese had was a partial disability settlement pending from the police department of the city of Philadelphia. He'd been injured in the line of duty, evidently.

"How did you get hurt?" I asked him once.

"What do you think?" Calabrese said. "Look, I was a cop. How does a cop get hurt?"

A rough-made man, stout but not soft, any age between forty and sixty, with bristly gray hair, he looked like a porcupine with a crew cut. Calabrese didn't live on the road like the rest of us, but on a driveway or lane a hundred yards long that he'd cut into the woods. The signs began at the road:

PRIVATE WAY: NO ADMITTANCE

PRIVATE PROPERTY: KEEP OUT

KEEP OUT!

DOGS WILL ATTACK INTRUDERS
DANGEROUS DOGS

"Why don't you stop in sometime?" Calabrese said. "Sure, stop in. Anytime."

2

Some days I could see a house on the side of the hill farthest to the east. What was I to make of it? A house painted white, or gray, or some light color, with a metal roof that shone in the sun. The house must have been six or seven miles away, air line. It was hard to tell its distance. Indeed, it was hard to tell exactly where the house was, which struck me as odd. After all, it was a real house. Wasn't it?

I got out my compass and took the bearing of the distant house from my own. Then I drew that bearing on the relief map of the district, which showed buildings. I found no buildings where the line I drew hit the nest of contour lines I thought stood for the hill I saw off to the east: Back Diamond Mountain. But the map was not new and the house may have been. It was also possible I had marked the wrong hill. I never claimed to be a navigator. And anyway, how much use are maps? Unless you know where a place is, no map will tell you, not in the way you need. I sat at my table with the map spread before me and I looked out the window across the valley to where the sun flashed off that roof on the distant hillside, and I wondered why we haven't found a better way.

I thought that house might even be over the line in the next town. How did you get to it? I couldn't think of a road over there that went anywhere near it, and, set in the woods at the top of its ridge, it must have had a steep and difficult approach. Maybe it had no approach.

Maybe you couldn't go to it at all. Maybe the house over the valley was under a spell of false distance, like a castle in a fairy tale.

Another queer point: Some days you could see the house and some days you couldn't. It had the quality of a mirage. Sometimes it would be there in the morning, other times in the afternoon. On clear days, it appeared—or it didn't. The same for cloudy days. Shadows or haze hid it, I suppose. One thing: I never saw it in the winter. The white house disappeared into the background of snow. Someday, I said, I'm going to go over there and drive around until I find that place. I'd like to stand in front of it and look back across the valley to my own place, my own life, myself looking out from here. We Noons know how to muse.

"Listen, kid," Calabrese said. "Here's the deal. I got to go down to the city. For my claim, you know? Something—I don't know. I got a lawyer in the city. There's a hearing. So tomorrow I got to go down. I need to get my dogs fed for a day or two, three. While I'm gone."

"Sure," I said. "I'll feed them for you. I'll be glad to."

"Don't say that," said Calabrese. "Don't say that yet. Here's what you have to do. I feed them once a day, in the morning. Meat on the bone, no dog food."

"Meat," I said.

"Yeah," Calabrese said. "I'll have meat for two, three days ordered down at the store. I'll do that now. They'll have it for you there. You pick it up, take it on up here, give it to them."

"Sure," I said. "I'll be glad to."

"Don't say that," said Calabrese. "Look, I'll give you twenty bucks—and the meat's paid for."

"You don't have to pay me," I said. "We're neighbors. Besides, it's easy. I'm right down the road."

"Twenty bucks," said Calabrese.

There was that in Calabrese that made you not want to get across him. And in any case, was I to refuse to give for pay help I was willing to give for nothing? So quickly do relations stop making sense—but we must resist absurdity even when we resist by ceasing to resist.

"Okay," I said.

"Okay," said Calabrese. "Now here's the deal. You drive up there with the meat. All you do is drive in and toss the meat out of your vehicle in front of the house. Then turn around and drive out. You stay in your vehicle. Throw the meat out. Drive away. Do not leave your vehicle. You got that?"

"Toss the meat out. Stay in the car," I said.

"Do not leave your vehicle," said Calabrese.

3

It's not nearness that makes neighbors. It's not space at all. What is it? Destiny. Neighbors belong together. They are fated. They are wed. Happily wed? Who cares? Their peculiar union is permanent. Yes, they change, they grow. They may grow together, or they may grow apart, but finally they are stuck with one another: It is the essence of their relations. Beyond the wooded hills to the east with their enchanted houses appearing, disappearing, the Connecticut River, and beyond that, in the bluest distance, a savage place, a land without the law, Heart of Darkness—a neighbor of a higher order—Vermont's evil twin: New Hampshire.

What is it about New Hampshire? What makes them so obstreperous over there? It isn't history: In history, New Hampshire has always been a far more venerable, more civilized place than Vermont. It has a gracious and prosperous Colonial past, as Vermont has not. It has more stately homes, more ancient and aristocratic academies and colleges, better architecture, superior antiquities. And yet New Hampshire wants you to believe that when you cross the river from Vermont, you move, politically, from a zone of failed socialism and decadent, near-tropical inertia into a state of nature, a wilderness, a kind of capitalist Dodge City, lawless, dangerous, free. They fancy themselves on the frontier over there. You expect the governor to wear a six-shooter strapped around his pinstripes; you expect the trim elderly women of the village garden clubs to carry Derringers in their reticules. "Live Free or Die," is what they say of themselves in New Hampshire—as though they didn't say the same thing everywhere else. There is over the river a busy culture of political self-congratulation.

And the question is, Why? For what? Well, believe it or not, the conclusion of the whole matter is that in New Hampshire you can buy a refrigerator without paying a tax and in Vermont you can't. Over there live a people whose proudest boast is that they pay no state sales or income tax. Now, understand me: I don't enjoy paying taxes. Who does? But to make not paying taxes the whole duty of man, as New Hampshire does, seems somehow to fall short. It seems ignorant. Imagine a tiny island in the far Pacific where the pagan natives, asked to exhibit their god, produce with absurd pomp and ceremony an empty fifty-five-gallon drum dumped from a passing freighter.

Nor is a negative obsession with taxes the strangest part of New Hampshire's anthropology. For we are talking about a country whose most treasured institution is the New Hampshire Primary. Here, perhaps, is the height of the curiosity that is our neighbor across the river. In the New Hampshire Primary, we find an episode that any sensible people would regard as a calamity—a relentless visitation every four years by the most energetic, the most appalling of the rogues, blowhards, madmen, charlatans, unincarcerated felons, and political riffraff that make American democracy the envy of the world. You or I would kill our beasts, scorch our fields, and flee in terror before such an onslaught, but in New Hampshire they love it. For at least eighteen months in advance of every presidential election, they open to the barbarian invaders not only their shops and town halls but also their homes, their churches, even the schools where their innocent children learn.

Why do they do this? There is no telling. In Vermont, we can only pray for them, our neighbors, and for ourselves, and renew our gratitude that the Almighty has made the long, leisurely, pleasant stream dividing our two countries to be in some sense a river of fire, impassable.

What's that house I see across the valley? On the side of Back Diamond, I guess. You know the house over there?

Tin roof?

That's the one. Right up on the top.

That would be Amanda Marlow's.

I don't know her.

No, I don't guess you do. She's only been up there since this spring. Came in from out west.

So she's new, like me.

Not like you, son.

No?

Not exactly. She's my daughter.

. . .

In those days, I had an old Volkswagen of the Beetle kind, yellow, a car about the size of a large bathtub. Everybody my age is required to have owned that same car at one time or another in his youth, just as we are required to have had measles in childhood and later to have read Kafka and Kierkegaard, or anyway pretended to. The first years on Bible Hill, when I neighbored with Calabrese and the others, were my Beetle years.

The day after Calabrese was to have left for Philadelphia, then, it was in that famous, well-beloved car that I drove down to Clifford's store in the village. They gave me two slabs of beef from the cooler in the back. The meat was wrapped in butcher's paper and tied with string, but blood had come through the paper and soaked the string here and there. I put a newspaper on the front passenger's seat and laid the meat on it. Then I drove back up the hill, past my place, and into Calabrese's driveway. I rolled unconcerned past his array of ugly signs with my chin in the air, my passport, my safe conduct oozing onto the newspaper by my side.

The driveway ran through woods near the road, then came out on a clearing. Stumps and big brush piles stood everywhere, but new grass grew between them. I hadn't realized Calabrese had cleared so much in there. The woods ended more than a hundred feet from the house.

The driveway approached the house in a long uphill curve. It was rough and rutted. It threw my little car around cruelly. I thought of stopping and walking the rest of the way to the house with the meat. Calabrese had said I wasn't to do that. I was to stay in the car.

Then I saw beyond the house at the edge of the woods a black pony with its head up, watching me. I hadn't known Calabrese went in for horses. But there was another one coming around the house to stand alongside the first. Where were the killer dogs? I drove on toward the house and the ponies.

And why, if he kept horses, hadn't Calabrese given me grain to bring them while he was away?

Now the two ponies broke and ran down the hill toward me. I stopped the car. Funny-looking beasts: tub-headed, long-legged, with a loose, seesaw way of running, unlike that of any horse I had ever seen. When I stopped the car, they came on faster, and they began to bark, a deep, muttering bark, not loud.

I rolled up my window. I leaned to my right and rolled up the other one. Then they were around the car, their great dish faces above the level of my head, teeth and jaws snapping at the window glass, foam flying, their stupid eyes hot and red. One got his forequarters up on the front of the car and tried to get at me through the windshield. I leaned on the horn, and he jumped back. The dogs stood on either side of the car and watched me through the windows.

I thought of trying to open a window just enough to pitch the meat out to them. Then I thought not. I feared if I opened the window even a little, they'd scent the meat before I could throw it on the ground and try again to come in and get it. I wasn't sure they couldn't do that.

So I put the Beetle in reverse and began to roll back down Calabrese's long driveway, his twin monsters trotting stiffly either side, like a cavalry escort. They kept up with me to the bottom of Calabrese's clearing, through the woods, and to the road, where they waited alertly while I backed around and drove off. I drove down to the village and left the meat in the cooler at Clifford's.

"No sale, I guess," said the woman at Clifford's. I didn't know her name. I didn't know what she knew of Calabrese and his place.

"I don't know what else to do," I said. "They'll have to go hungry."

"They won't go hungry," the woman said.

4

It's not distance that makes neighbors. What is it? Attention. Windows. Your neighbors are those whose windows, if you could see into them, you believe might show you something you need to know.

Past midnight, some nights, in those hours so late and empty, they make the night look like it will never end, I would get in the car and drive down the hill to the road and so toward the village.

I would pass Miss Drumheller's house, dark, its windows flashing like silver platters in the moonlight. I would pass Bracketts', where a light would often be on in the front room downstairs. Why? Who was up? What were they doing?

I rode on: left on the road and along the river, where in the spring frogs by the hundred flopped across the road, frogs silver like the spinster's windows, and the eyes of deer, hunting cats, and other creatures shone in the headlights. Into the village, then, and through it: dark houses, porches deep in moon shadow, empty chairs on the porches, and in the fall the slates of the steep roofs gray with frost. A light over the gas pumps at Clifford's, sometimes the only light in the village, sometimes not. There might be a light in a house upstairs, showing the ceiling of a room and the top of a wall with its paper, paper in some print . . . animals: farm animals, circus animals. A child's room? A sick child? A bad dream? The sleepy parents bringing comfort, soon to put out the light again? In another house, the queer blue coal mine light of a television.

I would pass through the village and turn around at the little dam, or maybe I wouldn't. I might ride on down through the next village, past farms where by this hour there were lights in the barns, past new houses and trailers set back in the broad silver fields. I might ride right down to Brattleboro and end up at the all-night place on the edge of town. There I would have a cup of coffee and something to eat and listen to the early customers, two or three, talking: other people's neighbors, not mine. Then when I left the all-night place to drive back home, I'd find out in the parking lot that it wasn't quite night any longer.

I won't say I learned anything that I thought I needed to know riding around late at night. I found out nobody's secrets. But I wouldn't have missed my night rides in those days. I peered and peeped and spied and saw exactly nothing, but I took note. I attended. Being the only one awake and abroad, passing all those dark houses, blank silver windows, lighted windows, made me feel I had more neighbors than I knew. Among other lives, other minds, my life, my mind, was present, too, and had its place. Or so I believed. We Noons are fairly odd ducks.

"Hey, what happened?" Calabrese asked me.

"Well," I said. "I got the meat. I went up there. They came on kind of strong, you know? I was afraid to open the window to toss the meat."

"The meat's still down at the store," Calabrese said.

"That's right. I took it back. I screwed up. I didn't do what I said I'd do. I'm sorry."

"Don't worry about it, kid," said Calabrese. "It was my fault. I'll think of another way next time."

"Were they all right?" I asked. "They . . . I don't know their names."

"The dogs?" Calabrese said. "They don't got names. They're working dogs. You ruin them if you give them a name."

"Working dogs," I said.

"I told you."

"Were they all right?" I asked him again.

"Oh, yeah," Calabrese said. "Sure, they're fine. They got a sheep, see? Cruikshank's sheep. Cruikshank's pissed."

"They ate a sheep?"

"Couple of them," said Calabrese. "Shit, if I'd known he had sheep over there, I'd have never bought all that beef, you know? You know what that cost, those steaks?"

"Yes," I said. "I'm sorry."

"What the hell?" Calabrese said. "Listen, you and me'll have them. I got some charcoal. We'll throw them on the grill. Get a case of beer. Come on over. What do you say?"

"I'll get the beer," I said.

"No chance," said Calabrese. "It's on me. I'm celebrating."

Calabrese was a happy man that day. He'd been meeting with the principals in his case for three days in Philadelphia.

"Philly," said Calabrese. "What a shithole, you know? My old neighborhood, South Philly? You know? Frankie Avalon. Frankie Avalon is what they've got. Frankie Avalon went to high school with my little sister. No kidding. They went on a date. Frankie Avalon took my sister to the movies. Of course, he wasn't Frankie Avalon then. But, what I'm saying, my father told Frankie Avalon to get my sister home by eleven or he'd kill him, and Frankie Avalon dropped her off at quarter till. That's what they've got. Do you know what I'm talking about? That's the top of the line. Frankie Avalon. And the rest of the city's like something at the end of World War Two. I mean, I was in the MPs, you know? I saw Berlin, at the end there. Fucking Berlin in 1945 looked better than most of Philly does now, you know? I mean, it's bombed out. I go down there today, like I just did? And after I get past Trenton, I start feeling like I'm going to puke. The claims board, the cops, those lawyers, reporters, the rest of them? What dirtbags, you know? I'm looking for seventy-five bucks a month. I got shot in the stomach, and I'm asking for seventy-five bucks a month.

"Well, fuck them," said Calabrese. "Just fuck them all. They don't matter. I'm going to tell you, I'm glad to be back. I would have never believed it. A year ago, I would have never. Look: what have I got up here? I got no electricity. I run into things in the night like I'm blind. I got no real heat. I freeze. I got no friends, no woman. I live with dogs. I got no plumbing. I shit in a hole in the ground. That's it, you know? That's what it is. And I couldn't wait to get back to it."

Amanda once asked me if I hadn't been too much alone on Bible Hill.

"I don't know, Noon," she said. "Isn't it kind of lonely?"

"Not anymore," I said.

"But before?" Amanda asked. "Before me?"

"Yes," I said. "It was."

"Kind of depressing?"

"You see," I told Amanda, "the things is, I like being depressed."

"Uh-huh," said Amanda. "Kind of hard to explain, I guess, right, Noon?"

"I guess," I said.

3. The Dumb End

1

Now, I set out to make a buck, but it wasn't the same. It was a different buck you made up here. Before I came to Bible Hill, I had tried to make the adult buck, the heavy buck, the buck that has a life attached to it. I had failed, partly from laziness, partly from native incompetence, but partly, too, from the extra weight of that life. The buck, I could lift—the life, not. I tried, or I thought I tried. But always the result was failure: effort misapplied, the task not mastered—the task, perhaps, not even understood.

THE SCHOLAR GYPSY

There are two kinds of college: colleges where the faculty is smarter than the students; colleges where the students are smarter than the faculty. The second kind is best. The second kind is the kind of college in which I found myself as an instructor in the English Department. It didn't go well. At first, I had no clear idea why that was. At the time, I had no clear idea about much of anything. What did I have? I had a fellowship that I was fairly sure I wouldn't have much longer. I had a thesis on Bret Harte and nothing to say about Bret Harte. I had two sections of freshmen and *The Norton Anthology of English Literature.* I had a room in a vast brown firetrap of a house near the university, a house covered with shingles laid like the scales of some rank and hideous fish, a carp or loach.

The Norton Anthology of English Literature is seventeen hundred pages long. It's a fat and heavy book. It will stop a bullet, but it won't cover your nakedness. Most of my freshmen seemed to know more about its contents than I did, and most of them knew they knew more, knew I knew they knew more, knew I knew they knew I knew . . . and so on. Their knowing, their ambition flashed like steel. After class, they stormed the lectern, citadel of my default, as I backed toward the door. I took to not showing up at all some days. We Noons do not seek pain.

My adviser was an Elizabethan scholar, a decent man, but he had studied at Oxford after the war and the experience had marked him. Another fucking Anglophile. He aimed for a kind of English shortness to cover his kind heart—though why cover it?—and he had a habit of turning important sentences into questions. He evidently thought the English spoke that way, and for all I know, they do.

"It doesn't seem to be going well for you, does it?" he said.

"Not really," I said.

"Is it true you haven't met one of your sections for two weeks?"

"Yes."

"Were you ill?"

"No."

"I'm told you gave one section a talk on some insect."

"Yes."

"Some moth."

"Yes."

"Well, but why? Why do that, Mr. Noon?"

"I don't know," I said. "It was interesting."

"I'm sure it was," he said. "I'm sure it was most interesting. But the point is, well, you don't seem to be taking hold, do you?"

"Taking hold?"

"That's it, yes. Not taking hold. Not jumping in, are you? It's a curious life here. Teaching here. You must take hold. You must jump in. I'm not sure it's for you, is it?"

What are you going to do, son? For work, I mean.

Work? I'm rich, Mr. Applegate. You and Usher made me rich. I don't have to do anything.

Well, rich? A hundred and fifty thousand? Not that that ain't a good round number, but I don't know, son. That house up there will take fifty thousand to keep it from falling into its own cellar by and by. Then, there's the Internal Revenue.

Internal Revenue? You mean I have to pay taxes on this?

Seems like you'd have to, yes.

I don't think that's fair, Mr. Applegate. I didn't seek this money. It came to me. I ought not to be taxed on money I didn't expect to have.

You could take it up with Mr. Connally, I guess. I ain't sure he'll see it the same way.

Mr. Connally?

He's the Secretary of the Treasury, son.

Well hell, Mr. Applegate.

My Virgil. My guide, philosopher, and friend. Mr. Applegate was a man between fifty and sixty, short, pink, a little plump: a good-natured man. A contented man, you would have said. I knew from the beginning that Mr. Applegate liked me. He let me know it. He didn't like everything. He was wry, and he was dry. Mr. Applegate had his limits. He sometimes took a dim view. He took a dim view of the people he knew because he knew them, and he took a dim view of the people he didn't know because he didn't know them. But me, he liked.

Mr. Applegate was by himself, a widower, it seemed. He was evidently one of the men who ran things in the town of Ambrose, not that there was much to run. He had a house in the village. He had a law practice, a sideline in real estate, another sideline in auctioneering. He had collections of old tools, old postcards, old wagon wheels. He had a daughter, a hell of a daughter. He had about all he needed, you would have said, but he didn't have a straight man. Then I arrived, and he had that, too.

Well then, Mr. Applegate, what do you suggest? What work is there?

Lots of things, son. Work in the woods. You ever used a chain saw?

No.

Nothing to it. Nothing at all. Of course, sooner or later, you kill yourself.

What else?

Well, cars. You know how to work on cars?

I can change a tire.

Mmm. Building. There's building. Milo might need a helper. We'll go see Milo. You ever hauled brick?

Not professionally.

You'd take right to it, son. I can tell.

2

Once you give up on having a good job, I discovered, you're free. When you go after the light buck because, in the place you find yourself, the heavy buck is not to be had, you get to figure out what a job is for: to let you live. Veils part before you. Difficulties fall away.

Milo Tavistock was a mason. He was working on the chimney of a house in Dead River Settlement the day Mr. Applegate drove me out one noontime in May. Milo was sitting in the back of his truck, having his lunch. Mr. Applegate told him I was looking for work. Milo's helper, Buddy, had decided not to come back from Florida that spring.

"He's got a job on a boat, he says," Milo said.

"This boy's in Littlejohn's old place up there," said Mr. Applegate.

"Is that right?" said Milo. "Well, okay, then. I can use you. I got to have somebody. My back. Slipped a disk a couple of years ago. Back's no goddamned good. I went to the doctor. Doctor made it worse."

"Try a chiropractor," said Mr. Applegate.

"Did," said Milo Tavistock. "Got worse yet. I don't need another doctor. I need a helper. How's your back?" he asked me.

"Fine," I said.

"You don't mind ladders, I guess?"

"No," I said.

"Can you pick up a bag of mix? You're big enough; you look like you could. It's a hundred pounds."

"Yes."

"Let's see," said Milo. He nodded to a pile of sacks waiting by the driveway. I picked one of them up. It was heavy, really heavy. But it was possible. I lifted it and put it on the truck beside Milo.

"Do that all day long?" asked Milo.

"I don't know," I said.

"Sure he can," said Mr. Applegate. "Look at him."

"Can you stretch a tape?" asked Milo Tavistock.

"You mean a measure?"

"Yes, a tape. Can you hold a line?"

"I can learn," I said.

"Well," said Milo. "That's okay. You'll do no harm. You get the dumb end."

ENTOMOLOGY

My Oxonian adviser wanted me to take hold, wanted me to jump in, but what I wanted to do at the time was sit in my room and read about bugs. Insects. For in a secondhand bookstore, I had discovered the patient, the curious, the infinitely consoling J. H. Fabre (1823–1915). For days, weeks, Fabre, in his village in Provence, watched caterpillars crawl along a straw; then for more weeks, he watched them crawl around the mouth of a jar. When Fabre was done watching, he knew a thing or two about caterpillars. Not much money in it, not much of the world, but then, how much do you need?

Wasps, beetles, locusts, grasshoppers, every kind of fly—these, too, were Fabre's treasure, and that spring they were mine, as well. I visited them the way the miser vists his gold, eagerly and in secret. Nobody could find me. My fellowship paid the rent, at least it paid the rent through June. To hell with the freshmen. To hell with *The Norton Anthology.* To hell with taking hold. To hell with jumping in. Fabre was able to investigate the insects so efficiently because he himself was part insect: automatic, repetitive, tireless. I would be the same.

The house where I lived was owned by the widow of a professor in the law school, and most of the rooms were rented by law students. My neighbor down the hall was one of them—or perhaps not quite. His name was Ned DeMorgan. He was older than the other students, older than I. Thirty? Thirty-five? Unmarried, evidently. At any rate DeMorgan lived alone. We nodded in the hallways.

At that house, you could do your laundry in the basement, if you wished. One evening, I was down there running a load through the dryer. I was sitting on a canvas lawn chair, waiting for my clothes to dry, reading Fabre on maggots.

Ned DeMorgan came down the basement stairs with a bag of laundry of his own. He saw me, nodded. He put his clothes into the washer, then tilted up the cover of my book so he could read it.

"Oh-ho, Fabre," said DeMorgan. "Good old Fabre."

"Right," I said.

"Fine stuff," he said. "I'm Ned DeMorgan."

"Mark Noon," I said.

"Noon?" said Ned DeMorgan. "That's a funny name. Is it Jewish?"

"Choctaw," I said.

"Exactly," said DeMorgan. "You're not law. I'd know you if you were. I am a man of the law."

"I'm in English," I said.

"Ah," said DeMorgan. He nodded at my book. "I'm not sure I see why Fabre is to the point."

"He isn't," I said.

"Exactly," said Ned DeMorgan.

I don't know, Mr. Applegate. I haven't had good luck with jobs.

Well, okay, son. But can't you give me a little help here? What can you do? What's your experience? What did you do before? Where was that place?

You mean the foundation?

That's right. What did you do there, did you say?

Well, different things.

What things, son?

Administration, analysis. You know.

I don't know. That's why I'm asking you.

Well, econometrics, resources, capital, trade, infrastructure.

Okay, son.

Different things.

Uh-huh. The thing is, we don't have a great deal of call for that up here. Not but what we could use it.

No.

What else?

Well, college teaching.

Not a college in town.

No.

It seems as though you might be looking at a kind of career shift here, son.

It looks that way, doesn't it?

THE PLAN

Finally, it was DeMorgan who opened the door, who touched the hidden spring and made the wall move slowly aside. Perhaps I ought not to have been surprised. Perhaps I wasn't surprised. June had arrived, exams were over, and the residence halls were emptying out. The lilacs that bloomed for commencement were past their best. My room was rented beginning the tenth by a Latvian poet who came for the summer sessions. I was packing my bag.

"Leaving for the summer?" DeMorgan had stuck his head through my open door.

"Not for the summer," I said.

"Ah," said DeMorgan. "Ah. I see." He came in, looked around my room, went to the window, looked out, then sat down on the sill.

DeMorgan's field was the law of the sea. He held a research position at the law school in the law of the sea. What is the law of the sea?

"What's your plan now?" Ned DeMorgan asked.

In those days, you had to have a plan. Having a plan was highly recommended. Because at that time, for ablebodied young men there was only one question: Are you or are you not going to Vietnam? And if you're not, what in the world are you going to tell the army? I had thought that, on the whole, I would just as soon let somebody else do Vietnam, but I was open on the subject. Too open, DeMorgan felt.

"Look here, you can't simply sit and wait for them to draft you," he said.

"I was thinking of joining up," I said. "That way, you have some choice of service, don't you?"

"Don't be silly," said DeMorgan.

"I thought of the navy," I said.

"Don't be silly," said DeMorgan.

"What's silly about it?" I said. "What else can I do? I've lost my exemption, or I will have. I've been sacked. I'm not a student any longer. I'm not even a teacher."

DeMorgan was quiet a moment. He stroked his chin. He tilted his head back and regarded me down his nose.

"Look here," he said. "How would you like a job?"

"What job?"

DeMorgan waved his hand.

"Well, you know, administration, that kind of thing. A foundation job, in fact. Writing reports, gathering data. I'm not certain, really. Central America. On south. A small private foundation that's active down there. Do you have any Spanish?"

"Not a word," I said.

"You'll pick it up. You're smarter than you look, Mark—well, you'd almost have to be. Know anything about Central America, do you?"

"The Panama Canal."

"There, you see?" said DeMorgan. "You're practically Foreign Service grade."

"I'd be writing reports on economic development in Panama?" I said.

"Not Panama, or not only. Latin America generally," DeMorgan said.

"What kind of reports?"

"Well," said DeMorgan, "research, surveys. Surveys, that's it."

"Surveys?"

"Exactly," said DeMorgan. "You know, surveys, econometrics, resources, capital, trade, infrastructure."

"For a foundation?"

"A small private foundation interested in issues of Latin economic policy—you know."

"I don't know," I said.

"There would be a certain amount of, ah, legwork, as well," said DeMorgan.

"Legwork," I said.

"Yes," said DeMorgan, "Actually, I'm talking out of turn. You'll have to meet the foundation's people, of course. I don't know in detail how you'd fit in. I know only a little of their work. If you learned more and didn't like it, of course you'd not go forward. But look here: You really must do something. You really must not simply wait for the draft."

"Working for a place like that doesn't get you out of the draft," I said.

DeMorgan looked at me again. He smiled.

"This one does," said Ned DeMorgan.

Well, but let's put our minds to this thing now, son. This ain't hard. You've got a lot going for you up here.

Is that right, Mr. Applegate?

You bet. For example, size. You're a big-enough fellow. What do you weigh? One ninety? Two hundred?

In there, I guess.

That's good. A lot of jobs around here are mostly a matter of beef, you know. Do you figure on indoor work or outdoor work?

I don't know.

Say outdoor.

Outdoor.

That's the boy. We'll go see Milo. You'll do for Milo. Sure, you're going to be just fine. You're a natural-born peasant, son.

HITCHCOCK

I ought to have known. In fact, I did know. I went in knowing, and as calamity piled on fiasco, I was embarrassed, I was humiliated, but I was never surprised. The signs were unmistakable. We Noons are among those on whom nothing is lost.

The Great Hitchcock had been Ned DeMorgan's classmate at Harvard or Yale or wherever you please. It was to Hitchcock I went, in New York, to a new building off Madison Avenue in the Fifties. In the elevator of the building, two young men, immaculately barbered and dark-suited like bankers, got on after me. Men my own age, but they were grown-ups and I was not. Could I be? They turned and faced the doors. We ascended together.

One of the grown-ups turned to the other, spoke. "I said to him,

'Look: Three into fifteen is five. Four into fifteen is three and three-quarters. Okay?' We're up against that here. That is what we are up against."

"And he said what?" the other asked.

"What did he say?" the first one asked. "What could he say?"

"Not good," said the second grown-up. "Fourth and a lot. Time to punt."

"Punt?" said his friend. "Punt? Time to fucking pray."

You knew those two had good jobs. Could I be like them? The elevator stopped, the doors opened, and they got off. I was left alone with five more floors to go before I reached Hitchcock. There was a red button that stopped the elevator. There almost always is a red button. You almost never push it.

Eighteen hours later, I stepped off the ferry at the capital. Hitchcock was already there; he'd beaten me. He met me on the quai. In those days, Hitchcock still met all the boats.

I worked for Milo that summer and fall, until he went to Florida after Thanksgiving. Then when he came back the next year, I worked for him again. From him, I moved on to others like him. I banged nails. I caught two-by-fours and fence posts coming off the saw at Jordan's mill in the village. I pumped gas. I painted, shingled, chopped, mowed, dug, carried. Always I stuck to the dumb end. I held the dumb end of boards, tapes, cables, chains, chalk lines. From the first day, I liked the dumb end. If you go to pick up the light buck, you must attend, you must concentrate. Because the nature of the light buck is that it's light because it carries no weight of life except time. The time delivers the buck. The life is up to you.

4. World Geography

Bible Hill rests on the 43rd parallel of north latitude and thus is on a line with Lourdes; Naples; Sofia; Tbilisi; Tashkent; Vladivostok; Hokkaido, the northernmost of the Japanese islands; Coos Bay, Oregon; the Wind River Reservation, Wyoming; the South Dakota–Nebraska border west of the Missouri River; Milwaukee; Grand Rapids; Niagara Falls. So many places. So many cities, ancient and modern; so many famous peaks, plains, rivers; so much geography.

And hasn't Bible Hill its own geography, as good as anyplace else's? Certainly it has; better, in fact, at least ostensibly, for geography hereabouts sometimes seems to be more than it really is. A measure of geographic inflation is at work.

Not everybody understands. In these parts, for example, a hill is called a mountain, a style that people from other parts of the country love to mock. They mock because they don't get it; we're too subtle for them. Sure, Diamond Mountain and Round Mountain in this township, even the higher country to the west, such as Glastenbury Mountain (elev. 3,748 feet), Stratton Mountain (elev. 3,936 feet), and Mount Snow (elev. 3,556 feet), are carrying too much name for you if you live in Denver or Missoula. But if you go on to dismiss Vermont's mountains and the people who have called them mountains as merely exaggerated, you miss the point. To call a mountain a hill is bragging, and anyone can brag. To call a hill a mountain is a joke, and to make a joke, you must be sly, you must have irony.

Irony: a way of knowing that has been well to the fore in these parts from the earliest days, evidently. Many of the place names in the town have been given in this same spirit of ambiguous, vaguely bitter fun. The steep wooded hillside above the village of Dead River Settlement shows up on old maps of the town as Squab City. The uninhabited, inaccessible top of Back Diamond Mountain, past where Amanda used to live, was known as Beartown. Both names ironically announce their places as what they conspicuously are not: cities, towns, human communities of any consequence.

Irony of another kind is evidently at work in the way some of our place names seem to project the geography of this obscure and insignificant township onto more famous geographies—in particular, the geography of the Holy Land. Hence the hamlet on the very western edge of town, known to the prosaic U.S. Postal Service as North Ambrose P.O. but better and more venerably known as Joppa—an analogue of the ancient Mediterranean port on the coast of Palestine, latterly Tel Aviv.

Other names were to preserve events and discoveries. The fairgrounds, where the flea market was laid out in my time, was called Scotch Plains, not from the nationality of the neighborhood, but from its onetime owner's suspected use of it as a transfer point for illegal whiskey brought down from Canada. Money Brook, an old name for the Quick Branch, played on the fact that during the last century, gold had been found in the brook's pebbles—gold in amounts utterly unprofitable, but gold nevertheless.

Bible Hill itself has an ironic name, given, probably, as a comment on the supposed religiosity of the hill's inhabitants, or anyway some of them. By now, that name, too, is plainly obsolete. There may be a believer or two left on the hill (my neighbor Mrs. Brackett has been seen in church), but they no longer predominate. We had best be thinking about another name, then, hadn't we?

It's also characteristic of the town that many of its features have had different names at different times, like a nobleman or a bank robber. On nineteenth-century maps of the town, Bible Hill is labeled Hammersmith Hill. Hammersmith was the name of the family who had the place below mine, the place that was later Miss Drumheller's.

Of the geographic features whose names have changed over the town's two hundred years, the most prominent is Round Mountain. At 3,177 feet, Round Mountain is by far the highest point in the township, most of whose northwestern quarter the mountain takes up. Round Mountain is in fact an elongated ridge that extends out of the town to the northwest, but from most of Ambrose, you look at it end-on, and from that angle, the mountain does indeed have a regular, round shape, like a great green cranium. Round Mountain dominates the town, and it is no doubt for that reason, because it has always been on everybody's mind, more or less, that it has had so many different names.

On the oldest map of the district, Round Mountain appears as Mount Ararat, a name I suspect, on no evidence, was given by the town's first settlers, veterans of the French and Indian Wars, Scripture readers, who, arriving safely at last at the end of their journey, after a hard haul over the hills from Brattleboro, hills that were then a wilderness, gratefully, devoutly gave that looming height the name of the biblical mountain where Noah landed the ark after forty days riding on the Flood.

By the time the first modern map of the township was published, in 1856, Mount Ararat had had its name changed to New Africa Hill, the name having been given by townsmen who remarked the comings and goings at a remote farmhouse on the mountain: fugitive slaves being moved to Canada on the Underground Railroad. Then in the next decade, a third map gives the name of the place as Bone Mountain; why, I have no idea.

The present-day relief map that includes the town of Ambrose was made by the U.S. Geological Survey in 1954 and revised in 1986. On it, Round Mountain is labeled with its current name: It's Round Mountain as far as Washington, D.C., is concerned, therefore, and has been now for fifty years.

The name of the town itself, Ambrose, is the title of a marquisate held in the eighteenth century by a family named Ormonde, long extinct, members of the second- or third-string English nobility with estates in Ireland and the West Country. The royal governor of the New Hampshire colony, in granting the land that became our township, put the name of the marquises of Ambrose on the patent to curry favor with the well-born. He did the same with half the towns in Vermont, whose names today amount to a pompous, faintly ridiculous register of the statesmen, courtiers, and aristocratic parasites of the reign of King George III.

The old maps of the town to which I have referred are a topic in themselves. If you pay any attention to them, they produce more confusion than they do understanding. That is because these maps are, variously, works of the imagination and of commerce at least as much as they are works of science.

There are three of them. The earliest is drawn in blotted and badly faded brown ink on a quarto sheet and purports to show the country between Fort Number Four on the Connecticut River in southern New Hampshire, and Montreal. It has no date but may have been made as early as 1750, probably by a British officer, Major Bascomb, or Barcomb, whose name appears faintly in a corner of the map. If all their military maps were as good as the major's, the British did well to hang on to their colonies in North America as long as they did; for the Bascomb map is mainly worthless. If it were accurate, Mount Ararat and the Dead River, both of which are clearly drawn and labeled and placed correctly relative to each other, wouldn't be on it at all. Bennington, Vermont, and Albany are on the Bascomb map, both located many miles north and east of where they belong. Montreal is on it, too, having been moved at least 150 miles south. Lake Champlain shows as a minor pond. The Bascomb map is easily available today only in facsimile. The real thing is in the collection of one of the libraries at Harvard, with the rest of the world's fiction.

The two nineteenth-century maps of the town of Ambrose are more accurate than the Bascomb map, certainly—or anyway their inaccuracy is better hidden. Both show the township on a folio page of its own, in a scale of about an inch and a half to a mile. Roughly, the township of Ambrose is a square six miles on a side, containing three hamlets or villages: the village, Ambrose, Dead River Settlement, and North Ambrose or Joppa. The town is divided diagonally by the Dead River. To the upper left of the river, and oriented parallel to it, two elevations, Bible Hill and Round Mountain; separating them, the Quick Branch of the Dead River, which joins it in about the center of the town. To the lower right of the river, level valley land, then the corner or rear of Diamond Mountain, most of which is in the towns adjoining Ambrose to the east and south. (Our share of Diamond Mountain, therefore, is known as Back Diamond Mountain.)

The older of the two nineteenth-century maps was published in 1856 by C. McClellan & Co., a firm of commercial mapmakers in Philadelphia. In addition to the lay of the land, McClellan maps the town's roads, and the households and other buildings of residents, each labeled with the owners' names. It all sounds pretty straightforward until you compare McClellan's world with reality. Then you find, for example, that his map puts the western half of Bible Hill not in Ambrose but in the next township over, and that at one point he seems to make the Quick Branch of the Dead River run smartly uphill.

The best old map of the township is by F. W. Beers, another Philadelphia concern, and was published in 1869. It's on the same principle as McClellan: farms, dwellings, shops, and so on all indicated, all owners named. On the road where I live, for example, Beers shows eight homesteads, labeled Madison, Hammersmith, Ballantine, Littlejohn, Brown, VanBuren, Scott, and Mrs. Tyler. It's just here, in its meticulous detail, that the map's failure lies. These maps weren't made for fun. Beers was in it for cash. The cash came from Madison, Mrs. Tyler, and the rest. The company's representative called on each householder in the town, explained the map project; discoursed on its technical sophistication, its utility, its permanence, its beauty; showed samples; declared that the householder's neighbors were already eager, fully paid-up participants in the exciting enterprise; and asked for his subscription, payable then and there. Those who came down right had the satisfaction later of finding their names inscribed on the published map. Others did not.

On this same road, a quarter of a mile up the hill from the house labeled Ballantine on the Beers map, are the remains of what must in Beers's time have been a considerable farm. You can see the cellar holes and stone foundations of a house, a large barn, and two other buildings. The Beers map shows no structures on that spot. Why doesn't it? McClellan's 1856 map places on the site a farm holding belonging to somebody named Emerson. What happened to him? It's not likely that such a big place was abandoned and allowed to disappear in the thirteen years between the production of the two maps. More likely is that Emerson refused to pay to have his name and property recorded and so, when the map fellow and his order book went on down the road, Emerson, as far as history would be concerned, ceased to exist. He was a man without publicity, and man without publicity, we know, is as a sounding brass or a tinkling cymbal.

TOWN OF AMBROSE, VERMONT

Table of place names

NAME	DATE	MAP	SOURCE
Mt. Ararat	c. 1760	Bascomb	Genesis 8.9
Dead River	c. 1760	Bascomb	A sluggish stream
Quick Branch	1856	McClellan	A rapid stream
Gold or Money Brook			Gold ore found
New Africa Hill	1856	McClellan	Fugitives
Bone Mtn.	1869	Beers	?
Round Mountain	1954	USGS	Shape
Scotch Plains	c. 1925	—	Rum-running
Hammersmith Hill	1856–1869	Beers	Name of resident
Bible Hill	c. 1900	USGS	Religionists

NAME	DATE	MAP	SOURCE
Squab City	c. 1875		Passenger pigeons
Dead River Settlement	1869–1954	Beers, USGS	Location on river
Beartown	c. 1890		A remote wooded district
Joppa (or Jappa)	1856	McClellan	A far-western district (cf. 2 Chronicles 2:16)
North Ambrose	1869–1956	Beers, USGS	P.O.
Pied Brook	1856–1954	McClellan, Beers USGS	Red stones
Diamond Mtn.	1856	McClellan	Quartzites
Sheep Desert			Overgrazing

5. Population

1

Is Bible Hill coming, today, or is it going? Clearly, the answer is the first. To be sure, decline and depopulation were the condition of the place for 150 years, but more recent numbers tell a different story. Take a look at the population reports for the town of Ambrose from the first U.S. census to the present. You find a V, steep on the left, less so on the right. From a maximum in the census of 1790 (1,566), the population drops off sharply through the nineteenth century and hits bottom in 1930 (662). Since then, the town's census has gradually recovered and now stands above—though not far above—its historic high. Furthermore, after about 1940, the rate of population increase accelerates: We passed our 1790 peak in 1997.

Who is behind this recovery? Mainly, people like me. Call us *flatlanders*: people from away. The case could hardly be otherwise, for a declining population is an aging one. Those lonesome Ambrosians circa 1925 were older by five or ten years, as a mean, than their forerunners and their successors. They were not having the kids; they weren't even reproducing themselves one of one, not close. If the town's population began to rise again, it was because the old-timers were getting some help.

The truth is, they might have been getting more help than they wanted. On Bible Hill alone, consider the past few years: Calabrese and I, flatlanders, immigrants, amount to an increase in population of 66 percent. We look like a tidal wave. You might make a like demonstration, no doubt, for half the back roads in the state.

That's your daughter's place over there? I didn't know you had a daughter.

You didn't know it, but it's a fact nevertheless, son.

What did you say her name was?

Manda. Amanda. Amanda Marlow, she calls herself.

She calls herself? Marlow's her husband?

Was. They split up.

What's she doing on Back Diamond?

That's my place she's in. We had it for a camp when the kids were little; then we rented it. Manda, see, hooked up with Denny Marlow and moved to California with him, was out there, oh, several years, five, six. Six years, I guess. Then when they split up, she needed a place to stay, so she went on up there. It'll do for the summer anyway.

What about her husband?

Mud season. It was in my second spring on Bible Hill that, some time around April Fools' Day, the bottom fell out of the road. This will happen in years when the spring comes all at once, rather than over the space of weeks: The dirt roads, which may be frozen down to a depth of many feet, abruptly thaw, producing mud, producing as well fear, rage, and failure. Producing, finally, a whole tradition of regional humor in the form of mud jokes like the story about the man who, on his way to town one day in mud time, came upon his neighbor sunk up to his neck in the road. Asked if he couldn't use some help getting out of the mud and and into town, the neighbor said yes, he could, but he didn't like to leave his horse. That kind of joke. That kind of mud.

If you live on a road like the Bible Hill road, you learn to tell when the mud of a section you're approaching is merely a foot deep and so, probably, negotiable, and when it is deep as the grave. There are subtle signs, having to do with the general color and sheen of the surface of the mud, but I didn't know those signs that spring, and so it was that, driving down to the village one noon, I got my little car sunk to its floorboards and very well and truly stuck. Presently, Calabrese came along, stopped, and offered to pull me out with his truck, which was big, lofty, powerful, and plainly up to the task. I thanked him. Calabrese drove into the mire behind my car, hooked a chain on, reversed—and got stuck himself.

"Still, you know," said Calabrese. "This is better than potholes. Potholes will really hammer your vehicle."

"Sure," I said. "This is a lot better. All we have to do is wait till the mud dries up, right? Not more than another week. A week at most."

As it was, though, Calabrese walked back to his place and returned with a tool, a kind of portable windlass. With it chained to a big tree by the side of the road and its cable extended by another chain, we were able, in an hour or so, to pull first Calabrese's truck and then my car out of the mud hole.

For the next few days, therefore, I had to get in and out on foot. Because of the mud, I had to walk. And so my story begins.

April Fools' Day: bright, not quite warm, small clouds passing, the thin, mild sun striking down through the unleaved woods. A prime mud day. A light blue Mustang, a powerhouse in its time but its time long past, a car even older than mine, over its axles in the Brown Impassible on Bible Hill road. A young woman sitting on the car's long hood, stretching her face and neck up to the reluctant sun, then turning to look at me as I came up on foot.

What I remember best about Amanda that day are her arms. They were bare. She'd taken off whatever she wore for a jacket or sweater, leaving her arms bare, round, and white. It's a long winter on Bible Hill—was and is—and the sight of a youthful female arm, the whole thing, uncovered, was about enough to raise the dead—was and is.

"Hi," I said.

Amanda didn't reply at first. Today I see that I was not, at the time, a figure to inspire confidence in a woman stuck alone on a deserted road a mile from any house. I was between jobs that spring. I shaved on a weekly basis, bathed likewise, and saw no reason to do frequent laundry when clean clothes became mud-covered in hours. So, if you were Amanda, here was a large, shabby, dirty, unshaven man appearing out of the woods.

"Hi," I said again.

Amanda looked me up and down one time, then again. She blinked.

"You are?" said Amanda.

2

What is a population? It's native-born and newcomers. You were born here or you weren't. That much is pretty close to pure logic, isn't it? You're here. That you came here either by nature or, so to speak, by road and rail would seem to be a matter self-evident, so obvious as to be of no practical importance. On the contrary. It is very often the single matter of practical importance. Around here, birth is what religion is in the Middle East, in the Balkans, in Ulster: not the biggest thing, the only thing. The gap between born here and not born here becomes a kind of intellectual black hole, sucking into itself and consigning to utter nonbeing every other, more substantial, question.

Thus it is that your every choice, your every opinion—on politics, baseball, the lumber industry, hunting, fishing, cars, schools, movies, music, farming, forestry, firearms, beer, law, property, septic tanks—all descend sooner or later to the level of born here, not born here.

Even the larger, more ancient and universal divisions in philosophy seem to be only surrogates for the real division, that of personal origin: free will or determinism; spirit or matter; the individual or the society; experience or reason; Aristotle or Plato; Burke or Robespierre; Hamilton or Jefferson—they all come down to from here or from away.

What we have here, evidently, is a permanent impasse, an insuperable intellectual gulf. The only sensible response is to ignore the entire business. That's what I did. Amanda once paid me a pretty compliment.

"You know what I like about you, Noon?" she asked me.

"Tell me."

"You don't belong here. You never will. But you don't seem to care. I like that."

What about her husband?

What about him? He's a nice kid. He's a smart kid, too. But he don't have any sense. They neither of them do. Denny figured he'd be an actor, why they went out there in the first place. He'd be a movie star. I don't know but what he might do it, but still, it ain't something you try to be, is it?

Why not?

Well, it don't seem like it makes much sense, that's all. Denny's Arthur Marlow's youngest, over here in Dead River. Arthur and Enid's. They must have four or five. Denny's the youngest, or maybe he's the next-to-youngest. Arthur's got the excavating business over there. He does all right. When they're building, he does better than all right. The other kids got big, went to work for their dad. Not Denny. He'd rather be a movie star. Well, so would I, I guess. Than drive a backhoe for a living? Sure, I would. But, I don't know, it don't make sense to me. It don't seem like it's something that's going to happen.

So what?

I don't know, son. Maybe it will, or maybe it don't matter. Anyway, Manda's up there on the mountain now. It'll do for her for the summer at least. After that, who knows? I doubt she'll stick it out here too long. She's impatient. The truth is, she don't much like it around here. Never has.

Her husband's still in California, then?

Far as I know. You see, what it was, she didn't even want to finish school. Her mother told her she had to. Her mother made her finish high school—but then she died. The thing was, she died, Edith did. And it looked like I never had the knack of talking to Manda, that way, as much, you see. Day after graduation, she and Denny took off in Denny's Mustang, which didn't look like it would get as far as Brattleboro. Well, it's the one she's got now. It got her out there and it got her back. Good car. She just got in beside him and off they went. I didn't know what to do. I didn't know how to stop her. I didn't know if I ought to stop her. I didn't know what to tell her. She'd been going to go to college. She was always going to be a vet—though I guess every girl's going to be a vet at some time, ain't they, son?

So what about her husband, though?

You asked me that already, son. What's your interest?

"Can I help you?" I asked Amanda.

"I don't know," she said.

"I could get behind you and push," I said.

"That's funny, right?" said Amanda.

"I'm trying to help you," I said.

Amanda looked down at the mud.

"I don't know if a push will do it," she said.

"Well," I said, "if it doesn't, I can go and get my neighbor's come-along. That will do it."

"Your neighbor?" said Amanda. "You mean there's people back up here?"

I left her, walked back to Calabrese's. Calabrese wasn't home, but I knew where he kept his little windlass. I found it, went back to Amanda, hooked up the windlass the way Calabrese and I had done a few days before, pulled her car out of the mud hole, started it up, backed it around, and got it pointed down the hill the way she had come. Then Amanda drove and I rode with her the rest of the way to the village.

"You really live back there?" Amanda asked me.

"Yes. Not far from where you got stuck."

"Where?" she asked. "In a cave?"

"In a house," I said.

"You don't mean Littlejohn's?" said Amanda.

3

Population is history. Compare the course of depopulation and repopulation in a place like Ambrose, Vermont, with the narrative of the United States, and you can discern the hard demographic structure that underlies the flux of history. Through the nineteenth century and half the twentieth, America is seen to have acted as a kind of vast historical pump on its decompression stroke, sucking people irresistibly out of these hills and depositing them in the farm states of the new Middle West and in the factory towns of southern New England. Then, after the turn of our century, the engine slowed . . . stopped . . . and began to run in reverse. Now it was pumping people out of the rest of the country and pushing them back up here. You can see it happen in the census reports. But those reports are only numbers; and numbers tell you only about other numbers. Population is not history; it's the opposite of history: the personal, the private, the unknowable. Amanda had gotten stuck on Bible Hill trying to find Littlejohn's place. She couldn't believe I lived there.

"You're kidding," she said.

"I'm not," I said. "Littlejohn's is my place now. I own it."

"Lucky you," said Amanda. "That's where I was going. I thought I'd passed it, or where it was. I'd have thought Littlejohn's would have fallen down years ago."

"How do you know about it?" I asked Amanda.

"We used to go up there when I was a little girl," she said. "I've been away. I don't know you, do I?"

"No," I said. "I'm new here."

"Lucky you," Amanda said again. "But God. Why?"

"Why what?"

"Why do you want to live way back there? Do you even have electric?"

"No," I said. "The line ends at Miss Drumheller's. I'm going to have it run in, though. Someday. It's expensive."

Amanda shook her head as she drove. She had curly light brown or red-brown hair, and on her bare right shoulder she had a spot of mud that I thought about removing for her but did not.

"I don't get it," said Amanda.

"Everybody has to be someplace," I said. "I'm there. I like it."

"You'd have to," said Amanda.

When both deliberate, the love is slight;
Who ever loved that loved not at first sight?

It's a good line, good enough for Shakespeare himself to have pinched it from Marlowe—not Amanda's sociopathic ex, but the other Marlowe. You can look him up in the *Norton Anthology*. We Noons are English majors. We know the players; we know their games. Therefore, we also know how to long; we know how to pine. We know how to serve an indifferent mistress. We know how to fail at love. Do we know how to succeed at it?

I didn't see Amanda for a week or more after our first meeting. The mud dried up, the road opened, and I began to work at the sawmill in the village, Jordan's. Mainly, I lugged boards from one place to another and shoveled sawdust. It was hard work, especially following a long winter doing nothing. For several days after I started at Jordan's, I was too broken down when quitting time came to buy groceries, take them home, and fix my supper. Instead, I'd stop in for a bowl of chili and a beer at the Weed.

The Weed's real name was Brown's Tumbleweed Inn. It was half a mile out of the village on the road to Dead River Settlement. The place amounted to a long barroom adjoined by a dinning room having maybe twenty tables: a medium-sized place, then, the only real restaurant in town.

In decor, the Weed was something of an anomaly in the neighborhood, in New England itself. Its look and spirit were of the Wild West. Most restaurants in this part of the country are content to align themselves with the established iconography of the region. Black-and-white cows, covered bridges, sap buckets, autumn hillsides, and the like make up their decoration. At the Weed, you had a lithograph of Custer's Last Stand, four by nine feet, hanging on the wall at one end of the bar, and at the other, a tintype of Front Street, Abilene, Kansas, in 1876. The owner, Brown, shortly after he opened the place in 1958, had found the lithograph of Custer's Last Stand at the flea market that operated on the old fairgrounds in Joppa. He'd bought it for two bucks, hung it up at the end of the bar, and gone on from there.

By the time I arrived on Bible Hill, the Weed had established a kind of schizoid identity in the district, a wild alternation of order and chaos, cycling on a weekly basis as though under the tidal influence of a small private moon. Through the week, the Weed was a lunch and dinner place for a fairly quiet, middle-aged crowd. The bar was empty. You saw your neighbors—all your neighbors—in the dining room, eating hamburgers, Brown's spaghetti and meatballs, London broil. They were with their children, grandchildren, and visitors from out of town. They drank a beer apiece with their meal, had a cup of coffee, went home.

Then, beginning Friday after work and culminating at Saturday-night closing, which was two o'clock Sunday morning, the Weed's moon drew close, too close. Its tug began to be felt. The noise level went up; the fuel changed; the crowd changed—changed drastically, and not for the better. Those nights, the Weed could be heard for miles around. There was yelling; there was fighting; there were roaring engines and screaming tires. The country sheriff's office and the state police were regularly on the premises early of a Sunday morning. One such night, it took three sheriff's deputies, all six troopers from the Brattleboro barracks, two game wardens, and elements of the Vermont National Guard to pacify the Weed.

Sunday was calmer. Mondays, Brown closed.

A witty place, too, the Weed, in its way. The bar was overhung by the head and shoulders of a bison, which dominated the room from its central place on the wall behind the middle of the bar, with Custer's Last Stand to its right, Abilene to its left. The mounted head was enormous; it must have been five feet high and weighed a hundred pounds, and it loomed over the bar, dark, shaggy, horned, its black glass eyes the size of billiard balls. But directly behind the bison's head, in the men's room on the other side of the partition, located where the rest of the living bison would have been, Brown had hung the stuffed hindquarters of a cottontail rabbit. Some people called the Weed "the Bunny-Ass Bar."

The Weed is gone now. They had a fire and Brown didn't reopen. Custer's Last Stand, Abilene, and the great bison burned up. The fire department managed to save the bunny's ass, though. They plucked it from the flames. Brown told them it was theirs and they hung it up in the trophy case at the firehouse.

Normally, the bar at the Weed was handled by a man named Potvin. Potvin liked to bet. In the spring I am telling about, he picked a five-thousand-dollar lottery ticket and took his winnings to Las Vegas for as long as they would last, leaving Brown in temporary need of help. So it was that on the day when I sank exhausted onto a stool at the bar of the Weed and waited for succor, I found myself looking not at Potvin but at the April Fools' mud queen.

"It's you," I said. "What are you doing here?"

"Filling in for Brown's regular," she said. "Are you okay?"

"I'm tired," I said.

"You look like you're dying," said Amanda.

"Can I have a beer, please?"

Amanda drew a glass of beer from the taps and put it before me. I got out my money to pay for the beer, but she stopped me.

"On me," said Amanda. "Thanks for helping get me out the other day."

"It's all right," I said. "Thanks for the beer."

"You're welcome," said Amanda. "What's your name?"

"Mark," I said. "Mark Noon."

"Noon?" said Amanda. "That's a funny name. What is that, German?"

"Cherokee," I said.

"Uh-huh," said Amanda. She moved away down the bar then to see to another customer, but later she came back, and when Brown left the kitchen to take the bar and give her a break, she sat with me at a table in the corner. I was never much for the club life, in any of its forms, and I avoided Brown's place during combat hours at the weekend; but I stayed late at the Weed that night. For a time, I was a regular. The Weed knew me well that spring. What can I say? I fell in love with a bartender.

You never been married, have you, son?

No.

No, but don't it seem to you . . . What I mean, Manda and Denny didn't think. They decided to get married, they got married. They decided to stop being married, they stopped. You see?

Yes. So?

Well, so, don't it seem to you like something's missing there? You got married, you made a deal, didn't you? You made a contract. You took a promise. You stick by that. You don't change your mind and undo it.

That's how it used to work, I guess.

You ain't hearing me, son. I didn't say used to. I didn't say in my day. I didn't say everything was better back in the past. I didn't say anything was. I know different. I was there. I'm saying if you take a promise, you do it; if you decide you don't want to do it anymore, you still do it. That's what a marriage is. It's a promise. Then, now, anytime.

You're right. As far as it goes, you're right.

With Manda, though, I don't know. She's stubborn. She goes her own way.

She does?

4

Today you have to look at the science, the real science: the molecules, the chemistry. What is a population, chemically? Only a reproductive mass, a soup of genes stirred by the great finger of God, or by the complex mechanisms of nature, or by whatever you please. Whether it's coming or going, whether it's born here or not born here, whether it's running to its history or away from it, a population is nothing but a place where genes combine. Which genes, what combinations, hardly matter.

"All right," I said to Amanda. "I don't belong here. I came in from outside. That's me. What about you? You were born here, but you left. You broke the chain. Now you're back, but you came back from away. So, does that make you belong here, or somewhere else?"

"Here," said Amanda. "Like it or not."

"Okay," I said. "What if you and I had a baby . . ."

Amanda looked at me levelly. She raised her left eyebrow.

"You and I are not going to have a baby, Noon," she said.

"Of course not," I said. "But hypothetically. What if we had a baby?"

"What if we did?"

"Well," I said, "would our baby belong here?"

"Yes," said Amanda.

"Even though I don't?"

"Yes."

"So it's like being a Jew, isn't it?" I said. "It goes by the mother's line. You've got a little matriarchy going up here. The guys don't count. They only think they do. Now I understand everything."

"You think so?" Amanda asked.

"Sure," I said.

"You're a scholar, Noon," Amanda said. "You're a dreamer."

"I know," I said. "I am. I dream about you."

"Say what?" asked Amanda.

Anyway, she's back now.

How long has she been back?

I don't know, a couple of weeks.

Why doesn't she live with you?

She don't want to. She wants her independence, I guess you'd say.

What does she do?

Well, she's working for Brown right now. When she's not working, she drives around in that beat-up Mustang. I don't care how good a rig it turned out to be; it can't last long.

Wait a minute. Brown's? A Mustang? What color?

Light blue. She met you up by your place, the other day, she said.

Quick-witted we Noons may not be, but how was I to tell that Mr. Applegate's wandering daughter and the new cupbearer of the Weed were one and the same? Ambrose was a smaller place even than I had understood, it seemed. So, quick-witted? No. Useful, though, and willing.

That's your daughter?

I know, I know. We are advised never to go to bed with anyone whose troubles are worse than our own—but how are we to tell? So often it happens that the bed part comes first, the troubles part later. Not that it was that way in our case. Amanda was in no hurry. But the principle is the same: first you jump; then you fall.

TOWN OF AMBROSE, VERMONT

Comparative table of population by census

CENSUS	USA*	VERMONT†	AMBROSE
1790	3,929,214	85,425	1,566
1810	7,239,881	217,895	1,521
1830	12,860,702	280,652	1,499
1850	23,191,876	314,120	1,417
1870	38,558,371	330,551	1,113
1890	62,979,766	332,422	952
1910	92,228,496	355,956	820

CENSUS	USA*	VERMONT†	AMBROSE
1930	123,202,624	359,611	662
1950	151,325,798	377,741	708
1970	203,302,031	444,732	900
1990	226,542,203	511,456	1,212

* United States Bureau of the Census.

† *Vermont Facts & Figures.*

6. Former Inhabitants

For human society I was obliged to conjure up the former occupants of these woods.
—Henry David Thoreau, *Walden*

1

Bible Hill was my Palestine, my Alexandria, my Troy: a place formerly greater, far greater, than it is found in the present to be; a place whose population, whose prosperity, whose confidence, whose very reason for being are no more than the ghosts of what has been. A kind of ruin, it was.

I liked it. Something in the declined, backward-looking condition of the place reached right to me. I liked its works, its remains on the land. I liked its cast of characters, now all but vanished. I liked its busted, obsolete tools, its pots and pans, its humble, flea market archaeology. From the first, I knew Bible Hill was my kind of place, even before I knew what my kind of place was.

I found at Littlejohn's, when I arrived, a cast-iron kitchen stove that burned wood, a cane-bottom rocking chair shaky and loud in the joints, a straight chair with no seat, a camp bed, a square oak table much cut and scarred and having a single shallow drawer containing three pennies, dated 1931, 1931, and 1938. I found an ax, a scythe, an iron kettle four feet high, cracked up and down like the Liberty Bell. I found a pile of Brattleboro newspapers from the year 1944, a trunk full of army blankets, another trunk that was locked. I found a hairbrush, a pair of wire-rim spectacles, and twenty-three empty bottles—not milk bottles. I kept everything. It seemed wrong not to, there was so little.

I found Littlejohn's stuff, therefore—and shortly I came to believe I might also have found Littlejohn himself.

In the middle of the night, a week after I'd moved in, I was awakened by a loud thumping and banging overhead. I thought a tree had fallen on the roof, but the noises continued, a heavy bumping and dragging, as though someone were moving furniture without enough help. It came from the attic.

At this time, the house had no electric power, and so no good light at night. I left my bed, took a flashlight, went out into the passage, and stood under the trap in the ceiling that gave into the attic. There were no attic stairs. I climbed onto Littlejohn's no-seat chair, opened the trap, got my arms up into the attic, and lifted myself. The bumping had stopped.

In the attic, it was not completely dark, for the moon, on its way down, was in one of the gable windows under the peak of the roof. I could see the empty attic, the pitched roof, the heavy old rafters. I could see the chimney. I could see Littlejohn's two trunks in the corner under the window, the one full of ragged blankets, the other locked. I switched on the flashlight. The locked trunk wasn't locked tonight. It stood open, its top flung back against the wall.

I hoisted myself all the way into the attic. I couldn't stand to my full height in there, but if I stuck to the middle of the space, directly under the roof beam, I was able to walk stooped. I got to my feet and, keeping the flashlight on the open trunk, I went to it. I put the light down into its interior. The trunk was half-full of books, little books and bigger books. I looked around the attic with the light. I put the light into every corner; I put it behind the chimney. There was nobody in the attic; there was nothing out of place there or otherwise amiss that I could see.

I dragged Littlejohn's trunk over to the hatch and got it down into the house. I took out one of the books and opened it. It wasn't a real book, but an old-fashioned school composition book written up as a journal or diary.

January 1, 1900. Clear, blows. Temp. 12M 20.
Snow pm. 20 centory

Flying squirrels.

No.

I'm telling you, son. You've got a bunch of flying squirrels in your attic. Pretty little silver-colored things. Live in hollow trees, live in sheds, live in attics. They love attics. Only come out at night; you don't know they're there. They go running around in the attic. Flying squirrels.

This was no squirrel. It was big and heavy.

Then it was a coon up there, or a porcupine. Remember, that place stood empty for I don't know—seven, eight years? More? Probably more. God knows what's living there—besides you, I mean.

No coon or porcupine opened that trunk.

A coon might. But, no—all right, son. Say they didn't. Where's that put you? You tell me. Are you saying it was Claude Littlejohn banging around up there? Claude died in '60, '61. Sixty-two? He's gone.

Not him. I'd have seen him.

Oh. I see. Now I get it. You're saying it's Claude Littlejohn's ghost living in your attic. You don't believe that, son.

No, I don't. But I believe something was up there the other night. Something made all that noise. Something opened the trunk. I went up. I looked. Nothing was there. I'm not saying I think it was anybody's ghost, but suppose I did think that. Does it make less sense to believe in a ghost than it does to believe in an invisible porcupine?

You didn't see a porcupine, don't make the porcupine invisible, son.

So a hard-to-see porcupine opened Littlejohn's trunk? Don't forget: The trunk was locked. Your coon, your porcupine, it had the key right?

That's a funny thing about that trunk.

I'd say so, too. I'd say it was pretty funny.

No, I don't mean that. I mean that it was there at all. And that book. A diary?

A lot of diaries. There are forty-odd of them. Some old pictures, too.

Yes. It's funny Claude kept up a diary. I never knew it. And it's funny Hugo didn't take it. Them. The books. He'd about cleaned Claude's place out, I'd thought. I wonder Hugo left it.

Maybe he didn't know they were there.

Oh, Hugo knew. He would have known. He knew what was there. It was his place by then.

On his own farm, ill and with only a few years to live, my predecessor, Littlejohn, had become the abject tenant of Hugo Usher, who bought him out but gave him a life lease of the place. Miss Drumheller knew about the arrangement. She had known two generations of Ushers, father and son both. She hadn't much opinion of the second.

"Hugo Usher was a vain man," she said. "Not vain—willful. Pigheaded. He didn't know what he wanted; he never knew. He only knew he wanted it. But he wasn't mean. He didn't have to lease back to Claude Littlejohn. Claude Littlejohn was destitute; he was crippled; he was drunk; he belonged at the poor farm. And he was no friend of Hugo's, not after their nonsense with that horse. But Hugo bought him out, paid his taxes, gave him a mortgage on his own place so he could stay there and have an income to live and pay his lease. He did it for his father's sake, I expect. Anson Usher had always admired Littlejohn's place, and he was another man who got what he wanted."

"It sounds complicated," I said.

"It wasn't," said Miss Drumheller. "Anson Usher wanted Littlejohn's place. He'd always wanted it. It was small, but it lay well, the land open and looking south, with an orchard and a sugar woods and some timber. Of course, that was fifty years ago. Now it's a mess, worthless, a jungle."

"Thanks," I said.

Miss Drumheller ignored me. "Anson Usher offered to buy the place from Littlejohn for a fair price," she said. "Not a fair price—a high price. He offered more than once. Claude Littlejohn wouldn't sell. Then, after Hugo's father's time, when Littlejohn was old, he got hurt; he couldn't work. Couldn't pay his taxes. Could hardly keep himself. Hugo might have had the place for the unpaid taxes by then, but instead, he made the same offer his father had made before, a generous offer."

"Littlejohn sold," I said.

"He did," said Miss Drumheller. "What else could he do?" She laughed. "He sold, but he made a condition. Claude Littlejohn made a condition. He said he'd sell to Hugo for so many dollars, the leaseback, and Hugo's agreement never to set foot on the property again, for any reason, while Littlejohn lived. Claude Littlejohn didn't even want to have to look at him."

July 4, 1900. Temp. 12M 77. Independence Day. Rain p.m. No parade

Yes, with Hugo and Claude, there was no love lost, you might say. Hugo always thought Claude foxed him about Dan.

Who was Dan?

Dan was a horse, son.

Littlejohn cheated him over a horse?

He didn't, really, or he didn't any more than was right. But Hugo had the idea he did. Hugo had a lot of ideas. And his father, Anson, was a funny old boy, too. I didn't know him, really. Hugo's dad liked to hold himself high, you know what I mean. You didn't get to know him. Hugo, now. I knew Hugo.

If he thought Littlejohn had cheated him, why did he let him stay on his place? Why not throw him off?

I don't know, son. Hugo wanted that place of Claude's, though. I don't expect it was the land he was after, exactly. Thing about him, I guess, was he was like the old story about the fellow who kept buying his neighbors out. You know that story? This fellow, any lot of land that came on the market, he'd buy it, didn't matter what it was: good, bad, mowing, pasture, woods, roadside, swamp. This fellow has to have it; he buys it all. So they ask him what he needs all that property for, and he says, "Don't like folks owning land next to mine."

2

Not that Bible Hill and Ambrose township, in the days of their strength, were to be known only from the memories of Miss Drumheller and Mr. Applegate. Not at all. Indeed, you could argue that they had missed the best of the show almost as much as I had. For hereabouts, the ruling century, for fame, was not theirs, ours; it was the nineteenth. During that long age, before the people were found to have deteriorated into yokels, shopkeepers, and eccentrics, there were giants in the earth and all this land was filled with faerie.

We had, right here, statesmen, warriors, heroic healers, even a kind of poet. Percival Munro (1842–1891), born in the Joppa district, was famous in his time for his verses and songs, somewhat after the manner of Stephen Foster. Munro was by way of being a professional Scot. His works had titles like "The Croft in the Glen," "The Maid in Mantle Green," and "The Laird of Lothian." In adulthood, Munro lived and worked in New York City, but Ambrose, Vermont, claimed him then, and would claim him still, perhaps, if it hadn't utterly forgotten him.

The town's other historic figures were more worldly. We had two congressmen and a superior court judge. We had better than that. Bible Hill itself was the birthplace of Julius Scott (1811–1883), United States senator from Iowa; later, an undersecretary in the Lincoln administration; later still, a senator again, this time from Wyoming; architect of the Scott Tariff Act of 1893; and thereafter, briefly, U.S. ambassador to the Austro-Hungarian empire; recalled after six months in Vienna, and, en route home, drowned in the wreck of the steamer *Agamemnon* off Montauk. The cellar hole that had been the Scott place was on my property line with Calabrese.

Ambrose village had for its chief nineteenth-century ornament Louisa Mackenzie (1819–1862), who, unmarried, went to the Civil War as a nurse in the great military hospitals in Washington, D.C. There, Miss Mackenzie quickly saw that, given the state of medicine at the time, hospitals were superfluous: The badly wounded, they couldn't save; the slightly wounded, they made worse. Nursing was essential, not in the rear, among the hospitals, but on the battlefield itself. To the battlefield, therefore, Louisa Mackenzie took herself, with three other women, in defiance of the War Department and at risk of arrest. The War Department didn't have time to arrest her. She and all her helpers were killed in the explosion of a Union battery behind Antietam.

Also connected with the Civil War was the township's most colorful, most ambiguous ancient hero, the abolitionist and later cavalryman Gideon Harkness (1802–1865), whose tireless work in aiding fugitive slaves from the South gave one of its former names to the hill where his farm was.

Gideon Harkness was a lesser John Brown. For years, beginning in the 1840s, he harbored slaves bound for Canada on the so-called Underground Railroad. He did more than take in fugitives and pass them up the line, however. Gideon Harkness, who was a childless bachelor, had at any one time a small community of fugitives working his farm on Mt. Ararat, as his hill was then known. No doubt the townspeople at the time were less than sold on Gideon; no doubt they told amazing stories about him and his changing black retinue. But, then as now, those same townspeople would leave you alone, mostly, if you let them. Gideon Harkness's slave-rescue station prospered, and the people called his part of town New Africa Hill and went about their business.

Then in 1850, the United States Congress passed the Fugitive Slave Act, and southern slave catchers began to come north to seize runaways and carry them back to their owners in Virginia, the Carolinas, Georgia. Late in 1860, two such officers arrived on New Africa Hill. Gideon Harkness's work there was hardly a secret. By then, he was famous, in a small way, throughout New England. The Carolina marshals knew where to find him. They didn't know, perhaps, that their advent was what Gideon, who was quite mad, had been waiting for for twenty years. He had armed and drilled his fugitives, put up an earthwork around his farmhouse, and mounted a four-pounder cannon to enfilade the lane. When the officers rode into the lane, Gideon didn't hesitate. He gave no warning. He opened on them with grapeshot, slightly wounding one and killing one of their horses. The sheriffs rode double right back to Carolina. Federal charges were filed against Gideon Harkness, but no local authority could immediately be found to bring him to book, and when the war began, months or weeks after his stand on New Africa Hill, the matter became moot.

Gideon Harkness, aged sixty when war came, raised a cavalry regiment from Ambrose and the surrounding townships and took it south. He led the regiment as its colonel through several of the eastern campaigns. He died in mysterious circumstances—not in battle, evidently—near Front Royal, Virginia, in the last month of the war.

In 1877, the state of Vermont provided a granite obelisk to mark Gideon Harkness's grave in the family plot on New Africa Hill. On the side of the shaft was a relief sculpture showing Colonel Harkness, in a kind of toga, leading a ragged pair of Negro children by the hand through an archway. The sculptor showed Harkness as a demigod, erect, tall, and the slave children as pop-eyed, woolly-headed gnomes. Altogether, it's not an image exactly to the taste of a later era—but no matter: The Harkness farm has long since been abandoned; the family plot has disappeared, and so has the obelisk. There is a market for such things, apparently, even the incorrect ones.

3

The books I found in Littlejohn's trunk numbered forty-seven. All were slender volumes cheaply bound in boards. Some were composition books, some were ledgers or account books, and some were little vest-pocket notebooks. All were filled—or mostly filled—with brief diary entries written in a firm, neat copperplate hand—Littlejohn's, apparently. The earliest diary was for the year 1898, the latest, for 1961. Littlejohn had skipped a few years entirely, and he had skipped parts of others; but he had worn through an impressive bulk of time, a matter of sixty-three years: two big wars, one little one, eleven presidents, the world made over by science, then made over again. A lifetime. Not that Littlejohn's record, long as it ran, can have been much of a chore to keep up. Most of his entries were confined to a single line; none ran longer than three lines.

I also found, slipped between the pages of one of Littlejohn's volumes (the one for the year 1920), two photographs. The photos were about five-by-seven. They were evidently a matched pair, tinted brown, and mounted on stiff cardboard. In the lower-right corner of each, in ornate script, ran the photographer's legend: *Angel's Studio, Rutland, Vt.*

One photo showed a woman in her early twenties, light-haired, dark-eyed, full-lipped. She was seated, and you saw her from the waist up. She wore a loose, cool white dress that left her long neck bare. Around her neck, she wore an old-fashioned close-fitting black velvet ribbon. Her right arm rested on a low column or pillar. She gazed boldly, straight into the camera's lens, unsmiling. On the reverse of her photo were the initials S.B., written in pencil.

The other photo was of a man, older, whose age was hard to fix—say more than thirty, less than fifty. He wore a dark suit and a collar and tie, but he didn't look like he belonged in them. He stood beside the same column that appeared in the woman's picture, resting the fingers of his right hand on its top. He had dark curly hair, dark brows, and a big dark mustache that hid his mouth. He was not looking into the camera, but to one side and slightly down. On the reverse of his picture, there was no writing of any kind.

Is that Littlejohn?

I wouldn't know, son. I guess it might be. Let me see it. I guess it might be Claude. Claude had curly hair like that, but of course when I knew him, he hadn't this much of it and it was white. I really couldn't say this was him.

And the woman?

No idea. These old photos, you know. They all look alike, don't they? She could be your grandma and you wouldn't know her.

S.B.?

Sarah Bernhardt, son. How do I know? Susie Blue-Eyes.

August 1, 1900. Warm. Temp. 12M 94. Dry
August 2, 1900. Temp. 12M 85. Well down

I thought it odd how hard it was to learn much for certain about Littlejohn. I owned his diaries. I read them. I knew what he'd done every day of his adult life, or close to it. I lived in his house, alone, as he had, among his things—the only house, the only things, he'd ever known. In a way, therefore, I lived on terms of some intimacy with Littlejohn. And, after all, Littlejohn wasn't part of the storied past. When I arrived on Bible Hill, he'd been dead about ten years. Not so long—but what was known of him? He was buried in the little Bible Hill cemetery, where his grave marker gave the year of his birth as 1879. He'd lived on Bible Hill, latterly as the reluctant ward of Hugo Usher, my legator. He'd died in 1961 at eighty-one or-two. He'd had the reputation of being a drunk.

"Is that Littlejohn?" I asked Miss Drumheller.

"Let me see," she said. She took the picture, held it under the lamp at her elbow. She handed it back to me.

"That's Littlejohn," said Miss Drumheller.

"Are you sure?" I asked her.

"I'm sure," she said.

"How well did you know him?"

"As well as I had to," said Miss Drumheller. "No better. When I first came to this house, he'd come down to chop wood for me for pay. He worked in the yard. He wouldn't come in—well, he would have. I didn't ask him to. He hadn't much to say. He was a good-enough worker, I suppose—not good, but good enough, when he was sober. He was nearly as big as you and very strong."

"Who's his lady friend?"

Miss Drumheller held the picture of Littlejohn in her right hand, the picture of the young woman in her left. She looked from one of them to the other.

"Do you know who she is?" I asked her.

"Yes," said Miss Drumheller.

"Is she you?"

"No," said Miss Drumheller. "My sister."

"S.B.?"

"Sibyl Bradshaw," said Miss Drumheller.

4

Go back much before 1800, and the former inhabitants of Bible Hill cease to have names and addresses. They become hypothetical, algebraic, mere quantities or counters in the game of history: Indians, explorers, soldiers, traders, colonists. They never interested me as much as their great-great-great-grandchildren did, but they have their scholars, plenty of them—more scholars, in fact, than attend on their descendants.

European man is old in this section. Long before the first settlements, British armies passed through the region on their way from Boston to the frontier outposts around Crown Point and Lake Champlain. Long before them, the French, in the character of missionary priests and coureurs de bois, crossed the region in search of savages to baptize and peltry to adorn the fashion of Louis XIV. The French and the British, especially their fighting men, left behind them vanished strongholds, buttons, clay pipes, nails, musket balls, their teeth, their bones—a small museum full of remains both rich and unequivocal.

There may or may not be an even older European presence. The question is open. What your view of it is depends on what you make of certain curious structures to be found here and there in the woods of the neighborhood. Mainly, these are small three-sided enclosures or chambers, built up of fieldstone like a dry-laid wall and roofed with enormous slabs of granite. A big chamber might be six or seven feet square, five feet high. Earth has in most cases been banked up around and on top of these chambers, making them into low mounds.

There were two stone chambers in the township of Ambrose that I knew about. One was in the deep woods on top of Round Mountain. It was roofless but unusually large, ten feet square, and had an oblong stone set on its end in the earth a few feet in front of its open side. The other was on the far side of Bible Hill, in the woods near Sheep Desert: a classic stone chamber, with an interior the size of a cut-down telephone booth and a single roof stone that must have weighed a thousand pounds.

The question is, Whose work are these? Nobody believes they were made by the Indians. Bible Hill's Indians, such as they were, apparently didn't build with stone. Therefore, the question becomes, Whom do you like for the builders of our famous stone chambers? Do you like Vikings (circa A.D. 700)? Do you like Icelanders (circa A.D. 500)? Do you like Irish monks (circa A.D. 200)? There is even a party that likes Phoenicians, the far-voyaging maritime traders of Homer's Mediterranean (circa 800 B.C.), as the builders of Bible Hill's artful, enigmatic rock piles.

Then there are the skeptics.

Pigpens, son.

Nonsense.

Pigpens. Cow pens. Sheep pens. Potato cellars. There's no mystery here at all. It's easy. No Phoenicians need apply.

You're crazy. Nobody builds something like that to keep his cow in. Think of the work.

People put those things up knew how to work, son.

Look, it's not believable. It would be like building a cathedral for a pissoir.

For a which?

An outhouse. You don't build a stone outhouse. Think about it.

You think about it, son. You ever built anything out of stone?

No.

I have. There's nothing to it. Now, that old place back of you? I've seen it. That's what—twenty-five or thirty big stones, plus the really big sucker up top? Sure, they're heavy. But they ain't all that heavy. Suppose the stone's handy to the spot; suppose you've got six, eight pretty rugged fellows and a team—they could do it in a morning.

Never.

And that's another thing, too, son, ain't it? You need equipment to do that kind of work. A tractor, a loader. If you're back then, you need a team. So what's that do for your Phoenicians? Are you saying they sailed their horses clear over here from China or wherever it was?

No.

No. Pigpens, son.

It's hard to win an argument with a skeptic. With a skeptic as thoroughgoing and as eloquent as Mr. Applegate, it's about impossible. Nevertheless, I resisted his banal view of the stone chambers of Bible Hill. I resisted it even though I came to feel that Mr. Applegate hadn't brought out the strongest argument against their being the work of vanished travelers from the ancient world. For if our mysterious stoneworks were made by European or Mediterranean visitors centuries before Columbus, then it follows they were here to be found by the first historical settlers of the region when they began to arrive in the middle of the eighteenth century. And if they were found in place by those settlers, how come we have no record of them from their discoverers? For, surely, to the settlers, stone structures in the wilderness would be remarkable, an astounding discovery—as though Lewis and Clark should have found beside the remote breaks of the Missouri River, where to their knowledge no white man had ever stood, a '59 Corvair, parked and with the radio playing. Would they pass over the thing in silence? Would they fail to make the least note of it? It's unthinkable. The fact that the earliest records of Bible Hill contain no mention of stone chambers on the ground proves the chambers weren't there when those records were set down.

All right, but what about the place on Round Mountain, the place with that tall stone set up in front? That stele?

That which?

Stele: a stone set upright as a monument or a marker of some kind. What about that?

What about it? It looks like when the boys got done putting up that pen, they had a rock extra. So they put it end-over that way. Why? For the hell of it, son. It wasn't all work, you know.

5

With his forty-seven volumes, Littlejohn was a diarist of extraordinary patience, but, my God, he was a spare one. This was no Pepys.

August 20, 1900. Fair. Temp. 12M 77. Shooting stars. Well still down

August 23, 1900. Rain. Temp. 12M 67

Each day Littlejohn noted the weather and the temperature, usually at 6:00 A.M. or noon. He recorded his work for the day, if any. He observed local happenings seldom, happenings in the nation or the world, almost never. I found on his brittle yellowed pages sixty-three years of this. I jumped right in. I read Littlejohn backward and forward, skipping over years, going back and burrowing through them. Then I read him again. Here was Bible Hill its very self, if only you could keep awake. We Noons are scholars.

When I moved into Littlejohn's place I found hung from a nail on one of the posts of the woodshed a broken thermometer, the same one, perhaps, from which Littlejohn had read off his daily observations. Or perhaps not, but it was an old one, a wooden scale a foot long, graduated in degrees Fahrenheit from −40 to 120 and printed at the bottom with the name of a hardware store in Wilmington, Vermont. The scale or back had brass staples to hold an empty glass tube, the top half of which was missing. Every day, Littlejohn had consulted this instrument or one like it and entered the temperature in his book. Often the temperature was the only entry he made for the day.

August 24, 1910. Rain. Temp. 12M 73
August 25, 1910. Rain. Temp. 12M 76. Well up

Sibyl Bradshaw. S.B.

You know how you can be driving along a road in winter and suddenly feel you have hit an icy stretch, though you don't skid? You go on, but you go slowly. All at once, you're careful, because all at once, the going isn't the same. So it was as I asked Miss Drumheller about her sister, S.B.

"Bradshaw," I said. "She's your half sister or something?"

"Something," said Miss Drumheller.

"Littlejohn had her picture," I said. "She knew Littlejohn, then?"

"Oh, yes, she knew him," Miss Drumheller said.

"She was around here, too, I guess," I said.

"For a while," Miss Drumheller said. "Not for long."

"She wasn't from here, then," I said.

"Certainly not," said Miss Drumheller. "No more than I."

"How did Littlejohn know her, then?" I asked.

Miss Drumheller gave a sharp little laugh.

"How?" she said. "What kind of question is that? They were friends—not friends, acquaintances. Not that, either. How does a man like Claude Littlejohn know a girl like Sibyl? How do you think?"

"Oh," I said.

"What's your interest in all this, young man?" Miss Drumheller asked me. "Why do you care anything about Claude Littlejohn?"

"To tell you the truth," I answered her, "I'm not sure."

"He's not worth it, you know," said Miss Drumheller. "There was nothing interesting about Claude Littlejohn. He lived on that place; he kept himself fed. He might as well have been a savage—not a savage. He might as well have been a cow or a horse. Except for his liquor. There was nothing interesting about him when he was alive, and there's nothing interesting about him now."

I shut up.

"And Sibyl Bradshaw wasn't my half sister," said Miss Drumheller. "She wasn't my sister at all. I only thought she was."

A sharer of Miss Drumheller's young womanhood, apparently, Sibyl Bradshaw, a schoolmate, perhaps, or another maiden teacher, a professional friend. A sentimental friend. Sibyl comes up for a summer visit—1920, 1921. She comes up on that ridiculous woodland railway from Brattleboro. Miss Drumheller meets her at Jamaica depot; she's hired a buggy for the ride home. The friends will have a couple of weeks together: long walks, reading aloud, listening to the rain, berry picking, ice cream. Peace and joy, a languid feeling interlude of delicate pleasures, delicate emotion—all violently busted up and trampled on by the rude, crude Littlejohn, who has the squalid slum up the road, and who bursts in upon the young women's idyll like an unlettered, unshaven, no-longer-youthful, and far-from-sweet-smelling Silenus, a bull satyr bent on—what, exactly?

What happens?

Does he sweep S.B. away? Does he play Zeus to her Leda, her Europa, the mortal virgin who excites the abundant lust of the Olympian studhorse? Does he ravish her? Does he do her wrong? Plainly, he does something, for Littlejohn was Miss Drumheller's enemy, in her mind, forever. Ten years dead, he was her enemy yet. Was he also her rival? What happened?

You'll never know. Apply the breaks gently, gently, slow down, and continue carefully until you're on a clear surface. And don't come back this way. Miss Drumheller didn't want to talk about it. Littlejohn was dead, and so was S.B.—at least she was no longer available; she couldn't be asked, and the present day, well supplied with more efficient pornography, furnished no Ovid to tell their story. At one time, I might have tried it, but my Latin really never was up to the job.

October 10, 1900. Fair & warm. Temp. 12M 74
October 17, 1900. Fair. Temp. 12M 62. Geese flying south over river. Seventy-seven geese fl. south 4 p.m.

Littlejohn would have been forty or forty-one the year Sibyl Bradshaw summered on Bible Hill—Sibyl a few years younger. What happened? Probably not much, but consider: A man's lifetime, his length of days, doesn't need much, if he can stand it.

6

Before the remarkable, gifted generations of the Civil War, before the colonists, before the dubious stonemasons, Bible Hill belonged to Indians and also to a whole bestiary of quadrupeds whose magnitude gradually decreased into historical times. About the Indians and their lives, little or nothing is known. They were a short-statured people, who had no fixed dwellings, but moved over the land from place to place. They evidently didn't go in much for jewelry or cookware or fancy funerals, and they weren't killers or conquerors on a big scale, and so inevitably they come down to us as a low-living, inoffensive people who had no adornments, a poor people who sat in darkness, if any people ever do. That is a harsh judgment we make, a judgment that comes out of our own lack of imagination. But at any rate, it's true this far: If Bible Hill's Indians didn't sit in darkness in their own time, they do today.

Of the animals who shared Bible Hill with these uncelebrated tribes, we have a clearer idea, perhaps, than we have of the tribes themselves, as we also have of the terrain they inhabited. We're to think of a cold, dripping land only lately laid bare by the retreating glacier; of rocky uplands, barren or covered with a quick, tough growth like heather; of bogs and sinks stretching for miles; of poor stands of birch, aspen, fir; of grassy river meadows. It's a landscape that makes the steepest, remotest wrong side of present-day Bible Hill look like a garden, and over it wander a population of beasts that make our fauna look like household pets. We know them by their bones.

On a night in January 1939, Orson Ware, whose place was on Back Diamond Mountain, a mile or two from the cabin Amanda later occupied, was driving home, not without difficulty, from the barrooms of Brattleboro when he, as the saying goes, swerved to miss a beer. Orson was driving a Model A Ford. It skidded and shot off into a frozen beaver pond that lay beside the road. The Model A, as was well known, went on ice like an Olympic competitor. For thirty feet, the auto, with Orson at the wheel, passed over the frozen surface, but the ice on a beaver pond is not reliable. The Ford hit a thin spot and broke through, sinking about halfway up the windows. Orson climbed free, got himself out of the pond, and walked on home, another two miles. He ought to have frozen to death, but alcohol has a low freezing point, and Orson's blood that night would no doubt have tested not far short of 90 proof.

The next day, Orson felt poorly and kept his bed, but the day after that, he brought in his brother-in-law and his cousin and his cousin's tractor and set about pulling his car out of the beaver pond. The brother-in-law put on a pair of rubber waders, went over the ice and into the hole around the Ford, and got a log chain on the bumper. They hooked up the tractor and drew. The Ford came out easily enough. One of the headlights was broken, so was the off-side window, and of course the motor was full of water; but when it was drained and given a little grease, it ran normally. The incident was closed—or not quite.

Sticking out the broken window of Orson Ware's Model A, and lying across the rear seat, was a rib bone six feet two inches long and weighing ninety-seven pounds. It was the color of strong tea.

The men agreed that by right, the rib belonged to Orson, but Orson decided he had no use for such a thing. His brother-in-law, Tristram Rand, who was married to a cousin of Mr. Applegate's, took the rib. He put it in the back of his truck, meaning to do something with it—but what? He forgot about it. The rib lay in the back of Tris Rand's truck with the log chain, some cable, and more or less snow and ice all through that winter and into the next spring. Then one evening in early June, Tris stopped at the store in Dead River Settlement for a fresh package of Lucky Strikes. On leaving the store, he found a tall, ruddy-faced man standing beside his truck, looking into the back. Tris knew the man but didn't know his name. He was one of the summer people.

"Help you?" Tris asked him.

"Where in the world did you get that?" the man asked.

Within a week, four cars full of polite young men had arrived in the neighborhood from the Museum of Comparative Zoology in Cambridge, Massachusetts. They set up a kind of encampment beside the beaver pond on Back Diamond, and they stayed there the whole summer, slapping black flies and mosquitoes and digging petrified bones out of the muck. When they finished, they had a nearly complete skeleton of a woolly mammoth. You can see it today in Cambridge. The goddamned thing is ten feet tall. In front of it is a sign identifying it and giving its likely date as 25000 B.C. The museum's sign records that the skeleton was discovered and excavated in 1940 by Professor Washburn of Harvard and his students at Mammoth Pond, Ambrose, Vermont. The Harvard people made up the name Mammoth Pond; that pond had, and has, no name.

November 10, 1900. Snow a.m. Temp. 12M 34. Snow does not stick
November 30, 1900. Temp. 12M 33

Always, I felt I had missed the best of Bible Hill. Not by much. In my time, the old life was still so near. Most of the old people from the last century were gone, but not long gone. On my arrival, I found their empty chairs, so to speak, still rocking very slightly back and forth. Their setting was not much changed, either, but it was lifeless in a way: The stage was dressed, its paint still pretty fresh, but the cast was gone, the orchestra, the audience, were gone. The stories came down to me by the dozen, but they were stories about people who had died or departed. Mr. Applegate, of course, remained, and Miss Drumheller, and others. But they were historians of Bible Hill, they were its interpreters, and so they stood at a remove from the real life that I wanted to know.

I believed the metaphor for my search for Bible Hill was Littlejohn's old thermometer: It survived—was, very likely, the same instrument he had used—but it was broken. It was still here, but it didn't work.

Sure, I well knew I was running a deep and foolish game on myself. For my predicament in having missed the best of Bible Hill came to this: The best was the past, and when I arrived on Bible Hill, the past was . . . past. So would it have been had I arrived a hundred years earlier with Bible Hill's vigorous soldiers and poets. So would it have been had I arrived twenty thousand years earlier with Bible Hill's Ivy League mammoth. I knew I was up against time, and I knew time wins. But still I believed that where Bible Hill and its best taste and feel, its best meaning, were concerned, there was a way through or around time, if I could find it. The road was at hand.

December 15, 1900. Temp. 12M 28. Snow p.m. Sticks
December 25, 1900. Temp. 12M 10. Mery Christmas to All!
January 1, 1901. Fair. Temp. 12M 0. Hapy New Years!!

7. Wildlife

1

As much as it was for any reason, it was for the animals that I came to Bible Hill. It was for the creatures of the woods and fields. Not to study them or follow them, not to hunt them, not even particularly to attend to them; but I liked the idea of living in, and not merely visiting, a place where you might look out your window and see a moose, a black bear, a mountain lion.

Not everybody needs that kind of casual access to the wild, but if you are one who does need it, nothing else will do—no zoo, no park. It's not the bear you need; it's the bear in its setting. And it's not the bear in its setting; it's the bear's setting's being your setting, as well. It's the intersection of the bear's free, everyday life with your free, everyday life. On Bible Hill, you have that intersection, and if you're here, you probably want it. Why?

For contrast. Contrast is all. Today, if you get an early start from Bible Hill, you can sit down at the poshest table in Manhattan in time for lunch—and that's driving your own car: no trains, no planes. The suburbs of the great, the ineluctable American future begin, in effect, no more than four hours' drive from Bible Hill, and they're coming closer every year. Hence the importance of the bear, the moose, and the others. They belong here, not there. They are proof of where you are. If you can see a moose in your backyard, if bears live in the woods behind your house, if your cat has been devoured by a fox or a fisher marten, then you know you're not in Greenwich or Winnetka. Not quite. Not yet.

So it was gratefully that I found myself sharing with the local wildlife a decaying house where sunlight and birdsong and soft, sweet air came in and out through the busted windows, squirrels and porcupines danced on the roof covered in brown pine needles, and wood thrushes, vireos, redstarts, and a hundred others were busy among the embowering trees. Outside my door, a green-and-yellow wood, the flickering shadow land, where owls hooted all night long and by day deer passed and repassed on their rounds.

Of other wildlife, I had rumor but saw little or nothing. The bears, the moose were about, for sure, but they kept out of the way. That suited me, too. You don't want your nature to arrive all at once, like a traveling show. Then, too, for some there are parts of nature that are never welcome.

"Noon? Come here, Noon."

"I'm on the roof."

"I know where you are. I need you down here. Hurry."

Not long after Amanda moved into her father's camp on Back Diamond Mountain, she discovered that the roof leaked badly at the chimney. I had been working at Jordan's all that spring, but Jordan's had slowed down and put me on part-time. Mr. Applegate decided I might as well fix Amanda's roof. What was he up to? Quite possibly, nothing; but in any case, I was willing. I was more than willing. Mr. Applegate bought flashing, tar paper, and shingles, and I loaded them, with ladders and tools, also Mr. Applegate's, onto his truck and drove them up to the camp. What did I know about roofing? Nothing at all, but Mr. Applegate expected I'd pick it up I guess, and then, the good thing about a bad leak is that even an incompetent workman can usually make a difference, at least for a while.

So I was aloft, uncomfortably astride Amanda's roof, tearing up rotten shingles, when Amanda called out. She was below, standing at a stack of old boards that were lying on the ground beside the porch. Amanda had been moving them to the burn pile at the edge of the yard. She had just picked up the last board.

"Noon!"

I came down off the roof, still holding the flat bar I'd been using on the shingles, and went around to where Amanda stood. She pointed to the ground. There, beside the board she had lifted and still held before her like a shield, coiled together and unmoving in the warm sun, was a large, quite handsome snake. It was more than a foot long, an inch thick, and curiously marked with tan and darker brown bands. The snake stirred slightly in its coils.

"Look at him," I said.

Amanda stepped back, away from the snake, keeping her eye always on it, as though she feared it would leap out at her the moment she looked away.

"Kill it," said Amanda.

"Don't be silly," I said. "He's harmless. I think he's a milk snake. He eats mice, bugs."

"Kill it, Noon," said Amanda.

"I won't kill it," I said. "It won't hurt you. There's no reason to kill it. I'll move it away, but, no, I won't kill it."

Amanda looked at me. She shook her head. At that point, the

snake, perhaps waking fully for the first time, put itself in motion and slid off into the tall grass between the camp and the woods.

"Are you hard of hearing, Noon?" Amanda asked me. "Did you not understand what I said?"

"I understood."

Amanda shook her head again.

"I don't know, Noon," she said. "It's my luck, you know? A whole state full of cowboys, and I have to end up with some kind of Buddhist."

"I told you," I said. "It's a milk snake. It's got no poison. It's harmless."

"How do you know it's harmless?" Amanda asked me.

"I know snakes," I said.

End up with? What, exactly, had she meant by *end up with*?

June 12, 1925. Rain a.m then clear. Temp. 12M 71. Pea flours
June 13, 1925. Fair. Temp. 12M 70. N. Grooms Bess foaled

FER-DE-LANCE

I know snakes.

Hitchcock belonged to a club catering to men from the embassies, the banks, the trading companies, and to local grandees of the highest standing. Obviously, it wasn't a place for the likes of me, but if things were going well at the station, Hitchcock might take me to the club for dinner. He did that two or three times. That he did it no more suited me.

Not that the club wasn't a pleasant place. It had a compound overlooking the harbor. There was a nice old house, deep verandas, white stucco outside, cool, dark wood paneling within; tennis courts, a pool, gardens of hibiscus, oleander, and prickly pear; smooth green lawns above which nodded tall palms and a kind of big shaggy pine that turned out to be casuarina. You could sit on the club's veranda and listen to the wind from the harbor rattle the hard, dry leaves of the palms and the sea grapes. You could watch the sunlight flash and dance over the double belt of razor wire that surrounded the whole place. You could mark the evolutions of the three guys with submachine guns who patrolled the club's narrow beach. Paradise.

Every Tuesday night, Hitchcock drove over to the club to play hearts and drink gin with three other young egregiosos who were thought to be rising men in the world of large affairs. The game always ended late, and Hitchcock, tight, would attempt to navigate himself back to the bungalow he and I shared at the time in Dolores, the gringo section of the capital, which we called "the Main Line." He always made it, but never without mishap. The next morning, Hitchcock's car would be found on the front lawn, or at the place down the road, or parked in the middle of the road.

"My God," Hitchcock would say.

"Next time, get a taxi," I said.

"Never," Hitchcock said. "Never. You can't. You can't do it. You don't know where they'll take you. Hear me, Mark. A lesson for life: Never take a taxi down here. Never."

Then the next week, he'd go through the same routine all over again. In any reasonable country, the police would long since have locked Hitchcock away for a hundred years, but in that part of the world, for people like Hitchcock, there essentially were no police.

Hitchcock's car was an exotic German rig with an unusual feature: heated seats. In cool weather, rather than turning on a blower to bring heated air into the car, you used a control on the dash to make your seat pleasantly warm. The seat warmers ran off the car's battery.

Often, returning far gone in gin from his hearts game at the club, Hitchcock would forget to turn off the seat warmers on leaving the car. If, as happened frequently, he also forgot to close the car's door, the result the following morning might be remarkable, owing to a cause that requires a digression into the natural history of the Latin tropics.

Down there, nature isn't an indifferent, parallel system the way it is in the north. Down there, nature seems intent; it seems to exert a constant fell pressure. Consider the wildlife. In Vermont, harmful creatures, though present, are rare, but in the jungle forests inland from the capital, they abound. Everything stabs, stings, bites, exudes, injects, is, in one way or another, armed.

Most formidably armed, I soon learned, is the hideous fer-de-lance, a tropical viper the length of a city bus, according to Hitchcock; whose venom, again according to Hitchcock, is based on an enzyme so potent that it consumes blood and even muscle, wasting the victim, turning him to liquid inside his own skin within half a day of the bite.

Now Hitchcock, it's true, was mostly full of shit, but the fer-de-lance was no campfire tale. It is a brown snake as thick as my ankle, and if it isn't as long as a bus, it is a good six feet, and it has the fangs of a tyrannosaur. I know this because on three occasions, Hitchcock, badly hungover on a morning following one of his drunk nights at his club, and having once again simply abandoned his car, emerged from our quarters to drive to work and found one of these same beasts asleep on the driver's seat. The fer-de-lance is a cold-blooded animal, of course, and it seeks warm places like sunny openings in the bush, like open lanes among the coffee trees, like the electrically heated leather seats of expensive Bavarian road machines.

The first time he found a fer-de-lance in his car, Hitchcock repaired to our bungalow for reinforcements—me. Together, we returned to the car. We peeped gingerly in. A big, big snake. What to do? Well, one might reach into the car, past the serpent, and switch off the seat warmer. In time, the fer-de-lance, no longer feeling the warmth, would surely go about its business. But one wasn't quick to try that course, not quick at all: really, the thing was enormous.

"Look at the bugger," said Hitchcock. "He's as big around as my leg."

"What do you think?" I asked.

"Fuck him, is what I think," Hitchcock said. "He can have the fucking car. I'll get a bike." Hitchcock was apt to be obscene when agitated.

But I have always liked snakes and felt I understood them. You handled the big ones with nooses, didn't you? Nooses and sacks? We rigged a noose of clothesline on a broom handle, got it around behind the snake's head, and dragged the monster out of the car. We stuffed it still bound, into a laundry bag and hurled the whole show—bag, noose, broom handle, fer-de-lance, and all—into the brushy ravine behind the bungalow.

The second time Hitchcock found one of the same creatures in his car, we put it in a metal trash barrel, drove it out into the countryside, and let it go. The third time, I think we did the same, but I may misremember. By then I was fed up with Hitchcock, the station, the capital, the foundation, and all of them. I was ready to move on.

When I came to Bible Hill, I'm saying, I felt I knew something about snakes and their disposal.

June 25, 1925. Rain. Temp. 12M 74. To Grooms to see foal

2

Of course neither on Bible Hill nor anyplace else can you learn the local wildlife on your own. You need other eyes and ears, other hands. You need collectors. Great Fabre had half the *petits enfants* and three-quarters of the village *curés* in the Midi picking bugs for him and carrying them to Sérignan.

No *curés* on Bible Hill, to be sure, and *petits enfants* damned few. Nevertheless, I, too, found a collector. I found a hell of a collector, one worth a hundred peasant lads, two hundred off-duty priests.

I refer to No-Name, the cat.

He was waiting for me at Littlejohn's house when I moved in. A good-sized cat, longhaired, black and white, and looking like a very large, broad skunk. A male, for sure, uncut, and hung like a pawnshop. Scruffy and uncared for, too, but not unhealthy—and wild as a lynx.

The morning after the first night I spent on Bible Hill in my new old house, I found the cat sitting in the dooryard when I went out. He wasn't afraid of me—he wasn't afraid of anything—but neither would he let me approach him. I put a saucer of milk on the step: What else do you do for a cat? The next morning, I found the saucer dry and beside it on the step a decapitated chipmunk. Milk for dead rodents was our transaction, then and thenceforth.

Through my first summer, I saw the cat, although not every day, here and there around the place. He was on the step with his saucer, in the dooryard in the sun, crossing the road in the beam of my headlights at night. I respected the ten or fifteen feet he seemed to insist on keeping between us. I didn't touch him, didn't try to. Obviously, I didn't own him, and so I didn't give him a name, any more than I would have given names to the coyotes that whooped in the middle of the night from the wooded ledges at the top of the hill. "They don't got names," said Calabrese. "You ruin them if you give them a name." No ownership, no name.

I laid on the milk, and the cat collected from the broad base of the local food pyramid, on which he sat right up near the top. Whatever was out there, in the woods, in the old fields, if it was a little smaller than himself, he'd bring it in. Chipmunks, he ate like popcorn, but he had a specialty in mice.

I have to end up with some kind of Buddhist, Amanda had said. What had she meant by *end up with*? Did she think she'd ended up with me? *Ended up.* Was this, then, the end, the payoff? So soon? *Ended up with.* Did she think she was with me? How, exactly? Not in the obvious way. Once, around that same time, Amanda asked me, "Are you good in bed, Noon?"

"I am," I said. "I sleep like a baby. I never snore. I don't sweat, don't thrash around. I awake refreshed and cheerful."

"It's not exactly what I meant," said Amanda, "but it's good to know."

No, we weren't together that way. Did Amanda, then, think we were together in another way? Was there another way? And what about me? Did I think we'd ended up with each other? Not yet.

A whole state full of cowboys, and I have to end up with some kind of Buddhist. Was it only a line? It might have been. Amanda was glib. She had no lack of lines; she wasn't Mr. Applegate's daughter for nothing. Was it more than a line? Had she meant it? Meant what? How was one to know? Well, one might simply ask her, but I thought I would not. We Noons operate from a certain diffidence.

I had been sitting beside Amanda on the grass. The milk snake was gone.

"I don't know," I said. "It's just you don't seem like the kind to be scared of things like that. Snakes—you know, the things women are scared of."

"I'm not," Amanda said. "That one surprised me. Suddenly, there it was. It wasn't the snake; it was the surprise. I don't like surprises."

"Why not?"

"We could talk about something else, Noon," Amanda said.

"Anything you like," I said.

"Plus, then," Amanda said, "you were here. I wanted to see what you'd do."

"You mean about the snake?"

"That's right," said Amanda.

"You wanted me to kill it."

"I wanted to see if you'd kill it," Amanda said.

"So you didn't want me to kill it—it was like a test?"

"Something like that," Amanda said.

"Well then," I asked her, "what? Did I pass?"

Amanda turned to look at me. She raised her eyebrows. She nodded her head. "Yeah," she said.

November 15, 1925. Temp. 12M 29. Snow. N. Groom wants $20 for colt Dan

3

With the untiring assistance of the black-and-white cat, over parts of the two years he was in my hire, I was able to identify on Bible Hill eleven different kinds of mice. Eleven. The mice, the cat, and I together about wore out our copy of *Wild Mammals of New England.* As I have said, we didn't have much to do with the more glamorous wildlife of the hill. We left them to the tourists. Fabre knew that it's down among the small, obscure, and numerous creation that you have the most to learn. On that humble base, you can rear some pretty lofty speculation.

We found house mice and field mice and white-footed mice; we found two kinds of jumping mice and three kinds of vole. There were mice with short tails and mice with long tails, and mice with no tails; stubby gray mice that lived in the fields and kept to themselves and sleek deer mice with fawn-colored flanks, snowy bellies, and shining eyes—beautiful little creatures that moved right into the house and seemed to want to talk things over.

Eleven different species in the area regularly ranged by No-Name the cat, a matter of, at most, ten acres.

My question is, Why do we need eleven different mice? For as a practical matter, I suggest, all these creepers, jumpers, long-tails, short-tails, big ones, little ones, pretty ones, plain ones, are the same animal. They are the Platonic ideal Mouse in different keys. Not scientifically, no: Our resident mice represent eleven different species and eight different genera. Perhaps they are as various as men and lemurs in point of their genes, or their chromosomes, or whatever you please; but empirically, morally, they're the same note eleven times repeated. Nature, which on Bible Hill has done a bear, for example, in one try and a deer in two (if you count the moose), has seen fit to make eleven runs at the mouse.

Nature, did I say? Or have we found down among the mice an intimation of something else, something larger, more consoling? I understand that according to evolution, the sole mission of every species is to reproduce, and so blindly to project its genetic material for another week, month, year. And I understand that the mice in their vast and unseen numbers are well able to do that. But wouldn't the task be done as well, and more efficiently, by a couple of species? If transmission of DNA is the only real purpose of the lives of organisms, wouldn't one or two different strings of the stuff be as good as eleven? Eleven kinds of mice looks to me like more than evolution; it looks like caprice. It looks like frivolity. And if you have a capricious, frivolous product, then you have a capricious, frivolous maker. We have eleven different mice on Bible Hill and only one bear because the Creator found making mice easy and fun, making bears long and boring.

So No-Name the cat and I, working in a theological backwater, with no seminary within a hundred miles and no more sophisticated materials than a few dozen dismembered rodents, have raised the neglected banner of Saints Thomas Aquinas and Anselm, the banner of Descartes and Pascal. We have proved the existence of God. Not bad for an English major and a cat without so much as a B.A.

A POOR COUNTRY

Bands of children ran in the streets of the capital. They begged; they stole; they slept in the alleys and gutters. Seven years old, eight, ten, they darted through the traffic, they crowded the pavements, they filled the spaces between the people, like pigeons or sparrows in a happier, healthier city, and, like pigeons or sparrows, they were ignored. And like pigeons or sparrows, they were out for themselves. They had to be. Who were they? Where were their parents?

"Their parents?" said Hitchcock. "Don't be silly, Mark. You'll be asking me next why they aren't in school."

"Well who are they?" I asked him. "Where do they come from?"

"The mountains, the bush—the interior," said Hitchcock. "There's no work there. There's nothing to eat. They're starving. They come here, to the city. This is a poor country, Mark."

The children flowed and eddied around you in the street, their hands stretched out at the ends of their dirty arms like sticks, their voices not loud or strong, but intent. Then they moved on down the street. I felt if I stopped, or if I lost my footing and fell among them, they would swarm and pick me clean to the bones in seconds.

"Actually," said Hitchcock. "Actually, they're better off here. They're Indians, for the most part, you see. They're not well liked. In the countryside, until a few years ago, the landowners hunted them from horseback with dogs and rifles."

A poor country. Journeying to such a place, contemplating such a place, is supposed to instruct you. It's supposed to open your eyes. It doesn't. It has the opposite effect. You're staring at the sun. You can't look for long, or if you can, it's because you're already blind.

At her father's place on Back Diamond, up on the roof, then down around the rotten mud boards or the porch steps, swinging my hammer, pushing my saw, I aimed to get to know Amanda. She didn't always make it easy.

"So, what about your husband?" I asked her.

"Denny?" she said.

"Yes. Is he still out west, then?"

"I hope so," said Amanda.

"Right," I said, "but where? Los Angeles, was it?"

"That area, anyway," Amanda said.

"He wanted to be an actor, your father said. Is he in Hollywood?"

"Not Hollywood," said Amanda. "Los Angeles is a big place, Noon."

"I know it is," I said. "I've been in Los Angeles. What does Denny do there now?"

"Now?" said Amanda. "Now, I don't know. He was a waiter."

"You can have your lawyer present, you know," I told her. "You can call your lawyer at any time, have him present. You can't be questioned without your lawyer, unless you choose to be. Do you need a dime?"

Amanda laughed. "Okay, Noon," she said. "What do you want to know?"

"Is he your husband?"

"Yes."

"But you aren't in touch with him."

"He'll call sometimes," Amanda said. "He'll call my father. They always got on. My father can get on with anybody, about."

"But you don't know where he is?" I asked her.

"Not right now, no," Amanda said.

"What happened with Denny?"

"What happened?" Amanda said. "What didn't happen?"

"I know I've got a dime here somewhere."

"Denny was disappointed," said Amanda. "Things didn't go his way; he got disappointed. Then things didn't go his way even more. He thought your life has to go up, not down, not sideways—always up. He saw his life wasn't that way. He reacted badly to that."

"Why did you marry him?" I asked her.

"Why?" Amanda said. "We were in high school. I was his girlfriend. I got pregnant. We got married. This is not new material, Noon."

"But there's no baby," I said.

"No," said Amanda. "I had a miscarriage. Like two months after the wedding. No baby after all. Denny was pissed."

"He wasn't ready to be a father," I said.

"He wasn't ready to be much of anything," Amanda said. "Well, that's not fair. Billy the Kid, Denny was ready to be him—or the guy who plays Billy the Kid in a Billy the Kid movie. Denny couldn't figure out if he wanted to be the guy or the movie star who plays the guy. Anyway, he wasn't around a lot by that time. He was off with his desert friends."

"Desert friends?"

"Yeah," said Amanda. "You know: They'd go off into the desert for days, weeks at a time. Camp. Be like the last guys left. Lots of beer. Lots of dope. Lots of guns. . . . How come it always works out that way, Noon? You're educated; you can explain it to me: How come the guy always gets to be the asshole, never the girl?"

"Who says it's so?" I asked her.

"You know it is," Amanda said.

"I don't know it at all."

"Sure, you do," said Amanda. "Nine times out of ten, the guy gets first crack at it, anyway. He gets to be the asshole first; he beats her to it. The poor girl, she's too late. She never catches up. You don't see it?"

"No."

"Think about it, Noon," Amanda said. "Think about yourself. Don't you have desert friends?"

"No."

"Not any desert friends?" Amanda asked. "Not one? Never?"

"Maybe once. No more."

"Do you wish you had?"

"No."

Amanda was looking at me. "How about that?" she said.

"So what was going on with Denny and his friends?" I asked her.

"I don't really know," Amanda said. "Like I said, I didn't see much of Denny the last year or so. Whatever they were doing wasn't good.

We had police at the house. We even had federal guys. They said that's what they were, anyway. I don't know. I didn't care. I had other plans."

"Me, too," I said.

"You?" Amanda asked. "How?"

"If one place doesn't work, try another," I said.

"Well, but you have to know where to stop," Amanda said. "You have to find the right place."

"That's right," I said. "You do."

"So, how do you do that, Noon?" she asked.

"Luck," I said.

November 20, 1925. Gray. Temp. 6 a.m. 27.
Told N. Groom $10.00 for colt Dan

4

In the fall of my first year on Bible Hill, when the frosts arrived, the black-and-white cat took off. His milk froze overnight in the saucer on the step. The mice went uncollected. No-Name was gone.

I mourned. I reckoned the cat had at last come up against a bigger set of teeth than his own. Not at all. He'd merely migrated. The next spring, No-Name turned up again shortly after May Day, looking not at all starved, but rested and well fed. Had he wintered in Florida like everybody else? No way to know, but our wildlife census—call it that—picked up where it had left off the year before. His first day back, the cat brought in a Gapper's red-backed mouse, a species new to both of us. Well, new to me anyway.

That Gapper's, however, was among the last new species of mouse that I was able to establish on Bible Hill. For it was toward the end of the cat's second summer that Amanda left her father's place on Back Diamond and moved in with me. Yes, that happened, and as a result, other things happened—one of them being the final and apparently permanent departure of No-Name the cat. He and Amanda did not get on.

"I don't like that cat of yours, Noon," said Amanda.

"He's not mine."

"You got that right," said Amanda. "He's nobody's. He doesn't let you touch him, stroke him. He doesn't purr or sit in your lap like a cat ought to do. He doesn't even come indoors. All he does is live outside and kill things."

"He's a cat. He kills mice. That's his nature. Besides, it's interesting what he finds. Do you know how many kinds of mice he's found just right around the house?"

"Different kinds of mice?" asked Amanda.

"Eleven."

"You're keeping track?" Amanda asked.

"Sure."

"You're, like, making a record of the mice he kills?"

"Sure."

"I don't know, Noon," said Amanda. "That strikes me as being a little odd. You know? A little bent? You've been on your own up here long enough. It looks like I might have gotten here just in time."

"It looks that way to me, too," I said.

They struggled, it seemed, No-Name and Amanda. Their wills struggled. Amanda won. One afternoon, she spotted the cat trotting toward the steps with a chipmunk dangling limply from his jaws. Amanda liked chipmunks. She stepped out onto the porch and dumped a bucket of water on No-Name. The cat screeched and shot off to the right, dropping the chipmunk, which, very much alive, shot off to the left.

No-Name was still wet when I found him at the edge of the woods. Rather, he found me, for in this crisis, the mouth of the cat was opened:

"What was that, man?" No-Name asked me. "What'd she do that for?"

"To save the chipmunk, I guess," I said.

"Save the chipmunk?" said the cat. "Come on, man. Save the chipmunk? Since when? What's that about?"

"I know," I said. "I can't explain it."

"We had a project going here," No-Name said. "We had our work."

"I know."

"We had it going good. Then her," he said.

"Well," I said. "Come to that, we'd about covered all the mice. Eleven different kinds of mice. We were about done."

"You don't know that, man," said the cat.

"That's what *Wild Mammals of New England* says," I told him. "Eleven species is about all we'll find in this range."

"That's a book, man," said the cat. "Don't tell me what a book says. What is a book? What is it? We were way past a book. For all you know, we were just getting started."

"Listen," I said. "I'll talk to her."

"No, man," said No-Name. "No talk. It's time to come down to the nut."

"Okay."

"Me or her," said the cat. "Choose."

"Don't do that."

"Her or me," said the cat. "Your call."

"Her."

December 5, 1925. Snow night. Temp. 12M 29. Bought colt Dan of N. Groom $17.50. Robed again

BIBLE HILL'S MICE AND THEIR ALLIES

ENGLISH NAME	LATIN NAME	REMARKS
Deer mouse	*Peromyscus maniculatus*	Moves indoors in winter.
White-footed mouse	*P. leucopus*	Hard to tell from *P. manic.*
Gapper's red-backed mouse	*Clethrionomys gapperi*	Rare: only one found.
Meadow vole	*Microtus pennsylvanicus*	Found everywhere afield but never indoors.
Rock vole	*M. chrotorrhinus*	
Pine vole *M.*	*Pinetorum scalopsoides*	Uncommon.
Southern bog lemming	*Synaptomys cooperi*	Uncommon.
Norway rat	*Rattus norvegicus*	Little ones compared to city.
House mouse	*Mus musculus*	Commonest mouse indoors. Cat never catches.
Meadow jumping mouse	*Zapus hudsonius*	Six seen.
Woodland jumping mouse	*Napaeozapus insignis*	Hard to tell from *Z. hudson.*

From A. J. Godin, *Wild Mammals of New England* (Baltimore: Johns Hopkins, 1982).

8. Treasures of the Snow

Hast thou entered into the treasures of the snow?

—Job 38:22

1

Never doubt that I entered into the treasures of the snow. On Bible Hill you didn't have much choice. Around there, the treasures of the snow were passed out with a free hand. Snow on Bible Hill had an importance that was not only practical but also moral. It gave the place its deepest nature. Snow was Bible Hill's tragic flaw: the heart of the heart, the epitome, the factor such that if it bored you, if you couldn't enter into it all, you'd probably be happier in another part of the country.

I entered right in. I learned to know the winter storms. There were two kinds: the northers, which came down from Canada, and the nor'easters, which came up from the south. Northers were the workhorses, reliable storms that accounted for most snow accumulation through a whole season. They were called by weathermen "the Montreal Express." Since northers were essentially the prevailing westerly wind doing its work in a cold season, they were the more frequent storms. They came in hard, their snow small and driving at an angle, like sand on the wind. If you stood still and listened outdoors, you could *hear* it snow; the snow landing all around you with a soft, even hiss, like a tiny surf. Northers started quickly, and on Bible Hill at least, I thought they were a little apt to begin in the middle part of the day. They also stopped quickly; when they were done, they were done, and you could start shoveling. I could get myself cleared out, then go down the hill to Miss Drumheller's and shovel her, and be drinking her magic coffee inside of an hour.

The southerly storms, nor'easters, were the thoroughbreds, the glamour storms. They came up the Atlantic coast softly, inexorably, like a tidal wave of down comforters. Their snow was bigger and it fell straight. There was often a lot of it. When one of these storms was going right out, it could snow an inch an hour. You watched the snow mount up higher, then higher, and you saw that, yes, this stuff was water and what you were in was a flood. Nor'easters, it was my impression, were more likely to begin at night and go on into the next afternoon. They started gradually and built, and at the end, they stopped, started, stopped, started. They piddled away. You did your shoveling. Then the wind came in and blew the new snow all over in a kind of rear-guard, no-storm snowstorm, and you'd have to start shoveling all over again.

There you are, son. Been getting on all right up there this winter, have you?

All right. I was snowed in the other day, though. Monday, was it? I couldn't get out.

They plow on past you, don't they? Sure, they do. They plow to Carlo's. They used to.

They still do. It's a question of when. The other day, they didn't get to me until about five o'clock.

They must have broke down.

That must have been it.

Still, there ain't many people on that road, you know. They plow where there's people. They get to you. They won't get to you first, and they might get to you last, but they will get to you. That's the snowplow's creed, son.

January 30, 1914. Weather. Snow p.m. Temp. 12M 27
January 31, 1914. Temp. 6 a.m. 10. Snow
February 1, 1914. Fair. Temp. 6 a.m. 5. Snow 22 in.

It's a canny phrase, too: *the treasures of the snow.* For snow, I learned, is like money: It is of no interest in itself, is interesting only as it is moved from one place to another. Snow is like money also in this: It mixes easily, too easily, with alcohol.

For some years in the 1950s, the driver of one of the town's two snowplows was Wild Bill Arbogast. Wild Bill had moved on by the time I arrived on Bible Hill, but the people remembered him well. Wild Bill was responsible for the roads in the northern and western parts of the township, including Round Mountain, Bible Hill, and the Dead River district—say thirty miles of roads. These he cleared with a huge plow mounted on an army-surplus deuce-and-a-half truck from World War II. In that antique, Wild Bill roared up and down the town roads through every kind of storm, day and night, often working around the clock. He plowed not only the public ways. In those days, on the lonely back roads, where houses were few, the town plow would swing in to clear your lane or driveway as it passed. You would then carry out to the weary plow driver a cup of hot coffee. Naturally, in recognition of the driver's exhausting, unending work, the miserable conditions in which that work went forward, and your gratitude for his care of your own drive, you would not allow that coffee to stand alone. You would pour into it a full measure of rum, whiskey, brandy, or whatever you liked. Rum was cheapest and had the weight of tradition behind it.

Some householders were more liberal than others with the assistance they gave the snowplow driver's coffee, but none stinted. None. There was a family of Pentecostals living on the road to Dead River Settlement. No member of that family had ever tasted alcohol or ever would, but they kept a fifth of Jim Beam in the cupboard for Wild Bill. My neighbor Miss Drumheller, a maiden schoolmistress, was known for putting enough rum to her plow coffee that you might have lit the cup off like a Roman candle.

In any kind of decent snowstorm, therefore, by the time Wild Bill got halfway through his plowing circuit, he himself was well up toward the red line. The snow got plowed, but accidents happened. Mailboxes flew off into the woods like steel partridges as Bill blew by. Parked cars got handled roughly. One night in the middle of a blizzard, Wild Bill, on his way down Round Mountain with a full tank, caught the corner of Errol Burgoyne's woodshed and plowed the whole affair all the way to the four corners before he understood what was happening. Burgoyne's tools, chicken feed, spare lumber, lawn mower, windowscreens, and three cords of his winter fuel were strewn over a mile and a half of mountain road.

Burgoyne was on the board of selectmen at the time. The board fired Wild Bill that spring. It also announced that the town equipment would no longer be used on private property under any circumstances, and that any townsman found to have served any beverage whatever to any member of the town road crew during working hours would be subject to prosecution.

"You can't do that," said Hugo Usher.

Mr. Applegate was town attorney at the time. "We just did," he told Usher.

"This is nothing but goddamned social engineering," said Usher. Usher had high-held ideas on individual liberty and personal responsibility.

"You want to be the one who pays for that shed?" Mr. Applegate asked him. "You want to pay for the wrecked cars—the ones he's already wrecked? The ones he'll wreck next winter? You want to stand liability for when he kills somebody on the town's time, driving the town's truck drunk? Are you offering to take care of that?"

"That's not the point," said Usher.

"What is the point?" asked Mr. Applegate.

"The point is, you're treating everybody like they were children," said Usher. "You're acting like you were my mother. You're not my mother."

"We're saying, No more drinks for the plows," said Mr. Applegate. "That's all we're saying. I don't see what that's got to do with your mother."

Today, no doubt, the sacked Wild Bill, who for ten years had worked sixty-, seventy-hour weeks for never more than two thousand dollars per annum and two weeks off, would hire a lawyer and, alleging wrongful dismissal, sue the town for every dime it would ever have, but those were simpler times. Wild Bill went quietly. He said he was ready for a change. He was tired. Wild Bill was deaf from the terrible banging racket of the plow as it ran over the rough dirt roads, his back and his kidneys were bad from the bouncing around in the cab, and, of course, his liver was shot. He took a hundred-dollar bonus from the board and what was left of the Pentecostals' bourbon, and he moved to Florida.

. . .

Hugo, you see, figured everybody's free, everybody gets to do what he wants and take the consequences. You'd best just let them go, let things work themselves out. You'd best not interfere; you only make things worse. Besides, you're not authorized. That's what he meant about not being his mother.

It makes sense.

Sure, it makes sense, son. It makes too much sense. Or it did with Hugo. The thing is, with Hugo, the town couldn't ever have a good idea and do it. You couldn't ever have a solution to a problem. You've got Bill Arbogast, drunk as a bat, banging around in a twenty-five-thousand-dollar piece of equipment that don't belong to him, that belongs to you. He don't care what he does. He's wrecking people's sheds, crashing into their cars. But you can't do anything about it, because to do something about it, you'd have to make a rule for people that they'd have to obey. You'd have to pass a law. God forbid.

Don't pass a law. Fire Arbogast.

Well, even that's making a rule, ain't it? Why did you fire him? Besides, you've got the rest of the crew doing the same thing, more or less, whenever they get the chance. You going to fire them all?

No.

No. Instead, you make a rule: Free drinks are no longer part of the job. They were, but now they ain't, and here's the reason. It's easy, but Hugo never could see it.

2

February 25, 1914. Fair a.m. Temp. 12 M 18. p.m. cloud, yello sky
February 26, 1914. Temp 12 M 24. Snow

Snow is like money also in that one wants to know where it will appear and in what quantities. The man who predicts its comings and goings will be listened to. Unfortunately, there are many such men and always have been. It can't have been difficult, even in the old, scienceless days, to predict the winter storms. You can feel them coming. Before each kind of storm, you can note a kind of changed, lowered feeling, a new purpose in the air. Sensing that, I would turn on the radio and find that, indeed, a storm was on the way. Littlejohn watched the sky; he felt the air to predict the weather. I watched; I felt, as well—to predict the prediction.

More difficult was the matter of foretelling not the several storms but the winter they belonged to. Some winters piled snow to the housetops; some were quite bare. Could you tell, say in July, which the winter ahead would be? The short answer was no. You couldn't and neither could the radio, neither could the almanacs. Not in July. But in December, you could venture a guess at the coming winter's weight of snow, not from science but from psychology. That was because, for the weather as in every other realm, life is education. Once a winter's succession of storms got established any given year, it would keep on the track, bringing in a storm regularly every week or ten days all winter long. That would be a deep, white winter. But a winter that had not been educated to snow, one that was indifferent or unformed in its infancy, might falter and produce a naked, inconsistent season of frozen browns and greens—beautiful in its way but at last unsatisfactory.

I came to think that an educated winter would reveal itself by December 10. If there had been shovelable snow by that day, then there would be snow to the eaves in February and plenty left in April. Little or no snow by December 10 meant a bare, weak winter.

It only remained to manufacture a feasible piece of antique weather lore, in the form of one of those quaint maxims, redolent of medieval superstition, that have given expression to rules like this one for at least a thousand years. *Butler's Lives of the Saints* (4 volumes, 1953 edition) in the Brattleboro public library answered the need perfectly. Thus we have:

> Snow on St. Gregory's Day [December 10],
> Snow in May
> Half a foot on Budoc's Day [December 9]
> Half a rod on Ubald's [April 9]

Never mind Saint Gregory, though, never mind Saint Budoc and the blessed Ubald (respectively a Pope of the eighth century, a Breton abbot of the sixth, and a Florentine martyr of the fourteenth). Ignore them, and ignore their rule. For like so many other weather maxims, these will hardly stand analysis. They seem to come down to this: If it snows a lot, it will have snowed a lot. So experience, when it is applied to predicting snow, dwindles away in tautology.

I sat in my kitchen window with a cup of coffee on the sill—unassisted coffee—and I watched it snow and snow and snow.

3

How did she get by before I came? I have wondered. Miss Drumheller, mean. For in the winter I began up here, it wasn't after the first storm that I stopped to help her, or after the second or the third. I didn't know she was to be helped, you see. And what did she do the winter before, the one before that?

I was working that winter at Clifford's store. I opened the place, swept up, took in deliveries, kept the shelves stocked, ran the register. There had been a big storm on a night in January, February. The snow had ended after midnight, and so I'd had some breakfast, shoveled out the car, and started down the hill to Clifford's. A bright morning, very cold. The snow lay to your hips all about, and along the road, the plows had thrown up a bank as high as your head. It had also left dams of snow across the entrance of every driveway. At Miss Drumheller's house, this dam was a couple of feet high. When I passed, she had managed to wade through the new snow from her house and to climb over the snowbank into the road. There she leaned on her snow shovel and contemplated her driveway, a small figure in an old blue coat, with a scarf tied around her white hair and on her feet thin ladies' boots trimmed with fur and now full of snow. I stopped, drew my car over, and got out.

"Hand me your shovel," I said.

I took her shovel and began to work on the snow blocking her driveway. Miss Drumheller stood behind me with her hands in the pockets of her coat and watched me shovel.

"You're the young man who's moved into Claude Littlejohn's," said Miss Drumheller.

I nodded.

"How did you find it?" she asked.

"A little run-down," I said.

"He lived like a hermit in there," Miss Drumheller said. "Not a hermit—an animal. He lived alone. He never cleaned. And he drank. He drank like a fish."

I saw she was shaking a little. The coat she wore wasn't up to much, and the temperature had gone to twenty below in the night, the way it does when a storm blows out in a big freeze from the north.

"Sit in my car," I said. "The heater's on. Go ahead."

Miss Drumheller waited in the car while I cleared her driveway and shoveled a path from it to her house. Then she led me into her kitchen and sat me down beside her stove, a wood-burner, which was going straight out. The furnace sighed and muttered in her cellar, as well, and she had an electric heater running under her kitchen table. The room was an oven.

Miss Drumheller took off her coat and scarf and hung them up in the hall. She moved around her kitchen slowly, a very old lady done up in three sweaters and a wool skirt, who, with all of them on, looked about eighty-five pounds. She sat and took off her boots. Her ankles were the size of my wrists. She went to the stove and poured out a cup of coffee for me and another for herself. She took a bottle of black rum from a cupboard and held it over my cup, looking at me and raising her right eyebrow.

"If you please," I said, and she poured a shot of rum into my coffee. She capped the bottle; then she uncapped it again and poured me another little tot. She screwed down the cap for good and returned the bottle to the cupboard. She had not dosed her own coffee.

"None for you?" I asked her.

She shook her head. "What's-her-name's coming," she said. "Nora. Not Nora. I'll think of it in a minute."

"Who is she?" I asked.

"Karen," said Miss Drumheller. "Not Karen. Maureen. Yes, Maureen. Maureen's coming."

"Who's Maureen?

"Maureen's a housekeeper," she said. "Not a housekeeper. 'Home visitor,' they're called. She comes Monday, Wednesday, Friday. I mustn't smell of alcohol when Maureen's here. She'd have it all over the town that I'm a drunkard."

I nodded.

"That's why I was out there," she said. "I don't need to get out. I don't even have a car anymore. But Maureen couldn't have gotten in. She won't shovel. You'd think they could do that, wouldn't you? But they won't. They're paid to help you, but you end up helping them. Maureen would have had to leave her car in the road and walk through the snow, and then I'd have had to listen to her complain about it all morning."

"She's a home visitor," I said. "She's not a shoveler. Leave the shoveling to me from now on."

Miss Drumheller raised her chin a fraction and gave me a long look. Gray eyes. She hadn't thanked me for shoveling her out that morning. She never did. That was the country schoolmistress in her. Shoveling was my chore, like beating out the erasers or raising the flag. You don't thank a pupil for doing his job. That would weaken him.

"What's your name?" Miss Drumheller asked me.

"Mark Noon," I said.

"Noon?" she said. "That's an odd name. Is it Irish?"

"Sioux," I said.

Miss Drumheller gave me a little more coffee, a little more rum. I heard the story of Wild Bill Arbogast for the first time from her that morning. I've heard it a dozen times since, but never again from her. Mr. Applegate, for example, told the story of Wild Bill, his swath of destruction, his high-principled defense by Usher, his downfall, at least once a year, never the same way twice. Not Miss Drumheller. Miss Drumheller was not repetitious. She let you have it once and expected you to get it.

February 20, 1914. Gray. Temp 5 p.m. 26
February 21, 1914. Fair. Temp. 6 a.m. 31. Stayed inn

For two years, living in this house in winter was like camping out indoors. To a degree, it still is. The snow still blows in under the doors and around the window sashes to lie in pretty, lacy fans and swags on the floor and sills, and in the coldest weeks, I still spend much of the day tending fires. But there is a real furnace in the cellar now, and electricity. There is hot water from the tap. The house in winter, today, is a house and no longer a kitchen surrounded by freezing, unvisited rooms. The army blankets are gone.

By Christmas of my first winter in Littlejohn's house, I found that if I was to stay there, I would have to make fundamental changes not only in the house itself but in how I lived in it. I was going to have to do more than keep the wood-burning cookstove in Littlejohn's kitchen going twenty-four hours a day, for one thing. Doing that sufficed to make the kitchen habitable, but in the bedroom upstairs, where I had set up my cot, the water in my pitcher froze solid every night. It was too cold to sleep.

There were two responses I could see: one demonstrating mastery, one submission. In my past life, being cold, I would turn up the heat, I would open the radiator. I would bring heat to where I was. Now I submitted. I brought myself to where the heat was. I moved into the kitchen. I ran my cot into the narrow berth between the stove and the wall, drew my one comfortable chair close, and slept in the kitchen, waking two or three times in the night to drop new wood into the firebox when I felt my ears begin to freeze.

Life in the kitchen was possible, I found, but the kitchen was a drafty place and took up most of the length of the house. It had seven doors. Each door led to other rooms or to the outside, and each of them admitted its own wind; Littlejohn's kitchen was like an old mariner's map, decorated around its margin with drawings of clouds having human faces and puffed cheeks, representing the several winds—the westerlies, the trades, or whatever you please.

I strung clotheslines around the height of the kitchen walls and hung blankets from them to enclose a space around the stove, a space of, say, twelve by fifteen feet, which shut out the wind from the doors and windows. The blankets, I found in one of Littlejohn's chests in the attic. They were worn, full of holes, brown, and one of them had US printed in a corner. Army blankets, for sure, but which war?

With the blankets in place, I had a very tolerable little cave inside my house. When the wind blew and made the blankets stir, the effect was like what you might imagine in the tents of the nomadic desert Bedouin: a safety that is more comforting just because of the same frail, temporary quality in the shelter that would seem to deny safety.

By New Year's, I was set up tight and snug in the kitchen. I figured I had done pretty well. There was a family of field mice—several families, perhaps—that had moved in from outdoors and lived in the kitchen. They were a superior class of mice, or they were lucky; however it was, they had escaped being collected by that scientific cat in the summer past, and now they quartered with me: good-natured little creatures, fearless, with bright, intelligent eyes. I sat in my chair beside the stove, and they sat on the clotheslines hung with blankets under the ceiling. From up there, they regarded me, I thought, with some admiration. "You," the mice said, "are a not unresourceful fellow." I felt their praise was deserved. We Noons know how to improvise.

Through the winter, I lived down there, and for the next winter, I did the same: moved down into the kitchen after the frosts, when the nights got cold, the days short. It was a straitened, shiplike life, certainly, but it worked. It answered. And if it got a little messy, a little close, if it came to smell a little funny in there, I found I didn't care. I had picked my ground and stood. I hadn't prevailed, exactly, but I was alive, I was still here; and if this was the worst winter did, I could stand it. I'd be here for some time to come.

Did Littlejohn feel the same in his time? *He lived like a hermit in there*, Miss Drumheller had said. *He lived alone. He never cleaned. And he drank. He drank like a fish.*

Precisely, I thought, but where had the old boy managed anything to drink? Perhaps he made his own. There was much to learn, but I had a start. My first Christmas on Bible Hill, I bought myself a plum pudding, put some warmed-up bourbon to it, fired it up, and had myself quite a little solitary celebration while the wind blew and the mice minuetted about on the clotheslines under the ceiling like the Flying Wallendas. God rest you, merry gentlemen, let nothing you dismay. I contemplated the blue fire that quavered about my Christmas pudding; I felt it warm me all the way down. Frank Lloyd Wright it was who said, "Take care of the luxuries and the necessities will take care of themselves."

4

Thus Miss Drumheller and I became friends of a kind: snow friends. After each storm, I stopped at her house and shoveled her out, then sat in her kitchen, steeping myself in poisoned coffee and in Miss Drumheller's unforgiving views of her neighbors—our neighbors.

She was pre-Freudian, Miss Drumheller. She believed in good and evil, mostly evil. Miss Drumheller was a Manichean. In a lifetime of teaching in country schoolhouses, she had come down to thinking that there were good children and bad children, and she had come to feel pretty confident she knew which was which. It was simple, really. The good ones were those who did what they were told; the bad ones were the others. Indeed, in practice, it was simpler yet, for the principle seemed to amount to this: The good ones were the girls, the bad ones, the boys.

She had taught nine-tenths of the town's population over parts of three generations, and the judgments she had formed of the townspeople as children, as curly-headed puppies, sometimes thirty, forty years earlier, were fixed and absolute. Of lawyer Applegate, for example, a leader of the community, a steady man, Miss Drumheller had a small opinion.

"He thinks he can talk his way out of anything," she said. "He thinks because he looks like a little angel, nobody knows what he's up to. It didn't get him very far with me."

"I bet it didn't," I said.

"Of course," Miss Drumheller said, "it was terrible, what happened."

"What happened?"

"To his boy."

"What?"

"He died."

"His son?"

"The way he died."

"What way?"

Miss Drumheller shook her head. "Ask someone else," she said.

With Miss Drumheller's and my down-the-hill neighbors, the Bracketts, she was more satisfied than she was with Mr. Applegate, but not by much.

"He's not the smartest thing going, you know, I don't care what he did in the war," she said. "Emmy's all right, though."

The other men of the town, for Miss Drumheller, likewise came up short. Burgoyne, the selectman, was an incompetent waffler. Gorsuch, at the bank, was a snoop.

Calabrese she pretended didn't exist. Miss Drumheller tolerated me, however. She tolerated me because she believed, mistakenly, that I was an educated man—or, really, just because I was from away.

So was she. Miss Drumheller came from Portland, Maine. She was a graduate of Mount Holyoke College, class of 1907.

"When I came here, this place might as well have been in another world," Miss Drumheller said. "Not another world—another planet. You came up on the train from Brattleboro. Half the time, the train didn't make it. It got stuck in the snow or it ran off the rails. And then, when you got here, where were you?"

"So why did you come?" I asked her.

"They needed a teacher," said Miss Drumheller. "I wanted to work. Not like some people."

That was aimed at me. Miss Drumheller felt I was wasting my life. She held me to a high mark, because she knew I had been to college, and even though my degree was from a state university in the Middle West, it had some small credit with Miss Drumheller, who was a college snob.

"When I came here," she said, "the only college graduate in the entire town, besides myself, was Anson Usher, Hugo's father. He was a graduate of Harvard," she added, "a scholar. He knew Latin and Greek." Miss Drumheller dearly loved a lord.

I sat in her kitchen and listened to her, and I wondered about her life. No, if I am honest, I have to say I wondered not about her life but about her body. Miss Drumheller, I gathered, had never married. What, then? Irresistibly, lifted on the fumes of Miss Drumheller's spiked coffee, my mind flew to the question of her—um—*experience.* Was I to imagine Miss Drumheller's youthful slimness clasped in the arms of the aristocratic Usher senior, the Harvard man? He had both Latin and Greek, she said. What, exactly, had she meant? Was she praising Usher's linguistic ability, or was her praise directed at forbidden arts, unnamed except in the ancient languages? The thought appalled. Was Usher not the one, then? Did Miss Drumheller in her time rather grapple with earnest normal school fellows in celluloid collars? Might she even have taken on a local, a rustic, a farm boy, a stud townie, an overgrown eighth grader? Littlejohn had chopped her wood for pay, she said. Had he chopped to other purpose for free? A grotesque montage of images swarmed before my mind as Miss Drumheller talked on, her pretty, perfectly white hair bright in the sunlight that came off the snow and through her kitchen window. It is God's mercy that our thoughts, at least, are hidden.

A maiden lady. So, had she maybe worked it the other way? Had the passionate life of Miss Drumheller been a matter not of crass fucking but, rather, of obscure pleasures languidly exchanged among suffragettes, or bluestockings, or whatever her youth had furnished, pleasures inverted, female, consisting as much of sentiment as flesh? Who was S.B.? What was she?

Maybe I was at fault, unable as I was to raise my eye from the mire in which I paddled. We Noons are a dirty-minded lot, altogether. Miss Drumheller might have been asexual, celibate, above the fray. Some are. She might be a maid of eighty-something, a kind of hill-country nun. Was she? I thought not. For with all her age, frailty, and disapproval, Miss Drumheller didn't seem to me to have the mind of a virgin.

"You're a big young man, really, aren't you?" she said one morning as I was taking off my coat in her kitchen. I had finished shoveling and was hot and blown.

"What?"

"I said you're a big young man. Turn around."

"What?"

"Go ahead," said Miss Drumheller. "Turn around. Let's get a look at you. How much do you weigh?"

"I don't know. A hundred and ninety?"

"You don't carry much fat, though, do you?" said Miss Drumheller.

"I guess not," I said. "Do you object to my weight?"

"Not at all," said Miss Drumheller. "A man's best when he's big."

Another day, she had given me a second cup of coffee and taken a tiny bit of rum for her own. Maureen was not expected that morning.

"What does she do, anyway?" I asked Miss Drumheller.

"She cleans. Changes the bed. Does laundry."

Miss Drumheller sipped her coffee. She looked at me over the rim of her cup.

"She bathes me," she said.

"Bathes you?"

"That's right," said Miss Drumheller. "Old people need help bathing, you know. Maureen helps me bathe—not helps: She doesn't like to. She's better at laundry. Laundry is her forte. You, now, I'll bet you're good at giving baths."

"I wouldn't know," I said.

"You ought to try it," said Miss Drumheller. "I'll bet baths are your forte."

I started to laugh.

"You know?" I said. "If I were sitting here drinking rum at nine in the morning and having this conversation with a woman half your age—no, two-thirds your age—well then I could make a pretty good guess where the rest of my morning was going to go."

"But as it is," said Miss Drumheller, "you've no idea."

Was she a good teacher? I don't know if you'd say she was. She taught some things that were plain not so, I know that. We had to learn the capitals of the states, you see. That was a big part of school. And she had this long wooden pointer and a map that rolled down like a window shade in front of the blackboard. She would point to a state and ask somebody the capital, and they'd better know it. The map hadn't any names on it—it was for school. She'd slap her pointer down on the map, on a state, say, "Orlando Applegate!" and you'd have to name the state and the capital. She'd slap it down again, say "Robert Huntoon!" and so on. If you didn't know a capital or called out the wrong one, she might even give you the pointer.

She'd hit you with it?

One of the girls it was who figured out you could get your own map and learn off the capitals at home, be ready for her. Nobody else had ever thought of doing that. It seemed like cheating to us, but it was only homework. We were pretty raw.

But if you didn't have the answer, she'd hit you?

She would if she felt like it. She'd had us learn that the capital of Wyoming was Casper. It ain't. It's some other town out there. Well, one day, it was Nancy Parrish, she was sweet on Errol Burgoyne, and she came to school and told Errol that the capital of Wyoming ain't Casper, but this other place.

Cheyenne.

That's it. And so Errol went to teacher and said, "The capital of Wyoming ain't Casper, either. It's"—what did you say?

Cheyenne.

"It's Cheyenne," Errol said. And teacher gives him a look, picks up the pointer, and cracks Errol over the head with it. "If I tell you it's Casper, then as far as you're concerned, it's Casper." She was that kind of teacher, you see. That's the only kind there was, in those days. Would you say that's being a good teacher, exactly?

It's a matter of discipline.

That's right, son. You're right. That was more her job: to keep us all in line until we got big enough to go to work. She did it by teaching. In the army, they do it by the manual of arms and drill and so on.

Still, you learned things. You're not dumb.

Thanks.

I mean, you're an educated man. You got that way from her, partly.

I'm self-taught, son.

5

The snow kept falling, and I kept shoveling it. Sometime in February of my first winter on Bible Hill, I had to shovel out my windows because the snow had about buried the house. Littlejohn's house had a steeply pitched roof, with two front windows under the eaves. The ground in front of those windows got the snow that fell on it directly, and it got the snow that slid off the roof. By February, most years, the snow in front of the house had mounted to the eaves, blocking the windows and giving life indoors a quality of gloomy, submarine endurance. Gloomy, submarine endurance we Noons can stand better than most, but I could feel it breaking me at last. Nowadays, of course, there are medications you can take when you reach that point, but thirty years ago, you had to do something. I shoveled out the windows. Doing it, I felt like a fool, but it worked; the light came in. Snow is like money, finally, in this: Too much of it makes you do funny things.

What is to become of snow? Now, we are told, the world is growing warmer. Soon snow will be no more. It will be a thing of the past, like diphtheria, like streets full of horse shit, like blank verse, and the particular conditions it has for so long imposed on people's lives and thoughts will be lifted. What will we do? Will Bible Hill become a tropic, a department of the visionary south? Will its brief, productive summer elongate, protract itself on either end, to curve, converge, and finally effect a kind of Mediterranean evenness varied only by the south wind and lit with the colors of oranges and lemons? Will its mind, its people change? Sure they will. They'll have to. But how? Will they exchange resignation for enjoyment, wit for passion, work for life? Will the hard, bleak Protestant underpinning, already long subject to erosion, at last dissolve altogether? If we find ourselves without snow, will we get over the idea that we'll prevail by shoveling?

Of course, they'll tell you it don't snow like it did, but I don't know. The thing is, I don't recall. I don't remember how much it used to snow, not really. Neither does anybody else. They tell you it don't snow as much, but they don't know. Nobody does.

Well, come to that, there are records, aren't there? You can just look up the records.

Well, come to that, I guess you can. If that's what you're after.

Well, isn't that what we were talking about?

Is it, son? We were talking about snow.

Mr. Applegate expatiated. Mr. Applegate instructed. Mr. Applegate interpreted. He deals in paradox, in metaphor. You will hear it said of the old-style New England hill-town dweller that he has few words or none: a silent, stolid fellow. But my own experience of the breed has been that you can hardly get them to shut up.

9. Rocks

Bible Hill is an elongated ridge rising to the south, its axis oriented southwest-northeast. Its elevation is 1,611 feet, its area, tough to estimate, but say three square miles plus, a little short of two thousand acres. In the Old World, the whole place would have about made a decent deer park.

The hill itself is a solid lump or plug of hard gray granite which, in the youth of the world, was exposed as layers of softer rock around and above it were weathered down. The last glacier mauled and scoured it into its present shape, roughly that of a tadpole swimming toward Albany. The glacier left Bible Hill with no soil, no vegetation to speak of—no life at all, perhaps—but with a terrifying abundance of rocks. The place today is a museum, a zoo, a university of rocks of every size, color, and kind.

The grandest are the glacial boulders, eight or ten feet tall, that stand unaccountably about in the woods, solitary, seemingly unrelated to anything in their surroundings. The glacier, as I understand it, ripped them from what are today the suburbs of Montreal and then, some thousands of years later, let them down here. There is one of them in the woods behind Bracketts' that is the size of a toolshed and entirely white.

Another such boulder, according to the annals of the town, stirred itself from its lodgment below my own place one morning in the spring of 1899 and started rolling down the hill. It soon got going at a pretty good clip. It flattened a hundred feet of woods, crossed the road, went through somebody's new corn, and fetched up in the yard of the district schoolhouse. There is a photograph of the boulder standing hard by the corner of the schoolhouse. It comes to just below the eaves. It's still there, though the schoolhouse isn't. They couldn't move the boulder, so they moved the school.

Glacial boulders are the biggest of our rocks, but in a way, they are the least of them. Certainly they are the least troublesome (as long as they stay put). For human purposes, it's not the boulders but the smaller rocks that give Bible Hill its hard heart.

Since the departure of the glacier, the succeeding fifteen thousand years have furnished Bible Hill with a mantle of poor topsoil, rarely more than eight or nine inches deep. That soil is full of rocks the way the sea is full of fish, the way good clam chowder is full of claims. The rocks lie in the ground in schools and shoals, in all sizes, at all depths. I once dug a ditch, no more than five or six feet long, to carry the spring runoff away from a patch where I hoped to grow early vegetables. I went down a little less than two feet. The digging took me half a day. When I was done, I had my ditch, and I had two piles of spoil: a pile of dirt and a pile of rocks. The pile of rocks was the bigger pile. I took a fancy to count them. My little ditch had contained 377 rocks, the smallest the size of my fist, the largest the size of an unabridged dictionary. All were more or less round. None was of any earthly use I could imagine except to grind down the spirit of the digger.

Worse than the rocks is the stuff they lie in, or most of them: a tough, sticky clay hardpan, light gray in color, which can scarcely be dug at all. It bounces your spade right back into your teeth and laughs at you. To dig down any more than a foot or so, you need a pick or a heavy bar to break up the hardpan. When you come to it, the hardpan may make you decide you don't need to dig as deep as you'd planned. Of course, sometimes you don't have a choice. I knew a man in the next town over who worked, when he was in high school, as a grave digger. He was part of a two-man team. They dug four and a half feet down—by law. A grave took the two of them a full day to dig, just because the hardpan had to be broken with a crowbar before it could be dug. You'd think in a country furnished with that kind of earth, the people would catch on to laying their dead to rest in trees or atop pole towers like the Sioux. But no, they keep on digging.

In some few years, now, of attempting to grow things on Bible Hill, I have found its thin, sour soil can support a reliable crop of garden peas and a tolerable radish. Beans also thrive. Other vegetables are uncomfortable on Bible Hill. Brought in and planted here, they don't fit in; they shrink, they faint, they grow morose, they withdraw like revelers who have wandered by mistake into a Quaker meeting.

Fortunately, however, the meager topsoil of Bible Hill and its inert, impossible substrate do produce one thing well: trees. On Bible Hill, the most ancient and irresistible forces of the earth, the vast orogenies, the eons of reduction by water and wind, the annihilating glaciers advancing, retreating, have wrought over half a billion years to produce poor farming in pleasant country. It's odd when you think about it, but the fact is that the same stubborn dirt that so defies the science and labor of the best farmer grows effortlessly a very pretty forest.

Bible Hill is wooded from top to bottom except around the houses of its few present-day inhabitants and over part of its northerly flank, an open, rocky hillside pasture once called Sheep Desert, amounting to, say, ten acres. The forest that covers Bible Hill is a hardwood forest: beeches, oaks, ash, and maples giving way here and there to belts and stands of pines. At the top of the hill, and starting down its steep north side, you are in fir trees and birches; then the better hardwoods return and take you down to the road at the bottom.

The woods on Bible Hill have been cut down again and again, though never systematically or all at once. Originally, the forest here was—who knows what? Perhaps an open parkland of the legendary king's pines: straight trees, white pine, ninety, one hundred feet tall, which were marked out for use as masts by the Royal Navy, perhaps a prehistoric version of the brushy mixed woods we see today. Certainly any original forest is gone from Bible Hill by now, although in the ravines on the dark north side there are enormous hemlocks that must be pretty old. And growing out of the stone walls that crisscross the hill in the woods are huge old oaks and maples. On this property is a wall maple whose trunk is more than fifteen feet around. That tree has been there for a long, long time. Still, it and the other wall trees can't be original growth, can they? For obviously, the walls are older.

At the turn of the twentieth century, the southern, eastern, and western flanks of Bible Hill were cleared land except along the fence lines. In old photographs, the hillsides are nude, and you can see the boulders and ledges that the forest now conceals. The shorn land looks sad, somehow, or abused; it looks like a battlefield. When I came to Bible Hill, there were plenty of men and women in the town who as children had gone down the hill on bobsleds and pungs, a long and giddy ride, a ride out of the last chapter of *Ethan Frome.*

Today it is no small job for the imagination to conceive of a rush down Bible Hill in a toboggan, and I don't suppose there are any of those fun-loving children left alive.

Not on Bible Hill, but not far from it, there was once thought to be gold in the earth. My teacher, Mr. Applegate, kept in the desk in his law office a brown stone the size of a walnut that had a plug in it of some dull yellow metal that might well have been gold, for all I knew. He'd had it from his grandfather, he said. His grandfather had found the goldstone in the Quick Branch, probably sometime in the 1870s or '80s. Believe it or not, there was quite a little gold panning in the township's streams in those years. Others besides Mr. Applegate's forebear claimed to have found color. The gold rush in Ambrose didn't last, though. I suspect the only reason for it in the first place was excitement among the people at having come upon an occupation that, on the land as it was found to be, made even less sense than agriculture.

Plainly, God never made Bible Hill for farming. He didn't make it for mining. He didn't make it for grazing, unless by the kind of animals, like sheep, that enjoy starvation. What did He make it for? Looking at, I guess. Looking at, and logging. And for what else?

10. Politics

1

What were the politics of Bible Hill? Not what you might expect; not, at least, if you got beyond party. Of party politics, Bible Hill hadn't much. It was not long before I arrived that the state legislature had passed a resolution declaring Democrats an endangered species in Vermont, along with the pine marten and the Canada lynx. Party politics were, at the time, predictable. Not so predictable, and far more debated, more passionately held, were what you might call "mental politics."

Politics asks, How are you governed? From what distance? By whom? Whom do you wish to be in charge? And a related question: Whom do you *imagine* to be in charge?

At Jordan's mill, on the edge of the village, there was a tall, thin, chinless fellow named Norton Rand, one of the innumerable Rands from Dead River Settlement and out that way, who believed the country—in fact, the world—was controlled from the brightly colored panel trucks that drove about everywhere over the back roads delivering Tip Top Bread. I worked at Jordan's off and on over a couple of years, worked with Norton Rand, and found him willing to explain.

Everybody knew the Tip Top Bread trucks. They were square, painted white, with large red, blue, and yellow dots to look like the wrappers on the bread they distributed. They went from house to house, in the villages, among the valley farms, and on out to the remotest homesteads back in the hills. A dozen times a day, you might see the Tip Top Bread men on their rounds—more exactly, you might not see them, so familiar a part of the setting did they and their silly trucks become.

It was Norton Rand's contribution to mental politics to realize that the Tip Top Bread men's harmless presence, in large numbers, in all seasons, and in every corner of the district, gave them a great and nearly invisible reach. And for what? The Tip Top men's ostensible errand was widely accepted, but it was one Norton couldn't, from his own certain knowledge, verify. Did he eat Tip Top? He did not.

"And another thing, too," Norton said. "You ever know anybody that drove for Tip Top?"

"Well, no," I said.

"Well," said Norton. "You wouldn't. You're new. But what I mean, neither have I. And I've known, oh, I don't know, guys drove for the oil company, drove beer, LP gas. I've known guys who drove milk trucks. But Tip Top? Nobody. Never. Who drives them? That's what I want to know."

"Right," I said.

"And who buys it?" Norton went on. "Who buys Tip Top? You?"

"No," I said.

"Not you," said Norton. "Anybody you know?"

"I'm not sure," I said. "Maybe. Maybe lots of people."

"But *nobody you know*," Norton said. "Me? No. Nobody buys the stuff. But there are those goddamned trucks, everywhere you want to look. Am I right?"

I nodded.

"So?" Norton asked.

"Gee," I said. "Here I thought the worst they were doing was screwing everybody's wife."

That was the joke. The Tip Top Bread man was supposed to be a backcountry Don Juan, a grinning male presence busy among the lonesome housewives stuck away out at the ends of the Star Routes. To them, he brought forms of consolation not made in any bakery. The Tip Top Bread man was the son of the egg man, grandson of the iceman, a figure out of *The Decameron*.

"Ha," said Norton. "Might be they're screwing more than that."

And here observe the acuity of Norton's analysis. For the Tip Top Bread man was *already* half-believed to be other than he seemed, and even so, he was ignored. The lie of his apparent role, exposed, ended the inquiry for most. Not for Norton. He discerned that to cover the grandest, darkest machinations, one lie is never enough. There must be two: the lie that is discovered and the lie behind that lie. The bread driver, and then the satyr in bread driver's clothing. And then what?

"Well, what?" I asked him. "Who are they, then?"

Now, for Norton, the Tip Top Bread men, once examined, revealed a force too large and penetrating to imply any ordinary purpose. You don't put an engine that big in a rowboat. In what is the essential move in the logic of mental politics, Norton deduced from the Tip Top Bread men's mystery, and from their subtlety, an authority commensurate.

"Who do you think?" Norton asked me.

"Well, do you mean they're from Washington, or what?" I asked.

"Washington?" said Norton. "Ha. You think what's-his-name—

Carter?—you think Carter tells those guys what to do? Don't make me laugh."

"He's the president," I said. "He's the commander in chief."

"He's nothing," said Norton.

"Well, then," I asked him. "If he's nothing, then what does he do? What do the rest of them do? Any of them. Take the Joint Chiefs of Staff. What about them? What do they do?"

"They're actors," Norton said. "They're nothing. They're a show. Somebody's got to be up there for us to look at. That's all they are, a show."

"Who runs them, then?" I asked Norton.

"You figure it out," Norton said.

At this point, the normal circuitry of mental politics begins to light up the old bulb of anti-Semitism. You prepare for a long discourse on the Jews, the bankers, the broadcasters, the Jews, Wall Street, the foundations, the universities, the Jews. Not from Norton Rand. Norton hated nobody. He feared nobody. Nor was he dumb, nor was he crazy—or not exactly. He was doing mental politics. Norton had looked about him. He had applied an entirely healthy skepticism to what he saw, and he had worked things out for himself. He believed somebody must be in charge. He knew it wasn't he. He refused to believe the world was directed by the buffoons who purported to lead it. Direction, therefore, must come from elsewhere. QED.

So far I was with him, but what about the Tip Top trucks? At first, I supposed Norton's fixing on them came from ignorance. After all, I thought, he's not an educated man.

July 10, 1947. Fair. Temp. 6 a.m. 66. To town. Dose for Dan $1.00

July 11, 1947. Fair. Temp. 12M 74. H. Usher here to see Dan

THE LIE

Politics with us is a sport and a pastime. We're right not to take it altogether seriously. In the capital, politics was the same, and it was different. It was both a less and a more serious business than with us. It was less serious down there, because down there it was a kind of show. It had a theatrical, eventful quality that made it fundamentally frivolous. Politics was more serious down there because down there it could get you killed.

Carlyle, in his book on the French Revolution, said that the origins of that cataclysm finally reduced to a single principle: A lie cannot be believed. A lie cannot be believed. Hence, the fall of the old regime, the murder of the king, the transformation of society. The regime, the king, the society were a lie, and a lie cannot be believed.

You couldn't prove it by the politics in the capital. There they knew how to produce belief. They did it by sleight of hand. Governments came and went like the silk scarves, white rabbits, and white doves of a stage conjuror. There were Communists and socialists and syndicalists and social democrats and Christian democrats and labor democrats and irredentists and nationalists and whatever you please. And always, there was the police, and always, there was the army.

"Sometimes, don't you see, the police is the army," Hitchcock explained. "And sometimes the army is the police. Other times, they're separate."

"What difference does it make?" I asked.

"Quite a lot, sometimes," said Hitchcock. "You can make a false step without knowing it. You don't want to do that."

Hitchcock was an old hand, and he knew what old hands know: At the end, all reasons are the same reason.

"Of course," Hitchcock mused, "you can argue that it makes no difference, since they both use the same . . . ah . . . measures."

Well, son, what makes you think he's wrong?

What? What do you mean?

Just that. Nort figures those bread trucks are important. How do you know they ain't?

Come on. You're not going to tell me you believe that about the Tip Top trucks. That's flying saucer stuff.

Maybe I don't believe it, maybe I do. Anyhow, we weren't talking about what I believe. We were talking about what you believe. Weren't we?

No. No, we weren't. We were talking about Norton's idea that the people who really run the country are driving around Bible Hill, here, delivering Tip Top. If that's the case, maybe you can explain to me what all those guys in blue suits are doing in Washington, D.C.

That's what I say. We're talking about what you believe, not Nort. You believe those fellows down there are running things. You believe it because they say they are and it's in the papers and on the TV that they are. That's good enough for you. It ain't good enough for Nort. Why's it have to be?

That doesn't make any sense at all.

It makes all kinds of sense, son.

Who are they, then? Who is it that's in charge, if it's not who it's supposed to be?

It makes no difference, not to Nort. You're telling him he can't know anything unless he knows everything. That ain't logical. It ain't even law. Like if you find a cow flop on your parlor floor, you know somebody got in there. It might have been a cow. It might have been the hired man with a shovel. You don't have to know which to know what. Put it this way, son: Nort's showing you the top side of reasonable doubt.

Okay. All right. Forget about Norton. I think he's wrong. What do you think? You, yourself, really. Are you going to tell me you think he's right? You're an educated man.

Maybe I ain't as educated as you think, son.

I could get nowhere with Mr. Applegate, any more than I could with Norton. Not, you understand, because of any failure of intelligence or education on the part of either of them, but, rather, because as countrymen they were constitutionally receptive to the hypothesis of conspiracy. Maybe Mr. Applegate did not believe in Norton's theory of government by the Tip Top Bread men. The point is, he understood it. He was willing to entertain an article of political lunacy that is, I suggest, characteristically rural. Those who live far from the seats of power, as country people by definition do, see that they have no control of great affairs, or even of middling affairs. They conclude that somebody else has, often some shadowy combination. The interesting thing is not that they arrive at that conclusion but how they react to it.

"I mean, doesn't it worry you?" I asked Norton.

Lunch break in the yard at Jordan's. Norton and I were sitting on a stack of new two-by-twelves. Norton had a fat ham sandwich. The air was full of the smell of mustard and of the new pine boards.

"What?" Norton asked.

"Well, the Tip Top trucks, you know?" I said. "Aren't you a little concerned about them?"

"Why would I be?" Norton took a big bite of his sandwich.

"Well, look at what they are," I said. "They control everything. They control you. You can't do anything about them. Doesn't that alarm you a little?"

"Why?" asked Norton, around his mouthful of ham sandwich. "What do I give a shit?"

Cheerful acceptance, you see? In the presence of an immense, irresistible, hidden will, a sinister influence dimly perceived but virtually omnipotent . . . No problem at all. Norton Rand exhibited mental politics at its best: analytical, detached, scientific. It needn't always appear so well—seldom does, perhaps. Certainly others in the neighborhood, persuaded by—or at least susceptible to—something like the same intimations, were less sanguine.

July 12, 1947. Cloud. rain p.m. Temp. 12M. 68. H.
Usher buys Dan $175!!

2

In my time, nothing remained of Usher's Hole but a hill of dirt in an old sand and gravel quarry off the Joppa road. The quarry, which was also Usher's, was exhausted: a scraped, dusty two or three acres grown up in hawkweed and sweet fern, with a rusty chain across the entrance and, around the perimeter, a ruined palisade of dead and dying trees that had fallen from the rim as the bank eroded. The place was a kind of oasis in reverse: a yellow desert amid the fertile green hills.

There it was that Hugo Usher, ten years earlier, had dug a bomb shelter, his end-of-the-world redoubt, into the side of the hill that the quarry had exposed. Recall that at the time—1960, 1961—the likelihood that North America would be spared a grand thermonuclear doomsday seemed no better than, say, 50 percent. Under the circumstances, those odds didn't seem wide enough for Hugo Usher. If there was any chance the whole country was going to go up in a big fireball, and if making plans and spending money could see you through the business alive, then Usher aimed to be among the survivors.

He used designs published by the Department of Defense. He hired geologists, mining engineers, architects, heavy-equipment operators, dynamiters. He bored a horizontal shaft thirty feet into the hill and finished it as a two-chambered bunker, like a pair of small house trailers, buried. Usher needed the walls and overhead to be of reinforced concrete eighteen to thirty-six inches thick. No local contractor knew how to put up a job like that. Usher brought in a firm from Albany.

"Listen," Usher told the foreman. "Here's what I want. If they drop the bomb right on this hill, right on it, and I'm down in here, I don't want to hear it. I don't want to feel it. I don't want to know about it at all until I turn on the radio."

When the construction was finished, Usher's shelter had all that New York concrete and sixty-five feet of hill between it and the sky. He bored an extra-large air shaft and installed a ventilator. He added a generator, a well. Then he provisioned. The Department of Defense had a publication for that, too. Usher got in dried foods, canned foods, water, medical supplies, reading matter, alcohol, tobacco, soap, batteries, aspirin, fuel oil, bottled gas, ammunition.

"What are you going to shoot?" he was asked. "It looks like if you got to go down there, everything up top's going to be dead. What's left to hunt?"

"I'm not hunting," Usher said. "I got to be able to defend the place."

"Against who?"

"Against you," Usher said.

. . .

Hugo, you see, figured, well, when the day comes, any kind of law and order, any kind of regular business, is going to be finished. It's going to be the end of the world, in a way.

Armageddon.

Well, or the Flood. More like the Flood. Hugo figured he'd be Noah. He'd get himself an ark. He'd get himself fixed up in there and wait it out. Now, you know, when the rain starts, the water starts to rise, that old ark starts to float, you know your no-good, useless neighbors are going to show up, wanting to climb aboard.

Too bad for them.

That's right, son. Too bad for them. There's food and water for one. Let everybody else go dig his own goddamned hole, what Hugo said. They try to move in on his place, he'll be ready for them.

Nice guy.

Armageddon, or the Flood, or whatever you please. Usher waited for it. He paid off his contractors, got his supplies in, locked the door, went home, and waited for the day when he should have need of his shelter. Usher waited, but he was the only one who did. Others did not delay. Others understood that many of the provisions Usher had laid up against the Last Days were at least as convenient, or enjoyable, or negotiable, or otherwise useful, in more settled times. Usher's bunker under the sand hill hadn't been completed a week when somebody broke the lock and made off with Usher's doomsday scotch. Seven cases. Usher double-locked the door, got in more scotch.

A couple of weeks later, Usher found the door of the shelter had been broken in, apparently with a sledgehammer. Inside, he found the place pretty well ransacked. A story was around the town that Usher had a bunch of gold in there, a box full of old double-eagle twenty-dollar pieces (some said a thousand dollars; some said ten thousand), so he'd have specie when paper money should be worthless. In fact, according to Mr. Applegate's memory, it wasn't so. Usher was a tough economist; in the state of nature, metal meant no more than paper, he reasoned, and it was nature he was preparing for, nothing less. There were no double eagles in Usher's redoubt. Still, whoever had broken in this time hadn't left empty-handed. Missing were found to be a quantity of canned goods, blankets, toilet paper, and all the rifle and shotgun shells.

"Goddamn it," said Usher. "These people are eating my lunch here."

He had the bunker fitted with a steel door. He got in new food, bedding, ammunition. New toilet paper. That fall, somebody evidently drove into the quarry with a tractor, put a chain on Usher's new door, and ripped it right out of the hillside. Then they went in and cleaned the place out once again.

Usher brought in yet another foreign contractor to install a second steel door. This door weighed half a ton. It bolted into the concrete bulkhead like the door of a bank vault. Usher refitted and restocked. Through the winter, the people let him be. That was the winter the East Germans barricaded the highways to Berlin and built the famous wall across the city, a wall that looked a little like the front of Usher's bunker. He checked the place pretty frequently that winter, you may be sure, but all was secure.

On a day in May, the heavy vault door was found standing open and the bunker rifled. Even the fixtures had been removed. The great door was undamaged. It had been opened from inside. Nobody could tell how the thieves had gained entrance, until the sheriff's deputy assigned to the break-ins at Usher's bunker discovered signs that somebody had been lowered down the ventilation shaft from the top of the hill above. By the size of the shaft, the intruder—or one of them—had to have been a small child.

Usher had provisioned and reprovisioned three times by now. "If they're going to start this World War Three," said Usher, "I wish they'd get on with it."

A PATRIOT

Lieutenant Hector was a graduate of Stanford. He was in the club, a friend of Hitchcock's. They played tennis. Lieutenant Hector was a handsome man, small, with a trim black mustache, even white teeth, soft hands, soft speech.

"Poor Hector." said Hitchcock. "Hector's a patriot. His country breaks his heart."

"My country," said Lieutenant Hector, "is like a man sitting in a jail cell, starving to death, being eaten by vermin. He sits there for years, tens of years. He suffers. He—what is the word?"

"He endures," said Hitchcock.

"He endures. He starves. Rats eat him," said Lieutenant Hector. "He sits in his cell. And do you know what? The door of his cell is not locked. Anytime, he can get on his legs, cross his cell, open the door, and leave. He never does. This makes me sad."

"Hector wants to do good," said Hitchcock. "But you see what he's up against down here. Do you know what the life expectancy in this country is?"

"No," I said.

"Neither do I," said Hitchcock. "Nobody does, really, but say twenty-six, twenty-seven years. It's a poor country. Do you know what the principal fatal disease, as far as we know, is? It's plague, Mark. Bubonic plague. Poor Hector. It must be excruciating for him, to look on, I mean."

"We help him, then," I said.

"Well, I don't know that I'd go that far," said Hitchcock. "We're not a charity, you know."

"What are we?"

"Not a charity," said Hitchcock.

Poor Hugo. The thing was, he reckoned that at the end of the day, everybody's on his own. Everybody's got to save himself, like Noah did. Everybody's got to make his own arrangement, not look to anybody else.

Come to that, I suppose he's right.

You think so, son? Well, come to it, maybe he is. Of course, Hugo was rich. He could afford to think like that.

True.

You're all alone, Hugo reckoned. I don't know. The thing is, Hugo liked the idea. He approved, you know? Poor Hugo, though. Noah's own people made a fool of him, too, didn't they?

Did they?

Sure they did. Read your Bible, son. It was the same with Hugo. His own people made a fool of him for his ideas.

August 2, 1947. Warm. Temp. 12M 81. To N.
Groom Jnr. to see horse. 3 yr old Bad eye

In the fall of that same year, it did seem as though Usher would get his wish at last, thanks to the Russian missiles to be placed in Cuba. You remember that week—or maybe you don't. (Maybe you weren't born.) Briefly, the Russians took out theirs and we took out ours, and for two or three days it looked like everybody might get wet. Usher moved into his shelter on October 25, 1962.

He stayed down there for five days. He drank a half-gallon of scotch, he told Mr. Applegate, read all of *A Treasury of American Sports Writing* and half of *A Conrad Argosy,* ate turkey hash and canned peas, listened to the radio, washed, and slept a lot. At the end of the time, he came out, he said, because he had begun not to feel perfectly right. Not once in five days had he moved his bowels.

It's not the case that the international situation improved after that time; on the contrary. Nevertheless, whether because he himself felt it had or for some more obscure reason, Usher never used his shelter again, hardly visited it. He had gone on to other things, apparently. For a couple of years, the town rented the shelter from him for a place to keep the road crew's equipment in, but that didn't last. With the ventilator shut down, the bunker became damp and everything rusted and rotted. The road crew moved out. Usher's project, which as a doomsday redoubt had been merely unsatisfactory, was, as a hole in the ground, a frank and flat failure.

It stood open and empty: Usher's Hole, a habitation of dragons and a court for owls. Children used it for camping out. Others, recently, though no longer, children, used it for bonfire parties, for beer drinking, for dope smoking, for assignations. At last, Mr. Applegate, acting again as the town's attorney, had to tell Usher that what his hole was was an *attractive nuisance* and that he needed to find some way of making it safe.

Usher reacted as Mr. Applegate knew he would.

"Safe for who?" Usher demanded. "Who's telling me it's not safe?"

"Look," said Mr. Applegate. "Sooner or later, somebody's going to get hurt out there."

"So what?" said Usher. "That's their problem. If they sue me, it's my problem. I can't see any way it's your problem."

"We'd just as soon nobody got hurt in the first place," said Mr. Applegate. "Wouldn't you?"

"I know where you're going with this, you know," said Usher. "You think I don't? Who owns that place, you or me?"

"You," said Applegate.

"Who built it?"

"You."

"That's right," said Usher. "It's my property, my improvements. But now I guess the town is going to tell me I have to pay to get it closed down so nobody gets hurt. Has anybody ever got hurt out there? No. Will anybody? Probably not. But the town thinks it can order me to undo my own work on my own land so somebody who might come along, somebody who *doesn't even exist*—that's what it comes to—won't break his ankle. For that, I've got to do all the work, pay all the costs, because the town says so. Well, the town can go right to hell. This ain't Russia. Not yet."

"We'll do the work," Mr. Applegate said. "It won't cost you nothing."

"Oh sure," said Usher. "Sure you will. You'd love to. You'd love to come onto my land with all kinds of equipment, all kinds of your people: snoopers, regulators, inspectors, cops. Goddamned bureaucrats. Goddamned social engineers. You'd love to figure out exactly what you want to do with my property and get your own people in to do it."

"I'm talking about the road crew," Mr. Applegate said. "Billy and them, one of the trucks, I guess. It might take an hour."

"Why don't you just take it?" Usher said. "Just take it right over. Confiscate it. Expropriate it. Why not? Take the land. Take the improvements. What's stopping you? What rights do I have when the state decides something ought to be done? Who am I to go up against the state?"

Just there was where Usher came down onto the rock. Politics asks, How are you governed? But the question presupposes a prior question: Are you governed? *No,* thought Usher: *Hell no.* He wasn't governed, didn't need to be, didn't want to be—or anyway, he wasn't governed by *you.*

"The which?" Mr. Applegate asked him.

"The state," Usher said. "You. You're the state."

"Well, then," Mr. Applegate said. "The state will make you this offer. We can force you to close that place up. We can sue you for it. We won't. We won't sue, and we'll do all the work. No cost to you. We'll seal up your improvement for you. Is that what you're calling it, an improvement? We'll unimprove it, free, for nothing. We'll hold you harmless. You agree never to improve it back again. What do you think?"

"I told you what I think," Usher said. "I think you can kiss my free and independent ass."

Mr. Applegate said nothing. There they left the interview for a long count of twenty-five.

"No cost to me at all?" Usher asked presently.

"Not a dime," said Mr. Applegate.

"No lawsuit? I'm covered?"

"That's what I said."

"Forever?" Usher asked him.

"Nothing's forever," Mr. Applegate said. "For as long as the state shall last. What do you say?"

"Close her down," said Usher.

So the town crew took a morning at Usher's Hole. They dropped a cement plug down the ventilation shaft, and they brought in five loads of bank-run gravel and used a bulldozer to push it into and around the door of the bunker. Now birches ten feet high grow on the hill in front of the hole, scrubby birches, and those poor cherry trees that come up on burned land.

Would you really have sued him?

Well, it wasn't up to me, you know. The selectmen would have had to decide. But I think so. Sure, they would have sued. They were irked. So was I. Nobody likes being called the state.

Amanda had known Usher's Hole well, especially in its next-to-last condition.

"Denny and I used to go there," she said.

"You did?" I asked her. "Why?"

"Come on, Noon," said Amanda. "Why do you think?"

"Oh," I said.

"Denny broke in there, before," Amanda said. "He claimed he was the first who did, right after Hugo had the place built. He and a couple of others. He had a bottle of whiskey he took from there. We shared it. We both threw up."

"You poor kids," I said.

Amanda laughed.

"Then, when the town was getting ready to close it down for good, Denny and I were out there one night and I lost my bra. My mom had taken me down to Brattleboro that week and bought me three new bras. So Denny and I were at the hole, and, I don't remember, I guess the constable came around with his light—they used to do that on weekends. Anyway, we had to leave quick, and later I found I'd left my bra at the hole. My mom couldn't figure it out, how she kept counting bras and coming up a bra short. She couldn't understand why."

"Couldn't she?"

"What's the matter, Noon?" Amanda asked. "Don't you like hearing about all the stuff I did? My wild high school days? You didn't think you could have wild high school days in a place like this, did you?"

"I don't mind hearing about you," I said. "Never. I'm not that interested in Denny, though, to tell you the truth."

"Yeah, well, what can I tell you, Noon?" Amanda said. "Denny was there. If you're going to have wild high school days in a place like Ambrose, Vermont, you can't pick and choose a lot, you know? You pretty much have to use the material they give you."

July 15, 1947. Fair. Temp. 12M 77. Bought horse New Dan of N. Groom Jnr for $125. $50 to good!

3

Usher, of course, I never knew, and Norton Rand not well. I don't claim to have seen through them—or anybody else, ever. But still, I hold that as practitioners of mental politics, they represent an attitude or style that is typical of Bible Hill and places like it. (Our adjoining state to the east, for example, as I have earlier indicated is practically a national park of mental politics.) Up here, there is a race of hill-country Cartesians, heroic doubters, who are willing to have every historical and political certainty dissolve and then to reestablish all knowledge on other ground. Let that ground be the Tip Top Bread men, let it be a crabbed, subterranean solipsism—Norton Rand, Usher, and many, many others hereabouts share a will to come up with a vision of their own and then to give effect to it, to live in it, in spite of cost, ridicule, disadvantage. It's that will, I'm saying, that belongs to country places, country people.

For myself, I knew I couldn't carry it off. I was city-bred, a distruster of visions, all of them; a distruster of systems, all of them. Visions are for the lunatic muttering on the subway platform, or they are for the saints, heaven-bound, and none of the systems work, none of them, not even the crazy ones. Or so it seemed to me then, and so it seems today. Mental politics were not for me. I couldn't take on the colors of a Norton Rand, still less of an Usher. As a Vermonter, I was never going to be a success. But then, I didn't have to be, did I? I didn't have to pass or pretend. I didn't even have to change. I didn't come to Bible Hill to be a spy. Whatever the reason I came was, that wasn't it.

11. Sounds

1

December 7, 1941. Fair. Temp. 12M 35. O. Applegate here p.m. Says China bombed Califonia

Bible Hill is no gallery. It's not a museum. It's a hall: Much of the best of it comes to you by your ears. If there were a philosopher of Bible Hill, a master of knowledge, he would be able to work entirely by ear. From sounds alone, his other senses deleted, he would be able to tell the spot, the season, the day, even the hour. I can partly do it myself.

Beginning around the first of August and continuing through the late summer and fall, I could hear from my dooryard chainsaws, three or four of them. Each saw had its own voice, like a hunting hound, and you could learn the meanings of the distant whines and pops of the saws, just as a hunter, sitting on his hill and listening to his dog coursing afar, can tell when it strikes, when it runs, when it faults.

Calabrese had two saws. One was a little one. It ran, idled, ran, idled. Its sound meant Calabrese was making sticks for his cookstove.

His other saw was a monster, with the biggest engine you could buy, and a deep, stuttering roar. It started, mounted, and kept on running straight out, on and on. Calabrese was cutting logs. Then, farther off, to the north, a pair of saws would start up nearly at the same instant and keep at it intermittently, strophe and antistrophe, all through a Sunday afternoon. That was Manfred Adams cutting firewood from his lot off the Branch road. Adams lived and worked in the village and got his wood in on the weekends. His boy helped him.

Sounds were the life of Bible Hill. I'm not talking now about sounds like the mysterious echo of the heavenly railway train that passed through the sky from Brattleboro each afternoon. I'm talking about real sounds made by real things, real people: carpenters banging boards, gunshots, engines, whistles, church bells. Their sounds carried for miles over this country, bouncing back and forth from hill to hill.

Even voices carried for miles and were heard and known. Early one morning in the fall, I was walking on one of the old logging roads that wander over the east side of Bible Hill, when I heard a woman's voice:

"Toby? Toby?" she called.

I stopped short and waited, expecting someone to appear out of the woods before me.

"Toby? Here's the bus, Toby."

Then I knew nobody was going to appear out of the woods. The voice wasn't coming from the woods, but from far, far off. Nowhere on this side of Bible Hill, as far as I knew, was there a house, a woman, a Toby. Was somebody camping out? Where?

"Toby? Damn it, TOBY!"

Oh. I was hearing Mrs. VanBuren trying to whip her ten-year-old out of the house and off to school. Their place was on the way to Back Diamond. Mrs. VanBuren's voice had come from their hill, across the valley, over the village, and up Bible Hill to me, a matter of two or three miles.

Some sounds are speech; some are mere noise. Some are both: the cries and calls of birds. Every bird on Bible Hill had its note. Crows, roosters, owls, wild geese, the ten million songbirds of the woods and thickets—you could hear them all in their seasons; you could know them all by their sounds. Or at least you could come to know them, with a little help.

For several years, there was one birdcall that troubled me, a strident whistle, falling a little in pitch, repeated once or, rarely, twice: *tiu, tiu, (tiu)*. It came from the woods immediately surrounding the house, close by, and it had an insistent quality that demanded attention, like the noise of a telephone left too long off the hook.

Tiu, tiu.

What bird was that?

I had no idea. I knew the birdcalls everybody knows: the crow, the jay, the cardinal. And I knew as well the voices of a few other birds, a little less familiar, whose calls figured in my setting on Bible Hill: the barred owl, the whippoorwill, the veery. The bird of the *tiu, tiu* was none of these. What was it, then? I felt I ought to give a name to whatever was making so distinctive a racket in my own backyard.

At first, I tried to spot the bird as it sang, but I never could. The woods from which its call issued were thick and dark, tough to penetrate even with binoculars; and, too, as with other birdsong, the call had a kind of sourceless, hallucinatory quality. It was like an echo, detached from its origin. The bird was a ventriloquist.

Tiu, tiu, it said.

I turned to the bird books then. I read up on the calls and songs of the species known to northern New England. I found descriptions of birdcalls: "a clear, whistled chant" (tufted titmouse); and I found attempts to reproduce birdsongs by onomatopoeia: *brrt, bjjt* (bank swallow); *tiddly-tiddly-tiddly-tiddly* (Blackburnian warbler). I even found, in older bird books, elaborate and often charming translations of birdcalls into English—for example, in the calls written as *I wish to see Miss Beecher* (chestnut-sided warbler); *Sam Peabody, Peabody* (white-throated sparrow); and—my favorite—*Quick, three BEERS* (olive-sided flycatcher). I found these antique attempts to converse with the birds quaint and somehow touching, but for the purposes of identifying a song in the real world, they were quite useless, as those same books' authors mostly admitted.

The trouble with trying to know a bird's song from written accounts in books, I discovered, was always the same: The descriptions of the songs were harder to understand, so to speak, than the songs themselves. Written transcriptions of songs in books would, no doubt, be found to be accurate enough *once you knew the song they described*; but they begged the question of their real use. To use them, you had already to know exactly the thing you hoped they would tell you.

There I about stuck. On went the strange bird, bleating away from the forest surround. Surely that wild, incorrigible *tiu, tiu* had lately a jeering, mocking tone?

I decided I no longer cared. I consoled myself, as so many wiser men than I have done, by reflecting that, after all, a name is unimportant. What's in a name? Does the bird know its name? Give the bird any name you please, give it none, its song is unchanged. I would enjoy the song for what it was and ignore the source.

I couldn't do it. Simply accepting the unnamed song as a gift, without inquiry or examination, proved to require qualities of mind I found I lacked: intellectual confidence, perhaps, patience, true philosophy. No doubt a seer out of the East could rest content with a familiar part of his daily experience going unexplained, but I could not. I'm a Westerner, after all. I can stand the pain of long, hard discovery, but not the pain of doubt. We Noons are men of science. We Noons are analyzers, classifiers. If you don't know the name, you don't know the thing. But how are you to learn?

Then Milo Tavistock, my sometime boss, came to my house to do a job of masonry. I had given Milo three days' work for no pay the week before, and he allowed he could come to me for a morning to point my chimney. (Six for one was the kind of exchange Milo could entertain.)

I carried Milo's ladder from his truck to the house, set it against the eaves below the chimney. I held the ladder while Milo mounted to the roof with his gear. I was at the foot of the ladder, holding on to the rails to steady it, and Milo was most of the way up, when the unknown bird began to sing, loudly, from the woods.

Tiu, tiu.

"What's that bird?" I asked Milo.

Milo stopped climbing the ladder.

"What one?" Milo asked.

Tiu, tiu, went the bird.

"That one."

"That?" said Milo, resuming his ascent. "Areole."

Of course. I about decided there's not much you can find out by yourself. By yourself, you can learn only what you already know. If you want to get forward, you need helpers.

June 6, 1944. Cloud. Temp. 12M 69
Bird in chimny. Set out 10 tomatoes

Some of the sounds that constitute Bible Hill today are not to be heard there, never were: a paradox.

Mild, silent Arthur Brackett was the rural letter carrier who served the RFD route that included Bible Hill. At one time, I coveted his job. He left his house, down the hill from mine, by eight each morning, had his mail sorted by ten, set out, and got to our road around one in the afternoon. He was home by three-thirty. Arthur did his trick in a green Jeep pickup truck. The post office bought his gas, his tires—or if it didn't, it ought to have done so.

I coveted his job, but then I learned the post office preferred to hire veterans. Fair enough. That way, Arthur Brackett was a man who had a good job coming to him.

Tubby, you know. Tubby was in the D day landings. He landed on that beach—what name did they call it? The American beach?

Utah or Omaha.

Omaha. Tubby was there. He's got a whole boxful of medals. He's got the Purple Heart, a couple of others. Tubby's even got a French medal.

I've never known anyone who was in that, D day.

Neither have I, son, except Tubby. But then, the age you are, your father must have been in the war somewhere, wasn't he?

He was in the navy.

Lot of navy people from town here. Errol was navy. You wouldn't think of this place up here for them, on account of no coast. They're here, though. The whole state has always been a good navy state, going all the way back. Hugo was navy.

What did he do to get decorated?

Hugo? I don't know that he was decorated.

I mean Tubby.

Oh. I don't know that, either. Something. Tubby never said. I didn't like to ask. Emmy's his wife. I guess Emmy knows; it looks like she would. He killed some Germans, I guess. Quite a sight of Germans, maybe. You wouldn't think it, would you, if you knew Tubby?

No.

Now I think about it, I don't think Emmy does know what he did. She once told my wife Tubby couldn't remember himself what happened then. He was blank, he told her. Anyway, whether he really couldn't remember or not, he wouldn't talk about it, even to his wife. He wasn't being modest. I don't know what he thought about it, but he wouldn't talk about the war. And I didn't like to ask.

2

Dogs, and the dog kind, made a signal contribution to the sound of Bible Hill. Not always a welcome contribution. Off the side of the road that runs by the west along the base of Bible Hill, on the left as you go toward Joppa, a family named O'Toole lived in a trailer on a little lot, another property that had been separated out of Usher's holdings. The O'Tooles moved around. O'Toole and his wife worked at Fellows Gear in Springfield. Their three children, boys, were in school in Ambrose.

The O'Tooles had a small flop-eared dog, like a beagle, which they were obliged to leave alone at their trailer each day, all day. When the O'Tooles went to work and their kids to school, the dog would be put on a chain fixed to a corner of the trailer. It had a wooden doghouse, but it was never known to enter it. Instead, the dog, every day, on being left, went out to the end of its chain, sat on its haunches, pointed its nose at the treetops, and commenced to bark, a kind of submusical mongrel hound's bark: three notes, spaced five seconds apart, then repeated.

Ike-ike-ike . . . ike-ike-ike . . . ike-ike-ike.

The dog kept that up pretty much from seven in the morning to three in the afternoon when the O'Toole kids got home from school. It never varied its bark. It never tired. I could hear it at my place, but not every day. By some trick of the wind, perhaps, or of the barometer, I'd hear it on cool afternoons. I seldom heard it in the morning. There were many days when I never heard it at all. And then, for me, the barking dog at O'Tooles' was a distant sound. I didn't mind it. The O'Tooles' neighbors on the Joppa road came quickly to feel less tolerant.

They complained to O'Toole. O'Toole shrugged his shoulders. There wasn't much he could do, he said. He was a workingman. He couldn't simply stay home. What would they have him do? Keep the dog indoors, the neighbors suggested. No, O'Toole couldn't do that, he said. They'd tried that. They'd kept the dog in the trailer when they'd lived in Oregon. The dog had eaten the couch.

At that point, the school year ended. The young O'Tooles were at home for the summer. They were a noisy lot, themselves, but at least the dog shut up. Then after Labor Day, the boys went back to school again, and again the dog was chained and left.

Ike-ike-ike . . . ike-ike-ike.

The neighbors returned to O'Toole. He simply could not leave his dog alone all day, they insisted. Not only was there the problem of its noise; leaving it chained for so long was an act of cruelty.

O'Toole threw up his hands. He'd about had enough. Whose problem was this? If his neighbors weren't around their homes all day, they wouldn't be annoyed by O'Toole's dog, would they? Didn't they work? O'Toole had to earn his living, didn't he? He did, and furthermore, O'Toole managed to leave the implication that some of his neighbors, perhaps, did not.

O'Toole's neighbors called the town constable. The constable called on O'Toole. The constable explained to O'Toole that unless his dog's noise was stopped, the animal would be impounded. And, as the world knew, impounded animals unclaimed after a week were disposed of, humanely but permanently.

At this, O'Toole's young raised a great cry. O'Toole's wife raised a great cry with them. The issue was no longer between O'Toole and his indolent neighbors. Their beloved dog was, in effect, under sentence of death.

About there, the matter rested for most of another year: unrelieved barking from O'Toole's dog; repeated complaints from O'Toole's neighbors; repeated defiance from O'Toole; repeated visits from the constable; repeated cries from O'Toole's wife and offspring. Nothing was resolved.

The fact is, the constable was in no hurry to act. Constables in towns like ours are in a delicate position today. Their authority, essentially obsolete, is poorly understood, and therefore it's precarious. Nobody knows exactly what the constable does, what he can do—nobody, including the constable. Therefore, a wise constable, in a matter like that of the O'Tooles' dog, will temporize. He will elect to kick the business along before him like a tin can in the road for as long as possible. He hopes the thing will go away before he has to stop at last and pick it up. At least as often as not, it does.

So it happened with the O'Tooles. School ended and the dog was quiet for another summer. Then in the fall, O'Toole appeared in a massive brand-new truck. He hooked his trailer to it, bundled into the trailer the wife, the kids, the dog, and drove away. The O'Tooles were on their way to Texas. Both of the senior O'Tooles, it turned out, were industrial engineers. What is an industrial engineer? Nobody knew, but the O'Tooles must have been pretty good ones, because they had taken jobs with the National Aeronautics and Space Administration in Houston. We'd see what would be made of O'Toole's dog by the Houston police, or the FBI, or the Texas Rangers, or whomever you please.

Mr. Applegate didn't like to ask Arthur Brackett about the war. I didn't, either, but I tried it once. In the fall, Tubby, Mr. Applegate, and I used to help get one another's firewood in. We'd go to Bracketts', then to Applegates', then to my place to saw and chop and load and carry. We had finished for the afternoon at Mr. Applegate's and he had brought three beers out back, where we sat on stumps before the woodshed. The day was warmer than it ought to have been, for it was November—in fact, the day after Election Day. Mr. Applegate had read in the newspaper the observation that we had just elected the first president in twenty-five years who had had no part at all in World War II.

"It's something when you think about it that way, ain't it?" said Mr. Applegate. He was talking to Tubby.

Tubby didn't answer. He was hard-of-hearing. He sat on his stump and drank his beer.

"Ain't it?" Mr. Applegate said. "The war?"

"Oh," said Tubby. "Sure."

"You were in it, weren't you?" I asked Tubby then.

"I guess so," said Tubby.

"What was it like?"

Tubby shook his head, tipped his beer bottle.

"What was it like?"

Mr. Applegate looked at the ground, covered in sawdust and fresh chips. Tubby looked over at me with a little smile.

"Noisy," he said. "You know, loud."

March 1, 1942. Rain. Temp. 12M 41. Town Meeting. A. Usher says his boy now in U.S. Navy

You know, loud. Somewhere I have read that in the summer of 1916, in the southeastern counties of England, the people could on many days hear the artillery firing on the Somme; they could hear the very guns that were turning their fathers, sons, brothers, husbands into white crosses in the vast military cemeteries of Picardy and Flanders. It was a sound like distant thunder that never brought rain, yet never went away. For a couple of summers, we had somewhat the same kind of noise in these parts, though less ominously.

A few years after I arrived on Bible Hill, the state Department of Highways set about straightening the main road through the town of Ambrose, where it went over the town line to the south. Doing that was a good idea. The road in that stretch came down a hill and around a curve, a sharp curve, the kind of curve that people pay to ride through at amusement parks. Then it hit the little concrete bridge over Pied Brook. On an icy night, the cars went flying out of that curve and into the brook as though they'd been shot from a sling. For years, the selectmen had begged the Department of Highways to work on that piece of road. At last they did.

The work took two summers, remade a mile of road, condemned thirty acres of various people's front and back premises. It cost, the newspaper reported, four million dollars. Not cheap, but you couldn't deny that for their money, the Department of Highways put on quite a show. For two years, they turned a mile of country road and its surroundings into a barren zone that looked like a strip mine on the moon. They brought in dump trucks the size of a small garage, with tires that were taller than I am. They brought in bulldozers of a like magnitude. They brought in battalions of engineers in white short-sleeved shirts, dark ties, and steel hats; and to direct traffic through the construction, they brought in a young woman with red hair, who on the hot summer days worked in a bathing suit. That she had the wherewithal, physically, to do that, there could be no question. Men came from all over the southern part of the state to inspect the progress of the work. I drove slowly by more than a few times myself.

Along with the enormous machines and the amazing traffic control, the Department of Highways brought in lots and lots of dynamite. To cut off the bad curve, they had to lay a new road along the chord of the curve's arc. The thing was, there was a hill there; that's why the road curved in the first place, right? The hill had to go.

Work started at seven. On Bible Hill, two miles distant and several hundred feet of elevation away, I heard the warnings: a long whistle, then two shorts, then the thump and rumble of the blast like thunder and finally the distant tremor underfoot. Over and over again through those two summers, the blasting went on.

At the end of it, the Department of Highways proved to have done exactly what it said it would do. I ought not to have been surprised, but I found I was—in fact, more than surprised: shocked, awed at the scale of their work and at the ease with which it remade not only the road but the land itself. You think the hills are permanent. Sure, they come and go over eons: That's geology. But as a setting for human lives, as a setting for your life, the hills are unchanging; you think. Not at all. The highway makers, given enough diesel, money, and explosive, could go on and on, until this country of steep hills and narrow valleys looked like a parking lot in Kansas.

September 25, 1944. Fair. Frost. Temp. 6. a.m. 27. Geese. O. Applegate here p.m Says Mrs. Ballantine's boy kild France. 18 yrs.

I never learned for sure what Arthur Brackett did in combat in Normandy to earn his battle decorations; whatever it was, it had some weight. For Tubby, you learned if you got to know him at all, was not as ordinary as he seemed. He was called by a note most others couldn't hear, like a talented dog. He had powers, and he had empty places. Once, on a terrible day in this peaceful township, I saw Tubby walk through blood, death, and wreckage as though he were taking a turn in the park. You can't do that if you carry a full set of human feelings; some part of Tubby had been amputated, and the decorations he never wore were hanging on the stump.

Mr. Applegate, for his part, hadn't been in the war.

I tried, son. They told me I had a heart murmur, and plus, I was too old. 'Course, I was sorry. But being honest with you, I can't say I was a hundred percent sorry.

Practically the whole town had turned to World War II in one way or another. Not from any local abundance of patriotism; that's the kind of war it was, evidently. Errol Burgoyne, the selectman, had served on an aircraft carrier. He had met Mrs. Burgoyne at a USO dance in San Francisco and brought her back east when he got out. Vernon Monroe had been the navigator of a B-17 bomber based in England. Tristram Rand was an artilleryman. He had been in it all the way from Africa to Germany.

I did my bit, though. Civil Defense. We had a plane-spotting station up top of Round Mountain. The Air Corps came in, cleared it all out in there, couple of acres. They put up a little tower, like a fire tower, but little. Little house on top. Phone line down to Patches' on the road to Dead River. You went up there and looked for enemy aircraft. If you thought you saw any, you called in.

Dull work.

Not really, son. We didn't spot a lot of enemy aircraft, it's true, but we kept busy. We spotted any amount of buzzards up there. Turkey vultures. Old Bob Polk didn't like them at all. He thought they were bad luck. Bob and I were teamed up as spotters. He'd bring his shotgun up to the tower when we had the duty and try to shoot them down.

Ridiculous.

Well, yeah, it was. But that is one tough bird, you know? I remember this one buzzard came over lower than usual. Bob upped with his gun and let him have it. Got him with the full load, too; you could see it hit. The damned thing just flapped its wings one time and sailed right on, didn't even slow down. Number-six shot, too, no pepper.

Mr. Applegate would tell you about his World War II as long as he could make a joke out of it, as long as he could turn it into a story. But not even he would tell you what he felt about the war, what it meant. So often, I found, that was the way for the men and women of that war, our parents. They must have learned things from it, but what they learned was so powerful and was learned at such cost that they couldn't teach it to us. They didn't talk about it.

3

Eight or ten times a year, somebody's house would catch on fire. Then the siren fixed on the roof of the firehouse at the end of the village would start up, its cry mounting in a prolonged ascent, from a low mutter to a high, sustained wail that carried all over the middle parts of the township.

When the siren sounded, every dog on Bible Hill heard it, and as its tone rose and grew louder, the dogs would join in, howling and barking from their various homes. Calabrese's monstrous guard dogs howled and roared. Down in the river valley, O'Toole's unhappy mutt would join in, until the O'Tooles moved to Texas. Mr. and Mrs. Gorsuch had a little dachshund. He was old and lived mainly indoors, but when the fire siren started up, even he would leap into the front window of the Gorsuches' house and bay.

It wasn't only people's dogs that reacted to the fire siren. If the siren went off at night, coyotes would set up their own peculiar wail to accompany the siren and the dogs. There can't have been more than a few of them, usually, but always it sounded as though there were a company of coyotes at least on Bible Hill, yelping, shrieking, and howling from the woods and rocks like a midnight picnic outing from a lunatic asylum. A coyote is a big, rangy, long-legged, long-jawed thing that looks like a starving German shepherd and travels in bands or packs. When they began their howls to the fire siren, the smaller dogs of Bible Hill would prudently fall silent, but Calabrese's great beasts would become more excited. They would roar the louder and race around their yard.

The coyotes' weird yodeling went on even after the fire siren had stopped.

"God, what's that? Is it Win?" Amanda sat up in bed. It was long past midnight. "Where's Win?" she said.

"Coyotes," I said.

"Coyotes?" said Amanda. "No, it's people. Where are they? Are they here?"

"It's coyotes," I said. "The siren got them going."

"The siren?"

"The fire siren. You were asleep."

"God, what a horrible noise. Where are they?"

"I don't know. All around. In the woods."

"Weren't you asleep?" Amanda asked me.

"No."

Amanda trembled in her nightgown. "God," she said. "There they go again."

I laid my hand on her back.

"Go back to sleep," I said. "Go ahead now."

You have noticed that I, who wasn't born until it was practically over, knew the language of World War II better even than Mr. Applegate, who lived it. I knew the names of the famous beaches in Normandy, not only ours but also the British and Canadian beaches: Omaha, Utah, Sword, Gold, Juno. I knew the names of the hot little islands and atolls scattered insignificantly over the western Pacific, where my own father lies at the bottom of the sea: the Solomons, the Gilberts, the Marshalls, Iwo Jima.

Brackett, Monroe, Burgoyne, and others who fought have a real, earned knowledge of the war. Mr. Applegate, who stayed home, has a real, earned knowledge of the war. I have none, but still I am persuaded that World War II belongs to me and to my own generation as much as—indeed, more than—it belongs to the generations whose experience it was; for the reason that the war is the condition of our entire lives, as it is not of theirs. Tubby Brackett went to war at nineteen. That's a great age, almost a complete youth, with its weight of learning, act, and eros, a youth unencumbered by the names and images of war. I haven't that kind of lightness. There is no fraction of my conscious life when World War II—by a long way the prime historical determinant of American experience in the twentieth century—hadn't happened. Mr. Applegate, Tubby, and all the others had their time before the war, however short. I had none.

Not that I mind. I'm with Mr. Applegate: I'm not sorry to have missed that war, except that I didn't miss it: for good and bad, its chronicles, its protagonists, its geography, its language, its science, its political consequences have been, will always be, my own either to embrace or to overcome.

In that, my generation is unique. The older people lived when the war hadn't been. The younger people forget it. They don't care. Why should they? What is to remind them?

Less and less. All the war's dead are long since dust. The old towns and cities overseas that the war destroyed are built again. The new towns that the war made, the army towns, the air bases, have become real towns, or they've been abandoned. On top of Round Mountain, there is today not the least trace of the observation tower where Mr. Applegate awaited the Luftwaffe. Kids will set a thing like that on fire for the hell of it, or perhaps the tower simply rotted, fell down, and disappeared in the forest. And now I read in the news that the seas are rising in the western Pacific. The hot little islands and atolls are awash. Soon they will be no more. It's tough on the natives, but I say, Let them go. Every war is forgotten sooner or later, after all, even that one.

May 7, 1945. Fair. Temp. 6 a.m. 57. Bloodroot. O. Applegate here. Says E. Drinkwater found dead Round Mtn. yestday. Kild by bear, was squirl hunting Round Mtn. Germany give up

If there were a philosopher of Bible Hill, a master of knowledge, he would be able, from sound alone, to tell the season, and on Bible

Hill, the season is everything. There were a few days in October when the air was tuned up so tightly that the dome of the sky seemed to ring like a crystal goblet. Overhead, the Canada geese passed to the south, flight after flight. They honked and cried among themselves constantly as they flew, and if they were high up, there would be a moment every year when I didn't remember what they were. A flight of geese a mile up sounds like a cocktail party. It sounds like a pack of hounds. It sounds like a musical ice-cream wagon in the next street. It sounds like everything but what it is.

Hearing the faint cries of the geese, I stopped my work at the woodpile and for a second stood puzzled. Their clamor seemed to come from nowhere, from the air itself. Then I remembered them. I looked aloft and spotted them at last, flying south by west, about on the line of the Dead River, in long, ragged echelons—a sign in the heavens more certain than any rainbow, a promise that this year would end with me upright on this spot, watching it go, and a promise implied that in the spring the geese would be back and I would be right here waiting for them.

12. Visitors

1

Visitors, looking for Calabrese. One afternoon in September, I picked up a dozen eggs at Clifford's store in the village. I took them to the counter near the door, and I waited for the girl working the cash register to put down her magazine and let me pay for them. I had had that girl's job from time to time—would, very likely, have it again one day. A dozen eggs and a quart of Ballantine's ale.

The door to the place opened and there entered a tall man in some kind of uniform: black suit, white shirt, dark tie, black peaked cap. Like a policeman, but not a policeman. What, then?

The man came to the end of the counter and spoke to the girl at the register. He had an accent. Which one?

"Calabrese?" he said. "This guy is living here? Carlo Calabrese?" The girl's name was Kristin. She was one of the St. Justs' daughters, either the middle or the youngest. She might have been sixteen. She worked at the store weekdays after school. She glanced at me. I shook my head slightly.

"Carlo Calabrese?" the man asked Kristin. "Please?"

"I don't know him," Kristin said. The man nodded, looked at me, turned, and left the store. Kristin added up my eggs and beer, put them in a paper bag, changed my money, and picked up her magazine. I took my bag and went out the door the way the man in the black suit had gone.

A chauffeur, a driver, was what he was: That was a chauffeur's uniform he wore. Parked in front of Clifford's, a Mercedes limousine, black, long—not the longest one they made, perhaps, but long: the kind of car that has running water. I had to pass it to reach my own, and as I did, one of the rear windows ran down and somebody called to me, not the driver.

"Excuse me?" said a woman's voice.

I went over to the limousine. In the back was a passenger, a woman with her face at the window and her hand resting on the top of the door; not a kid like Kristin, no milkmaid, no simple high school girl, and not your sister, not your aunt. This one looked like she cost real money: blond hair, piled up; long neck; long fingers resting lightly along the polished rim of the door; red nails; red lips.

"Do you know Carlo?" she asked me.

"No," I said.

She looked up at me from the car's dark interior. She smiled.

"You do know Carlo, don't you?" she asked.

I didn't answer her.

"It's so important we find him," the woman said. Her face was pale. I saw she wore some kind of dark fur jacket or stole around her shoulders. "Where does he live?"

"I can't help you," I said. I could see the driver in the front. He looked straight ahead over the wheel. His hands were out of sight.

"Go after him," the driver said without looking around. "Follow. Follow this guy. Go where he goes."

"We could do that," the woman said to me. "What if we follow you?"

"You don't know the roads," I said. "I'll lose you in five minutes."

In the front of the limousine, the driver turned in his seat to look back at me.

"You think?" he said.

" "No, Dmitri," the woman said. "There's no time. They'll be waiting." She raised her window. The glass was smoked or tinted somehow, and when it rose, she disappeared. The driver started the engine. The long car rolled away from me into the road, turned around, and went south out of the village.

Later, I spoke to Calabrese at his place.

"You had visitors," I said. "At Clifford's. A woman out of a glamour magazine. Chauffeured Benz about half a mile long. Foreign driver, some kind of Russian, in a monkey suit. They were looking for you."

"A woman?" asked Calabrese.

"Very much of a one," I said. "A blonde. Hundred-dollar hairdo. Manicure. Fur coat. Smells good. Probably bathes every day. A beauty."

"Oh, yeah," said Calabrese. "Her."

June 15, 1920. Rain. Temp. 12M 73.
Visiter to teachers from city

There is something on Bible Hill that people want. What it is, we ought, perhaps, not to be too certain we know. In any case, it hardly matters what it is; people want to partake of it. And so we have visitors. That's lucky for us, for we need visitors. We're told we need visitors. We need their money, and we need as well their stimulus. Visitors are our livelihood, we're told, and they're our education. Everybody needs a livelihood, certainly, but does everybody need an education?

The visitors to Bible Hill are of three kinds: summer people, year-round summer people, tourists.

Of the three, summer people are the strangest. They are the closest of our visitors to us, and they are the most remote—like a distant, hardworking father. Normally, the difference between a visitor and you is plain: The visitor *goes* home; you *are* home. Summer people, however, as they reside on Bible Hill and environs, are home, too—and they are not. They have two homes, maybe more, of which Bible Hill is only one. Their conduct is that of people who are at home—and yet they leave. So their position is ambiguous; they are partly familiar, partly unknowable. Summer people are like the moon: a whole side you never see.

Yes, you wind up with the damnedest people, don't you? You know that house on Back Diamond, below Manda's, big old place, right on the road, needs paint? Summer place now? You know the fella that has that place, comes up here for the summer?

I don't think so.

Sure, you do, son. Little fella, lots of white hair, sticks out? Nachtigal? You know who Nachtigal is?

I've told you I don't.

That little guy is some kind of professor in Boston. At MIT. He's got the Nobel prize.

The Nobel prize?

Yes, sir. Nachtigal. He's got the Nobel prize for physics or chemistry or some damned thing. What I mean, he's famous. But up here, he's not famous. Up here, he's just another flatlander. Must be he likes it like that.

Must be he does.

He's kind of a funny old boy, too, Nachtigal. To be smart enough to get the Nobel prize, it looks like you'd have to be. But Nachtigal, I don't know. Like one day I was over there by his place, thought I'd see if there was a trout in the brook there. This is, oh, ten years ago. I used to go fishing up there, had my pole and everything, went in through the woods, and when I got to the water, there was Nachtigal, sitting on a rock in a pool in the brook—butt naked, not a patch on him, playing a clarinet. Nobel prize winner. What do you think of that, son?

June 17, 1920. Fair. Temp 12M 77.
To teachers for wood. Visiter S.B. her cousin?

In the way of summer people, then, the town of Ambrose had its lump of teachers, lawyers, doctors, and men of business, and it had its leaven, its famous and important men: the eccentric genius Polycarp Nachtigal, a Nobel prize physicist, and until recently, two others, as well: a former secretary of the Treasury and a Broadway producer. The cabinet secretary was old, however; he seldom came to his place now, even in the summer. The producer was gone. He had lately sold his property to an ophthalmologist from Boston, an important man, too, but not a famous one; lump, not leaven.

In addition to the pure summer people who come and go there is a subgenus of the same family: summer people who come and don't go—year-round summer people. Calabrese and I were year-round summer people. So, come to think of it, was Miss Drumheller, though she was too old to be typical. On average, year-round summer people are, by comparison to the defining summer type, younger, poorer, less important, and less interesting. They are like new furniture: suddenly, there they are, and you have to take account of them. You have to walk around them, but they aren't always bad. They can be useful. They can be quite comfortable. As I have suggested earlier, however, the year-round summer people's irreducible difference must not be lost sight of; that they like the water doesn't make them fish.

I'd keep clear of Carlo, son, if it was me.

Why's that, Mr. Applegate?

Fella like that, comes up here, buys a place out in the woods, gets in a couple of big dogs. Keeps to himself. He's running away from something. Carlo's not the first to do that up here, and he won't be the last.

Running away from what?

That's the question, ain't it, son? You don't know, but either way, it's best to keep clear. What I don't understand about people like Carlo is what makes them think this is a good place to run away to in the first place. I don't understand that at all. Do you suppose we've got some new state office now that advertises down country to people like Carlo who can't take it anymore where they are? Like the board of tourism?

All that's for the skiers, I thought.

Carlo look like a skier to you, son?

No.

No. So what's he up to? What's he want up here?

A cure. A balm for the soul.

How's that, son?

He wants to rest. He wants to be healed. Is there no balm in Gilead?

I wouldn't know, son.

You tell me to read my Bible. You do the same. Is there no balm in Gilead? It's not a question. He wants to be soothed, a soothing oil. A balm for the soul.

Whatever you say, son. Ask me, he owes money. That or he needs a place where his wife won't find him.

June 19, 1920. Rain. Temp. 12M 66.
To town. Teacher and S.B

2

Calabrese didn't want visitors. He had told them at Clifford's, at the post office; he had told me: We were not to direct strangers who might inquire about his place. We did as he asked. But in the event, when company began to arrive in town looking for him, Calabrese found the negative cooperation he had asked for and been given wasn't enough.

"Look, kid," Calabrese said to me some time after the incident of the elegant woman in the limousine. "Look," he said, "We need some kind of system."

"System?"

"Yeah," said Calabrese. "I almost wished we had the phone in up here."

"You do?"

"No," said Calabrese. "But I've got to know if somebody's on the hill looking for me. That thing at Clifford's, that was one thing. What if they come here?"

"What if they do?" I said. "They can't see your house from the road. They'll stop at my place. If I'm here, they'll ask me if I know you. I'll say no. They'll go look someplace else."

"They won't," said Calabrese. "They'll come. I've got to know they're coming."

"The dogs will scare them off."

"The ones I'm thinking of, they won't," said Calabrese.

"Who are they?"

"Nobody," said Calabrese. "People I don't want to see, okay?"

"Okay," I said. "But why not? I would. If that lady from the other day comes back and you don't want to see her, send her right down the road. I'll see her. Tell her to bring an overnight bag and her checkbook and come on down."

"Yeah," said Calabrese. "Ha, ha. You don't know what you're asking for, kid. May you never find out, okay? Look, here's what we might do, though. Do you have a gun?"

He asked you if you had a gun?

He wanted to give me one.

What do you know? Sure, I thought Carlo was a little off from the start, but I didn't think he was that kind of trouble. You don't look for that sort of thing.

I didn't know what to do.

I'll give Carlo one thing, though: He minds his own business. I'll give him that. Not everybody does the same.

No?

No, son, they don't. Take Considine.

The selectman.

That's the one. Considine moved up here from someplace in Connecticut. He retired up here. He could have retired anywhere he wanted, but he came here. You'd think that was because he liked it here, wouldn't you?

Not necessarily.

Well, but he did. He said he did. He's been waiting to move up to a place like this for years, he said, years. When he finally did, he might have just sat back and enjoyed things. He didn't do that. He hadn't been here six months before he started going to the selectmen's meetings. Just to listen, he said.

What's wrong with that?

Nothing, son. But when somebody turns up at a selectmen's meeting and just sits there, doesn't want anything, doesn't complain about anything, it makes the selectmen nervous. It makes them uneasy. They didn't have to have worried, though. Considine started in speaking up soon enough.

What about?

Everything. Considine worked in New York for thirty years. He was in the advertising business. He knew how to advertise the hell out of cigarettes, cars—I don't know—toothpaste. It turned out that meant he also knew everything you can know about how to run a little town up in Vermont. You might not have thought the advertising business would teach you that. Well, it does. Considine knew it all. He figured we needed a lot of work up here. We needed a five-year town plan, a ten-year town plan, a hundred-year town plan, a town economic development committee, a town forester, a town publicist, a town whatchamacallit to the state tourism board.

What?

What do you call that?

Liaison?

That's it, son: liaison. Considine was available. He ran for selectman. He lost. He kept on coming to meetings. He ran again the next year. He lost again. He decided the selectmen were joined up against him. He filed a grievance with the state election commission. The selectmen decided,

The hell with it, it's not worth it. So Errol, he'd been on the board for years, he was about done anyway. Errol got off. Considine ran again. He won. There he is.

So, he'll grow into the office. He'll learn.

He can't learn. How can he learn, son? He knows everything already. He knows everything, and we get the benefit. I tell you, I'll take Carlo any day, guns and all.

I didn't know what to do.

Well, do you have a gun?

No.

Did you take one from Carlo?

No.

Good. That's good, son. I told you Carlo's trouble. I wonder who it is that's looking for him?

As for guns, have them if you want them is what I think. Have them for collecting, for killing tin cans and clay pigeons. Have them for making noise on the Fourth of July. But don't have them because you think they will keep you from trouble. With a gun, unless you're one in a million, in ten million, no trouble it gets you out of is worse than the trouble it gets you into.

HITCHCOCK SORTIES

East of the capital, the dry brown mountains rose up out of the coastal jungle, never more than ten miles from the sea. That whole country was cruelly squeezed between the coast and the cordillera. It was as though the place did without law, government, rational politics, peace, not from any lack of aptitude on the part of the people, but just because there was no room for them.

In the mountains, there were tin mines and silver mines and gold mines and whatever you please. "It's a poor country, but it's a rich country," said Hitchcock. "See what I mean, do you, Mark?"

"No," I said.

"Resources, Mark," said Hitchcock. "There are resources here."

"I see; It's just that they don't do anybody any good," I said.

"Oh, I wouldn't say that," Hitchcock said.

"The resources are rich, but the people aren't rich," I said.

"Some of them are," said Hitchcock.

Hitchcock had contacts in the mining companies. He didn't much go to the mining country; he met with his people in the capital. There was a time, though, not long after I got down there, when he had to go into the mountains, because the parties he was to meet wouldn't come to him.

"Do you know?" said Hitchcock. "I feel a bit peaky about this. I believe I'll go armed."

"You're joking," I said. I didn't know Hitchcock then.

"Not at all," Hitchcock said. "Look here."

He opened a drawer of his desk and brought out a pistol. He laid it on the desk before him and took from the same drawer a box of cartridges. Hitchcock picked up the pistol, pushed the little button behind the trigger, and dropped the magazine onto the desk. He began to load cartridges into it. Hitchcock grinned.

"My uncle brought it back from the war," he said.

"You're taking that with you tonight?" I asked him.

"I am," said Hitchcock.

"Why?" I asked him. "Are you going to shoot somebody?"

"Don't be silly, Mark," said Hitchcock. "I'll merely have it. If need be, I'll show it. Merely showing it will keep anything from happening, don't you see?"

"No," I said.

"The idea is, you show you're prepared to make trouble, and so you avoid trouble," said Hitchcock.

"You do?"

"Yes," said Hitchcock. "Of course, I may have to fire a warning shot."

He fitted the magazine into the butt of the pistol and slapped it with his left hand to drive it to its seat. He grasped the top of the pistol at the rear and drew the action back, let it snap forward. He set the safety.

"I might have to put one across their bows, mightn't I?" said Hitchcock. "Put a decent fear into them? Eh, Mark?"

The Lord keeps the fool, but for how long?

June 21, 1920. Fair Temp. 12M 83. To teachers for wood. Teacher & S.B. gon to Bratt. in cars

Calabrese had come to my place. We stood in the yard.

"Look, kid," said Calabrese. "Here's what we might do. Do you have a gun?"

"No."

"Okay," said Calabrese. He went to his truck, reached in through the driver's window, and lifted out a shotgun. He brought it over and handed it to me. It was heavy, not very long, the kind you operate by working a slide back and forth under the barrel. Quite a weapon: The muzzle looked like the entrance to the Lincoln Tunnel.

"You know how to use one of these?" Calabrese asked me.

"No."

"Nothing to it," Calabrese said. "Pump it, hang on tight, pull the trigger, then pump it again."

"Right," I said.

"Okay, then. This one's yours. That's a two-hundred-dollar gun. It's yours. If people come here wanting me, you use it—"

I put up my hand to stop him.

"Wait," I said. "No chance. I'm not going to shoot somebody just for coming onto my own place. I'm certainly not going to shoot them for coming onto yours."

"Slow down, kid," said Calabrese. "You didn't let me finish. Nobody's going to shoot anybody. If they come here for me, all you do, you send them on their way. Then you get this, you go out back, and you fire two. Two shots. I'll hear you. Fucker makes a lot of noise."

I handed the shotgun back to Calabrese.

"No," I said. "No guns."

Calabrese took the shotgun back.

"I'll do this," I said. "If people come looking for you, I'll send them on their way. Then I'll hit my car horn twice. Two long beeps. You'll hear that as well as a gunshot."

Calabrese looked at me. He shook his head.

"I wish you'd take the gun," he said.

"No guns," I said. "I'm superstitious. Guns are bad luck."

"Well," said Calabrese "I can't tell you you're wrong about that."

July 1, 1920. Rain a.m. Temp. 12M 74. To teachers for wood
July 2, 1920. Fair. Temp. 6 a.m. 58. To teachers for wood.
S.B. Talk. S.B. teacher too

HITCHCOCK REGROUPS

Two days after he had left for the mountains, Hitchcock was found lying in the road on the edge of one of the capital's abject suburbs, a place where houses made of cardboard, scrap plywood, and plastic sheeting stood amid their own filth and garbage, and the streets ran with urine, the blood of chickens, and orange water from the factories. Hitchcock had been left for dead, evidently, not without reason. He was concussed, his left leg and arm were broken, he had two cracked ribs and a collapsed lung, and his spleen was injured. He'd been naked when he was found, and the barrel of his uncle's war souvenir pistol had been forced into his rectum. The pistol had not been fired.

I went to the clinic. Hitchcock lay in a bed in a dirty hallway. He looked like a sackful of overripe strawberries, and he was in some pain, but on the whole, he was pretty bright. You overestimated Hitchcock; then you underestimated him. You admired his manners, his grace, his utter confidence, but you soon dismissed him as a mere clubman, a butterfly, an aristocratic nitwit, because that's what he wanted you to do. In fact, Hitchcock came of the old Puritan stock from the Massachusetts Bay and those people are tougher than they may look. They will not stay down. Hitchcock was undiscouraged.

"It might have been worse, Mark," said Hitchcock. "They might have pulled the trigger, for example."

"That would have been worse," I agreed.

"Or they might have taken Uncle Ted's Luger," Hitchcock went on. "I wouldn't have lost it for anything."

"Where is it now?" I asked him.

Painfully, with his unbroken arm, Hitchcock shifted in the bed, reached under the sheet that covered his legs, and brought up the pistol. He flourished it.

"Put it away, put it away," I said.

Hitchcock put the pistol back under his bedcovers.

"What happened?" I asked him.

"I'm not sure, really," Hitchcock said. "I was to have met one fellow and I met six. From the start, it was clear the thing would not go off well. I drew my gun and pointed it at them. They seemed not to care. I thought, Shall I put one across their bows now? Is this the moment? Presumably, it was, but it seems I didn't shoot. I don't remember much else."

Hitchcock spent ten days in the hospital. When they let him go, they gave him a cane to help him walk until his leg was fully mended. Hitchcock liked the cane. He kept on using it after he had recovered. So the matter was not a total loss for Hitchcock. Discovering the right accessory is worth some pain.

3

The best of our visitors are in a way the least: transients, people passing through. Tourists. Tourists are the least of visitors in that they are the most ephemeral; they come and go so quickly and in such numbers that they're hardly here as individuals at all. They are the best of our visitors in that they afford us the richest fund of story, experience, literature.

The literature of the tourist is essentially a comic literature, based on the view of the tourist as a kind of child: willful, lucky, gifted in a way—but fundamentally inferior because he doesn't know how to live. Setting out for Bible Hill from wherever his home is, the tourist leaves behind his manners, his good nature, but especially his wits. Hence the cars dangerously stopped in the middle of the highway through October as the driver admires the colors of the autumn leaves. Hence the busload of tourists from, as I recall it, Rahway, New Jersey, that got wedged in the Joppa bridge simply because it's a covered bridge and therefore formed an essential part of the tour. The driver neglected to allow for the low clearance.

And hence the thousand jokes about travelers who are lost and countrymen who are not, my favorite of which is this:

"Say, friend, can you tell me how to get to Bible Hill?"

Long pause . . .

"If I were going to Bible Hill, I wouldn't start from here."

The comic literature of the tourist has another side, however. For when any one group consistently, historically, makes so much fun of another group, it's because they're afraid of them. We fear the tourists. Why? Do we fear them because we see they're richer than we? Because we suspect they're smarter than we? Because they seem to be having more fun, a better time, a better life than ours? It would be tough to demonstrate that any of those propositions was ever true except the first, and that seldom. But so what? Where these visitors are concerned, we don't care about what's true. We know how we feel.

July 4, 1920. Fair. Temp 12M 81.
Parade. Saw S.B. with teacher. No cousin!

Tourists get no break. Whoever they are, they always lose. They never finish in the money.

The bank branch in the village of Ambrose was held up once by two men and a woman from Pennsylvania—not tourists, exactly, but like tourists in that they had no faces, they were in a hurry, and they parked funny.

I discovered that everything of real importance in the annals of the town had happened a few years before I arrived. The robbery of the Vermont Agricultural Bank's office in Ambrose was an instance. It occurred in 1965, on a Monday in July. The whole business took between five and ten minutes. The three visitors got to the bank about half past eight in the morning. They were driving a Chevrolet station wagon a couple of years old. They parked it in front of the bank slantwise, with the rear up on the sidewalk and the front end in the road. It was the way they left their car that attracted the attention of Mr. Applegate, whose law office was across the street from the bank.

I thought it must be some tourist who couldn't be bothered to get his rig out of the way, that or an old fellow that didn't know how to drive. When I was a kid, you know, there still weren't too many cars in town. The old people parked them that way, just anyhow, like they still hoped the car would turn into a horse and buggy. So I took notice of the car. I guess it made it easier for those people to drive off from the bank, parking like that.

I don't see why.

I don't either, really, son. Maybe they just screwed up. Nobody ever said these people were the first team for bank robbers, you know. Any rate, by the time I took notice of them they were already in the bank. Or the two of them were, the girl and the man. The other man stayed with the car. I could see him at the wheel. Then I saw the other two come out of the bank, walk down the steps, and go to the car. They didn't look like they were in a hurry. I didn't notice that they were carrying bags or cases or anything that might have had money in them, but I guess they must have been. They came down the steps, got in their car, the girl in back, drove off, not fast, going toward Brattleboro.

You didn't think anything of it?

Nothing. There was nothing to think of it, really, except for the parking job. Well, but then Bob Gorsuch, the manager, came out the door, and the two women who worked there with him, Lucy Browning and the other, a loaner filling in from the main office in Brattleboro. They came out, all three, and stood together on the top step, looking after the car.

You thought that was odd.

I did. And then a sheriff's car came down from the other way, fast, and then the state police. So I left my office and went on over.

What did they get?

The bank wouldn't say, but Lucy thought not more than three thousand—in bills. They said they had a gun, but nobody saw it. They took what the cashiers had; that was it. The cashiers, the manager, are trained: Give it to them. Everybody was real calm, except for after. The cashier filling in from Brattleboro lost her breakfast and they sent her home at noon. She had a delayed reaction, seems like.

So did they catch them?

Sure. Gorsuch read their plate. They were well off by the time he got out to the street, but Bob's a wing shot; he's got good eyes. He couldn't read what state it was, but he could read the numbers. New Hampshire state police got them the same morning. They'd checked into a motel in Peterborough, to count up the money, I guess. They hadn't even switched cars. Like I said, they weren't the first team.

July 7, 1920. Fair. Warm. Temp. 6 a.m. 66.
To town. S.B.

Another visitor for Calabrese. A helicopter passed low over my place. For a moment, I didn't know what it was: a great thumping and flailing overhead, a great chastisement of the air. What in the world kind of bad weather was this, now, that nobody had told me about?

I ran outside. I saw the helicopter. It circled, beating against the air, returned, passed over, hovered, and descended to the west. It dropped down below the treetops. It must have been looking for Sheep Desert, the biggest opening on this side of Bible Hill. It was going to land there. Why? I knew why. It hadn't come to see me. Going through the woods, I was at Sheep Desert in ten minutes.

The helicopter was the kind with a glass fishbowl for a front end. It crouched like an iron grasshopper amid the juniper islands of Sheep Desert. The pilot sat at the controls. He hadn't shut down the engine entirely; the machine's rotor continued to revolve in a slow sweep. Two men had left the helicopter and were standing off from it, looking at what I took to be a map, which they held between them. I went to them.

One of the men was my size. He wore no hat, a blue windbreaker, gray flannel trousers, and polished low shoes, city shoes. He had blond or light brown hair, a crew cut, and wore horn-rimmed glasses. He saw me first, spoke to the other man, pointed my way. The other was his boss. He was a black man, bigger than the other, bigger than I, six and a half feet tall, and broad through the shoulders and chest. He wore the full uniform of an army officer, pressed and brushed. On the left front of his jacket, a row of campaign ribbons, and above them, a black-and-white name bar that said DONOVAN.

The smaller man took a step to the officer's front so as to meet me as I came up to them.

"Can I help you, sir?" he asked me.

"I was going to ask you that," I said. "What do you have, engine trouble?"

"No trouble," the man said. "Do you live around here, sir?"

"Not far," I said.

"Do you know Carlo Calabrese?"

"Who?"

"Calabrese," the man said. He looked at his map. "This is Bible Hill, right?" he asked. I saw he wore a radio receiver in his left ear like a hearing aid. Its wire went down into his shirt collar.

"This is Bible Hill," I said.

The officer came up beside the other man, who had been about to reply but fell silent. The officer smiled at me. He had a good face, open and kindly, though perhaps not indefinitely so. He looked around at the grassy pasture, its rock ledges and seams, its juniper carpets, the woods surrounding it, the neighboring hills, the hills farther off. Sheep Desert is a high spot.

"Nice country you've got up here," the officer said.

I never knew what to reply to that remark. After all, I don't have the country. The country isn't mine. "Thank you," I said.

"Can you tell us how to get to Calabrese's place?" the officer asked.

My cue, at last.

"If I were going to Calabrese's," I said. "I wouldn't start from here."

The officer nodded. "What's your name, son?" he asked me. I didn't know how much I liked his calling me "son." He wasn't Applegate.

"Mark Noon," I told him.

"Noon?" the officer said. "That's a funny name. What is that, Dutch?"

"Mohawk," I said. "We're Mohawks."

"Me, too," said the officer.

"Is that right?"

"You can call me Major Jefferson," the officer said.

"Your tag says Donovan," I said.

The major looked down at his chest, made as if to cock his head to one side to read his name tag.

"So it does, son," he said. "Where's Calabrese?"

Just then, the smaller man pressed his forefinger to the receiver in his ear. He listened. He spoke to the major.

"They're in place," he said.

"All right," said the major. "Nice talking to you, son," he said to me. "Tell Carlo Major Jefferson was here. Tell him I'm real sorry I missed him. Tell him I'll be sure to stop by again when I'm in the neighborhood. Tell him he can count on it."

I didn't answer him. The two men turned and went to the helicopter. The major climbed into the front and took the seat beside the pilot. The smaller man took a jump seat behind. The rotors picked up speed. I stepped back. The helicopter rose right up out of Sheep Desert, thrashing, pressing the air down harder and harder on the juniper mats, spreading them apart to their roots. It rose, pivoted, and flew off over the trees toward the east.

Later, I told Calabrese about the helicopter, the major's helper, the major, his color, his size, the name he wore, the name he gave, how I knew he was lying to me, how he knew I was lying to him, how he didn't care, what he said.

"So, you know him?" I asked Calabrese.

"Oh, yeah," said Calabrese. "Fucker's no Mohawk."

Why do we mistrust the tourists? They enrich us; they entertain us. What are we afraid of, then? Well, we're afraid because we suspect they are on the right side of history and we are on the wrong side; afraid that Bible Hill is moving toward the tourists and away from us. Bible Hill will belong to them, and never again to us. The tourists are the mammals of our epoch: weak, contemptible, but fated to prevail over ourselves, the great lizards, majestic, dominant, and presently to be extinct—or so we suspect. Is it so?

July 9, 1920. Rain. Temp. 12M 61. S.B.

July 10, 1920. Fair. Temp. 12M 73. S.B

You plan on staying up here for a while, son?

A long while.

Like it, then, I guess?

I do.

Why?

What?

Why? Why do you like it? What do you like about it?

I don't know. I like the country, the woods. You know. The hills. What everybody likes.

Uh-huh. What else?

Your daughter.

I can see that. What else?

You. I like you.

Oh. Well.

13. Housekeeping

Every man looks at his woodpile with
a kind of affection.
—Henry David Thoreau, *Walden*

1

Littlejohn's place, as I found it on Bible Hill, was a sawed-off Cape—that is, a plain story-and-a-half house, about four square, with a front door, seldom used, at one side, two windows left of it, business door in the opposite gable end. The balance of the house—two more windows right of the front door, lighting a sitting room or parlor—wasn't there, hence, a half or *sawed-off* Cape. Really, the place was tiny, a good size for one, tight for two—unless they stacked vertically.

Stacking vertically was not part of Amanda's plan for our sharing quarters. She was to have her own room. Upstairs at Littlejohn's, under the pitch of the roof, were two tiny bedchambers, one for Amanda, one for me.

"I don't know, Noon," Amanda said the day she moved her things from her father's cabin on Back Diamond. "You don't walk in your sleep a lot, do you?"

"Never," I said. "You?"

"No," said Amanda.

"Ah," I said. "Well, if you decide to try it, you know where to go."

I wanted to believe Amanda came to me out of the beginnings of love, or affection, or anyway curiosity; and certainly she wouldn't have come without some little push of the heart. Mainly, though, I admit, she came to me for heat. Her father's place, where she had been living since she arrived from the west in the spring, was a hunting camp. You couldn't do the real winter there, not the whole winter. Littlejohn's house was not greatly better, perhaps. It was far from snug. It was drafty and dilapidated. But Littlejohn's house was a house.

Amanda wouldn't go to her father's house in the village for the winter. I didn't know why not. I didn't ask. I wanted her on Bible Hill, with me. If she came less from her heart's, her body's inclining to mine and more because of my stove, my woodpile, my storm windows, my insulation—well, that would do for now.

"I don't know, Noon," said Amanda, looking the place over, "you've got an awfully high hermit factor up here."

"Not anymore," I said.

"The deal here, with us?" said Amanda. "Together, here, but not? The deal is a little weird, you know?"

"So what?" I said.

So Amanda and I began on Bible Hill that fall like Hansel and Gretel: cautious, wondering, chaste. The deal was a little weird; but, for my part, if a weird deal was the terms on which I could have Amanda, I'd take it and hope for better, closer days. We Noons know how to wait.

February 2, 1927. Fair. Temp. 6 a.m. 5. Cut wood around high lot

February 3, 1927. Cloud. Temp. 12M 17. a.m. cut wood big beech. Snow p.m.

"I don't know, Noon," Amanda said. "The place needs work."

"You should have seen it when I came," I told her. "Windows were out; the walls were full of holes; the roof was bad, the chimney."

"Who fixed them?" Amanda asked.

"I did."

"You're handy?" said Amanda. "I wouldn't have thought."

Not handy, but formerly handy, was what I was. At the time Amanda moved in, I had about retired from being handy. For two or three years, I had been a busy workman, a tearer-out of the old and the rotten, a renovator. At Littlejohn's, when the house came to me, you had to be. Littlejohn's was the king, emperor, and god of all fixer-uppers. You fixed it up or you died. The place was a wreck. In particular, as I have written, the wind blew through the walls and sailed around the house with the freedom of a swallow flying about a ruined abbey. In my first fall on Bible Hill, I found one day a partridge sitting on the kitchen table. It might have come down the chimney, but I believed it came right through the wall. Therefore, I began with insulation.

My early years on Bible Hill were around the peak of the Age of Insulation. Doctrine at that time, the mid-1970s, was that if you had enough insulation of the right kind, you didn't need heat. Bears and bobcats and foxes and the rest, after all, don't heat their dens; they rely on insulation. It began to seem as if heating your house was a sin, as if you neglected insulation at the peril not only of your comfort but of your immortal soul.

In the Age of Insulation, Littlejohn's house was hopelessly reprobate. The place was made of timbers a foot thick, pegged together as post and beam. The outer walls were planks rough from the saw, covered with clapboards; the inner, split lath, wet-plastered. The wall cavity resulting was deeper by two or three times than the wall cavities of a modern house; the north wind whined and moaned in Littlejohn's walls as it might in the rigging of a clipper ship. The insulator's task was to fill the walls with the correct stuff.

What was the correct stuff? A vexed question. In my time, there were many schools of insulation. The best, most up-to-date scholars, however, favored the new synthetic foam products. Some of these, we learned, had been developed for use in insulating satellites and vehicles that were fired off into space. As insulation, those materials must assuredly work, for it's cold in space. Insulating foam was easy to install, too; it was injected into walls in a kind of shaving-cream state, then promptly hardened, and there you were.

For all its effect and convenience, however, foam insulation failed to gain in this vicinity, owing to a particular disadvantage it presented, a disadvantage brought out for us by the painful case of a couple named Armstrong, who around that same time built a house near the Four Corners. Determined that their place should be as economical in its need for heat as science could make it, and advised by a visionary young architect from Cambridge, Massachusetts, the Armstrongs made the perfectly logical decision to skip over the conventional steps in construction and build the whole house out of insulating foam.

The result looked like the house of elves or gnomes, but it was perfectly practicable and comfortable, even luxurious: three rooms upstairs and four down, modern kitchen, baths, a small garage. The walls were three feet thick and entirely of foam, poured and shaped with simple forms: The amazing stuff needed no reinforcement. The house went up in two days. The whole place was easily heated through the winter by a single wood-burning stove and half a cord of fuel.

The Armstrongs were delighted with their new house. They were more than delighted; they were beatified. In the religion of 1974, they were sitting on the Ark of the Covenant. They were drinking their camomile tea out of the Holy Grail.

It was not to last, their idyll of insulation. The Armstrongs had a boy, Sean, say twelve at the time, a good boy, but mouthy when crossed. One evening in the deep winter, asked to wash the dinner dishes, then asked again, Sean told his mother to go fuck herself and was ordered to his room. An hour later, the Armstrongs realized that they were feeling what had never been felt in that house before: a draft. They went to their son's room, to find him gone and a gaping hole in the outside wall, a tunnel in the foam that you could have pushed a wheelbarrow through. Sean they found at the neighbors', watching TV with the neighbor's boy. He had dug his way to freedom with a teaspoon.

Now it was discovered that the foam of which the Armstrongs' house was made could not by any means be fixed: No patch, no fill, no effective repair was possible. There was nothing for it; the Armstrongs had to move out. They left town. They finally took the place as a total loss. You can see their house today, half a mile from the Four Corners store, in the woods to the right as you go north. Visit anytime you like; there's no hurry, for the house's material does not degrade or decay. It lasts forever. The foam house today is as good as new—except for the hole.

The Armstrong debacle produced a level of skepticism among us with regard to foam insulation. The town of Ambrose would hold on to its heat by other means. Fortunately, other means were ready to hand.

Feathers, they had, one place I heard about.

In the walls? You're joking.

No. Alcott's place in Dead River, right past the bridge there. Alcott was adding on a room, something like that, so they had to tear out a wall. When they got started, they found the wall was full of feathers. Course, they all busted out when the walls got opened. Feathers all over to hell and gone, like a pillow fight in a female academy. Quite a job to get it cleaned up.

Why would they insulate with feathers?

Well, they used what they had, it seems like. Somebody recalled how years back whoever had that place—oh, long ago—raised geese for market. He had a whole flock. Feathers, you see.

I guess so. Fiberglass for me.

That's that pink stuff like wool? I wouldn't have that in any house of mine.

Why not?

That's bad stuff; you can tell by looking at it. Kills you to breathe it, too.

It's shut up in the walls; you don't breathe it.

Whatever you say, son. It's your place. Ask me, though, you're going about this thing the wrong way. What you ought to do, go on down to Brattleboro, get yourself an oil burner in up there, biggest one you can find. Get yourself a blower, bunch of ducts, the whole show. Crank that thing right up to the top notch, and leave it there. Be comfortable.

At whatever oil costs a gallon now? No chance.

I thought you were rich.

Not that rich. Besides, no oil truck will come up that road.

Find one that's got a long hose, then.

Two miles long?

You got an answer for everything, don't you, son? I didn't say it'd be easy. You got to be a little resourceful here.

. . .

Amanda knew Littlejohn's house. She had been there as a girl.

"Sure," said Amanda. "My dad was big pals with old Claude. He used to bring us up here to see him. It was supposed to be fun. Some fun, you know, Noon? Claude and Dad would sit on the porch step, drinking beer, and Win and I would sit in the yard, looking at them. I'm talking about the whole afternoon. Great, huh? One time, Dad drove us into the ditch on the way home. He and Claude must have been hammered."

"I'd heard Littlejohn liked a drop," I said.

"They both did," said Amanda. "We'd come up to Claude's every week or so. It wasn't just to drink, though. I don't mean that. Dad wanted to see how Claude was getting along. He was pretty broken-down by then."

"What was he like?"

"I was afraid of him," said Amanda. "He was old and rough and dirty, had a bad leg; he limped around. He smelled. He dipped snuff, and so he was spitting brown juice all the time. He had a couple of fingers missing from one hand, I remember: That was pretty scary all by itself. He cussed and swore. Sometimes we'd help him get his wood in. Once, I remember, Claude chucked a stick at Win when he didn't move fast enough for him. Claude wasn't exactly what you'd call warm with little kids."

"What did your father do?" I asked Amanda.

"He didn't see it," she said.

"Was Littlejohn mean to you, too?"

"Not really," said Amanda. "He acted like I wasn't there at all—a girl, you know."

2

March 15, 1927. Fair. Cold. Temp. 12M 11. With Dan to high lot. Drew wood
March 17, 1927. Fair. Temp. 12M 29. Drew wood
March 30, 1927. Cloud. Temp. 12M 40. Drew wood. Mud. Robbin

So I set to ripping out Littlejohn's lath and plaster walls and ceilings to expose the space within and prepare it for fiberglass. This was work of destruction, and it went quickly enough, especially as Littlejohn's walls were in tough shape to begin with. In the front room, there was a place where the lath seemed to be peeling away from the studs at the top of the wall, from time to time letting drop slabs and lumps of plaster like icebergs. In a corner of the kitchen, the wall was in place, but it appeared someone had gone to work on it with a sledgehammer: A dark hole the size of a dinner plate gaped through lath and plaster, both.

I tore out the crumbling walls, cleared the dirt, spiderwebs, and mouse nests from between the studs behind them, hung fiberglass blankets in the space, fixed plastic sheets in front of the fiberglass, and got ready to restore the walls. It was at this point that I encountered the big panels of that product called variously gypsum board, wallboard, plasterboard, drywall, Sheetrock. I quickly came to hate and fear the stuff and to understand that it goes by so many names because it's both powerful and evil.

Sheetrock, I found, was awkward in a way that was almost wonderful: The panels were exactly of a weight and size that could not quite be managed by someone working alone. I worked alone. I improvised step-on levers to raise the Sheetrock to the correct height so I could nail it in place on the wall. I invented Sheetrock clamps and clips. I rigged a gin pole to hold up one end of a Sheetrock panel to the ceiling while I worked on the other end from a stepladder.

With all these aids, I made slow and painful progress. Part of the difficulty came from the structure I had to work with. Littlejohn's house was a place of many angles, but not one of them was a right angle. The floors sloped east, the plates sloped west, and the doorways were cocked up or down like a villain's eyebrow. As a result, nothing fit, nothing. The Sheetrock panel that I had aligned neatly to the floor at one corner missed the floor by two inches at the other. Sheetrock had to be trimmed, shimmed, and otherwise pieced out. Sheetrock asked for either an artist or a butcher. I was neither. I sweated, I itched, I wept, I raged. Once I hauled off and tried to drive my fist right through a Sheetrock panel. I failed, and hurt my hand quite badly. It's strong stuff, altogether, Sheetrock.

I found the solution to my struggle with Sheetrock after the struggle had mostly ended. The solution was a helper, the right helper. After Amanda moved in, she and I worked together to put Sheetrock on the walls and ceiling of her room upstairs. Instead of a lifeless pole holding up the other end of a ceiling panel, I had Amanda there, a warm, living thing. I could talk to her, look at her. When Amanda stretched her arms high above her head to support the Sheetrock, the T-shirt she wore lifted up over her belly, revealing her navel in its soft declivity. I regarded it. The Sheetrock flew up and into place as easily as a flock of doves that seeks its roost. Here, I saw, was Sheetrocking as it was meant to be.

I brought with me to Bible Hill one pair of shoes, six shirts, two sweaters, four pairs of pants, underwear. I brought a sleeping bag, a steel teakettle, a cup, a fork, a spoon, a camp cooking outfit of nesting pots, pans, and plates that might have belonged to the Boy Scout I never cared to be. I brought a Swiss army knife, a can opener for beer, a flashlight, twenty feet of clothesline, a compass. I brought three cardboard boxes full of books.

Look at all this stuff, son. Anybody would think you're going to camp out. You got a house up there, you know.

Call it that.

What would you call it? Look at all these books. Are you going to read all these?

I have read them.

Why carry them, then?

So I can read them again.

Uh-huh. Look at this one. This ain't even English. French, ain't it? You know French, son?

A little. You?

Ha. No, son. No French. Not me.

It pleased Mr. Applegate to pretend to be no reader, as though the texts on civil and criminal procedure, on probate and tort law, as though the six or seven feet of *Vermont Statutes Annotated* in his office, the volumes of Parkman's *France and England,* Prescott's *Conquests,* de Tocqueville's *Democracy,* Beveridge's *Marshall,* Malone's *Jefferson*—as though these somehow didn't count. In the keeping of his own intellectual store, clearly, Mr. Applegate meant to have more on the shelves than he had in the window. To me, that made him something new. Mr. Applegate was the first honest man I ever met who wanted you to believe he was dumber than he was, not smarter.

What's the rope for?

I don't know. I thought I might need it.

Oh. I wondered if maybe you were planning on hanging yourself when it got to be winter.

Hanging myself?

Well, son, if you don't get cracking up there—get the roof fixed, get the busted windows fixed, get some wood in—hanging might be the best thing for you when winter comes. That or go to Florida like everybody else.

The roof's not too bad.

The windows, then? The wood?

It's July. There are two busted windows—no, three. I'm working on them.

The wood?

Wood won't be a problem. There's plenty of wood around there.

There is? Where, exactly, son?

What do you mean, where? They're woods all around the house. You've seen it.

That's trees. Trees ain't wood. Who's going to chop it? Who's going to split it? Who's going to truck it? Takes time.

All right, but come to that, I can buy wood.

You won't buy oil, but you'll buy wood.

Wood's cheap.

You're inconsistent, son. Don't you see? You're both ways and no way. You say it's July? Sure, it's July. In three months, it's October. Don't lose track of that rope.

"Win was older than you?"

"Five years," said Amanda. "He'd have been fourteen, fifteen then. He was afraid of Claude, too, but he wouldn't let him see it. Win would give it right back to him. Once we were there with Dad and they were sitting out front having beers and Win and I were in the yard. We were throwing a ball back and forth. Well, Win threw one wild, and Claude barked at him. 'You're a goddamned poor shot, ain't you?' And Win came right back. 'Maybe, but I ain't a goddamned drunk.' How Claude laughed at that.

"Then one day when we drove up there, it looked different. It looked like there was nobody around: no smoke coming out of the chimney, no lights. So Dad told Win and me to wait in the car, and he went in. Then he came back out and we drove home to phone. He'd found Claude on the kitchen floor. He'd had some kind of attack. That was my last trip up here."

"Until now," I said.

June 3, 1927. Rain a.m. Temp. 12M 65.P.m. sawed wood. Saw brok

June 9, 1927. Fair. Temp. 12M 77. Sawed wood

3

Littlejohn's house appeared on the F. W. Beers map of the town of Ambrose, so it had existed at least since that map was published in 1869. If, at any time in the intervening 105 years or so, the place had supported a square inch of paint, there was no sign of it today. The clapboard walls were weathered to a kind of blue-gray-brown, the color of a winter deer.

It seemed wrong to me, an unpainted house, I don't know why. My first year on Bible Hill, I was insulating, Sheetrocking, glazing. I had no time for paint. But I was more and more aware of the house as needing paint, and I decided paint was to be my first job after the weather turned the next year.

Slow down, son. You don't want to jump into this thing.

Why not? The place looks like hell. It hasn't had paint in a hundred years, more.

That's what I mean. If Claude and them didn't paint, maybe they had a reason.

What in the world are you talking about?

Maybe the place oughtn't to be painted. Maybe there's some reason we don't know.

That's stark nonsense. What reason could there possibly be?

And then another thing: That place has sat up there for a hundred years with no paint—you said it yourself.

Yes?

You said it yourself, a hundred years, more. So why's paint going to make it better all of a sudden?

Look, I can't talk to you. We've got a philosophical gap here. The thing is, I own the house. It's mine.

Sure is, son.

And I want to paint it. So I'm going to paint it. I don't like the way it looks. So I am going to paint it.

The way it looks? Why didn't you say that was what's on your mind?

What? What are you saying? What else would be? It's paint. It's got to do with looks, nothing else.

Well, as far as looks . . . Here's what you do, son. Get yourself a bucket of white paint. Gallon'll be plenty. Paint the trim. Not the walls, just the trim, you see? That way, the place will look like it's all new painted, even though it ain't. You'll see. You'll like it. Go ahead.

To oblige Mr. Applegate, I tried it. I found he was right: White trim at the windows and doors, white corner boards, white mud boards, they picked the place up beautifully. Now, instead of looking like a winter deer, it looked like a summer deer. That was just right. A complete paint job was unnecessary—would, in fact, have been wrong.

Mr. Applegate was my Socrates, my Zen master, my priest: the one I could learn from, if I would. His way was always to do the least work, and yet he was by no means a lazy man or a careless man. He was for the least work, the best job. He meant that work should fit, that things in general should fit. It's a Greek idea, surely. Where Mr. Applegate can have picked it up, I have no idea.

"You know what I like about you, Noon?" Amanda asked me once, not long after she'd moved in.

"What?"

"You're not in a hurry."

"Who says I'm not?" I asked her.

"Well," said Amanda. "You don't act like you are."

"That's not not being in a hurry," I said. "That's good manners."

"There you go, Noon," said Amanda. "That's what I mean. You're a gentleman. You're a college boy. You're educated. Now, you take me: I never had the opportunity."

"Come on," I said. "Don't give me that. What are you, dumb? Poor? If you'd wanted to, you could have gone to college perfectly well. You still could."

"But why, though, Noon, you know?" Amanda said. "You went. You went for the whole shot, right? What, four years?"

"Closer to eight, all told," I said.

"Well, there you go," said Amanda. "You went eight years. Eight years. And look where you are. You're pumping gas. You're carrying bricks. Eight years. You're chopping wood, Noon."

September 2, 1927. Fair. Cool. Temp. 12M 66. Split & stak
September 10, 1927. Fair. Temp. 12M 56. Split & stak. Geese

4

At last, I retired from fixing up. I had apprenticed myself to myself as a carpenter, so I was pupil and master, both. On the whole, it hadn't gone well, and when my apprenticeship ended, I skipped right over journeyman and hung up my tools.

I went into the wood business. To get through the winter at Littlejohn's, Mr. Applegate told me, I would need between five and six cords of firewood, all to feed the big black iron range in the kitchen, which at the beginning provided the only heat the house had. A cord of wood is a rectangular pile the size and shape of a CEO's desk. In contemplation, five or six of those piles don't seem to be as much as they turn out to be in action—just as the distance between Boston and, say, Portland, Maine, doesn't seem to be very great, until you start to make the journey on your hands and knees.

My first year on Bible Hill, then, I began by undershooting badly in the wood department. Throughout that fall, I was working regularly for Milo Tavistock, maybe three or four days a week. I planned to fit my wood chopping in here and there between working for Milo and spells of fixing up. I didn't see a problem in doing that. I had an old ax I'd found at Littlejohn's. I had a new saw, a businesslike orange thing about a yard long, with a keen blade hung on a steel bow. I had some five acres of woods that seemed to hold plenty of dead and down trees and branches. I even had the promise of Mr. Applegate's pickup truck when I needed it. Where was the difficulty?

I busted the head off the ax my first afternoon in the wood business, and I learned that putting up wood in quantity with a one-man handsaw is a job for pyramid builders. At the end of a few days, my woodpile was not the size of the CEO's desk. It was not the size of the CEO's Jack Russell terrier's desk. I looked upon it with no kind of affection. As the days became shorter, I began, indeed, to look upon it with a kind of apprehension.

I'm not going to make it for wood.

No, you ain't.

I need some help.

You do. You also need to get some equipment going for you up here.

Mr. Applegate knew a man named Kirby Rackstraw, a logger. For fifty bucks, Kirby drove up Bible Hill with a crane truck stacked ten feet high with cordwood in the log. This, he unloaded in my front yard, a little hill of logs.

It will take me awhile to cut that much wood to size with my saw.

Take you the rest of your life, son. Hang that little saw up on the wall with the pictures and the books—the books in French.

What about the log pile?

Forget it's there. It won't run off. We'll take care of it. All we need's a nice weekend.

The hill of logs sat in my yard for four weeks, then for six weeks. Then, on a warm Indian summer Sunday at the end of September, Mr. Applegate turned up at my house with Arthur Brackett and Potvin, the barman from the Tumbleweed. They brought with them three chain saws and a case of Ballantine's Ale. By dusk, when we started on the Bally's, we were all four half-deaf from the saws and much wearied generally, but otherwise uninjured. The hill of logs was a lesser hill of round chunks, and we walked about the yard as on an ocean beach, treading soft hummocks and dunes of yellow sawdust.

Well, I don't know how to thank you.

Say what?

I said, thank you, for all this.

Thank us when you've done splitting it and stacking it up, son. We did the fun part.

It was fun, wasn't it?

Sure. Any work's fun as long as it ain't yours.

"So when I found you stuck in the road last spring, you'd been driving around up here to see Littlejohn's place again, to remember those times with your brother, was that it?" I asked Amanda.

"No, Noon," said Amanda. "I don't have to do anything to remember that; it comes all by itself."

"What were you doing, then?"

"I was looking for you, Noon," said Amanda. "My dad told me there was some crazy flatlander living up here at Claude's old place, living out in the woods like some kind of—I don't even know—porcupine. I thought I'd better come right up and see for myself. So I did. I came looking for you."

"You did?" I asked her.

"Found you, too, didn't I?" said Amanda.

October 10, 1927. Frost. Temp. 6 a.m. 23.
Done wood. 7 cord inn!!!

Work's fun as long as it isn't yours. Firewood wasn't my work at first, in a way it never has been; but an impartial observer of my life might find that tough to prove. For wood does look like being a permanent feature of my going out and coming in on Bible Hill. Bible Hill has seen me unmated, mated, reunmated; it has seen me drunk, sober, both, and neither; employed and unemployed; Democrat, Republican, in between, and none of the above; cat owner, dog owner, no beast's owner; it has seen me up and down, contented and pissed off—but it has never seen me entirely out of the firewood business. Each year around midsummer, I begin to give over some part of my life to the need of getting in my five or six cords for the winter to come. I have worked it about every way you can. I have bought wood as logs, the way we did the first year. I have bought wood cut into sections for me to split and stack. I have bought no wood, but, rather, I have cut up and split blowdowns or the knockdowns and treetops left behind by loggers. I have even gone into the woods myself, there to kill and butcher my own trees.

There have been stretches, including the period of the composition of these reminiscences, when getting in the wood has been about the only honest work I have done from year's end to year's end. It's good hard work, too, always, make no mistake, and I'm a lazy man, always. But I liked getting wood better than ever I liked fixing up. In firewood, I found at last my competent, physical male soul's true home. It seemed I was not the intellectual equal of a piece of Sheetrock, or a sagging floor, or a crumbling wall; these and other parts of the business of fixing up proved to have depths I couldn't sound. But I was and am smarter than all but a very few blocks of maple, oak, or beech. We Noons do what we do.

14. Water

The town is a web of water. It is caught in a net of moving water. The Dead River runs diagonally through the township, the state's seventh-biggest little stream, here a matter of seventy-five feet across. It breaks into rapids as it passes over granite shelves above the village of Ambrose; elsewhere, its bed is made up of round stones and boulders. It's a changeable stream, the Dead. In August, it can barely find its way from one rock to the next along its course—hence its name. In April, it boils along from bank to bank in a lead-colored flood that every couple of years drowns a canoeist or rafter who comes to the river for an afternoon's fun on the water and gets more fun than he needed.

The Dead River has two tributaries in the township: the Quick Branch and Pied Brook. The Quick Branch is a short, lively brook that drains a string of beaver ponds on the saddle between Bible Hill and Round Mountain and flows easterly to enter the Dead River in the middle of Ambrose village. Pied Brook is longer, four or five miles long. It rises across the town line to the southeast, in a spring on top of Diamond Mountain, and runs west down through the woods to join the Dead River a half mile above the village. Its name comes, perhaps, from the pebbles, dappled red and brown, that fill its bed near the village, perhaps from a man who farmed its upper reaches a hundred and more years ago—a man named Pye.

The town's three streams—Dead, Quick, and Pied—are trout streams. Brook trout, brown trout, rainbow trout are pulled from their waters, mainly by peasants dropping earthworms, but also, regularly, by gentry waving thousand-dollar rods to float tiny feather flies that may very well look like insects, to a fish. Both ends of the long social ladder that is trout fishing do pretty well in our waters, I'm told. I don't know it from my own experience, though. I have little interest in chasing any fish I can see, any shallow-water fish that is barely wet. I prefer to send my hook deep down into an element where I can't follow it except in imagination, thence to pull up fish that have seen strange sights. That makes me a still-water fisherman, a lake and pond fisherman, and of lakes and ponds (except for beaver ponds), the town of Ambrose has none. So I save a good deal of time for other things.

By volume, much the most part of the water in the township runs not in its rivers and river branches but in rills, creeks, and minor brooks too small to have names. In the town as a whole, there must be two or three hundred such. On Bible Hill alone, there are twenty or thirty, I'll bet. Littlejohn's place has two brooks, one small, the other tiny. Calabrese's land, adjoining, has two more that I know about. That's four brooks in an area a half a mile square.

The unknown, unnamed brooks are dark and fast, a couple of feet across at most. They run through the woods. They are streets for mink, otter, and raccoons, fountains for the deer. They belong to the frogs and salamanders and the insects that make their way over the surface tension of the black water. There are trout in the tiny brooks, too, I guess, but there can't be many of them, and they would be tough to catch: The brooks are mostly a hell of a tangle. They run under trees fallen across them, under low branches and brush. You'd be fishing in a brier patch.

The nameless brooks come and go. They dry up in August and September, sometimes in June. They quite disappear. You can't see them; you can't hear them, not as a trickle. To find them, you must follow their trails: black rocks tumbled together at the bottom of little defiles, windrows of pine needles, last year's leaves, branches, and other trash swept into bends and against rock outcroppings in high-water months. But even in the driest month, the least of our brooks, or the silent places where it has been, has a kind of cool, damp memory of water.

And then in the spring, when the brooks are up, they dash down their courses in a noisy free-for-all, falling all over one another and filling the air with their clamor, as though you'd turned loose a kennel of puppies.

There were mills on Pied Brook and the Quick Branch from the earliest years of settlement. Water power was everywhere up here. Even the tiny, come-and-go brooks back in the hills, many of them, were made to turn mills. Little one- or two-man water mills in this township made boards, posts, bowls, bobbins, shingles, clapboards, staves, hubs, tubs, ax handles, pick handles, hoe handles—if you could tinker up a way to rig a rotating shaft to make law or art or sound democracy, some clever fellow with a brook at the bottom of his pasture would have gone into the thing, at least for a while. Ambrose was a factory town, in a small way, a kind of cottage Detroit.

Not for long, though, not really. It's an odd thing how the past seems to go on forever. The periods or ages of history seem so prolonged—but they aren't. When you look at the matter with any attention, you find the past turns over pretty quickly. The great age of water power in these parts, for example, was good for no more than, say, fifty years. By the end of the last century, the mills were mostly broken up. Water power—or, anyway, the power you got from water like Pied Brook and the rest—turned out not to be the kind of foundation on which could be reared a permanent industrial edifice. We weren't Detroit, after all.

The issue was consistency. The trouble with those old mills was that for half the year, when the brooks were dry or frozen up, they hardly ran at all. Then every few years, there would be a big spring melt, and the mills would run too much: The brook would carry away the mill dam, the mill wheel, the mill itself. Everything would have to be rebuilt, and then everything would be destroyed all over again a few years hence, and so it went until somebody figured out you could move to Michigan.

I came to Littlejohn's house in July of a dry summer. On first going over the place, I was puzzled to find in the cellar a channel or ditch dug into the floor. The cellar floor at Littlejohn's was plain dirt, the walls fieldstone laid up without mortar, exactly as in a stone fence. The channel in the floor, nearly a foot deep by another foot wide, ran diagonally across the cellar. It made the cellar look like a sandbox where children have been playing with their toy cars and trucks but have taken them and gone home. I couldn't see why that ditch was there.

The summer continued dry, finished dry; but in September, there came a week of rain, sometimes heavy rain. From the kitchen of Littlejohn's, I began to hear the pleasant chuckling sound of a brook.

Where was it? Not outdoors: The grass and the woods were wet and dripping, but they weren't flooded. I realized the brook was in the house. The ditch that crossed the cellar floor now held a considerable flow of water, which entered the cellar under the stone wall to the south, ran through the cellar in the ditch, and ran out under the opposite wall.

I learned that anything more than a moderate fall of rain over a day or two would make the stream in the cellar commence to run. In the spring, when the snows melted, the stream became a river—an indoor river. Was I happy to have a river in my cellar? Not entirely. Certainly a river in the cellar was not the way a household was supposed to work where I came from. But it did work, didn't it? Littlejohn had dug and ditched, and the digging had worked. Look, I thought: The water runs into the cellar, but it also runs out.

Bible Hill isn't far from the tilt point of New England, indeed of the whole eastern seaboard. Twenty miles west, the brooks and rivers of the land begin to flow into Lake Champlain, into the upper Hudson River system; they begin to be part of the westerly mass of America. Back here, however, although we may feel a certain tug of continental gravity, we're still on the stay-home side. We're Connecticut River people.

On Bible Hill, the water in your potted geranium, your kitchen sink, the mud puddle in your dooryard, the river in your cellar, the nameless brook that passes under your road through a steel pipe, the Quick Branch, the Dead River—every ounce and drop of water winds up in the Connecticut River and is borne along down-country for 150 miles, swooning finally into Long Island Sound, the great wet barnyard, where even our humble waters, now carrying God knows what impurities, soluble and otherwise, will arrive at last off the elegant, leisured north shore of fish-shaped Paumanok, there to lave the nymphs and satyrs who copulate in the foam of Oyster Bay, a foam constituted in minute part from the limpid tears of Bible Hill.

15. Higher Laws

Blessed is he that readeth, and they that hear the words of this prophecy, and keep those things which are written therein: for the time is at hand. —REVELATION 1:3; 19:11-13

1

Not on Bible Hill itself, but a couple of miles to the west, in the Joppa district, there was a woman named Althea Tavistock, who believed in the end of the world—that is to say, she believed the Last Days were coming.

"When?" I asked her.

"Soon," said Althea Tavistock.

You understand what it was that Althea expected. She meant not world war, not epidemic or any other kind of cataclysm in nature, but the literal enactment of the Revelation of Saint John the Divine, the whole nine yards: the voices, the angels, the trumpets, the thrones, the books, the seven stars, the seven lamps, the seven seals, the beast, the dragon, the lamb, the fallen Babylon, the numbers, the women crowned, the New Jerusalem.

"Why?" I asked Althea.

"Why, what?"

Althea worked at the Joppa store. She ran the cash register, took in the deliveries. She might come out and pump your gas for you. Althea was probably fifty. She had a gap between her front teeth, weighed not less than three hundred pounds, and possessed the most beautiful, illuminated smile. An even-tempered woman. Althea didn't mind my questioning her faith in the Apocalypse. Why should she, after all? If she was right, then there was little point in minding much of anything.

"Why do you believe it? You believe all that is really going to happen, right?" I asked Althea.

"I know it," said Althea.

"But how? How do you know it? Because it's in the Bible?"

"No," said Althea. "Because it stands to reason."

Stands to reason?

January 15, 1929. Gray. Temp. 6 a.m. −25. Prety savage
January 17, 1929. Freeze holds. Temp. 12 M 8. Well froze
January 20, 1929. Thaw. Temp. 12 M 36. Snow p.m.

She said that?

She said it stands to reason.

Well, I don't know, son. I can see it, I guess.

You can?

Sure. Have you ever read that, in the Bible?

The Revelation? Yes, I have. Have you?

Sure.

You're not going to tell me you believe it?

No. But what I'm saying, if it's true, that's going to be quite a show there, ain't it?

I won't deny that.

Well, think about it, son. You're Thea Tavistock. You're in there, working at the store, year in, year out. Working for Newt Thurber. How'd you like working for Newt Thurber?

I wouldn't.

No. Then, quitting time, you go home to your husband, Junior Tavistock. You know Junior.

I do. Milo's brother.

You're Thea, now. You get to work at Newt's all day. Then you get to go home, clean up Junior's house. Then you get to do Junior's dirty laundry, cook Junior's dinner, serve it, do the dishes, watch a little TV—and then later, for a reward, you get to lie down, or sit up, or stand on your head, or do whatever else Junior's got in mind that night to satisfy his, uh, animal needs, if you follow me.

I'm with you.

It don't sound like much of a deal, does it, son?

No.

You need more, if you're Thea. You need something more. In your life, I mean. I don't mean more fun, exactly—though more fun wouldn't hurt, either—but something that matters, that's important.

Yes.

You know there's got to be something that's important. You know it sure ain't working for Newt Thurber and being Mrs. Junior. Could be it's the end of the world. Most people would say that's important. Yes, the end of the world might be it. You could say it stands to reason.

Wait a minute. You're arguing a fallacy here.

I ain't arguing at all, son.

I once thought Mr. Applegate that day was patronizing Althea Tavistock—that he was patronizing me. But now I think not. On the contrary, Mr. Applegate pays us a compliment. We aren't dumb, he tells us. We aren't sheep. We refuse to be satisfied with mere products, advertising, TV, shopping, credit cards, lotteries, movie stars, politicians—with the phantasmagoria our time offers us as real life—an offer tempting, perhaps, to an eight-year-old boy of average intelligence. No. We are adults. We won't settle for that. We will resist. We will strike out. We demand the momentous, the terrifying, the beautiful: Armageddon.

WHAT HE LEARNED

I was in the capital for not quite nine months. I'm not guessing, I've counted: 258 days. The point is, that's not much time at all. And yet every day, every hour I spent in the place is inscribed on my memory with a clarity and depth unlike those of longer matter. The hot, heavy wind, the sand, the rattle of the palms, the lap of dirty water in the ferry slip, the drab plaza with its martial statue of Bolívar—Bolívar, who hadn't the remotest connection with the place or its history—the big scruffy pelicans that sat on pilings along the quays: They and the sense of exhilarated uncertainty of which they were the setting are before me today, thirty years on, where places and feelings fade that belong to my life by better right. It looks as though if I were to live to a great age, those 258 days would prove to be the hard, igneous nub of my life, enduring at the end, long after the softer matter surrounding them has eroded.

And that despite the fact that for all the vividness and permanence of those sights, those sounds, I still don't understand the capital. I never did. Hitchcock, the foundation. Peabody, Lieutenant Hector: What were they about? I never knew for sure. The shoals of miserable children who clamored in the streets, yes. They were trying not to starve. Them, I understood. The rest, no, even though I took it into my head and mind forever. You could say I didn't learn much down there, but I learned it good.

I remember people's very words, their gestures.

"It's a poor country, Mark," Hitchcock was fond of explaining. He had a way of shrugging his shoulders and flicking his hand away when he said it. "It's an unlucky country."

February 6, 1929. Snow. Temp. 12 M 20
February 10, 1929. Temp. 12 M 21
February 13, 1929. Snow. Temp. 12 M 25. New snow abt. 1 ft.

Course, Althea, too. Althea always was what you might call religious. She used to drive Hugo about crazy.

Usher? How did she fit in with Usher?

She worked for him. She worked up at Hugo's, cooking, helping with the house. Althea went up there every day. Junior would drop her off on his way to work, pick her up after. She did that for, I don't know, six or seven years, until Hugo lost it about the TV. You heard about that, I guess.

You haven't told me about it, have you?

No.

Then I haven't heard about it.

No. Well, Tavistocks lived—well, you know where they live—on the way to Dead River, right down in the hollow. They had TV, but they couldn't get much of anything on it except buzzing and, you know, sand. No reception down there, and of course no cable TV in those days. So when Thea started working at Hugo's, it looked to her like Hugo ought to get pretty good TV because he was up on that hill. So she asked Hugo to get her a TV for the kitchen. Thea asked him, and he did.

He hadn't had one before?

No. Not many had. This was, I'm guessing, 1957, '58.

So he didn't like it.

He did like it. Everybody likes TV, son. They may say they don't. Sure, Hugo liked it fine.

So what was his problem?

I'm telling you. In those days, TV was mainly cowboy shows, you know. Westerns. Hugo liked those all right. Watching Westerns on TV after dinner beat reading the paper and playing solitaire, which is all he had to do else. The thing was, Thea wanted to watch the religious shows—the Gospel-preaching shows. It seems like that's what got her started on the end of the world in the first place, but I could be wrong about that. Thea had been going to the Living Water Chapel there past Dead River, Mort Pickle's place. Mort used to come down pretty heavy on the end of the world, I understand, so maybe Thea picked it up from him. Anyway, point is, she wanted the TV for the religious shows and Hugo wanted it for the Westerns. They couldn't agree.

Why didn't he get another TV?

That's what I told him. Hugo came to me. He was hot. "I don't know what to do," he said. "I wished I'd never got that goddamned TV. I wished I'd never got her. I'm just getting ready for Tales of Wells Fargo, *and here she comes and switches to goddamned Billy Graham. Then we fight about it. It's like we're married." But no, he wouldn't get a TV just for Thea. "That's even more like we're married," Hugo said. "Junior married her, goddamn it, not me." "Well," I said, "then I don't know what you're going to do." And Hugo said, "I do."*

Oh boy, stop.

What is it, son?

I know what's coming now.

What?

He shoots his TV.

You're right, son. You have so heard this, then.

No. Somebody in a book I read did the same thing.

Is that right? Well, this was no book. Hugo shot it right out. One day when Althea was getting ready to switch channels on him, he went and got his gun and blew out the TV set with a bunch of double-aught shot, right there in the kitchen. Also cut himself over the eye with flying glass, busted a window, and started a fire in the gas range. They had to get the fire department up there. Of course, Thea quit: no more TV in the kitchen, and plus, she'd begun to have doubts about Hugo.

Why? It's a perfectly reasonable reaction, in a way.

You think so, son?

Well, extreme, yes. But it took care of his problem. And, say what you like, it was his TV.

That's how Hugo saw it, too. You and Hugo'd have gotten on good, son. I wouldn't have thought that, but I see it's so.

I have read someplace that a third of the general population is convinced that the end of the world, as in the biblical Revelation, will occur in their lifetime. That's more people than are convinced that the earth goes around the sun. Those believers expect to see with their own eyes the Last Things: monstrous, annihilating things, and they are not afraid. On the contrary: They're comforted. They feel the consolation of the Apocalypse: at last, the real; at last, no more bullshit. Althea Tavistock felt that consolation, but, then, Althea hadn't much to lose by the end of the world—that was Mr. Applegate's point, perhaps. Usher did have a lot to lose, however, and yet he, too, felt the sweet pull of the end. He must have. What more apocalyptic gesture can you make today than shotgunning the television?

February 20, 1929. Fair. Thaw. Temp. 12M 40
February 21, 1929. Cloud. Temp. 12M 35. Rain night
February 22, 1929. Weather making. Temp. 6 a.m. 12.
End of thaw

2

And I saw heaven opened, and
behold a white horse: and he that
sat upon him was called Faithful
and True, and in righteousness he
doth judge and make war. His eyes
were as a flame of fire, and on his
head were many crowns; and he had
a name written, that no man knew,
but himself.

It was an apocalyptic kind of place altogether (in its own way), Bible Hill. For example, doesn't the Bible tell us that at the end of days, Israel will return to do battle for its kingdom? And didn't we have some of that action, too?

Goldhammer was hard on me. He accused me of running away to Bible Hill. Goldhammer accused me, when in truth the one who was running away was Goldhammer. I didn't know that at time, though. No one did, except Goldhammer.

Goldhammer was Bible Hill's Scarlet Pimpernel. I knew Goldhammer when he went by the name Declan Fitzgerald. One summer, we both worked painting houses for Bucky Polk. We spent a lot of long days side by side on the ground, on ladders, on roofs, scraping, scraping, scraping. Painting houses, we learned, you scrape, you caulk, you putty, you patch and piece, but you almost never actually paint. Bucky Polk would come around Friday noon with three-quarters of what he owed us in pay for the week. We'd have the balance when he collected for a job to be finished Monday, Bucky said.

Fitzgerald didn't believe him. Fitzgerald didn't care for Bucky Polk. He called him a "schmuck." I hadn't heard that word in some years. Fitzgerald didn't talk Vermont.

"Why should I?" said Fitzgerald. "I'm a New York Jew. I shouldn't even be talking to you."

"A Jew named Fitzgerald?" I said.

"We changed it," said Fitzgerald.

"Changed it from what?"

"Never mind," said Fitzgerald.

There was always something off about Fitzgerald, something withheld. He lived in a room he rented above the Tumbleweed, where he also worked in the kitchen. He was in Ambrose when I came and for a year or two after, working at Jordan's, working for Bucky, working at what came along. Not much mystery about that—and indeed, any mystery about Fitzgerald may have appeared only after he had departed as he did. Certainly everybody seemed to like Fitzgerald. Yes, they kept a little distance from him because he was an exotic, a flatlander, but then, so was I and so did they keep a little distance from me. The distance was part of the fun.

Everything that was known or believed about Fitzgerald came retrospectively, from what happened to him one day in the spring of, I think, 1975. About noon, a long and ominous line of vehicles arrived in town from the south, came over the bridge, and stopped in front of the Tumbleweed. The town constable led them in his truck. The other vehicles were state police cruisers, sheriff's department cruisers, an ambulance, a National Guard troop transport, and two of those battleship gray Plymouth sedans that you never see parked at the supermarket or waiting in line for a drive-through window: U.S. government issue.

Six men in business suits got out of the gray cars and, following the constable, went into the Tumbleweed. Less than five minutes later, they came out again, with Fitzgerald. Fitzgerald was in a kind of box formed by the government men. His hands were manacled behind his back, and the government man on either side of him kept hold of one of his arms. They put Fitzgerald in the rear of one of the gray cars and drove away.

Brown came out of the building.

"What was that?" he asked the constable.

"Don't know for sure," said the constable.

"Where are they taking Fitzgerald?" Brown asked.

"Rutland, they say," the constable answered. "He ain't Fitzgerald, either, they say."

"What do they want to take him to Rutland for?" Brown asked.

"I don't expect he'll be there long," the constable said.

"Who's going to wash the dishes?" asked Brown.

Well, you know the rest. Fitzgerald was tried and convicted in the federal court for the Second District, in New York, on charges of attempted murder, conspiracy, and destroying government property. Fitzgerald, it turned out, was an interstate fugitive whose real name was Avram Goldhammer.

Avram Goldhammer had been a bright lad indeed. Born in Fort Washington, the Bronx, in 1951; a graduate of the Bronx High School of Science, where he performed as a near prodigy in mathematics and physics; entered Harvard at sixteen; dropped out in his third year. Goldhammer became political. His movements began to be hard to follow. At some point, he swapped coasts. He was arrested in San Francisco in 1971, and soon after his release, he was, according to his indictment, part of a group that blew up a laboratory in Berkeley. Goldhammer disappeared, lived underground, moved underground around the United States and Canada, and eventually wound up in Vermont as Declan Fitzgerald, Social Security card, passport, and Minnesota driver's license all correct. He was hardly alone. In those days, it sometimes looked like half the people in the state were part of one underground or another. I myself might have looked that way, to some.

February 28, 1929. Fair a.m. then cloud. Temp. 12 M 27. Weather making p.m.
March 1, 1929. Temp. 6 a.m. 25 Snow
March 2, 1929. Temp. 6 a.m. 23 Snow
March 3, 1929. Temp. 6 a.m. 21 Snow
March 4, 1929. Fair. Blow from n. Temp. 12 M 16. Snow to eves

What will they do with him?

Put him in jail for a while, it looks like.

For how long?

How would I know, son?

Well, you're a lawyer, aren't you?

That's right, I am. Okay, for long enough. How's that? After all, he's some kind of Communist, it turns out, ain't he?

He's a radical, not a Communist.

What's the difference, son?

You can be a radical without being a Communist. You can be a Communist without being a radical.

I see. Well, he was bound to be something of that nature, though, wasn't he? That Fitzgerald?

Was he?

Sure. Up here, like he was, a smart fellow like that, working like he did?

What of it? I'm the same.

You ain't the same, son. You're one thing. That Fitzgerald's another. Anybody could tell he was some kind of Communist. Radical.

They could? You've known that? You've known he was in hiding?

Not known. But I ain't surprised to hear it.

You didn't turn him in, though. You didn't say anything.

Why would I? That Fitzgerald was a nice fellow enough as far as I could see. Did his work. Minded his own business. The rest of it wasn't any affair of mine, was it?

March 7, 1929. Fair. Temp. 12 M 44. Mud in road
March 8, 1929. Fair. Wind s. Temp. 12M 49

DODGE CITY

Down in the port section, along the quays, they were shooting off fireworks. You could hear the *pop-pop-pop* and see the flashes. Or perhaps it was another firefight. From a distance, I found, they look and sound a bit alike, at first.

Hitchcock sat in a rocking chair on the veranda of the club. His injured leg was propped on the railing. He was smoking a fat cigar. He was drinking cognac from a snifter as big as a fishbowl. He was wearing his seersucker suit, jacket off, tie loosened. He looked like a seventh grader in a class play—an inappropriate class play—*Rain,* perhaps, or some swampy piece by Tennessee Williams, mounted by a rich school where something has gone badly wrong. Behind us, in the dining room, plates and glasses clinked together as the waiters cleared off. Dinner was over.

Hitchcock stuck his long nose into his brandy glass and inhaled. He was reflective; he was downcast. That morning, I had put in my notice; I would be leaving the capital in a week.

"You just got here," Hitchcock said. "They'll send somebody else, and I'll have to start all over with him."

"I know," I said.

"And your plan," Hitchcock went on. "I don't understand your plan at all. Going to Vermont. Vermont puzzles me, Mark."

"Why?" I asked him. "I have a place there now. I've come into some property there. You know that."

"Well, yes, of course," said Hitchcock. "But so what? So what? It doesn't mean you have to live there, does it? My father came into property in the Florida Keys at one time. He sold it. He didn't go live in the Florida Keys, for God's sake."

"Vermont isn't Florida," I said.

"No," said Hitchcock. "It isn't. It's far worse. Have you ever been in Vermont?"

"No."

"Not that there's anything wrong with it," Hitchcock said. "Vermont's all right, as far as it goes. Pretty in the fall. I've driven through it, more than once. I had a cousin who went to camp in Vermont one summer, as a matter of fact. Girls camp, it was. People go to camp in Vermont. People ski in Vermont. People fish in Vermont. People hike in Vermont. People who have just been married go to Vermont to fuck. But, my God, Mark, nobody goes to Vermont to live."

"I am," I said.

"You won't like it," said Hitchcock.

"Then I'll come back down here and take up my old job," I said.

"Hah," said Hitchcock. "I think not. In any case, we'll be gone. We won't be here. We haven't long, have we, in all honesty? Listen to them."

Plainly it was no festival that was going on in the port. One of the warehouses was on fire, and then sirens could be heard and flood-lights began to play here and there over that whole quarter of the town.

Hitchcock leaned his handsome head back against his chair. He sighed.

"Dodge City," said Hitchcock.

Now the burning warehouse blew up. A red ball of flame and smoke burst a hundred feet into the air, hung there, and a second later we heard the blast like thunder.

"Not Dodge City," said Hitchcock. "Cheyenne. You're leaving Cheyenne, Mark. Good-bye, Old Paint."

Goldhammer had been willing to bring the whole world crashing down about his ears. So, figuratively, had Usher. Althea Tavistock would have been happy to watch and cheer them on. The three are allies. They are allied in apocalypse, and they are allied in futility. For the secret of the Apocalypse is this: It's not going to happen. You'll have to settle for something less, far less. What did Usher's apocalypse amount to? You blow up your TV, cut your eye, bust your window, almost burn down your house, and stampede your cook.

Did Goldhammer do much better? It would be hard to prove he did. Certainly Goldhammer's apocalypse didn't last very long—though its consequences for himself did—and certainly the destruction it caused was less than apocalyptic. You could say it was the opposite of apocalyptic. Goldhammer and his band had aimed to blow up one of the engineering labs at Berkeley that did work on contract for the Department of Defense, but in the event, the lab they destroyed was part of the vet school. No one was hurt. The saboteurs broke a lot of glass and killed several hundred white rats. Goldhammer had the wrong building, evidently. For the rats he destroyed, Goldhammer's apocalypse was a serious thing—no question. But otherwise, the towers of Babylon were not seen to tremble, or not much.

Still, if Goldhammer hadn't toppled Babylon, it wasn't his fault. Babylon's cops saw it that way, anyhow, and so did Goldhammer. He was in the fight for good. Underground as he was, Goldhammer, at least when I knew him, was never discreet. He made no effort to hide his politics. Even as Declan Fitzgerald, he was a fighter, or anyway he sounded like one. He didn't like it that I was not.

"So what are you doing up here?" Goldhammer asked me.

"I'm on vacation," I said.

"You're on vacation?" said Goldhammer. "You're not on vacation. You're in retreat. You're doing nothing. You're part of nothing. You see the system. You see what it does. How can you stand by and do nothing?"

There is no answer to that, and so I made none.

"You're running away," Goldhammer said to me.

It occurred to me later, after his arrest, that Goldhammer might have thought I was running away literally, that I was a fugitive, like him, living underground. He might have been forgiven for thinking that. After all, on Bible Hill, I was placed much as Goldhammer was: on my own, from away, happy to be here but, at the same time, not quite here. I might have been Goldhammer, I suppose.

I wasn't, though. I was nothing like Goldhammer. Goldhammer was a Harvard man, he was of the elite, and I was a peasant, as Mr.

Applegate had said, with a peasant's durable skepticism. I never believed in Goldhammer's apocalypse. Sure, I had seen the struggle, the convulsions, just as Goldhammer had; that struggle, those convulsions were my generation's exhibit. But Goldhammer took fire at the sight, and I never did. When you have seen one cop on horseback urge his steed up the steps of a college library, you have seen all cops do it. When you have seen one dentist's son from Winnetka, formerly president of his high school's student council, hurl a brick through the window of that same library, you have seen them all.

Goldhammer was wrong about me. I wasn't underground. I might have run away from time to time in my life, as any sane man does, but not on Bible Hill. On Bible Hill, I wasn't running away, though I might have looked it. I didn't believe in the end of the world, or in miniature, ship-in-a-bottle apocalypses like Goldhammer's and Usher's. I believed the Revelation of Saint John the Divine was a dead end. It was the last chapter of a very long book, nothing more. And I had a long book of my own: Littlejohn's.

Littlejohn's diary offered a kind of solace, or anyway it did for me, and it offered a kind of promise. I found that the utter spareness of Littlejohn's daily entries somehow suggested a way of upholding the good and resisting the fraudulent, a way that got around the necessity for unavailing destruction. I don't know why, but I believed Littlejohn's diary was more than the monotonous record of an obscure and undistinguished length of days. It was a manual for living, a primer, a document full of hope, a book of life. Littlejohn's diary was the Bible of Bible Hill.

March 10, 1929. Fair. Temp. 12M 49. Sap run. Mud. O. Taft stuk in rd. Puld him out

March 11, 1929. Rain. Temp. 12 M 40. Sap run. Late this yr.

That was the trick, perhaps. Not anger, not struggle, but concentration.

Keep it low.

Keep it simple.

Keep it exact.

March 15, 1929. Cloud. Temp. 12 M 41. Sap run
March 18, 1929. Fair. Sap done. Poor

Trust not to gear.

Avoid self-satisfaction.

Believe little.

Be alert.

March 21, 1929. Rain a.m. Temp. 12 M 51. Robbin

Above all, take your time. Take your time. Take your time.

Sure, it looks like hiding, it looks like running away. It isn't. You give what you have, not what you don't. You don't get honey from the cows; you don't get milk from the bees. Goldhammer accused me of never believing in anything, of never doing anything. About the first, he was more right than not, perhaps, but about the second, he was wrong. I have done something. I'm doing it now.

16. Farming

1

Now, I never aimed on Bible Hill to be a farmer. Lord no. No farming, no husbandry: no cattle, no sheep, no fowl. No crops. Let others farm. Many do, even today. The town no longer has whole farmers, but it still has any amount of half farmers, quarter farmers, sixteenth-farmers. They have a goat, a few chickens, ducks. They go in for maple sugaring, plant a quarter-acre vegetable garden, keep bees. They farm more or less. Some are born to farming, some farm for fun, and some farm because they hold any of two or three different ideas about farming, about living—ideas in every case unsound.

Not I. From the beginning, I knew farming was a life better recommended than lived. "Praise great estates, farm a small one," said Virgil—but he was a poet. I would go Virgil one better: Praise small estates, farm none. Somehow I came to that wisdom without having to learn it. Farming was one mistake I was never tempted to make.

Others were not so lucky. They felt the farm's pull. They moved to a little place, fixed up the barn, built coops and sheds, got in some animals—and began to make discoveries. They discovered the farm's servitude. They discovered that you keep the animals, and the animals keep you. They discovered filth. Most painfully, they discovered that farming is the business of death. Death by accident, as when the coon kills your chickens or the neighbors' German shepherd devours your lambs; and, sooner or later, death by design, death as the necessary end and purpose of all real husbandry. You raise up to strike down.

Not everyone can accept that, and so the hills are full of unslaughtered livestock whose tenderhearted owners funked farming's ultimate moment. Past Joppa, almost over the town line, lived a family named Lippincott, new to the area and having seven kids and not much money, who thought to buy a spring piglet for fattening. They built a pen out back for it. The older kids fed it every day. These novice farmers knew better than to make a pet of their pig. They didn't give it a name, they didn't play with it or talk to it. Even so, they knew it would be difficult, in the late fall, when the pig had made its weight, to kill and butcher it. The Lippincotts knew that would be difficult, but they didn't know it would be impossible. November came, December, and Lippincotts' pig still lived. It wintered. By the next spring, there was no question of eating it. The Lippincotts enlarged its pen, enlarged it again. In the summer of the pig's fifth year, it broke out of its pen at last and escaped to the woods. That fall, it was shot by a hunter on Round Mountain. He had taken it for a bear. Lippincotts' pig field-dressed at 625 pounds.

June 1, 1933. Fair. Temp. 6 a.m. 59. Began to cut high lot.
J. Ballantine & P. Scott to help. Dan & Scotts team
June 2, 1933. Holds fair. Temp. 6 a.m. 63. Done high lot
begun back.
June 3, 1933. Rain. Temp. 12M 66.
June 4, 1933. Fair. Temp. 6 a.m. 57. Done back.
To Ballantines p.m.

Amanda was reluctant. She was reluctant, and she had a little mole on the front of her left shoulder. On hot days, the first summer I knew her, when she lived in her father's cabin on Back Diamond, she would show up in a pair of overalls worn, as far as I could tell, on top of nothing, or anyway not much. The mole on her shoulder rode just inboard of her overalls strap, on the way to the hollow under her collarbone. Amanda in overalls on a warm afternoon was the best argument for a farmer's life I could imagine. It was all the argument I needed. But Amanda was reluctant.

"I don't know, Noon," Amanda said. "What are we talking about here? Are we talking about this afternoon? Are we talking about a matinee?"

"This afternoon. Tomorrow. The day after."

"Wow," said Amanda. "So, not just a matinee?"

"No."

"So, more like the real deal? You and me?"

"That's right," I said. "Like that. You move out of here, come over to my place. We live together."

"Live together, huh?" said Amanda. "It sounds like a marriage."

"It is like a marriage."

"I'm already married," said Amanda.

"No, you're not."

"But I am," said Amanda. "I've been a wife, Noon. I told you about it. It didn't go real well, you know? I don't know if I want to get back into that."

"You married Denny," I said. "I'm not Denny."

Amanda laughed. "You got that right," she said.

"Ask your father," I said. "He'll stick up for me."

"I'm sure he would," said Amanda. "That's one of the things I don't know about, about you. You and my dad, you're a lot alike."

"A girl's supposed to like that in a boy," I said.

"I know she is," said Amanda, "I know she's supposed to like that, but I don't know if I do. No, you're not Denny. But what are you? That's another thing, isn't it? You're up here all by yourself. You seem to like it. That could be trouble. You've got a lot of—I don't know—solitude about you, Noon. You know? A lot of distance."

"I'm right here," I said.

2

From its beginnings in the eighteenth century, farming on Bible Hill has had an illusory quality, a quality of advertising and unreal optimism. The first settlers, arriving before the American Revolution, chopped down the forests and scratched the dirt between the raw stumps to plant corn, oats, rye, living as they did so in tents and hovels, or in holes in the ground, like woodchucks. After a couple of years of this, if they hadn't given up or died, they might have achieved a dank, unwindowed house with a mud floor, a mud fireplace. They might have acquired a scrawny cow, some stone fences, a dollar or two of hard cash in a box. Did they despair? Did the weakest of them fall away? Did the strongest set their jaws grimly and resolve, if they could never know ease, at least to endure? Not at all. They believed they were in the money. Farming in Vermont was a snap, they found; they would soon be rich. They were rich already. Hanging on to their absurd, impossible few acres, living on filthy porridge and salt pork, working themselves to death, they wrote fulsome letters to their cousins in Connecticut and Massachusetts, urging them to come north and join the fun.

Even at its busiest and most productive, farming hereabouts had the vague, exaggerated unreality of dream. For a generation or two around the turn of the nineteenth century, Bible Hill and vicinity were the pantry of New England. Our farmers assembled great herds of cattle, sheep, pigs, even fowl, and drove them over the execrable roads to the slaughterhouses of Boston. There was a place in Dead River Settlement in those days that raised geese. Every year, ten thousand geese would be driven down out of the hills and off to the south. Think of it, ten thousand geese on the hoof! It's a vision from a nightmare, for the goose is a violent, disorderly fowl and also a profoundly messy one. Think of the 150 miles of road to Boston, a ruin of greasy goose feathers, slimy green goose shit, and the bad air that must follow the passage of that much goose aggression.

By midcentury, the illusion of prosperity by farming had become narrower and more obsessive. The farmers of Bible Hill had abandoned general agriculture and turned to sheep. Railroads and canals had put the old drovers out of business: in Springfield and Hartford, it was now easier and cheaper to get a goose from Ohio than it was to get one from Vermont—if you wanted a goose in the first place. But the mills of Massachusetts and New Hampshire were woolen mills. Someplace was going to get rich growing the sheep that made the fleece that supplied those mills, and it might as well be Bible Hill, especially since the introduction of a certain breed of Spanish sheep that produced a hundredweight of wool per head per month, ate practically nothing, and so would surely thrive on the less and less prosperous fields of the old hill farms. Those longhaired Andalusian sheep would be the philosopher's stone that turned the unprofitable seawater of Bible Hill's husbandry into gold.

For thirty years, the shorn hillsides were covered with sheep, as in a plague of very large brown caterpillars. Furthermore, history shows that two or three sheep barons did in fact do pretty well off the game. The rest went broke. By, say, 1880, the smart sheep had moved to Nevada and Australia, along with the smart shepherds.

Bible Hill entered the era of its last agricultural solution: It became dairy country. It became dairy country not so much because Vermont is an especially good place to raise milk cows as because of the limits of transport at the time. Nobody in Boston wanted to drink a glass of milk that has come in unrefrigerated on the slow train from Wisconsin. But with the little narrow-gauge railroads that began to thread up the river valleys after the Civil War, a farmer on Bible Hill could milk at 3:00 A.M., drive to the depot, load his milk onto the milk train, and have it for sale in Boston the same evening. That worked, one way and another, for fifty years or more, but with a difference from the older farming on Bible Hill: This farming was unillusioned. For no sane dairy farmer can make himself believe he is having an easy life, or ever will, or that he is getting rich, or ever will.

June 6, 1933. Fair. Wind. Temp. 6 a.m. 61. To high lot with J. Ballantine & W. Brown. Tossed

June 7, 1933. Cloud. Temp. 6 a.m. 66. Began back. Rain. Quit

June 8, 1933. Temp. 12M 66. Rain

Amanda was reluctant, but I thought she became less so. Through the summer she lived on Back Diamond, I saw her practically every day. I helped her with the roof of her father's place. I stopped at the Weed to see her before the bar got busy after five o'clock, and when her old car at last gave out, I picked her up there after closing and drove her home. I took her to the movies in Brattleboro. I held her hand. I aimed to be her friend, but I also aimed to be more, and I wanted that known. It worked. Amanda liked me, I thought. Who wouldn't? We Noons are hard to resist.

"I had a dream about you, Noon," Amanda said.

"You did?"

"I was on this boat, a big boat, like a liner. We were tied up at the pier. We were getting ready to sail, but we couldn't until all the visitors had left the ship, and they wouldn't go. There was this party—or, like a meeting, or it might even have been a trial—going on, and they wouldn't go. The captain kept on trying to get the people to leave the ship so we could sail, and everybody kept on not leaving."

"Where do I come in?" I asked her.

"No place special," said Amanda.

"Oh."

"I mean, you were there," Amanda said. "You were kind of off to the side, but there. We didn't talk to each other, but I knew I knew you and I knew you knew me. You were one of the other passengers on the ship."

"I was hoping I'd be the captain," I said.

"No, Noon, you couldn't have been the captain," said Amanda. "The captain was John Lennon."

"Well, hell," I said. "Look: I can't go up against John Lennon."

3

For me, the work of farming on Bible Hill consisted of undoing the farming of my predecessor. Littlejohn, in his solitary prime, had milked a dozen cows, but his prime was fifty years in the past. His little barn had mostly collapsed by the time I arrived. The timbers on one side had rotted and finally failed, pulling the whole structure over and allowing the roof to sag to within four or five feet of the ground. Littlejohn's barn looked like an enormous condemned pup tent.

There was no repairing it. One winter day, following Mr. Applegate's advice, I set it afire and watched it burn to its underpinnings. The next year, there grew up on the ashes of the barn a jungle of blackberries with stems as thick as my wrist and great thorns like dragon's teeth.

There was more such work. Every dairy farmer has to do with massive, slow-moving creatures whose placid minds are patiently devoted to getting away from where the farmer wants them to be. A cow won't jump over or break down a fence the way a horse or a bull might, but it will *lean* against the fence, and lean some more, reaching for whatever it covets on the other side, and so in time it will lean the fence right over. Therefore, Littlejohn through the years had strung up on his place a couple of miles at least of barbed wire. He stapled it onto trees in the woods around his pastures. As his farm declined, his herd dwindled, and the woods closed in on his pastures. So he ran new courses of wire from tree to tree inside the old perimeter. Elsewhere, he hung wire from posts of black-locust wood or from long stakes of iron. Surrounded by all that wire, I found living at Littlejohn's was like living in a prisoner of war camp long after the war has ended.

Littlejohn wasn't the first to put up barbed wire on Bible Hill. His forebears had hung their share, as well. Littlejohn's woods were a museum of barbed wire. Some of the wire had flat barbs; some barbs were twisted; some had two points, some three, some four. The wire was rusty and broken. Here and there in the woods, big oaks and pines had swallowed the wire stapled to them years before, which now seemed to run through their hearts.

I would have it all out of there. Littlejohn's wire tripped me up as I went about. It tangled my feet. It tore my clothes, my skin. I got a pair of cutters and began to cut it out. It took me a couple of years, but at last I got it all—all except for the wire that lived on inside the old trees.

By the time Amanda came to me, Littlejohn's wire was about gone. Barbed wire wouldn't have held Amanda on the place, I knew, so it might as well be away. Littlejohn had fenced. I unfenced.

June 9, 1933. Fair. Temp. 6 a.m. 61. High lot spoilt some. Done tossing back. P. Scott here

June 10, 1933. Fair. Warm. Temp. 6 a.m. 70. To Scotts, tossed. Some spoilt

June 11, 1933. Cloud. Temp. 6 a.m. 59. Waggon to Ballantines. P. Scott & W. Brown & J. Ballantine. Loaded all day. Dan & Scotts team

If you are a scholar, you can get an idea of farming on Bible Hill through history by consulting the tables of farm production compiled for each township and county by the state of Vermont's Department of Agriculture. You find that for any era, farms are much alike, though from one era to another, they may change almost past recognition. In 1850, there were almost twenty thousand sheep in the town of Ambrose. In 1980, there were four. We farm otherwise now. Indeed, the stock that is tended in these parts today, such as it is, would make the farmers of other times rub their eyes.

On Bible Hill today, the farm has become a zoological garden. In fields where safe and sound cattle, sheep, horses once safely grazed, you now see some pretty bizarre creatures. We have llamas, a pin-headed, swan-necked, low-rumped camel from the Andes. We have emus, ostriches, and beefalos. Chinchillas. Nutrias. Calabrese's place was for a time taken over by a man who bred a species of small kangaroo called LaGrange's wallaby. His project was to extract from the testicles of the males an oil known to be much prized by the Chinese. (He went broke in the end. The Chinese didn't prize his oil as much as he needed them to. Another fool who tried to hustle the East.)

"If I come, Noon," said Amanda, "if I come, I get my own room."

"Your own room?"

"That's right," said Amanda. "My own room. My own bed. What do you think, Noon?"

"Nothing," I said.

"Nothing?" Amanda asked. "You wanted this to be like a marriage. You said it. Okay, it will be like a marriage—also unlike. Can you do it that way, Noon?"

"Yes."

July 1, 1933. Warm. Temp. 6 a.m. 73. Began second cut at Ballantines

July 2, 1933. Fair. Wind. Temp. 6 a.m. 65. Finished at Ballantines. To high lot. J Ballantine & P. Scott & Scotts boy

July 3, 1933. Clouds. Temp. 6 a.m. 64. Done high lot. Begun back. To Scotts. Same two

July 4, 1933. Indep. Day. Temp. 6 a.m. 62. P.m. to Scotts. Done him

4

Some farmers on Bible Hill today farm because they are born to it, some farm for fun, and some farm from an idea, a powerful idea of individual freedom. They will subsist, they say. They will be self-sufficient. They will take care of themselves. They farm independence.

You could say that these subsistors have brought farming on Bible Hill back around to where it started. Our first settlers fought to make their places give up barely enough grain and meat to keep the farmers alive. Some of them succeeded at that. At the time of the seventy-fifth anniversary of the town's settlement, about 1850 a historian recorded the statement of an old couple who farmed out on the Quick Branch: In sixty years of married life they declared, they had never bought a pound of meat or flour. There is self-sufficiency, if you like. The new subsistors think they will do the same.

They're kidding themselves. Nobody takes complete care of himself: not I, not you, nobody. Certainly not the ancestral farmers of Bible Hill. They depended on one another utterly, for labor, for supply. They lived in one another's lives as neighbors to a degree nobody would accept today. They hoped to survive as a community, not as atoms. They knew better, perhaps.

Their imitators today misunderstand the old subsistence. They aim to set up for themselves alone. They forget the famous line of Aristotle: Whoever is able to live without society may be an animal, or he may be a god, but he is no man. The new subsistors aim to be more than man, and so they become less.

They wander into solipsism, into dark fantasies, in particular the fantasy of self-defense. Hugo Usher lived out that fantasy, or anyway a mild version of it, in the making of his famous bomb shelter. It's a fantasy of inexorable degrees. You need the cow so you'll have milk and meat and so on without trade. Next, you need the gun to shoot the guy who comes to steal the cow. Then you need a bigger gun to shoot the cop who comes to get you for shooting the guy who came to steal the cow. And so you go on down, down, down. You're in a nursery rhyme for madmen. You're farming not independence, but fantasy.

The fantasy of subsistence farming today proposes a kind of critique of pure freedom. You think if only you can subsist, if only you can achieve self-sufficiency, then you'll be free. The fact is, the more you're self-sufficient, the less you're free. I thought freedom was either overrated or misunderstood. The beasts of the field subsist. They take care of themselves. But are they free? Would you choose to be free like them?

Not I. My aim on Bible Hill was allied to the aim of the subsistors, perhaps, but it was different. It was no more than to keep things comparatively simple. Walk lightly over the world, I thought, and maybe the world will walk lightly over you. Amanda made me out to be solitary, distant. I was less so than she thought. I never thought by my light step to float free of my world, my place. Rather, I hoped by lightness to belong to it more and more.

"Okay," said Amanda. "Okay, I'll give it a shot. Sure I will. A girl could do worse than you, Noon."

"Thank you."

"One thing," Amanda said. "Don't hold on."

"Hold on?"

"If I want to go."

"How could I hold you if you didn't want to be held?" I asked her. "I told you: I took out the fences. The wire's all gone. How could I hold you without a fence?"

"You might try," said Amanda. "Denny tried."

"I'm not Denny," I said.

"You said that before, Noon," said Amanda. "We'll see. Anyway, okay. Here we go."

July 6, 1933. Rain a.m., then fair. Temp. 6 a.m. 52. Toss Ballantines rowen. P. Scott & boy

July 7, 1933. Fair. Cool. Temp 6 a.m. 56. Toss high lot. W. Brown & Scott boy here

July 8, 1933. Fair. Temp. 6 a.m. 66. Done high lot rowen. Begun back

Other vain farmers on Bible Hill today seek not self-sufficiency but, rather, salvation—or, say, conspicuous election. They think by farming to lead a blameless life, a life of moral vegetarianism. They will be better than those of us who go into the marketplace to get and spend. They farm virtue.

Why farming should, from time immemorial, have been thought to be more righteous than other occupations isn't clear to me; but today, at any rate, I believe the idea sometimes has to do with an approach to education. I have listened to people who claim to farm because they want their children to see where the food they eat comes from and not to imagine their stomachs are filled by the A & P. It seems a feeble foundation on which to establish a way of life. Why not simply explain to the kids that bread is grain and grain is grown in vast fields and harvested with vast effort, that hot dogs are pork and beef, the meat of certain large animals? Let the baker, the butcher, the packer do their work, I say; no one should feel compelled to be a farmer by a regard for truth in the upbringing of the young.

The fact is, farming won't get you into heaven, and it won't get your kids there, either. Most people figure that out soon enough. I have noticed that those who go in for farming because they hope by doing so to disabuse their offspring don't usually stick with it very long. The instructiveness of farming is quickly spent. One chicken with its head lately cut off is like another.

And then, there are different kinds of education available from farming, and different kinds of innocence. Maybe a kid can do worse than believe hot dogs are born at the A & P.

Sure, we kids had a new lamb every spring. It was ours, special. We took care of it. We'd have to give it a baby bottle at first, some of them, so it would eat.

It would be your pet, then.

Sure. It would follow you around, just like the song. We had a black lamb one year, I remember. We had one we called Lulu, and another Ozzie. I don't recall the others' names.

You'd play with the lamb?

Sure, like I said. Of course, in November it went into the locker.

What a bummer, right?

Not really, son. We knew there would be another lamb next year.

I wrote a minute ago that the last farming to be followed effectively on Bible Hill and vicinity was dairy farming. It's not so. I had forgotten a style of invisible agriculture that thrives in the hills today, thrives better, probably, than making milk ever did. I say *probably,* however, because the crop I'm considering is hard to get a true picture of: The statistical summaries of the Vermont Department of Agriculture scarcely help. You can only guess at the magnitude of this sector of our farm economy by extrapolating from the portion of the annual harvest that never makes it to market; the portion that is bundled out of the hills in the trunks and backseats of police cars.

Cannabis sativa (Linnaeus): From hidden fields and woodland clearings on the sunny sides of Diamond Mountain, Round Mountain, even Bible Hill, the locoweed was brought out and piled for official burning. Stacks of six-foot, seven-foot plants appeared, dope plants, with their strange, spreading leaves like gigantic lupines: harvest home. Of course, you could go to jail for farming that way, but you can go to jail for many things, and this crop was worth the risk if any was. You could consume it yourself, unlike the extract of wallaby testicles, and you could sell it for real money, unlike milk.

Sure, you had to be careful. The authorities, usually, would get word sometime in the summer of a dope patch growing off in the hills, and they'd stake it out in late August, September, when the plants were ready to harvest. If those plants were yours, and you went to gather them at the wrong time, you'd be sorry. But, of course, you didn't do your dope farming to the music of a brass band; you didn't tell the world. You were discreet.

The summer Amanda lived on Back Diamond, we were walking in the woods near her father's place one afternoon when we met a young fellow on the path. Amanda seemed to know him.

"Hi, Steve," said Amanda.

"Oh, hi," said the young man. "You're back? Where's Denny?"

"I wouldn't know, Steve," said Amanda. "What are you doing way out here?"

A pause.

"How do you mean?" asked Steve.

"I mean what are you doing way out here?" Amanda asked him.

"Oh, fishing," said Steve. Steve had no pole, no line, and there was no fishable water within a couple of miles.

"Okay, Steve," said Amanda.

"Okay, Amanda," said Steve, and walked on.

"Who was he?" I asked Amanda.

"Stevie Groom," said Amanda. "His big brother was a pal of Denny's."

At the end of that summer, the sheriff's office reaped a quarter-acre of dope on Back Diamond, not far from where we'd met the fisherman Steve. The deputies thought Amanda was helping grow the stuff, and maybe she was, though she said not. The sheriff's men hauled the dope down to the road. There they piled it in a turnaround, doused it with kerosene, and burned it. That was the immemorial custom—the last authentic harvest festival to be enacted in these parts, perhaps. A ceremony out of the *Golden Bough,* it was: ancient, ecstatic, full of death and life and dark joy—and pretty well attended. Sheriff's deputies, state police, town constables, firefighters, game wardens, dog officers, and even selectmen from all over the southern part of the state gathered each year to help Ambrose destroy its dope harvest.

You know the stuff, I guess, don't you, son?

I've tried it. You?

Tried it.

What did you make of it?

Being truthful with you, I can't say it did a lot for me.

Ah, you were fighting it. You were afraid it would be too much fun, weren't you?

That could be, son.

5

July 10, 1933. Haze. Warm. Temp. 6 a.m. 70. To Scotts. Load rowen. P. Scott & A. Perry & W. Brown. Dan & Scotts team

July 11, 1933. Haze. Warm. Temp. 6 a.m. 72. To high lot load all day. Same 3

July 12, 1933. Fair. Temp. 6 a.m. 62. To back lot load all day. Same 3. Done it 2:30 p.m.

The question comes up: What is to become of Bible Hill? What is to become of its farming? The sheep and cattle are, for all practical purposes, gone. When the llamas and the emus have gone with them, what will we farm on Bible Hill—apart from marijuana? Perhaps nothing. After all, go back far enough and most everyplace was a farm. London was a farm. Rome, Paris, Chicago, Manhattan—all former farms. Is Bible Hill to go that way? Is it Mineola and Anaheim in the egg? Is it moving into a destiny in which its farms are not even to be found as ruins?

I suspect the answer is yes, and that makes me sad. But I can't lament sincerely, for I'm part of the same destiny, am I not? For two hundred years, this land of Vermont has given to the nation whole cities and states full of useful men and women who fled screaming from the life of the farm—and it has taken in return at least one, less useful, who feels the same way.

No farming for me. Lord no.

Amanda was reluctant, but I kept after her, and in the end I prevailed. We Noons never quit. I wooed Amanda for all I was worth. She came to like it; she came to count on it. And, as I have suggested somewhere, she needed a warm place to live in the winter. Over the summer, Amanda's skin had become a kind of dark gold color, her hair a lighter brown, near blond, the color of certain honeys. She came to Bible Hill for good on a day in early September: two trips in her father's truck, me driving. She brought her own bed. She moved into her room. Amanda was there.

Platonically, she and I settled in to wait for the winter on Bible Hill—but the winter didn't come. It held off. The warm yellow days continued, and it was on one of them, when we went on a picnic to Sheep Desert, that I at last beheld Amanda out of her overalls.

"What are you looking at, Noon?" Amanda asked me.

"That mole," I said. "Right there."

"That mole?" said Amanda. "What about that mole, Noon?"

"I've been looking at that mole all summer," I said.

TOWN OF AMBROSE, VERMONT

Table of agricultural production: livestock, 1800–1980

	1800	1850	1900	1980
horses	149	222	195	16
milk cattle	74	41	836	51
beef cattle	1,499	777	28	2
sheep	61	19,444	1,599	4
swine	112	464	71	4
fowl	944	189	351	11
llamas	0	0	0	39
rodents, etc.*	0	0	0	235
ratites	0	0	0	7
marsupials	0	0	0	84

* I.e., chinchillas, nutrias, ranch mink

17. Economy

1

There was no money on Bible Hill. That suited me. I had taken a vow of poverty. I aimed to live cheap. I aimed to jump off the merry-go-round of getting and spending. I thought in a place like Bible Hill you could do that. Because Bible Hill supplied nothing to live on, I reckoned you could live there quite well on nothing. Not at all. Living on nothing costs money, I discovered. Could I afford to live in poverty? I wasn't sure.

What do I have? I asked myself. Well, I had the wages I got from the part-time, off-and-on, dumb-end jobs I picked up, the kind of job where you finished the week with a wad of greasy tens and twenties from the boss's pocket and the impression that his plans for the next week, as they affected you, were as yet unformed.

So far, not so good. But I also had what the old-fashioned novelists called a small private competence, in the form of my legacy from Usher via my mother: Littlejohn's place and a bank account producing between six and seven thousand a year. I thought I was rich, and so I was. Any money you don't have to work for is riches. But as always with money, the only important question is not whence or what kind, but how much—or, not even how much, but how much *exactly*?

Well, son, let's figure it out. We can do that: It's nothing but arithmetic. You've got seven thousand a year just for getting down to the post office, is that about it?

Six or seven.

Nice work if you can get it, like they say.

Nice? It's unbelievable. It's extraordinary. I had no idea. I'd hardly even heard of Hugo Usher. He was somebody my father knew in the war, but I never even saw him, you know? And here's all this.

"All this?" Well, let's see. Six thousand a year? Five hundred a month.

That's right. Five hundred dollars a month. Think of it.

You think of it, son. What I mean, five hundred bucks. A pretty good used car. Half your taxes. Two-thirds of a roof that don't leak. A winter's worth of number two oil, with luck. You see what I mean?

I suppose I do, if you want to be strict.

What other way's there to be son? We're doing arithmetic here. You've got free money but you ain't got a whole lot of free money. Then, plus, you've got your earnings. What's Milo paying these days?

Forty a day.

All strictly off the books, of course.

Of course.

Five days?

No.

Four?

It varies.

Three?

Sometimes.

But call it a hundred, hundred twenty-five a week.

Call it that.

So, all told, six twenty-five a month.

In summer.

In summer. Comes to seventy-five hundred a year, in there.

Mmm.

And that's the whole of it? No more's coming in?

That's it.

Well, it ain't nothing.

No.

No. But it ain't a lot. It looks like what you've got to do is, if you can't make the number over the line bigger, you better make the number under the line smaller. You see what I mean?

I see.

Thus far, Mr. Applegate. It was easy for him to talk: He wasn't trying to jump off the merry-go-round of getting and spending. He might drop as much money at the Joppa flea market each Sunday as I had made in the week past. Mr. Applegate had taken no vow of poverty. I grew weary of his arithmetic. I grew weary of his homilies. Nevertheless, a homily is partly true, or it wouldn't be a homily. Mr. Applegate was worth listening to, especially for me. I needed him. For, in living as in navigation, early error increases quickly.

June 1, 1921. Fair. Temp. 12M 72. To store a.m. nails @ .75/5 lb.

June 5, 1921. Rain a.m. Temp. 12M 65. To store. Hinge @ .05, screws @ .01

If you can't make the number over the line bigger, you'd better make the number under the line smaller. I gave up coffee, cut back on the beer. I quit smoking. Then I quit eating at the Weed and began cooking my chops at home, on the stove. Then I began cooking my hamburgers at home, then my eggs, then my beans, then my rice. I quit buying books, got a library card. We Noons know how to stretch.

It worked. I didn't die, didn't starve. I might have lost some weight, but I couldn't say for sure, as I owned no scale.

How's it going, son?

Great. I haven't eaten since yesterday's breakfast, I can't get my car out of first gear, taxes are due next week, Milo's gone to Florida, and I have three dollars and seven cents about my person.

You sound bitter, son.

Not at all. It's only that it's starting to get cold, being October. Have you noticed?

Matter of fact, I have.

I've been thinking about a winter coat, you know? One of those down-lined coats?

Those are good ones. Got your eye on one, have you?

Yes. I found a nice one in Brattleboro. On sale for seventy-nine ninety-five.

Is that right?

Yes. Did I tell you where the winter coat fund stands today? Three oh seven.

So you said. But look: A coat's only a coat, ain't it? Consider the lilies of the field, son.

2

June 9, 1921. Temp. 12M 77. Glass @ 1.00, pins @ .04, lemon @ .02

Littlejohn kept close account of his cash expenditures in his diary. In a flush week, he might lay out a buck and a half. I read him not without a certain wistfulness. In Littlejohn's day, surely, it was easier to be poor. But wait. *Easier to be poor.* It sounded uncomfortably, like a joke I didn't quite get. Still, there was one way in which Littlejohn clearly had an easier poverty than mine.

What did he tell you about your car, son?

New clutch.

That don't sound good.

No.

You took it to Raymond's, over here?

Yes.

Well, if Ray told you you need a new clutch, you probably do. What did he say for money?

Three hundred.

Three hundred. That means two hundred. Have you got two hundred?

No.

Can you drive it?

No. It's sitting out back of Raymond's. He won't fix it and send me a bill.

Of course not. Ray's been down that road before.

So have I. He's right. But what am I going to do for a car?

Look, son. Look here. I'm good for two hundred. Let me get that. Pay me when you can.

No. Thanks, but no.

Why not, son?

I'd never pay you back.

Sure you would.

I wouldn't. Anyway, I can get two hundred. I'll set it aside. Take awhile. But I'll be starting at Jordan's in another week. Milo's gone, so I don't need a car for him. I can walk to Jordan's.

Your car is your hardest master. You can't starve it; you can't neglect it. Having a car, for a poor man, is like having a violent creditor. You can deny yourself, but you can't deny him. You can only pay up.

"Take it, Noon," said Amanda. "Two hundred won't break him. Go on, why don't you?"

"I don't like to," I said. "I don't like to owe him that way."

"You wouldn't owe him," said Amanda. "You wouldn't have to pay him back; he doesn't really mean you should."

"I know he doesn't. I like that even less," I said.

"He wants to help you," said Amanda.

"I know."

"I don't get you, Noon," said Amanda. "You say you're trying to get by. You need two hundred dollars. Here's two hundred dollars. But you won't take it. That makes me wonder if you're for real here."

"Would you?" I asked her.

"Would I what?"

"Would you take two hundred from your father?"

"No," said Amanda.

"Why not?"

"It's different for me," said Amanda.

"Why?"

"It just is, Noon," said Amanda.

3

August 20, 1931. Warm. Temp. 12M 97. Dan lame. To livery, shoes @ .25

You come to understand that you can't jump off the merry-go-round of getting and spending, just because there is no place to jump off to. You can, however, slow it down some. And in doing so, you find you're not alone. You find you're not the only one who has taken a vow of poverty. You have joined an order. You have rules, monastic traditions. You have, really, a whole culture behind you, a cut-rate, job-lot culture of militant thrift. I learned, for example, that for every durable good, there is a secondhand market, if you can find it and if you do not insist on 100 percent function. Not only cars and books but clothes, furniture, appliances, machinery, tools, building materials, art, glass, crockery, sporting goods—if you could wait and if you could settle for an item a little off your need, they were to be had for nickels and dimes.

Beside the road to the Joppa district, on the old Mountain Fair grounds, a flea market was held on weekends from May through October. Over an area of three or four acres, there spread out an entire universe dedicated to the practice of poverty. At the flea market, you could buy a perfectly good coffee grinder without a handle, and you could buy a fifty-one-card deck of playing cards. (Why? For target practice.) And you could buy five-year-old copies of *National Geographic* and *Vermont Life* (sold by the bale). For any merchandise whatever, if it was out-of-date or didn't quite work, it would turn up at the flea market in time, and the price would be right. People who were interested in living cheap, either from necessity or as amateurs, went to the flea market in season the way pilgrims went to Canterbury.

I went to the Joppa flea market with Mr. Applegate. He was a regular there. In the gray dawn, Mr. Applegate loped along the periphery of the flea market with his tongue lolling, as a prairie wolf lopes beside a herd of buffalo. He was looking for calves, naifs, innocents who had cleaned out their dead aunt's attic and knew not what they had, knew only that they did not want to pack it all up and take it home again, unsold, at the end of the day.

Mr. Applegate picked up an eggbeater bearing a one-dollar tag. He examined it. He turned the crank, found it the least bit stiff.

"Can you take a quarter?" asked Mr. Applegate.

August 30, 1931. Fair. Temp. 12M 80. Dan heaves. Dose @ .10

Mr. Applegate took me to school to the flea market. You have to be sharp, but not too sharp, look hard, but not too hard; for finally, at the flea market as elsewhere, you advance by saying yes, not no. You can look and you can trade, but at last you must close.

"What's this, Noon?" Amanda asked.

"It's a tricycle. I got it for a dollar," I said.

"Why?"

"Well, I thought it might be good to have, you know?"

"Why?"

"Well," I said, "if you were to find yourself pregnant one day? If we were to have a baby one day, I thought."

"I found myself pregnant once before, Noon," said Amanda. "I didn't much like it. I'm not in a hurry to do it again. No babies, Noon. If you want to have a baby, have it by yourself. Leave me out of it."

"All right," I said.

"Besides," said Amanda, "look at this thing. It doesn't have all its wheels." Amanda didn't miss much.

"Look," I said. "It cost a buck. For a buck, you don't get new. Those little back wheels? You can pick them up anywhere. I'll find one, stick it on. Then if we should ever need a tricycle, we'll have one, that's all. Or we can sell it, for two dollars, for five, even ten. It's an investment. You ought to thank me."

"You puzzle me, Noon," said Amanda. "You're so cheap. You use tea bags twice. Then you come home with something like this. What's it all mean, you know?"

"Who says I'm cheap?" I demanded.

"Listen," said Amanda later. Evidently, she had been turning that exchange over in her mind. "If we did have a baby, she would have a new tricycle. Hear me? A new one. Brand-new. No flea market. You've been spending too much time with my dad, you know that?"

4

September 5, 1931. Temp. 12M 77. To livery. Fixx harness @ .50

Burning some oil, ain't you, son?

Some.

What's Ray say?

Valve job.

I'm real sorry to hear that. What's that cost, about, does he say?

Seven hundred. Eight hundred.

Uh-oh. Well, at least you can drive it this time.

Not for long, he says.

Another eight hundred. Is that right?

That's right. I'm tempted to walk away, you know?

Can't do that, son. You just got done paying for the new clutch. You can't stop now, can you?

I'm thinking about getting a horse.

Ha, ha. Who can blame you?

I'm not kidding. I'll have put a thousand bucks into that car in three weeks. I know perfectly well that next month something else will break on it. I know that, do you see?

Don't do it, son. It don't pay. Hugo tried the same thing, with horses. He lived to regret it.

No, wait. Here's the way I've got it figured. Ray will give me two hundred for my car, he says. I can get a horse for four. I've already got the shed; I can keep him there. I've got grass. I'd have to buy, like, hay, grain, tack. That's it. It looks pretty good to me.

I'm telling you: Don't do it. Don't think of it.

Why not? There's Mrs. Chadwick, the one you see riding around town on her horse. Hepburn's got that little pony cart; you see him running it all over. You see it parked out front of Clifford's. He's even got a sleigh, for winter. No more clutches, no more valve jobs, no more gas and oil, no more tires. It looks like business to me.

Mrs. Chadwick and Fred Hepburn have horses because they like horses. Do you like horses?

Well, I don't dislike them.

That ain't going to do it for you, son. Forget about it. Getting a horse to save money on transport's like washing your socks in scotch to save on water. If you're old car's had the course, Ray will sell you another one.

I don't doubt that.

Of course, Mr. Applegate was right. When you take the vow of poverty and join the order, you become a dreamer of a certain kind.

Most people dream of riches. They dream of spending a lottery win or they dream of an inheritance as unforeseen as mine and far, far larger. In the order, we dream the other way: We dream of horses, of windmills and tiny turbines and other ingenious feats of engineering. We dream of snug, warm, convenient houses built of hay bales or discarded telephone poles or old tires or plastic milk jugs. We dream of a life like Littlejohn's—indeed, a life where it's easy to be poor and you can cruise along from one year's end to the next handling thirty, forty dollars in cash, no more.

April 1, 1934. Rain. Temp. 12M 47. Dan sick. Dose @ .75

Hugo was of your same way of thinking exactly, son. He was always trying to think how to cut his living expenses—which was a little peculiar, because Hugo was about the richest man in town. Maybe not the richest, but not far from it. And it seems as though the rich can live cheap if anybody can, but Hugo never had any luck with it. He had the same idea you had for horses: no gas, no oil, no tires, no tune-ups, no repair bills; eats grass, which Hugo had plenty of, and a little grain. Plus, Hugo already had a two-wheeled runabout that had been his father's when they'd had horses on their place years ago. He decided he'd get a horse to pull it and go back to simpler days. This was right after the war, and a lot of people were thinking along those lines. I don't know why. Hugo went out looking for a horse to buy. The only one in town was Claude's Dan.

Littlejohn wasn't selling, he told Usher. Hell no. Not Dan. He needed Dan around the place. Maybe he didn't have cows anymore, but he still farmed, didn't he? How was he going to keep the mowings open, how was he going to draw wood, how was he going to gather sap without Dan? No, he didn't like to sell Dan.

Besides, Dan was no ordinary horse, Littlejohn explained. He was smart. He knew his way to Littlejohn's from anyplace in the town or the towns adjoining; many times, Littlejohn had simply gone to sleep in the back of the wagon and let Dan carry him home. Then, too, Dan was versatile. You could put a saddle on Dan whenever you liked—not the case with all farm horses. In fact, Dan was a jumper, which saved time putting up and taking down bars, and he could climb like a goat. Littlejohn couldn't part with Dan for less than a hundred dollars.

Usher had his checkbook out.

But then, Littlejohn said, he needed to think it over: He was damned if he'd let himself be euchered here. Dan was a steady horse, a working horse, a horse in his prime. And he was also a bred horse, out of the original Morgan line from the state farm. Littlejohn had the book on Dan someplace; he knew he had. What had he done with that book . . . ?

"We'll say a hundred and twenty-five," said Usher.

Not so fast, though, Littlejohn told him, because, after all, it looked like he was going to have to buy himself another horse when Dan was sold, didn't it? And he had to have something to show for the deal besides an unknown animal, didn't he?

"A hundred and fifty ought to take care of it," Usher suggested.

The truth was, Littlejohn had been thinking about a small tractor, like Cruikshank had gotten. He'd even talked to a dealer in White River who traded used. Littlejohn wasn't young, after all: A tractor might be the best thing. No grass, no grain, no stabling. In White River, the young fellow had a used Ford he'd let Littlejohn have for three hundred dollars. Two hundred for the horse, then, was Usher's cost.

Now, it was not lost on Usher that his transaction with Littlejohn seemed to be running in reverse. In bargaining, the numbers are supposed to get smaller; Usher's numbers were getting larger. He was bargaining backward. Nevertheless, he meant to have that horse.

Then a couple of days after Hugo gets Dan back to his place, he goes out to the barn one morning and Dan's lying in his stall, barely breathing. So Hugo calls the vet, and the vet comes out and looks Dan down one end and up the other and tells Hugo there's nothing wrong with him except that he's a very, very old *horse. Probably the exertion of moving all the way from Claude's to Hugo's was too much. Nothing the vet can do—apart from charging Hugo thirty bucks for the call. The next day, he has to pay another thirty to get Arthur Marlow to bring his backhoe over and bury Dan. Keep clear of horses, son.*

But Littlejohn cheated him.

Did he? How? Claude never told Hugo any lies about Dan—at least he didn't tell him any lies a half-wit would believe. All Claude did was let Hugo do what he wanted to do, which was buy the horse. It wasn't any great deal for Claude, either, in the end. Selling Dan, nobody made out. Claude didn't get a tractor; he got another horse for his place, but this time he got too much horse.

I still say Usher was right about getting a horse in principle. He was right economically.

Economically, son?

5

July 20, 1921. Fair. Temp. 12M 70. Pea flowers. To store, pepper @ .08

July 21, 1921. Fair. Temp. 12M 70

Mr. Applegate said that if I couldn't increase the numerator, I was to decrease the denominator, and so hold a living ratio. I would go him one better, I decided: I would take myself out of the cash economy altogether, take myself right out of it. I would sing for my supper, not for the penny that bought the supper. We Noons are resourceful.

"What were you thinking of doing, exactly?" Amanda asked me.

"Barter," I said.

"Yeah, but with what? What's your end? You're already working at the mill."

"I'm working for Noble Groom, too," I said. "I started yesterday."

"Doing what?" Amanda asked.

"Pumping gas."

"Well, then," Amanda said. "You're working two jobs for wages. How are you going to find time to work another for no wages?"

"I'll make time," I said. "You have to improvise."

"I don't know, Noon," Amanda said. "I'm still not sure what it all means, you know? Here you are. You've got all this college; you're a smart guy. You're running from one end of town to the other, working two lousy jobs, looking for a third. I don't see why you don't just get one good job."

Skeptics. I was surrounded by skeptics. Mr. Applegate with his numerator and his denominator, with his doubts about the horse. He was blinded by skepticism. Amanda, too. Amanda loved the pilgrim soul in me, I thought; though she might not know it yet. But she, too, was blinded by skepticism. Amanda was a skeptic on barter; she was a skeptic on getting out of the cash economy. There, she might have been in the right, I decided. It wasn't easy. Your tax collector, your insurance company, your bank aren't interested in having you cut their grass or wash their windows in lieu of payments you have contracted to make in U.S. funds. I didn't get much further with Raymond, at the garage.

"Let's see what it is here," said Raymond. "I'm going to put new valves and rings into your vehicle, and you're going to do . . . what?"

"Whatever you need," I said. "Cut the grass, wash the windows. Anything."

"I don't think so," said Raymond.

"Well, something else, then," I said. "Painting. Do you need anything painted?"

"Maybe," Raymond said. "You buy the paint?"

"Well, no," I said. "You buy it. But I do all the painting."

Raymond shook his head.

"It don't work, you know?" he said. "Let's keep it simple. I fix your motor. You pay me."

"That's not simple," I said. "This is."

"Maybe so," said Raymond. "But here's the thing. We've got our oldest boy, Raymond junior, started at Princeton last year, you know?"

"Princeton?" I said. "Boy. He must be a pretty bright kid."

"Math whiz," said Raymond. "They gave him half his tuition on scholarship. So he's down there. He's doing real well. Do you know what it costs, even half off?"

"I don't want to hear," I said.

"Neither do I," said Raymond. "But I do. I hear every fall and every spring. And Princeton, you know, they don't need me to fix their cars or cut their grass when tuition's due. You know what I mean?"

"Yes."

"I'll work on your vehicle for six hundred. I'll do that. But I've got to have cash."

It almost looks like none of us can jump off the merry-go-round of getting and spending until we all do. We must join hands and leap together like lovers going over a cliff. It's not going to happen.

Shall we admit, at last, that we are pretty much stuck on the aforesaid merry-go-round? That the flea market is a field of fantasy, barter a delusion? That the vow of poverty is today somehow vain or irrelevant? And shall we then go on to blame good times? After all, in Littlejohn's day, when seven or eight people out of ten scarcely had a pot to piss in, the entire national economy was contrived so as to keep them alive, for who else would make it go? It was easy to be poor because almost everybody was poor. Now, seven or eight people out of ten are doing comparatively well, and two or three out of ten possess the kind of wealth formerly enjoyed by a tiny fraction. Youthful stockbrokers, bankers, lawyers, and traders, people of no unusual talent or force, who ought to be delaying gratification, who ought to be anxiously computing their meager household budgets at the kitchen tables of cold-water flats, are buying town houses, country houses, cattle ranches in Montana, boats, airplanes. In the state of Vermont, historically a place of little wealth, there are said to be between seventy-five and a hundred taxpayers reporting annual incomes in excess of a million dollars. In this very township a year or two ago, one of the old houses on the village common—by no means the best house—was sold for $650,000, a price that must amount to the grand list for the whole town over the entire nineteenth century, summed.

No wonder it's hard to be poor. The poor are obsolete. What happened? Shall we blame the rich? No. Pass them by, ignore them.

Don't let them distract you from your duty, your service. The rich, you have always with you.

August 22, 1921. Rain. Temp. 12M 65. To store, glue @ .07, ribon for S.B. @ .79

18. Casualties

1

Somebody had gotten into Calabrese's. They had broken down his door. They had turned his place over. Where were his dogs?

Calabrese had taken a second-shift job at one of the printing plants in Brattleboro. He got home past midnight. He found his door down, his little house ransacked. At one o'clock, he was at our place. November: into the cold nights. Calabrese woke us up with his pounding on the door.

Had we seen anybody on the road, anything, a delivery truck, a car we didn't know? Calabrese demanded. Had we heard anything? No.

"Anything," Calabrese said. "A car, a dog, shots, talking—any sound?"

Nothing. We'd heard nothing.

"What did they take?" I asked him.

"I don't know," Calabrese said. "Maybe nothing."

"What about the dogs?" Amanda asked. "Why didn't the dogs keep them out?"

"I don't know," said Calabrese.

"Where are they?" Amanda asked him. "The dogs?"

"Gone," said Calabrese.

He had been excited when he came to our door, but he wasn't excited now. Now he was thinking. Calabrese had been angry, but he wasn't angry now. He shut up. He sat on the couch.

"There's nothing we can do tonight," I said. "Tomorrow morning, call the sheriff."

"The sheriff?" said Calabrese.

"It's almost two," I said. "What do you want to do?"

"Do?" said Calabrese.

"Stay here," Amanda said. "Stay here tonight; then in the morning, we'll see."

Calabrese nodded.

He lay on the couch, then, and Amanda and I went back to bed. I didn't sleep again that night, and neither did Amanda, or not much—and neither, I expect, did Calabrese. He lay on the couch with his eyes open, thinking. You could hear him thinking. *Carlo's trouble,* Mr. Applegate had said. Calabrese had trouble; he had an affinity for trouble. But what exactly the trouble was, he didn't say.

Trouble. Bible Hill was a place not without trouble, of course. How otherwise, being, whatever else it was, a patch of earth populated by mortals, by mortal, cutable, bruisable, breakable flesh? For, touching on trouble, I aim here to be quite elementary. I'm not even beginning on the troubles of the heart or the spirit, but confine myself to the material, to accidents: falls, breaks, blows, collisions. The subject is first-order trouble, whose theory comes not from the likes of Saint Augustine or even Sigmund Freud but simply from Sir Isaac Newton: Slip, trip—and you fall.

There were farming accidents and logging accidents and hunting accidents and mill accidents. In our time, there were a light million at least of car crashes, but if you went back, there was much more: train wrecks, stage wrecks, even sleigh wrecks.

These kinds of trouble belonged to the past. The past had its own species of trouble, as, for instance, the realm of domestic animals, trouble with which Bible Hill was well supplied, oversupplied. Principally, the accident-prone animal was the horse. There were people who fell from horses, horses who fell on people. There were crazy horses; runaway horses; kicking, biting, bucking horses. Nor were horses the only dangerous beasts of the farm. There were people killed by bulls, stepped on by cows, butted by goats. Burgoyne, the selectman, had a boy whose arm had once been broken by a pig, and Mr. Applegate knew of a man in Dead River who had lost an eye to an angry chicken.

Wild animals made their own trouble. Rabid foxes, rabid bats, rabid raccoons had added many a gravestone to the cemeteries of the town. There was a legend from the time of the first settlements of a boy killed by wolves. The wolves were gone, of course. There were no longer the kinds of wildlife on Bible Hill that anyone could believe would take a child. But there were other beasts of the field that were unpredictable and might go against type to make trouble. The books will tell you that the black bear of the New England woodlands is harmless to man, for example, but in the year of my birth, a squirrel hunter named Eldon Drinkwater was killed by a bear on Round Mountain. Exactly how it had happened was uncertain: Evidently, the bear had rolled over on him.

Yes, trouble was abundant on Bible Hill. But, there as everywhere, trouble—or anyway first-order, Newtonian trouble—was not as common as it seemed. Even on Bible Hill, there there have never been nearly enough falling trees, runaway teams, or poisonous mushrooms to go around. I myself, even as I enter middle age, have never broken a bone. You can't count on accidents for your trouble; sometimes you have to go out and make your own.

THE WORLD AS IT IS

Hitchcock and I left the capital the same night they began burning the embassies. We left in a Fiat taxi that might have been manufactured in the time of Mussolini. The bridge across the harbor was guarded, but we got through because Hitchcock bribed the guard. Another roadblock had been set up on the boulevard that led out of the capital through the rich suburb of Esmeralda. There were palm trees beside the boulevard, big ones, seventy-five feet or more tall. One had been cut down and made to fall across the boulevard. That was the roadblock. Ten or fifteen men, some in army uniforms, some apparently drunk, all armed, guarded the barrier. Hitchcock got us past them, too. He spotted the guard who was in command and gave him five hundred dollars U.S. The commander shouted to the others. They crowded around the top of the cut-down palm. The commander shouted again. Working together, the guards seized the end of the great trunk, raised it, and moved it out of the way enough for our taxi to pass. When we were through, they moved it back.

Hitchcock had gotten us out of the burning capital. He had done it by understanding instinctively whom he had to pay off. I couldn't have managed it, but Hitchcock always knew who was in charge. As long as he had unlimited money about him, he could do anything.

We arrived at a village on the coast, twenty or thirty miles north of the capital. The taxi wouldn't go farther, but Hitchcock thought we could get a bus in the village. The new day had begun, though the sun was still behind the long mountains to the east. They stood black and sharp with the pale light increasing behind them in the hard dawn of that country. Hitchcock and I sat on a bench before the square in the village. The square was gray in the dawn shadows, but there were people about and much poultry: chickens and some other like birds that might have been guinea fowl.

"Don't worry, Mark," said Hitchcock. "Storm in a teapot. In six months, we'll be back, business as usual."

"Not me," I said.

"No, of course not," Hitchcock said. "Not you. You're for Vermont. The Robert Frost thing, isn't it? Rusticating? The simple life? Chop wood. Milk the cow. Pick apples. Make a little maple sugar when you feel like it. Don't do it, Mark. You'll hate it."

"Maybe," I said.

The bus from the south drove into the square and stopped. Several women began to chase the fowls that scratched in the street. They caught them, put them into crates. The chickens were taking the bus, too. The sun rose clear of the cordillera and in an instant the village was full of heat and flat, glaring light. In an hour, the square would be as hot as a griddle. Hitchcock and I got ready to follow the women onto the bus. The chickens and other fowl squawked and screamed as the women passed their crates into the bus. Some of them could not be made to go into their crates. They squawked and screamed and flapped their wings, and the women did the same. Hitchcock and I followed them.

"Look at it, Mark," said Hitchcock. "Fix it in your mind. It's a poor country, but it's alive. They're alive down here. See it? This is the world as it is, Mark. Vermont? Vermont is not the world as it is. Vermont is the North. The North is over and done with. Don't go there, Mark. Don't take the wrong path."

November 1, 1952. Rain. Temp. 6 a.m. 57. Stayed inn. Leg bad
November 3, 1952. Fair. Temp. 6 a.m. 42. P.m. to schoolteachers for wood 1/2 cord. $5

2

Accidents. So many accidents. On Bible Hill, we were brained by falling branches, blown up by our own dynamite, crushed by our own tractors, hewn by our own chain saws. Littlejohn was crippled by the horse he'd bought to replace the aged horse, Dan, he'd sold Usher.

"Kicked him," Miss Drumheller said. "Broke his thigh. He never walked right after that. He could never really work again. He lost his place. It was the beginning of the end for him, that horse. No reason for it. A horse doesn't need a reason. One day he went to feed, the horse kicked him. They do that—did that. Something went wrong; the bone didn't set straight, I think. It got worse and worse. But, really, all the farmers were the same way; they were all injured one way or another: missing fingers, hands, broken legs. Claude Littlejohn had a couple of fingers gone himself, along with all the rest."

Not that any of them had much of Miss Drumheller's sympathy in their misfortune, not even forty years later—in particular, not Littlejohn.

"Pity the poor guy," I said. "He had bad luck."

"He was stupid," said Miss Drumheller. "Not stupid, worse—insane. Certainly he had bad luck. Everyone has bad luck. What do you do? is the only question. What he did was insane. You don't expect farmers to be intelligent, but you expect them at least to be practical, rational people in their own way. You find they're not. You find they're as crazy as the rest."

For six weeks, Littlejohn had been unable to walk. Neighbors did his chores, kept his place going as best they could, but neighbors were few. At the end of six weeks, Littlejohn was still laid up. He was about at the end of his rope. He was alone. He was broke. He was in pain.

At last, he found himself able to hobble about on a stick. The first day he could, he loaded his deer rifle and limped to the barn, but the new horse saw the gun and wouldn't lead. Littlejohn left the rifle outside the barn, returned to the horse, got a bridle on it, and painfully led it out of the barn, down the yard, over the brook, and into the pasture. He left it there. He went back to the house, got the rifle, took it into the pasture, waited until the horse began to graze, and shot it a little above and between the eyes, the way you're supposed to. He left it for the crows. It had taken him most of a day to get the horse shot.

"Insane," said Miss Drumheller. "For, now, where things had been difficult, he'd made them impossible. With no horse, he had no farm. He had no way to live. He went on the town. He became a charity case. Eventually, he had to sell out to Hugo Usher."

"You told me," I said.

The day after Calabrese's place was broken into, I went back there with him. The door looked as though it had been hit above the lock with a sledgehammer or a heavy ram; it had ripped out of the frame, splitting off the woodwork inside. Nothing else was damaged.

Clearly, the place had been searched. Every drawer stood open; a footlocker had been overturned and its contents scattered on the floor. The bed had been stood up on its side. Cabinets in the kitchen were open. But Calabrese said nothing had been taken. He had a radio that ran on batteries. It sat on the kitchen table. There was a bottle of rum two-thirds full on the counter. Calabrese's shotgun, which he had once wanted me to use to warn him of intruders, stood in the corner.

Kids, I thought for a moment. Half the high school boys in the town kept up a sideline in breaking into places like Calabrese's; it was a form of sport with them. But if kids had gotten into Calabrese's, they would have smashed and broken, and they would have taken things, maybe not the radio, but probably the shotgun, and certainly the rum.

"These weren't kids," said Calabrese.

And what about the dogs? For the five or six years that Calabrese had lived on Bible Hill, nobody had made an attempt on his place because of his brace of dogs, which were known by all to be killers. Now there was no sign of either of them. Had the housebreakers shot them? No: Amanda and I would have heard shots. What, then? Poison? Calabrese and I searched the area of the cabin, then went into the woods, but we found no hair of the two great dogs, no track, and as far as I know, they were never seen again.

I wouldn't be surprised if they hadn't just taken off.

Taken off?

That's right. Carlo didn't much do for them, did he?

No.

He left them outside, didn't feed them much.

To keep them keen, he said.

You can keep a dog too keen, son. Carlo didn't shelter them. Didn't pet them. Didn't feed them. Didn't even give them names. Dogs ain't dumb, you know. I bet they decided they could make themselves a better deal someplace else.

No way of knowing, I guess.

No, there ain't. But that's my guess. They just took off. Partly it's the time of year, you know? Getting dark, getting cold. We had a frost down here last night. Did you?

No.

Well, you're up on the hill there. But it's coming. Frost. Winter's coming: Next time it rains, it might snow. They get restless this time of year. They take off.

Dogs?

Not just dogs. You see how the deer are moving around this time of year? The turkeys? Everything is apt to just pick up and go. Bears.

Bears don't go anywhere. They're looking for a den. They're looking for acorns, beechnuts, berries, fattening up for the winter.

I guess. But it ain't only game. Not at all. It's a bad-luck time of year, it just is. Fall. Deer season.

Bad luck for the deer anyway.

It ain't only the game. Not at all. For instance, it was this time of year that Hugo took off. November. I don't think Hugo was looking for beechnuts and berries and the rest, do you? There's something in the time of the year that's bad luck. Deer season.

May 15, 1955. Cool. Temp. 12M 67. p.m. to schoolteachers dug garden. Worms. $3
May 19, 1955. Holds cool. Temp. 6 a.m. 53

I was about to say that the worst accident to occur in the township in my own time was the crash of the small plane that turned its pilot and his passenger, Connecticut men, into spare parts. Maybe it wasn't the worst, in one way, as its victims were strangers, but it was bad enough: It was like nothing I had ever seen or imagined, before or since. Arthur Brackett and I were the first to find the crash. We saw it all, or anyway one of us did.

The plane went down on a Saturday in May, just as the springtime arrived for good and the hillsides assumed their green. The pilot lived in West Hartford. He was a lawyer, or he worked for one of the insurance companies, or he was in real estate: Whatever his line was, he was doing well enough at it that he owned an airplane and knew how to fly it. He and his brother-in-law took off from the airport at Windsor Locks for an afternoon of buzzing around over Vermont, following the spring north. They took off about ten in the morning. At half past twelve, they flew into the side of Round Mountain.

The state police had alerted the county sheriff's office and the Ambrose fire department. A search was organized. Nobody knew exactly where the plane had crashed, for no one had seen it go down and there had been no fire. But Ingrid St. Just had been working in the garden behind her house on the Joppa road and had heard the plane pass overhead with its engine coughing, popping, evidently failing. Therefore, we began to search up the mountain from back of St. Just's. They sent us out in pairs. I was with Tubby.

We were on the south side of Round Mountain, which is thickly wooded and goes up by a series of shelves: a level pitch, a steep pitch, another level. It's tough hiking. Tubby and I had been out for an hour when he stopped and pointed.

"There it is," said Tubby.

A hundred feet ahead, where the hill began to rise sharply again, a thing that looked like a big bedsheet hung from the branches of a little stand of firs. We approached it. To our right were more pieces of the same stuff, and beyond the firs was a place where the trees were knocked down and their tops smashed, with a few broken right off. The bedsheet was some kind of light metal, evidently part of the plane's body. We went around it, around the firs.

As we did, I became aware, almost in an instant, of several things, several ways in which, I now quickly understood, I had been wrong about the experience I was about to have. I had expected to find dazed, injured people and help them, as in a car wreck on the highway—but that was not what we would find. I had expected to find an aircraft, more or less beat-up—but that was not what we would find. What was it that we would find? When Tubby and I came out of the firs into the opening where the trees were broken down, I thought for a second we had found the wrong wreck: This was no airplane; somebody had crashed a butcher's van up here.

With no warning, my stomach flew up into my throat. I turned right around and stumbled back into the firs.

Tubby paid no attention to me. He went ahead into the opening. He went out among the ruined trees, into the blood and matter hanging from their branches and flung over the ground, over the new ferns. Tubby picked up something and set it carefully out of his way. He stepped over something else. He looked around, turned, and came back to where I waited. I was on my knees, panting like a dog. Tubby's clothes were spotted with blood. Blood had soaked the cuffs of his trousers the way the dew will soak them when you walk through ferns or long grass early in the morning. There was blood in his hair.

"You okay?" said Tubby.

He didn't care. He simply didn't care. He walked through it. I've never seen anything like that before. Yes, I've seen dead people, bad ones. I've seen people shot. I've seen blood. But never like that. Tubby? It didn't seem to affect him one way or another. He walked through it. I don't know how that's possible.

Well, son, you're never seen anything like that before, but Tubby has.

Where? How? You mean in the war?

He meant in the war. Tubby walked unmoved through an encounter that no one should have to endure even as a nightmare, unmoved because of the war. Whatever hell accident could lay out on a mountainside in southern Vermont, Tubby had passed through a thousand times, ten thousand times worse on a single morning in 1944 on that famous French beach. He had come through it, but not whole. Here he showed his scars, his withered limbs. The war had killed his heart; it had turned him to stone, had burned forever the circuit that leads from blood to fear and pity. They can't give you a medal heavy enough to pay you back for that. Tubby was a monster.

"You okay?" said Tubby. "It looks to me like they told us to find them and we found them. There ain't nothing we can do here, so we might as well go on down. You okay?"

"What did he say?" Amanda asked me.

"Nothing," I said. "Somebody broke in. They didn't take anything. They were warning him, I guess is what he says."

"Who was?"

"He won't say."

"Warning him about what?" Amanda asked.

"He won't say," I told her. "Something is wrong from before he came up here, but he never says what it is."

"So, kind of like you, right, Noon?" Amanda asked me.

"Like me?"

"That's right," said Amanda. "Your old job, you know? Down south? You won't tell me what happened down there."

"Sweetheart," I told Amanda, "if I knew what happened down there, I'd tell you."

THE WRONG PATH

For a day and a night and another day, Hitchcock and I rode the bus north along the coast. We left the cordillera and came out onto a high rolling desert, brown and white, with the level gray sea appearing and disappearing far off behind blue headlands that came and went. The women with their poultry left the bus, and other women, also with poultry, got on. Toward sundown on the second day, we arrived at a town big enough to have a hotel. There, Hitchcock put us up.

"We part here," Hitchcock said.

"We do?"

"Yes," said Hitchcock. "You go on by rail, cross into Mexico. You're ticketed right through to Guadalajara. Then you're on a flight to Dallas. You ought to be there Friday."

"And you?"

"I stay down here for the present," Hitchcock said. "I'll be working down here with Tompkins."

"Tompkins?"

"I'll explain at dinner," said Hitchcock.

Hitchcock explained nothing at dinner, but he did produce Tompkins, a plump red-haired fellow dressed like a tourist. Hitchcock said Tompkins was a major in the air force, and for all I know, he may have been just that. Whatever he was, Tompkins said hardly a word through dinner but sat in his chair and put down, by my count, nine large bourbons without visible effect.

Hitchcock, on the other hand, became quite merry, then quite somber.

"We won't meet again, Mark," he said.

"No?"

"I'm afraid not. You're completely unfit for the work we have to do down here. You'll agree with me on that?"

"Yes."

"Completely unfit. Still, you're not a bad fellow. I've grown to like you, Mark."

"I like you, too."

"Do you?" Hitchcock asked. He was tight. "Do you, Mark? Yes, I expect you do. You have a kind of charm, an honesty. I like that about you, Mark. That's why I hate to see you make a wrong turn. Take the wrong path. This business of Vermont, Mark: It won't do. It's the wrong path. You have fucked up down here, God knows, but that's not a reason to take the wrong path; that's not a reason to go flying off to the opposite extreme like some sort of . . . some sort of . . . Do you see what I mean, Mark?"

"Yes."

"Vermont is extreme," said Hitchcock. "It's the wrong path. Vermont is a snare and a delusion, Mark."

"I'll have to see for myself," I said. "If I don't like it, maybe I'll be back."

"You're joking again," said Hitchcock. "Don't joke, Mark."

The next morning, Hitchcock took me to the station in a taxi. Tompkins was among the missing.

"Under the weather. He drinks, you know," said Hitchcock, who seemed himself to be bright as a bird. He gave me an envelope containing my tickets, five thousand Mexican pesos, two thousand dollars U.S., and a passport having my name and photo but issued by Canada. Thank God for our brother to the north, our good twin, vast, cold, harmless.

Hitchcock shook my hand, and I climbed on board the train.

Hitchcock stood on the platform, waving. I entered the car, found a place by a window that let you see down onto the platform, but when I took my seat and looked out for him, Hitchcock was gone.

3

In shooting the horse that had broken his leg, Littlejohn had lost whatever chance he'd had to return to the only life he'd known. He might as well have shot himself. *Insane,* Miss Drumheller had said: He had committed an impulsive, irrational act. I thought I understood Littlejohn better than she. Miss Drumheller hadn't followed her own logic as far as it would go. Littlejohn had lain up for six, seven weeks after the horse kicked him. Then he'd risen and shot it. That was no impulse. If Littlejohn had destroyed the life he'd known, maybe that had been his purpose.

For the years left to him—eight or ten—he became Bible Hill's sexton, a lowly workman about the sacred precincts, obscure, nearly invisible. He worked for the Bracketts, for Miss Drumheller, for the summer people. He mowed lawns, chopped wood, hauled trash. He did hammer-and-nail repairs around their houses. They would pay him a few dollars, more than the work he did was worth. He had as well poor relief from the town. He didn't need much.

"Oh, he'd do what he could," Miss Drumheller said. "For years, I had hired him to get in my firewood. He still did that. He couldn't get around well, but he could do that. It took him a long time, because he couldn't move fast, but he was still very strong in the arms and shoulders, and he stuck to the job—not like the people you hire now. He was a good worker, I suppose.

I'll grant that. I'd give him five dollars, ten dollars. He wouldn't only work on the wood. He'd do whatever needed doing outside. I wouldn't let him in the house."

"Why not?" I asked her.

"I was a woman alone here," said Miss Drumheller. "It wouldn't have been right. You wouldn't understand. You're a different generation. Look at you and Amanda Applegate carrying on up there, living together openly. You couldn't have done that thirty years ago."

"Yes, we could," I said.

Miss Drumheller didn't hear that.

"He didn't care," she said. "He needed whatever work he could get. He was glad to have it. And I'd feed him, bring out cookies, lemonade, coffee. Give him some to take home with him. We all would. Give him bread, garden stuff, even a hot dish. No alcohol, though. No beer. He wanted beer. 'You wouldn't have a cold bottle of beer?' he'd ask. He'd always ask for beer and he'd always ask about Sibyl. Had I heard from Sibyl?"

"Had you?"

"No," said Miss Drumheller.

"He kept on asking for her?"

"He did," said Miss Drumheller. "He had his reasons."

She looked at me: a thin smile.

"Where is she, then?"

"I have no idea," said Miss Drumheller. "I don't imagine she's still living."

September 30, 1957. Frost. Temp. 12 M 60. Took Nachtigal's old sink to dump. $2

October 1, 1957. Temp. 12M 55. Rain. Stayed inn. Leg

I never really got the whole story there.

You mean Hugo? Neither did anybody else, son. There ain't a lot to get.

He went out into the woods and never came back?

That's it. Hugo disappeared. This same time of year, the way I said, 1963. Hugo went up there to Round Mountain, right behind his place. Took his rifle, said he'd see if he couldn't get a look at a deer. Deer season, the way I said. He didn't come back. They looked for him most of two days, searching the woods up there. Had the state police, had dogs, the whole thing. Then a big storm blew in, the way they will that early every few years. Foot of snow, foot and a half. No point in looking for him after that.

So what happened is, he went up Round Mountain and shot himself.

Don't know, son. It's possible.

Well, isn't that the inference?

It's your inference.

What else could have happened to him?

About anything, it looks like. He could have had some kind of stroke, some kind of fit. He could have had an accident, a fall, busted his leg, his back, no way to let anybody know, died in the snow, when it came. He could have kept right on going over the mountain and down the other side, caught a ride, caught another ride, and be having a drink right this minute in Paris, France. Nobody knows.

You don't believe he's in Paris, though.

I can't say I do, son. Hugo's dead, but what happened to him nobody is ever going to know. That bothered me for a time after he took off, but it don't anymore.

I say he killed himself.

I say he didn't. Hugo didn't have any use for the world. The world outside, the world right here. He didn't have a high opinion of people.

The law, the government, Hugo hated it all, he said. It looked to Hugo like it was all going straight to hell. It pissed him off, all of it, all the time. That type don't usually kill themselves. They did, they'd miss out on seeing how much worse things can get. It's the contented ones that kill themselves—them and the ones that don't care.

June 15, 1957. Gray. Temp, 12M 61. p.m. to Bracketts to burn brush. $4

Calabrese was still thinking. He was thinking through his next move. I helped him put his busted door back up and straighten his scattered effects.

"What were they looking for?" I asked.

"They weren't looking for anything," said Calabrese. "They were talking to me. They were telling me, We know where you're at."

"Who was?"

"A bunch of people," said Calabrese. "What's it matter? Fuckers. They found me; let's see if they can take me."

"They who?" I kept asking him. "The same ones that were here that time: the lady in the Mercedes, the major?"

"Never mind," said Calabrese.

"What's going on?"

"Look, kid," said Calabrese. "I could tell you, but then you'd know. You know?"

"What are you going to do?" I asked Calabrese.

"I can do two things," he said. "I can stay here, try to make some kind of deal—I don't know what—or I can get moving. Again."

Calabrese was quiet for a minute. He shook his head.

"That's my choice," he said. "It's not a choice. You know what I mean? The fucking choice is not a choice."

THE BORDER

Hitchcock told me to go to Dallas. I didn't go to Dallas. I tried, but at the airport in Guadalajara, I found my new Canadian passport set off every alarm they had. Two policemen took me from the passport-control desk to a room behind, where they sat me down in a chair, told me to wait, and locked me in. I sat there for an hour, for two hours. The time for my flight to Dallas came and went. What was I to do? Well, I still had most of the money Hitchcock had given me. Hitchcock would use that money. He'd give some to the policemen, some to their captain, and walk away. I could do the same; I could try Hitchcock's way. But I doubted Hitchcock now. Hitchcock had said that passport was safe. It wasn't. Had Hitchcock been misinformed? I thought not. I never knew what Hitchcock's game was, but I always knew he had one. At least one. I sat in the room in the airport in Guadalajara.

It occurred to me that waiting for the police to come back and begin whatever they thought came next was not the best thing to do. But they had locked me in, hadn't they? Had they? I remembered Lieutenant Hector's image of his country: a prisoner of itself alone. I got up and tried the door. Yes, it was locked. On the opposite wall was a high window. I went to it. I pushed it. It opened: hot air and diesel. Outside was a parking lot surrounded by a chain-link fence. Beyond it seemed to be a highway. I stood on the chair, went out the window, crossed the parking lot, and climbed the fence. I had walked beside the highway for not more than two minutes before a truck stopped and picked me up. Mexico is a hitchhiker's paradise, or it would be without the conviction that a third of the drivers will kill you for the buttons on your shirt.

The highway went north by west. West was not the way I had been supposed to go, but I liked that about it. I stayed a couple of days in Durango, or it may have been a week, then got a bus to Mazatlán, on the coast. My idea was to ride on along the coast, then follow the highway to Nogales and Tucson. But at Mazatlán, I thought I saw somebody I knew at the bus station, so I changed my route and hitchhiked back east, then north again toward El Paso. I would cross the border at El Paso. But at the bus station in Chihuahua City, I again saw somebody I knew, so I sheared off to the west once more.

No, I was no longer thinking clearly. I had been out of the capital for a matter of three weeks. It might have been six weeks. I was running out of money. I was hungry. I was seldom sober. I had begun, once again, to doubt my biography. I felt that the several turns I had taken up to now had carried me down, and down, stranding me at last in a kind of underworld, a realm of shades, where I had no wish to be, no idea what to do, a place where I could neither speak nor understand the speech of others. Hitchcock, with a ration of gin in him, had lectured me on the wrong path. Hitchcock himself was the wrong path. Whatever path had led to where I was now—that was the wrong path. We Noons know how to face the facts.

I sheared away from El Paso, therefore, and crossed the border at last below Presidio, on the Big Bend of the Rio Grande. I crossed in a truck carrying scrap metal. Somewhere I had joined forces with two sisters, nurses, who were traveling from Monterey. One of them worked in Presidio and lived in a kind of motel on the old highway. I wound up there, too, with twenty-seven cases of beer, the nurses, their cousin, and I think from time to time, their mother. We all drank beer all day and lived in our underwear or in nothing at all. There I stayed for a week, or it may have been a month, or it may have been longer.

4

Trouble changes you, Saint Paul said. It makes you better, stronger. It makes you patient. It gives you patience, so in time you get experience, and with experience, you gradually come to know what the world is. That far, I was with him. But there was more. Experience gives you hope, Saint Paul said; it lets you hope. I didn't see exactly how that worked. On the contrary, I thought, experience shows you you're a fool to hope.

So much trouble, so many accidents. I haven't mentioned the people on Bible Hill hit by lightning, burned up in house fires, electrocuted by downed wires. I haven't raised the lid on the world of trouble that doesn't come to you at all but hits your lover, your brother, your sister, your parents, your friends, the kind of trouble that hits your child—the worst trouble of all—and so takes you from behind, striking deeper even than you immediately understand. The cemeteries are full of children, each stone marking the grave not only of a single young one but of the peace, the pride, the real life of others, more than one, more than two.

I thought it curious that so much trouble seemed to adhere to Round Mountain, like the smoky gray fog that comes in March and April when the snow melts too fast: the plane crash, the bear-killed hunter, the disappearance of Usher, the death of Mr. Applegate's boy, Amanda's brother, Win. There was nothing on Round Mountain—hadn't been for a hundred years—and yet accidents happened there.

It doesn't seem as though much could go wrong up there, does it? But a lot has.

That place is bad luck, son.

Can a place be bad luck?
That one can.

October 10, 1959. Frost. Temp. 6 a.m. 25. P.m. to schoolteachers for wood 1/2 cord

October 11, 1959. Rain. Temp. 12 M 60.

October 12, 1959. Fair. Temp. 12 M 58. Leg. To schoolteachers p.m. Wood done. $5. Cookies

19. Roads

For the care of its roads and highways, the town employs two road commissioners. One, appointed by the selectmen, is an ex–U.S. Marine lieutenant with a short temper and the habit of command. The other, appointed by nobody, is I. The ex-marine enjoys a salary of thirty-five thousand dollars per year. My services are unpaid. The ex-marine has charge of the town roads used by people and their vehicles. I have charge of the roads used by deer, porcupines, black bears—or by nothing at all. He's the commissioner of good roads, I of bad.

The town has two principal roads, roughly in the form of a lazy Y: a main stem following the Dead River through the township from south to north, with a branch going off obliquely to the northwest. These two roads are state highways. They are paved. They amount, together, to about ten miles. The remaining good roads belong to the town of Ambrose. They are mostly unpaved. They form more or less minor branches of the main roads, branches leading from them to Bible Hill, Round Mountain, and Back Diamond Mountain. The town's good roads, paved and unpaved, amount to seventy miles.

Until the end of the last century, the town was furnished with a total mileage of roads greater than that by at least a third. Something like twenty-five miles of road have been abandoned by the township over the years. In its roads, then, as in so much of its life, the town is less today than it was. The abandoned roads appear today as impassable stretches of existing roads, or as people's driveways or lanes, or they have been given up altogether and allowed to return to forest. You might call them ghost roads.

It is of the ghost roads that I have appointed myself commissioner. Nobody else was after the job, it seems, though it duties are not much. You don't have to plow the ghost roads; you don't have to fill them or gravel them or grade them. Mainly, the job of the commissioner of ghost roads is knowing where they are—knowing where they are, and appreciating them. Perhaps it would be more correct to say I am the *curator* of ghost roads.

They need a curator, or a commissioner—they need somebody. Today many of the old, forgotten roads are hard to find; some are impossible. Finding a ghost road in the woods can be a little feat of perception, like picking a fawn out of the thicket in which it hides. You don't look for a road; you look for runs of fallen stones walls, parallel and some fifty feet apart. You watch out for old trees growing beside the walls, oaks and sugar maples far bigger than the trees that surround them. You make yourself receptive to a kind of sunken, worked-over look about the terrain, to a particular order of rocks and boulders. Forget what you know of roads as they are. You won't find an old road by looking for a new one. You have to remember that roads built in the time of those that are your care didn't always go where roads go today.

As a rule, the ghost roads connect branches of present-day roads, via the hills that newer roads go around. Roads built by ax, pick and shovel, and a team of horses don't fool. They don't go where they don't have to. The abandoned roads are straight, as new roads cannot be. When they come to a hill, they go right at it, up, over, and down, not around. As a result, they're steep. If you follow the ghost roads, you come sooner or later to pitches that no auto road would stand. Not far from Littlejohn's and my place is a stretch of ghost road so steep that walking up it is easier than walking down. It's on Calabrese's land. A hundred and fifty years ago, that piece of road was on one of the stage routes between Boston and Albany. Today it's a rocky gully where the sun never shines and in summer the mosquitoes grow to the size of chickadees.

Other of the lost roads are fairly new—that is to say, their loss is fairly recent. It need be no less complete for that, however. The road that used to go over the flank of Back Diamond, in the woods behind Mr. Applegate's cabin, where Amanda lived, was given up by the town about 1920. Today it has essentially disappeared. When the town authorities resolve no longer to maintain a roadway, the road is said to have been "given up." It's an apt expression, aptly implying surrender and defeat. For in Vermont, more than in some other places, a road is an act of will. It's a frail stop against inexorable chaos. Once you quit fixing a road in these parts, once you quit putting back the dirt that the spring runoff and the summer thunderstorms have washed away, it doesn't take long for the road to die, especially over the steep sections. You come to places off in the woods where the ground drops away in front of you, revealing a narrow canyon full of boulders. You've found another ghost road.

The old roads are quiet, lonely places, haunted places, in their way. It wasn't for their quiet that I came to love them, however: on Bible Hill, we're not short on quiet. I loved the old roads for their sense of quiet succeeding life, for their sense of extinct activity. I liked it that these nameless places off in the woods, where from one year's end to another the only human visitors, besides myself, might be a lost deer hunter, had once been—not crowded with people, exactly, but the setting of a certain amount of human business, effort, folly. The old roads, I found, were not unmodified nature, but nature returned, nature reestablished, and therefore they proposed a pleasurable intimation of mortality. I'll take a ruin over a wilderness, if I can get it. We Noons are Romantics.

Put it this way: I loved the old roads for their junk. Along them, you could find all kinds of cast-off gear. The great-grandfathers and-grandmothers of Bible Hill were a careless, slovenly lot, perhaps; they tossed their empties. Bottles, crockery, china, tinware, every kind of busted ironwork—anything that wouldn't too quickly rot away—were to be found half-buried in the leaf mold beside the given-up roads. Near the top of the old track behind Calabrese's reposed the rusting body of a Chevrolet coupe from the mid-thirties, its engine, wheels, axles, seats long gone, its original color undistinguishable, its windows smashed. How in heaven's name had it come there? Had it fallen from the sky? The road to where it rested was little more than a fall of boulders and ferns. And yet somebody had driven, pushed, hauled that Chev up there. Was it possible? Had the road been that much better a short forty years earlier? Well, yes: necessarily it had. The car, rusting away out in the woods in a spot at present inaccessible, demonstrated the condition of a former world, like a fossil clamshell on a mountaintop.

It was by accident that I became commissioner of bad roads. One afternoon in September, the year after I arrived on Bible Hill—or it may have been the year after that—I got lost on Round Mountain.

I had been exploring the woods over there. I left my car beside the town road, followed a brook into the woods, followed a logging road, a stone wall, another brook, another wall, working generally uphill.

At some point, I realized that I didn't know where I was, had no idea how to return to where I'd started, wasn't sure whether the second brook I'd crossed was another part of the first or a different brook.

I became a little frightened. No: more than a little. Being lost in a place on the next hill from your home brings a subtle kind of fear, but fear is what it is. I now saw that the afternoon, which had been warmly sunny, had turned gray. The sun was gone, and surely it had gotten colder. Time, too, had changed: It had sped up. I had started a little after noon and had been out there three or four hours—but now my watch said it was past five o'clock. In another hour, it would be getting dark, it was getting dark, it was dark already. How would I get out before night?

I felt a nearly irresistible need to be up and moving, moving fast. Moving where, in what direction? It didn't matter; I had to get going. That was wrong, wasn't it? We're told to stop if we're lost. We're told to stop, sit, think things through, wait for somebody to come and find us. It isn't easy.

I stopped and sat. I thought things through. I thought that it was certainly fast getting darker and colder. I thought that nobody was going to come and find me. I thought that at the place I'd come from, nobody would know I was gone.

Of course, Round Mountain isn't the great Beardmore Glacier, it isn't the Hindu Kush: Wherever the nearest house was, it probably wasn't more than half a mile from where I sat. You won't die of being lost on Round Mountain, will you? Still, being lost is being lost. I got moving.

I knew that if I was going to get unlost, it wouldn't happen by my moving up the mountain. I needed to go down, head south, keep on south, toward the valley. I turned around and started downhill, holding to my right because that seemed the easier walking. As I went down the mountain, the woods got darker, and as they got darker, I went more quickly.

Then I stopped. I looked around me. I realized I was standing in a road or track, a fairly broad one. There were the bordering stone walls with the big old trees growing up beside them, there was the sunken way of the road itself. Without knowing it, I had for some time been walking along an abandoned road.

I went on, and in another quarter of an hour, now at the end of the daylight, I came out into the rear of a farm: yard, sheds, big barn, and big white house. The barn was empty and the house closed up and silent, but I knew it. It was the Usher place. If I went past the house and down the lane, I'd come to the town road, and if I turned right there, I'd come, in two or three miles, to my car, where I'd left it. I'd gone up Round Mountain to the west of north, apparently, gotten turned around somewhere near the top, started down headed due east, not south, and hit the old road that had led from Dead River Settlement right over the mountain to the hamlet at Joppa.

Usher's was the last place on that road. Beyond Usher's, the road had been given up long ago. It had about disappeared, but it had served me. It had gotten me unlost. It had put me out at Usher's place. You couldn't die of being lost on Round Mountain, but Usher had, hadn't he? I decided the bad old roads might be good for something after all.

Since then, I have followed the old roads, the ghost roads. I have sought them out and found them even where the years have nearly obliterated them. I have carried out my commission in all parts of the township, in all seasons, in all kinds of weather. In so doing, I have, much of the time, been as turned around, as out of reach, as unsure of my whereabouts as I was the first afternoon on Round Mountain, but I haven't been lost, for I have known that whenever I liked, I could turn and follow the bad road home.

Many of the given-up roads are property lines. Landholdings from the last century that were bounded by a road may have the same bounds today, though the road has ceased to exist. Hence the bold yellow signs, nailed onto trees, that you'll sometimes happen on even far into the woods:

POSTED
PRIVATE PROPERTY
Hunting, Fishing, Trapping or
Trespassing for Any Purpose
is Strictly Forbidden
VIOLATORS WILL BE PROSECUTED

There are people who hate these signs, hate what they mean. Time was, you will hear, when such signs were unknown, and a hunter, a fisherman, a trapper could go where he liked as long as he put the bars back up behind him. In those days, in the state if Vermont, there was no such offense as trespass. That more and more land is posted today is a sign of the end of a free way of life, a rural way of life based on trust, community, and shared tradition. Now a mean and fearful generation has need of posted signs. Angry people, finding posted signs in their way, rip them from the trees and trample them into the ground. They hack them with knives, fill them with bullet holes.

I don't blame them. I don't like the signs, either. When I come upon a line of posted signs out in the woods, I, too, feel my spirit sink. I let the signs alone, though. I don't let them make me angry. I understand that they don't apply to me. For I consider their plain language: *Hunting, Fishing, Trapping, or Trespassing for Any Purpose.* . . . Am I hunting? No. Am I fishing? No. Am I trapping? No. I'm the commissioner of bad roads and my work is not to be forbidden. I am not hunting, not trapping . . . I'm not trespassing for any purpose, I reflect. Not at all. Rather, I'm trespassing for no purpose. That sign isn't talking to me. And so I go my way.

20. Antiques

Say not thou, What is the cause
that the former days were better
than these? for thou dost not
inquire wisely concerning this.
—Ecclesiastes 7:10

1

A yellow ambulance turned off the road and made its way through the parked cars and into the flea market on the old Mountain Fair grounds. Passing among the stands and tables spread with their treasure, the driver found it necessary two or three times to let off his siren in short whoops. People's heads came up. They looked around. They began to follow the ambulance. The driver brought it bumping over the old pasture to us. The ambulance was an odd color: yellow and black. It looked like a giant bumblebee. Here it came.

Mr. Applegate was down. Some kind of falling, some illness, took him at the flea market, where he shopped for his tools. He fell among the hammers, planes, and augers. He didn't know what the trouble was. Then he did, and for the longest time, nothing was the same.

A Sunday morning: Mr. Applegate and I had gone to the flea market together, as we sometimes did. Mr. Applegate made for the tools. I found a man near where you parked your car who had ten or twelve boxes of secondhand books set out on blankets on the dusty grass. Mr. Applegate went on ahead.

I might have been ten minutes with the books, not more. There was a whole library of paperback Western novels, I remember, three quarters of them by Louis L'Amour. That was a man who knew how to drive his pen. The flea market bookseller also had a copy of *The Annotated Walden* which I would have bought, except the guy wanted five bucks. Mr. Applegate would have talked him down—would have tried anyway. You were expected to haggle at the flea market. But I was never much of a haggler; if I couldn't stand the price, I preferred to do without. We Noons take it or we leave it. I followed Mr. Applegate.

He was behind a row of tables, on which were spread the old tools he so admired. Mr. Applegate was collapsed in a lawn chair somebody had shoved under him when he began to fall. He was conscious all right, and he was calm, but he sat in that chair as though he'd been dropped there from a great height, and his face, normally pink, was the color of dirty snow. Four or five people were around him, trying to learn what was wrong, trying to help.

There you are, son. Where did you get to?

No place. Over there. What's wrong?

"He's had a stroke, looks like to me," said Bob, the tool seller at whose table Mr. Applegate had dropped down.

Don't know. I feel like they let all the sand out of me.

Are you in pain?

No

"It's his heart," said another of the helpers. "He's having a heart attack. Look at his color."

Is it your heart?

Don't think so. It's still going, ain't it? I guess it's still going.

I put my hand on Mr. Applegate's chest and felt his heart strong and steady beneath.

Did you pass out?

It don't seem like I did. I got over here to Bob's and I felt light-headed, a bit, and then it seemed as though I couldn't stay on my legs.

"What it is," somebody said, "he's having a blood-sugar fit. He needs sugar. Somebody get him something to eat."

"Honey," said another. "Somebody get him some honey."

Ten or fifteen people had gathered.

I'm okay now.

No, you're not. Can you get up?

Sure.

Sure he could get up, said Mr. Applegate. But he couldn't. He couldn't even try. And then we heard the siren at the end of the flea market field. Somebody had gone for the medics, and the ambulance was slowly bumping toward us along the dirt aisles between the tables full of junk, the driver letting off his siren in low, short growls to get the people to clear the way.

At one time, Mr. Applegate had collected wheels. In his garage, his cellar, his closets, in his attic, in the corners of his woodshed, he had wagon wheels, carriage wheels, wheels from velocipedes, from bicycles, from prams; he had wooden wheels, iron wheels, wheels of brass. Mr. Applegate collected hammers. He had, probably, a hundred claw hammers. He collected old postcards, specializing in views of Vermont and of the Rocky Mountains. The postcards had to have been written on and mailed; otherwise, they were of no interest to Mr. Applegate. He had a postcard of the Bennington Battle Monument, mailed in 1927 to an address in Troy, New York, on the back of which, in a woman's hand, was written, simply, "NO."

I didn't get it. We're meant to travel light through the world. I believed that; I believe it yet. I believed Mr. Applegate was of the same mind. Why surround yourself with so much that has so little use? Perhaps some of Mr. Applegate's hammers had a kind of plain, vernacular beauty—but a hundred of them, all alike?

They ain't all alike, son. They're all different.

Yes. They're hammers: There are bigger ones and littler ones. So maybe you need two. You must have a hundred.

A hundred and thirteen.

I don't see it.

It's simple, son. You see a thing; you like the way it looks. That's all. It don't cost much, so you buy it. Then you find out there's more like it. You buy another.

Mr. Applegate collected more than wheels, hammers, and postcards. He had a shelf on his office wall where he kept his collection of objects he called "ringers." These were obsolete devices, whose use was unknown. They had cranks, shafts, knobs, teeth, blades, arbors, hinges, bearings, dies all more or less ingeniously contrived to do—what? You could only guess. Well, no—in fact, you could do more. You could send such an item, or a picture of it, over to *Yankee* magazine in New Hampshire. *Yankee* had a page each month identifying and explaining forgotten implements submitted by its readers. Mr. Applegate never consulted *Yankee.* He didn't want to know for sure what a ringer did, I don't think. He preferred to speculate.

Mr. Applegate held up a hinged wooden thing the size of a cigar box; it looked like an oversized ham sandwich with teeth.

Now, this, I bet you used to shell some kind of grain or nuts. That or make cloth. Look at that, son. Look how that's made, in there.

Amazing.

See that plate on there? That's copper. See that? E. W. HAYNES

PAT. WATERBURY, CONN. Old Bob was selling the thing mainly for the plate. He wanted fifteen bucks. He'd take ten, he said. I gave him seven fifty.

The question is, Why?

Why? That's old, son. That's an antique.

2

Mr. Applegate thought that, no, he wouldn't ride in the ambulance. He sent the medics on their way. He waited at the flea market for half an hour. I stayed by him. Somebody brought him a doughnut and a paper cup of coffee. He said he felt better for them. It looked to him like that idea about low blood sugar might have had something to it. His color was coming back. He got to his feet at last, and we made our way out of the flea market to the car. I kept a little behind Mr. Applegate and to his side so I could catch him if he began to fall again. I didn't hold on to him, didn't touch him. Somewhere, I had gotten the idea that you're not to help people who don't want help.

He felt well for a week, two weeks. Then he fainted during a meeting with a law client. This time, the ambulance took him to the hospital in Brattleboro. They went over him there, kept him overnight. Before the hospital let him go, one of the doctors there told him he needed to have tests done that they couldn't do in Brattleboro. They did those tests in Hanover.

"Hanover?" said Amanda. "Oh boy, Noon."

"What's wrong with Hanover?" I asked Amanda.

"What's in Hanover?"

"Dartmouth."

"What else?"

"I don't know," I said. "Nothing that I know of. Some kind of hospital, I suppose."

"Now you're getting it, Noon," said Amanda.

I hadn't been to Hanover at the time, knew it only for its hearty old college. During Mr. Applegate's illness, I learned more about Hanover than ever I wanted to know. For Bible Hill, and indeed for half the state of Vermont, Hanover, New Hampshire, thanks to its medical school and associated teaching hospital, is the Delphi, the capital of Bad News. Hanover is where you go to learn what ails you when what ails you is so obscure, or so complex, or so abundantly awful that the local medical men don't know or can't bring themselves to reveal to you what it is. Hanover is the house of the Long Friends. You can jump from a tall building in New York City, and if you should chance to land on a passing hay wagon, say, you might survive the fall. But if you find yourself called to Hanover, you had best see to it you are paid up, testated, and right with the Lord.

Look, I'll drive you. They'll give you some tests. You'll be there a few hours. You have to know what's going on here.

I don't know if I want to know, though, son, you know?

It could be nothing. It's probably nothing. You'd find out it's nothing.

If it's nothing, I don't need to find out. If it ain't nothing, then, like I said, I don't know if I want to.

Well, if something is the matter, they'll tell you what you can do about it.

Thing is, a lot of the time, what you can do about it's worse than it.

But either way, you'd know.

I already know, son.

You do?

Sure.

What is it, then?
Not nothing.

That's old, son. That's an antique. Is it? What is an antique? What is the charm of old wheels, hammers, postcards, unnamed gadgets? The question comes up, especially on Bible Hill, for it's charm those things apparently have—charm, but little else, perhaps. Charm, but little worth. The idea of the antique as the invaluable, irreplaceable product of superior art, or as the authentic embodiment of a distinguished history—the prestige of the antique—scarcely applies to the flea market trash that passes for antique in these parts. On Bible Hill, we are in the realm of the *subantique,* and so we are game for snobs.

"What's the matter with him?" Miss Drumheller asked me.

"He doesn't know," I said. "They want him to have tests."

"Tests?" Miss Drumheller asked. "What kind of tests?"

"I don't know," I said. "In Hanover."

"Hanover?" said Miss Drumheller. "I don't like that."

"No," I said.

"I was told he collapsed at that junkyard," Miss Drumheller went on.

"The flea market," I said. "That's right. I was with him."

"You were? What were you doing at that place?"

"We go there," I said. "He likes to look for things there."

"What things?" asked Miss Drumheller.

"Antiques."

Miss Drumheller scoffed.

"You're talking about the old milk bottles and bent nails those people have for sale every weekend, aren't you?" she asked. "They're what's considered an antique around here."

"Why not?" I asked her. "They're old."

Miss Drumheller snorted.

"By rights, that entire market belongs at the town dump," she said.

"I won't deny it," I said.

"Come with me," she said. She led me from her kitchen through a short passage and into a dim parlor that looked out on the road through curtained windows. A fireplace, cold and sour-smelling in the early summer, stuffed chairs, a sofa; on the floor, an Oriental rug, good but a little frayed. Miss Drumheller showed me a small table standing on a footed pedestal, its top round and having a raised rim, the whole affair made of some hardwood, polished and polished to a deep luster, like satin.

"*That's* an antique," said Miss Drumheller. "You won't find one at your flea market. That was made in London before 1750. It belonged to my great-great-grandfather. It was an antique in *his* time. He was captain of a China clipper. That table was in his house in Newburyport."

"Boy," I said.

"You can touch it," said Miss Drumheller.

"I'd better not," I said.

"Don't be silly," said Miss Drumheller. "Go ahead."

"I might hurt it," I said.

Miss Drumheller looked at me.

"Are you laughing at me, young man?" she asked me.

"Certainly not," I said.

3

Three weeks after Mr. Applegate became ill for the first time, Amanda took him in hand. She talked to his doctor, made the necessary arrangements at the hospital in Hanover, and got ready to drive him up there. I offered to take him, but Amanda said he wanted her to do it. He would go with her, she said.

"He wouldn't otherwise," Amanda said. "He wouldn't go at all. He's scared."

"Sure he's scared," I said. "So am I."

"Yeah," said Amanda. "I wish he would go alone though. Or let you take him. I wish it didn't have to be me."

Of course she wished that. Nobody wants to follow his declining parent around from one degrading station to another, explaining him, carrying his bags, propping him up, picking up after him, like some kind of macabre valet. Nobody likes the sick, even his own sick. Nobody likes an unlovely and too-close mortality.

"I don't know, Noon," Amanda said. "He and I get on okay as long as we keep it light, you know?"

"Yes. So?"

"So, this is a tough one to keep light," said Amanda.

There you are, son. Where did you get to?

No place.

I guess you heard, then? I guess Manda told you?

I heard.

It's funny, you know? I feel all right, now. I feel fine, like nothing was going on—have all week.

That's good.

Your pancreas? I don't even know what your pancreas does, do you?

Not really.

I didn't even know for sure where it is. That doctor had to show me. It's kind of tucked in there behind your belly.

Is that right?

Damnedest-looking thing, too. Yellow, six, seven inches long, fatter at one end. Looks like the biggest tadpole you ever saw. I bet you didn't know any of that.

You're right.

No. Well, inform yourself, son, is my advice. Keep that pancreas attended to, keep her turned up. When she goes wrong, you've got a problem.

So what kind of treatment are they talking about?

Oh, the fellow in Hanover lays it all out for you: You can have X rays, I guess, and there are drugs of one kind and another. Thing is, with this kind of deal, a lot of times they don't much help. Maybe they get you a little time.

I see.

On the other hand, a little time's not a bad thing to have.

No.

So I've got to decide here, I guess. What would you do, son?

Do you mean would I take the treatment or not? I'd take it.

Would you?

Sure.

Manda said the same thing.

Mr. Applegate waited. I drove him to Hanover for his next appointment. He felt good. His appointment went well. That was how you talked about this business: *Your appointment went well.* Not *You are better*. Not *You are worse*. Not *You won't die very soon. Your appointment went well.* Hanover, capital of Bad News, was also the capital of Circumlocution.

The oncologist in Hanover wanted to get Mr. Applegate on a treatment regimen. Mr. Applegate put him off. I think he figured he might have all the time he needed, in any case. Needed for what? How old was Mr. Applegate anyway?

"I'd have to think," said Miss Drumheller. "His father died young, too, I think. Certainly he did, and he had something like the same thing, some rare cancer. He must have been about the age Orlando is now, I suppose. Orlando has bad luck. His boy, and then Edith. I liked Edith. Edith was solid. She was the brains of the family. Orlando wasn't up to much after she died. And with the girl, Amanda, running wild? I never had much opinion of Orlando Applegate, but I would not have wished for him the life he's had. That family has always been unlucky. Bad luck runs in families, you know, like left-handedness, like red hair."

"I wouldn't know," I said.

4

What is the value of the flea market antique, the subantique? For the true antique, value comes from conspicuous excellence of workmanship, from English or European provenance, and from great age—for example, Miss Drumheller's venerable tea table, made in England before 1750. In the realm of the subantique, value is another thing—almost the opposite thing. It seemed that for the junk at the flea market, picked over so lovingly each weekend by Mr. Applegate and others, the cheaper, the commoner, the more banal a thing was, the more value it had. Miss Drumheller's little table would have sat forlornly at the flea market, neglected, a swan among the ducks, while pipe tobacco tins struck off in 1960, dead vacuum tubes from obsolete radios, and unwashed Moxie bottles went briskly in commerce.

Why? It can only be that the value of the subantique is not intrinsic, but instrumental. You don't realize that value in exchange, but only in possession. The subantique is plain rather than fine, honest rather than foreign, and used rather than old. You can't buy it low and sell it high. You can't profit from the subantique, but you can use it. The subantique is a talisman, a ticket. For those so inclined, the subantique is their admission to the past, but a past that is accessible in a way the past of the real antique is not. Perhaps the past they want to possess by way of the flea market is their own past. Mr. Applegate, I, and the other devotees of the flea market went there to rub up against and so to participate in and reanimate the past—not the distant past, but yesterday or the day before, last week.

The flea market version of the antique was the collective memory. Its charm was the charm of reminiscence, and so it was very much implicated in the setting that was Bible Hill, for Bible Hill is itself a kind of subantique.

Mr. Applegate's predicament was simple. It was elegant. He seemed almost to savor it. It was this: If he took treatment at Hanover for his illness, an aggressive, incurable, and absolutely terminal cancer of the pancreas, then the pain, the misery of the treatment stood to make what time he had left unbearable. If he didn't take treatment, then what time he had left stood to be short.

It's what you call a dilemma.

That's what you call it, all right, son. But it ain't a dilemma if you know what to do.

Exactly. Mr. Applegate knew what to do. If you know how to die, then you know how to live, said the philosopher. Mr. Applegate was a philosopher himself, perhaps, the rarest kind, a philosopher in action. He conducted himself, always, as though at some fundamental level, the right way is the easy way. When at last you take the right key from your ring and fit it to the lock, it sails in and turns the wards like cherry pie: There is no resistance.

"Wait a minute," said Amanda. "You mean he told you he won't be treated?"

"No. He didn't tell me anything."

"But that's what you think?"

"Yes."

"He can't do that," said Amanda. "What is he, sixty-two? Sixty-three? He can't just give up and die."

"He wouldn't see it as giving up," I said.

"He'd be wrong, then," said Amanda.

I don't think so, son. Going up there every week, maybe more? Having them work you over, the way they do? Having it maybe make no difference? The way they talk about it up there? I don't think so. I think I'll sit it out down here and see what happens.

You know what happens.

Well, sure. But I've got some time, they say. I feel okay now. I believe I'll stand pat.

I could understand that if you were seventy-five. As it is, I think you're nuts.

You think I'm nuts, son?

Amanda, too.

Manda. Well, but she don't have it to do. Neither do you. I do. Tell you what, son: You and Manda feel like if I was seventy-five, not letting them work on me would make sense. Okay, tell you what: I'm sixty-six, almost, so we'll call it a wash, plus or minus ten years. Tell you what,

I'll spot you my ten. You can have them. I'd rather go ten years early than ten years late.

You see? Easy.

5

Bible Hill is itself a subantique, is itself a kind of flea market, a flea market of signification, a way into the collective memory for those who feel they need one. And here observe its failure; for the collective memory is no one's memory. It's memory so acute that it leads you to recall what never happened. In a way, that dear, well-worn, trivial stuff at the flea market is illusory. It never existed at all. Those who hope to use old postcards, old books, old tools—those who hope to use old places—to roll back up the thread of their lives are kidding themselves, supremely, and they must know it. The intellect of man, aided by his will to self-deception, can accomplish almost anything, but it can't reverse time, not by science, not by medicine, not by the contemplation of E. W. Haynes's suppositious corn cracker from Waterbury, Connecticut.

Mr. Applegate and the rest of us can use these things to learn about the past, but that's the only use they have. And it's not what we want. We don't want to learn about the past. We want to summon it.

As his illness grew upon him, as his appointments in Hanover went less well, Mr. Applegate neglected the flea market. He took less interest in summoning the past, perhaps. Perhaps when you discover at last the proportion the past really bears to the whole of your life—the higher and higher proportion—you find less in it to love. Did Mr. Applegate still reckon he had enough time left? He quit going to Hanover. He fired his oncologist. He would be examined by a doctor in Brattleboro. Amanda drove him down there each week, or I did.

There you are, son. Where did you get to?

No place. Amanda says you're through with the doctor.

That's right. I gave him his walking papers. Fired him. Didn't like to do it, but the boy won't starve.

Why?

He tires me out, son. Well, he doesn't. He's a nice fellow. But that place tires me out. The hospital. More and more, you know? No, it ain't the doctor. He's all right. But, the way I look at it, they can count in Brattleboro as well as they can in Hanover.

Count? Oh. Well, yes, I guess that's right.

Sure it is.

I wish you were feeling better.

So do I, son. But I'm okay. I'm okay, only not quite as.

I know. I'm sorry.

Well, it'll work out. You can stand about anything as long as it don't hurt and don't go on too long.

As long as it don't go on too long.

"What did they say, the last time?" I asked Amanda.

"Nothing for sure. Maybe six months, less."

"But not a year?"

"Probably not," said Amanda.

"Boy," I said. "It goes fast. He thought he had enough time. That was in the summer. Now he thinks it won't last too long. I wonder if he thinks he has enough time now."

"Well," said Amanda. "He made his choice. It will have to be enough, won't it?"

"Yes," I said.

"We're into something, here, aren't we, Noon?" Amanda asked me.

"We are," I said.

"Keep it light," said Amanda. "Always keep it light. We're into one that's tough to keep light, though."

"Tough," I said. "Maybe not impossible."

Miss Drumheller said bad luck runs in families. I thought that was a partial truth at best, as though there was something that didn't run in families. Everything runs in families, I came to think. You have to look for the effect, however. That's what I was doing. Everybody, if he's lucky, gets to learn, really learn, a family not his own. The Applegates were mine.

21. Remarkable Providences

1

Amanda had seen a man in the woods. I thought it might have been Calabrese. It wasn't Calabrese.

"No," said Amanda. "This was somebody else. This guy was as tall as you."

"Brackett's tall," I said.

"Tubby?" Amanda said. "I know Tubby. He's light. His hair, his eyes. This guy was dark. It wasn't Tubby."

We had been together on Bible Hill through the long fall and most of the way through the winter. We no longer kept separate rooms. I liked it. I took right to it. I found having Amanda in the house, in the kitchen, in the bathroom, in the bed, was easy. It was familiar. It made a setting that reminded me of my childhood; it reminded me of real life. I settled right in, I'm saying, but Amanda didn't.

"Who was that, Noon?" she asked me.

"I don't know," I said. "It's turkey season. Maybe it was a turkey hunter. Maybe it was Tris Rand. He was up here for turkeys last year."

"A turkey hunter would have had a gun," Amanda said. "This guy didn't. And it wasn't Tris Rand. I know him, too. I know everybody around here, Noon. Better than you."

"People come to see Calabrese, sometimes," I told her. "Maybe it was somebody looking for Calabrese."

"Maybe," said Amanda.

October 2, 1935. Fair. Warm. Temp. 12M 67. Apple picking

Later in the winter, she saw him again. He was across the road, walking along the edge of the woods at the end of a pasture, walking over the snow; a dark figure on the long white reach of snow, against the gray of the woods.

"He was carrying something on his shoulder," said Amanda. "That's all I could tell."

I went to look. Amanda wouldn't go with me. I found deer tracks in the snow and smaller tracks that might have been made by a fox, but no others.

"Don't tell me I didn't see him, Noon. Don't tell me that."

Suddenly, she wasn't making sense. Why? Amanda was brave. She had walked away from her crazy husband in California. On her own, she had come clear across the country in a junk car that broke down again and again, stranding her beside the empty highway up on the continent's vast, scary middle, alone with the rattlesnakes, the cowboys, the gunslingers, the *posse comitatus*, and worse. Alone, she had made it. Then she had lived alone in the cabin on Back Diamond, a place far more isolated than mine, and she had gone to work at the Tumbleweed for the four-to-closing hours, a shift that was short on green tea and watercress sandwiches, long on fights, cops, and broken glass. Plainly, Amanda could take care of herself. What was on her mind, then?

She thinks there's somebody sneaking around in the woods.

Is there?

No, but she won't hear it.

She wouldn't. Manda's what you might call strong-willed.

I noticed that.

Well, then.

Are you warm enough?

Oh, sure. Thanks.

Appointment's for two o'clock. You want to roll?

Let's roll her, son.

Amanda decided the man she had seen was Littlejohn. She had looked into Littlejohn's diaries and found the photographs he'd kept. She held up the photo of the man.

"That's the guy I saw," said Amanda.

"That's Littlejohn," I said.

"That's him," said Amanda.

"He's been dead for fifteen years," I said. "Besides, you knew him when you were a kid, didn't you? You'd have known right away if it was Littlejohn you saw."

"No," said Amanda. "I knew him when he was old. He didn't look like this." She pointed to the brown old photograph, to Littlejohn's heavy mustache, his black brows. "Dark, big. It's the same guy."

"Look," I said. "It can't be."

"Same guy, Noon," said Amanda.

I believed Amanda had dreamed the man she thought she saw. In dreaming, Amanda was no amateur. She dreamed often, and she dreamed elaborately, vividly. Working the combat shift at the Weed, she was tired the following day. She would nap, off and on. She had napped, surely, and had dreamed of a man in the woods, a man across the white pasture. Did the man she'd dreamed of look like Littlejohn? Well, then, she'd seen Littlejohn's picture in another place, or she remembered him better than she knew from her girlhood.

"This was no dream," said Amanda.

"How do you know?"

"What do you mean, how do I know? How do you know anything's not a dream? It just isn't."

"Oh."

"Do you think I want to see him, Noon?" Amanda asked. "Do you think I'm happy he's there?"

2

October 5, 1935. Fog a.m. then fair. Temp. 12M 66. Apple p.

Amanda didn't like Littlejohn. She didn't like him and she didn't like his book. It bored her. Well, it was a boring book.

"What's this *M,* Noon?" Amanda asked me.

"M?"

"Yeah. 'Temp. twelve M.' What's *M*?"

"Meridian," I said. "Midday. Noon. You know: A.M., before noon; P.M., after noon. M noon."

Uh-huh," said Amanda. She shut Littlejohn's diary and held it in her lap. "You think this is interesting stuff, right?"

"Yes," I said.

"Why?"

"I don't know, exactly," I said. "Something about it. It's steady, you know?"

"It is that," said Amanda.

October 6, 1935. Fair. Temp. 12M 61. Apple p.
October 7, 1935. Fog in valley. Then fine. Temp. 58.
Ten bushll a.m.
October 10, 1935. Rain. Temp. 12M 61. Blow p.m. Apple drop

"Steady," said Amanda. "Have you read this whole thing, Noon?"
"No," I said. "But I will."

April. Amanda told how on a fine spring day she had taken a walk through the woods to Sheep Desert. She felt as though she had been shut indoors all winter, she said; she longed for the feel, the smell of sun and fresh air. At Sheep Desert, when she came out of the woods and onto grass, she had taken off her shoes and gone barefoot. She sat on a rock ledge in the sun. She saw Littlejohn coming up the hill toward her.

"Don't tell me I was dreaming, either, Noon," said Amanda.

"All right," I said.

"He was down near the road, like he'd just left the road, and he was walking up the hill. He wasn't in a hurry, but he was coming on. The same big guy, big black mustache. He was even wearing a suit like the one he has on in your picture."

Amanda had hurried back to the house. At that time, I was working for Noble Groom, pumping gas at his station on the Dead River road. I had the car, so Amanda was stuck at home. When I got to the house that afternoon, I couldn't open the door. Amanda had wedged a piece of kindling wood into the jamb to keep the door closed tight. We had no locks in those days.

"It was daytime, and I wasn't tired; I didn't work last night. I was wide-awake, okay, Noon?" Amanda said. "If you tell me I was dreaming this time, I'll throw something heavy at you."

"You weren't dreaming," I said.

Maybe she wasn't, but what, then? Need one believe in ghosts for that? There were ledges and juniper clumps all over Sheep Desert. I didn't know exactly where Amanda had been sitting when she saw the figure approaching up the hill. But if she was anywhere near the top, and he was down on the road, the distance must have been a hundred yards and might have been twice that. How could she know it was Littlejohn she'd seen?

She knew.

March 29, 1937. Fair. Temp. 12M 55
March 30, 1937. Rain. Temp. 12M 61. Geese

"I don't know, Noon," Amanda said. "There's not much here, is there? Work. Birds. He writes them down. In the winter, it's cold; he writes it down. In the summer, it's hot; he writes it down. He's just there, you know? Day after day, he gets up, he—I don't know—eats. He writes his little note. That's it."

"Right," I said.

"I've got to tell you," said Amanda. "I don't get the appeal, you know? This guy doesn't have much of a life, does he? Like I said, he's just there."

"But he's *here,*" I said. "Right here, on this spot, is where he was. The time, the days, all passed right here, on this piece of ground. That's the thing: We're in the same place."

Amanda shook her head. She didn't get it.

"I'm interested in his life," I said. "You say he didn't have one, but he did. He did, and I want to know about it. You say that doesn't make sense. But you believe you see his ghost. Does that make more sense?"

"Cheap shot, Noon," said Amanda.

"Besides," I said. "How do you know nothing ever happened to him except little things?"

"Well," said Amanda. "That's all he writes about, isn't it? If anything were happening, he'd write about it, wouldn't he?"

"Would he?" I said.

3

Littlejohn never came near. He was in the woods, across the pasture, down the hill. Once, Amanda saw him up in a tree. I never saw him, though twice I was with her when he appeared.

"There, look," Amanda said. "There."

"Where?" I asked.

We were driving home up Bible Hill. We were a quarter of a mile from home. The road bends right. Amanda saw Littlejohn ahead, standing beside the bend in the road.

"There, on the left. There, look."

"I'm looking," I said.

Ahead, where she pointed, a deer crossed the road, walking, then bounding.

"Deer," I said.

"Past the deer," said Amanda. She looked. "He's gone," she said. "He went into the woods. You saw him, though, right?"

"I saw a deer," I said.

We drove on to the place where Amanda had seen Littlejohn standing. We stopped the car. We looked into the woods, summer woods, where within a few yards vision became lost in curtains of green, changing, passing, mingling, bright sun and dark shadow, bright shadow and dark sun. Littlejohn might have been in there with a regiment of infantry, and if they held still and shut up, you'd never see them.

She thinks she's seeing Littlejohn's ghost.

Does she? Well, you thought about the same thing at one time, it seems to me.

No. I thought I heard him up in the attic one *time. I never said I saw him.*

That's right, son. Now I recall.

Two times I've been with her when she's seen him. I don't see anything. Does she?

I don't know, son.

Have you seen Littlejohn?

Sure. Hundreds of times.

You know what I mean. I mean since he died.

Well, once I thought I did.

Where?

On the Joppa road. Not too far from your place. If you're going to see Claude, that's where he'll be, it seems like.

When?

Oh, a few years ago. Fall. I was on my way to the flea market, you know. It was early, not long past dawn. There was a lot of fog. I saw somebody up ahead hitchhiking. I thought it was Claude. It looked like Claude. But, like I say, it was first light and foggy. When I got up to the place, there was a deer ran off into the fog. I don't think it was a deer I saw, but it might have been.

Or it might have been a man, but not Littlejohn.

That's possible, son.

But you don't think so.

I don't.

February 26, 1937. Fair. Temp. 12M 28. Wash buckets
February 27, 1937. Gray. Temp. 12M 25. Took buckets to woods. Snow to wast in woods.
March 1, 1937. Snow a.m. Temp. 12M 39. Sap run

Littlejohn never spoke to Amanda. He made no sign. He seemed unaware of her; he seemed to be going about his business. What was Littlejohn's business these days, he being fifteen years dead? Goofing off, perhaps. The last time Amanda saw him, he was up in one of Calabrese's apple trees.

There had evidently been quite an orchard on the southwest slope of Bible Hill, between Calabrese's place and mine. The wood had long since grown up wild there, but the old apple trees were still to be found, slowly dying under the overtopping oaks and maples, which themselves grew beneath scattered tall pines. Calabrese, from his end, had begun to clear out the woods and release the apple trees. He had opened a half acre or more of the grown-up orchard and exposed twenty-five or thirty poor old trees.

Amanda and I went over there one fall day, a keen little wind blowing, to help Calabrese gather apples. Those apples were small and hard and marked by worms or some other bug. You couldn't eat them, but Calabrese thought he'd make cider.

Most of the apples had fallen. We stooped under the stubby, twisted old trees and combed through the grass. We picked out the soundest, least spotted apples, and put them into baskets—cold work that's hard on the back. Amanda straightened up and left me to drag the full basket out into the open.

"Noon," she said.

I left the basket and went to her side. The wind blew her hair into my face for a moment. Amanda was looking out across the orchard. She had seen Littlejohn in one of the apple trees Calabrese had released from the woods that same summer. It was clear across the open space, a couple of hundred feet from where we stood. Amanda pointed.

"In the tree, Noon," she said.

And for an instant, I thought I could see him, too, a dark mass in one of the trees, indistinct but having limbs, seemingly, as though a suit of clothes or a straw-stuffed scarecrow had been flung up into the lower branches of the tree. I thought I saw Littlejohn, too; but I couldn't be sure. Those old trees hadn't been pruned in seventy-five years. They were dark and tangled, like thickets suspended in the air. I looked again, and then I saw—we both saw—Calabrese stand up under another tree where he had been gathering apples, a tree no more than twenty feet from the one where Amanda saw Littlejohn climbing.

We called to Calabrese. We waved. He waved back. We pointed. Calabrese looked.

"What?" Calabrese called to us. "What?"

Amanda and I went across the orchard to Calabrese. The tree where Littlejohn had been was empty.

"Did you see him?" Amanda asked Calabrese.

"See who?" said Calabrese.

Then I thought I began to understand. Only natives could see Littlejohn, only those who belonged on Bible Hill by right of birth. No transplants, no flatlanders had the gift. Littlejohn's apparition was no ghost, but yet another principle of difference. To Amanda and her father, Littlejohn was available; to me, never.

Bitter irony. For Amanda wanted nothing to do with Littlejohn. He threatened her; he frightened her. But mainly, he bored her. *Work, birds. He writes them down. In the winter, it's cold; he writes it down. In the summer, it's hot; he writes it down.* And that's what there is and what there will ever be. Exactly that life, that monotony, was what Amanda had been willing to exchange for a doomed liaison with Denny, a squalid narcissist who was able to rise from the swamp of his damaged self only long enough to abduct her into an idle, violent demimonde three thousand miles away on the crazy coast. Even all that trouble and woe had looked better to Amanda than the long days of Bible Hill, Littlejohn's days. Littlejohn was what Amanda despised, and he watched her, pursued her, waited on her, waking and dreaming.

Whereas for my part, I loved Littlejohn. He fascinated me. He was my oracle, ever curious, ever apt. I longed to know him, to converse with him, to see him—even his shade. And I could not. Wanting nothing more than access to Littlejohn, his life, his time, I had none, apart from the dry pages of his daily log. Wanting nothing more than to put Littlejohn and his life from her forever, Amanda found he followed her around like a bill collector.

I understood that now. I understood more, as well: Our being here together wasn't going to work. Amanda wouldn't remain on Bible Hill. She wouldn't remain with, me. Littlejohn wouldn't let her. Littlejohn would drive her away.

March 7, 1937. Fair. Temp. 12M 37. Sap
March 8, 1937. Rain a.m. Temp. 12M 45. Sap

What is a ghost, I ask? Not what we think, perhaps. A ghost is no remnant, no essence, no spirit. A ghost is no argument for immortality, no argument against it. A ghost is a product of time, a projection of the past. It is the impress on the present of the past, a faint and fleeting impress. You think a ghost, or your belief in a ghost, has a purpose and a place. It hasn't. A ghost isn't even immaterial; it isn't even an illusion. It has nothing to do with you.

I keep thinking that when all this is over, you know what I mean, that I'll get to see Win again.

How?

I don't know, son. That's the thing. I've got no idea how it works. But I do think he'll be there. I don't know if he'll be, you know, older, or the age he was, but I believe he'll be there. I never thought that before.

What would you like him to be?

Oh, the same age, I guess.

Then that's it. Why not?

You don't believe it, though, do you, son?

No, I don't guess I do.

No. Well, but like I said, neither did I. Never. You get to where I am and see how it looks to you then.

I can wait.

For sure, you can. Wait as long as possible, son. I would.

July 25, 1940. Warm. Temp. 12M 77. Saw deer on road

"Do you love me, Noon?" Amanda asked.

"I do."

"But how, exactly, you know? I mean, suppose I didn't like it here. Suppose I thought about moving away. How would that be?'"

"That would be difficult."

"Would you love me just the same, then?"

"Yes," I said.

"Would you come with me?"

"No."

"There you go, Noon. Don't you see? How much can you love me if you won't follow me?"

I said nothing.

"The thing is, you and I come out of different places," Amanda went on. "You worked hard to get here. I worked hard to get away. You made it. I didn't. Now I'm back. It's not bad—I don't mean it's bad. It's certainly not as bad as I thought it would be before I came. I didn't know you'd be here, for one thing. Your being here makes it easier. Easier, but not easy. It's still a place I didn't want to be."

"It's just a place," I said. "If you love somebody, then isn't it that person who's important and not the place where that person is?"

"I could ask you the same question, Noon," said Amanda.

Amanda said love is a book: It has a setting, it has characters. Which is most important, Amanda asked? She thought she knew the answer: In love, the characters are more important than the setting. Maybe they are. But maybe, as well, Amanda's question was a question that can't be answered. She thought you could choose the way you make your book, but can you? I don't know that you can. You can choose the book you read but not the book you write.

22. Real Estate

1

On Bible Hill, the best property belongs to the dead. The old Bible Hill cemetery sits on a sunny slope near the foot of the hill. It's a square enclosing a half acre, more or less. It has a southern exposure. It's convenient to the road. It has several old sugar maples. It even has a good spring of water, something a cemetery, perhaps, hardly needs. As real estate, it's one of the nicest lots in the township, but of course it's not for sale. You can no longer get so much as a piece of it, even by dying: The Bible Hill cemetery is full up at about a hundred customers, though nobody knows exactly how many are buried there. Call it 110.

All told, the town has fourteen cemeteries, which would seem to be more than enough for a small place, except that eleven of them are like the one on Bible Hill, fully subscribed. Space has been a problem. Mr. Applegate once assured me that when he was a boy, the town cemetery commissioners, to make the available ground go further, ordered that burials be vertical.

Come on.

True fact, son. They put you in standing up and you had to have a yard of overhead. Anson Usher, Hugo's father, was about six and a half foot tall. That was quite a hole.

Ten feet deep?

Near enough. Course, they had to stop burying upright after a few years.

Why?

Couldn't find anybody to dig the graves. Do you know how much work a hole that deep is? Funny shape, too: eight, nine foot deep and three foot square. Like a well. Got so they couldn't find anybody who'd do the work for what they could pay. People your age don't want to work, it seems like.

So you keep telling me. Wait a minute, though. When was this, did you say?

Oh, I don't know. Forty, fifty years ago.

Your time, then, not mine, right? So it looks to me like people your age didn't want to work, either, did they? Ha.

You might have something there, too, son.

None of it was so. Nobody was ever buried standing up, not in these parts anyway. Mr. Applegate was once more having his little joke, and not any joke this time, but the ripest, best joke of all: death and dissolution. And to give Mr. Applegate his due, he was all of a piece in the matter. His illness grew upon him gradually, then not so gradually; and the closer his own death came, the more he reminisced, the more he jested, the more he was amused.

Amanda hated that.

August 25, 1921. Cool. Temp. 6 a.m. 58. To Mountain Fair. Reed's Tim took 1 tun pull. S.B.

August 26, 1921. Rain a.m. then clear. Temp. 12M 71.

Calabrese was selling up. He was leaving Bible Hill, leaving the state. He wanted to put his place on the market—or, better yet, he wanted to sell it to me.

"Twenty acres, five hundred feet of frontage. I bought it for ten thousand, raw land. It's yours for twelve, cash, kid. That's with the house, the driveway. The driveway alone's worth twelve grand."

"I don't doubt it," I said. "But I haven't got twelve thousand."

"Make me an offer," said Calabrese.

"I can't make you an offer," I said. "I've got no money."

"Bullshit, you got no money," said Calabrese. "You're rich, kid. Everybody knows it."

"Then they know more than I do," I said.

"This is your big chance here," said Calabrese. "Don't you want to be a land baron? It starts right here."

"No," I said.

Calabrese shook his head.

"All that work you put in over there," I said. "All the clearing. The driveway. Work on the house. So much work."

"Fucking A," said Calabrese.

"It's too bad," I said. "You've been there—what, five years?"

"Over six," said Calabrese.

"Why leave?"

"You think I want to?" said Calabrese. "I don't want to. I told you: I got no choice. They found me. I never thought they would, but they did. They fucking found me, and now I can do two things. I can wait for them to make their move, or I can move myself. I ain't waiting."

"Look," I said. "Okay, I know I don't know what you're talking about. I know you won't tell me. But I don't see why you can't get help. Go to the sheriff. Go to the state police."

Calabrese only laughed.

"I ought to have known better," he said after a moment. "I thought this was the place: so far away, nobody around, nothing going on, nobody knows you. I ought to have known. This ain't the place."

"What is?" I asked him. "Where are you going?"

Calabrese gave me a sly look.

"I thought about Italy," he said. "I'm a guinny, you know? We all want to go back."

"Or so you say."

"Yeah," said Calabrese. "So you won't make me an offer, right? Listen: You could rent the house out, get some income there, you're so-poor."

"I can't do it," I said. "I can't afford to, and anyway, I've got enough land."

"You won't think so when somebody comes in and builds a hundred and fifty shitbox ranch houses all over my place," said Calabrese. "We're talking about your neighbors here. You can't have enough land, kid."

"I'll plant shrubbery," I said.

"The hell you will," said Calabrese. "You're making a mistake here, you know—but it's your call. I'll go see Applegate, then, I guess. Tell him to list the place."

"Get somebody else," I said.

"Why?" Calabrese said. "I bought it from Applegate. He sold it once, he can sell it again."

"There are agents in Brattleboro," I said. "Get one of them. Applegate's sick. I doubt he'll want to take on anything new."

"Sick with what?" Calabrese asked.

"Cancer."

"Cancer?" said Calabrese. "I hadn't heard that. How is he doing with it? Okay?"

"No."

"Shit," said Calabrese. "I'm sorry for that. Applegate's all right, for a woodchuck. Listen: Ask him anyway, okay? If he can't do it, ask him to get me a name. I'm going. I need a name. I'll be in touch with whoever sells the place."

"What do you mean, you'll be in touch?" I asked Calabrese. "When are you leaving?"

"Soon," said Calabrese.

"So, if your friends come looking again, I'll tell them you're in Italy, is that it?" I asked him. "It's a big place, Italy. Where are you thinking of? Rome? Naples? Milan? What shall I tell them, when they come?"

"Tell them they can kiss my ass," said Calabrese.

2

Is it wrong to like cemeteries? Is it depressive? By no means. Cemeteries give you the aspect of death, its emotion, without its pain. That can't be wrong. The earth belongs to the living, said Jefferson, not the dead. Cemeteries are meant to be visited, to be enjoyed; why else do we take such pains in their improvement? Cemeteries give you death without loss, or at any rate they do as long as they aren't your cemetery.

Mr. Applegate's family was buried in the cemetery on the hill above Ambrose village; their stones leaned this way and that underneath the yellowing elms. There were Applegates there who had fought in George Washington's army, and there was a Dyer, an Applegate cousin, who had been in Congress. Mr. Applegate's own headstone was waiting for him, a slab of plain gray granite, already crowded—in fact, overcrowded:

APPLEGATE

ORLANDO APPLEGATE 1911–

EDITH APPLEGATE 1914–1964

WINTHROP APPLEGATE 1941–1957

WHEN TO QUIT

Outside the Trailways station in Presidio, four boys were fighting. Three of them were beating up the fourth, who was down. They were kicking him. Nobody seemed to care or even to pay much attention, so I went in to break them up. The three ran off. I helped the down boy to his feet. He was all right, maybe a little cut. He didn't speak English. He took off, too. What had I expected, thanks? I would thank myself. I would have a beer before I bought my ticket north. There was a café across the street from the bus depot. At the bar, I found my wallet was gone and, with it, all my money.

Enough, I thought. Get me out of here. Point me north, anywhere north. I had not done well by the South, and the South had not done well by me. Hitchcock thought the South so rough, so real—let him have it, then. I would give it up. We Noons know when to quit.

Once I had admitted myself knocked down, stripped, and beaten, my luck began to change. Hitchhiking again, I got a ride with a rancher who took me clear to Roswell, New Mexico, a matter of three hundred miles. Hitchhiking is easier in that country, I found. In Vermont, the driver who picks you up lives two miles down the line; you're back on the roadside before you have figured out what the funny smell in his car was. Not in New Mexico. There, everybody has at least a thousand miles to go. They drive in a trance, and their vast land pours under their wheels like a river in a dream. In Roswell, I was picked up by a kind of cowboy. He listened to my misfortunes, bought me a dinner and the beer I'd missed in El Paso, and drove me to Raton, another four hundred miles, in a busted Cadillac. He was going to the rodeo in Raton, almost on the Colorado line. He was a bull rider. We drove out the day, with the sun going down in the west like the end of the world, flaring scarlet and vermilion behind the crazy sharp mountains, or mesas, or buttes, or whatever you please, and ahead and on the right a flat dark tableland void of life except for rattlesnakes and jackrabbits. They will tell you that dry, dry country was once an ocean, those red mountains once a coast, wave-lapped. And if you believe that one, they'll tell you another.

By noon of the day after those clever kids had cleaned me out in El Paso, I was in Trinidad, Colorado, five hundred miles from the border, two thousand miles from the capital and its dank tropical complexities. I was waiting for a ride on a highway that went east. East. Get to Boston and make a left. (Those were my new instructions.) I believed I could just about smell low tide in the Atlantic bays, just about smell the spruces and balsams that cover the tops of the Green Mountains. Of course, I hadn't eaten anything, I hadn't slept, in thirty-six hours.

August 27, 1921. Cloud. Temp. 12M 76. Saw S.B. on road. To M. Fair with her Fri.

"What was the Mountain Fair?" I asked Amanda.

"Mountain Fair?" Amanda said. "Mountain Fair was like a farmers' fair when I was little, like an ag show. Mountain Fair. You know: livestock, pies, preserves. They had it where the flea market is now, on a day in summer sometime. July? August? I don't remember. There hasn't been a Mountain Fair in years."

"Did you go?"

"Sure," Amanda said. "Everybody did. They had rides, too, and games. That was about all there was to it when I went. There used to be more. Why? What about Mountain Fair?"

"Littlejohn writes about it in his diary."

"When?" Amanda asked.

"Several times. The time I'm thinking of, 1921."

"Oh," said Amanda. "Back then, Mountain Fair was a lot bigger thing. Ask my dad about it. Mountain Fair went on for days. People came from all over the state. They had races, shows. My dad could tell you. Mountain Fair used to get kind of rowdy, I think. Ask my dad."

"Littlejohn went three times that year," I said.

"I bet he did," said Amanda. "What else did he have to do, Claude? Mountain Fair would be the biggest thing in the year for him."

"That year's was anyway," I said. "He took a girl."

"A girl?" Amanda said. "What girl?"

"I think a friend of Agnes Drumheller's, another schoolteacher."

"Claude and a schoolteacher," said Amanda. "Wow. That must have been a match."

3

Not in the Bible Hill cemetery, but in the cemetery, even older, on Round Mountain was the grave of a man named Nash, who died in 1859 at the age of forty-seven and whose stone bore this epitaph:

Reader, regard me
As in Death's Embrace
At Heaven's Gate I stand,
Delivered by our Savior's Grace,
A PICKLE in my hand.

What was that about? What craziness was there given its final expression?

Another stone, from 1861, read simply:

An Unbeliever just
Proved wrong, we trust

Another, perhaps marking the grave of a bridge player:

I pass

What is going on here? Every cemetery in the township, every cemetery in New England cackles with the same silent clamor of bad verse, forgotten obsession, wisecracks, and one-liners. These people thought they were funny, and never more so than when newly dead and buried. Not all of them, though. Not all the dead are comics. Only the older sections of our burying grounds keep up their hollow laughter; gravestones from our own century are mostly mute. They seldom bear any epitaph at all, and never one that has the impudent wit of stones from the century before.

Why not? Why don't we go in for witty epitaphs anymore? A whole form of literature has gone extinct. Evidently, death doesn't crack us up today. Why doesn't it? Is it because we fear it more than our great-grandfathers did, or because we fear it less? Is it because we have less religion than they? Maybe so, but I don't believe it. I think that fact that our graves today are only graves and no longer tablets on which we inscribe our precious exit lines has nothing to do with death but comes instead from something worse: loneliness.

Our forebears were less lonely than we are, and more hopeful. If you take the time and pay the cost to arrange for a silly remark to be cut into your tombstone, you do so because you expect someone to read it, and not a casual stranger, but someone you know, your inheritor, or anyway someone who is connected to you closely enough that he'll get your joke. That expectation is what the old people had and what we have lost. They thought they left behind others who might care. We know better. They thought they were talking to somebody. We know better.

Nash believed his taste for pickles, or his mania for pickles, or his skill in making pickles, or his transaction with pickles, whatever its nature may have been, would live on through his funerary verses and bring an understanding smile to the lips of his friends and townsmen and their descendants. We know he was wrong. We know that very soon almost everything to do with our lives will be forgotten and left behind, and that nobody will remember, or care, or even see.

Littlejohn had a stone in the Bible Hill cemetery, too, and his stone was an exception to the rule of twentieth-century burials free of literature. Littlejohn had an epitaph.

CLAUDIUS LITTLEJOHN
1879–1961

Stayed behind
Gone before

Who put that there?

Mr. Applegate couldn't sell Calabrese's place for him. Even if he had been in good health, he was retired from the real estate business, he said.

Yes, I had to let the real estate go. I haven't done anything that way in two, three years.

Why not?

Well, it got too busy. You've heard that old story about the lady goes into the store in one of these little towns up here?

Yes.

She goes in there, asks for a box of, I don't know, Alka-Seltzer. And the clerk says, "We don't carry Alka-Seltzer anymore." And the lady asks him why not, and he says, "Well, Alka-Seltzer got to be so popular, we couldn't hardly keep it on the shelf, so we had to quit stocking it."

You're right. I have heard that one.

Sure, you have, son. Probably from me. It was the same with real estate, you see. When I opened my office here, right after the war, there weren't any real estate agents—well, maybe there were a couple in Brattleboro, but that was it. There was no real estate business to speak of. Nothing ever came up for sale, and if it did, nobody bought it, because nobody had any money then. It wasn't worth anybody's time selling real estate. Real estate was a nuisance. You couldn't make a living.

You can now.

You bet you can, son. I took on the real estate business as a sideline to the law office. Plus, I did some auctioneering in those days, for estates mostly, so it all fit together pretty well. For a long time, I was the only real estate man in the valley, and still I don't suppose I handled more than two or three properties in a year. Today, Lord. There must be seventy-five or eighty real estate offices right here in town.

There are three, I think.

Like I said. Real estate people are some thick on the ground now, even here. In Brattleboro, I bet there are a couple of thousand of them, agents, and every one of them is younger and smarter and stronger and better-looking than me.

And richer.

Richer by a lot. It got so I was bringing in—I don't know—fifteen, twenty thousand dollars a year in commissions, and I could see it was only going to get worse. I had to get out while I could.

So I'll tell Calabrese you're retired. Who shall I say can help him?

Tell him to call young Ginger Browning, works out of her house out past Dead River. She's just trying to break in. Sharp as a tack. Hard worker. She'll do a job for him. Tell Carlo to call Ginger. But not me. No, real estate ain't what it was.

I still think it sounds like the game for me.

And I still think you're wrong, son. You couldn't stand the pace.

The pace? What do you mean? I'm strong, and anyway, how bad can it be?

It will kill you, son. Ha.

August 28, 1921. Warm. Temp. 12M 81. Haircut
August 29, 1921. Temp. 6 a.m. 72 To Mt. Fair.
S.B. Photographer. Asked her

THREE TRAVELERS

There seemed to be a third man in the car now. I must have slept. From where I lay curled on the backseat, I could see the green lights from the dash glowing on the face of the driver and, beside him on the front seat, the head and shoulders of a passenger. The driver must have stopped for another hitchhiker while I slept. Wouldn't that have wakened me?

I sat up in the back and looked ahead past the driver and the new rider at the night highway unrolling like a shining rule in front of us. On either hand the silver roadside, then the blank, flat country.

The driver was an Indian, or he said he was. He had picked me up about suppertime. When I sat up, he turned his head toward me a little, nodded.

"Mmm," said the driver.

"Where are we?" I asked him.

"Oh, Wyoming someplace," the driver said.

That couldn't be. He had picked me up at a truck stop on Highway 50 outside La Junta, Colorado. He was going to Garden City, Kansas, he said. We were headed east. If I had slept for a couple of hours, we might by now have crossed into Kansas. Wyoming wasn't that way.

"How long was I out?" I asked the driver.

"Oh, for a long time," he said.

"How long?"

"Oh, a long time," said the driver.

"I thought we were going east," I said.

"Change of route," said the other man. He didn't turn toward me as he spoke. All I could see of him were his head and shoulders. He must have been a big man, broad, and wearing some kind of overcoat.

"I'm going east," I said. "Maybe you'd better drop me, next place we come to."

"Let's talk," said the new man. "You know: Here we are, out on the road, middle of the night, long drive, strangers. We might as well talk. What's your name?"

"Noon," I said.

"That's a funny name," said the passenger.

"You think so?" I said.

"Well, yeah," the passenger said. "Scotch, right?"

"Abenaki," I said.

"Is that right?" the man said. "He look like an Abenaki to you, does he, Charlie?"

"Oh, I guess so," said the driver.

"You're up from the South, I bet," the man said. "Whereabouts?"

"Around Roswell," I said.

"Nice town," said the passenger. "But you didn't start there, did you?"

"No," I said.

"I bet you came up from El Paso," the man said.

"Yes."

"Was a nice town," the man said. "The army ruined it. And then, then, before El Paso, I'm thinking you were right on down there with the tortillas and the *cucarachas,* am I right?"

"How did you know?"

The passenger chuckled.

"I could tell, you know?" he said. "Young fellow like you, gringo, crapped-out, wasted, dirty, hitchhiking, no clothes, no bags, hasn't eaten, hasn't slept, hasn't got two cents? Looks like he's been fucked in the ass by a telephone pole? Boy's been in Mexico. How did you like it?"

"Not much," I said.

"I bet," the man said. "But, let me see. You didn't start from Mexico, either, did you? Oh, no. You'll be on your way from much farther down, all the way down: We're talking about snakes, vines, bad water. You started way down there, didn't you? Do you know a guy named Hitchcock?"

"You know I do."

"What exactly did you do for Hitchcock down there?" the man asked me.

"You know?" I said. "I was never sure. What if I asked you?"

The man laughed. He shook his head.

"Knowing your ignorance, that's the beginning of wisdom, wouldn't you say?" he asked. "Be a shame to get in your way now you're finally on the right track. You wouldn't happen to know where Hitchcock is at this time, would you?"

"No."

"Or where he was headed?"

"No."

"You wouldn't, uh, hold out on me, now, would you?" the man said. "We're friends and all, but I've got to tell you, holding out on me would not be wise."

"I don't know where he is," I said.

"I believe you," said the passenger. "Boy, what a mess down there, though, huh? A confused situation. Were you there when they burned all those buildings?"

"Yes," I said.

"Just a badly confused situation. You were smart to get out. And, serious people, down there, wouldn't you say? Down there, they don't fool. You were lucky to get out."

"Yes."

"How did you happen to get out?" the passenger asked.

"Hitchcock."

"Where are you headed?" the passenger asked then.

"Back east."

"New York?"

"New England," I said.

"Boston?" asked the passenger.

"Vermont," I said.

"Vermont?" said the passenger. "That's part of Mass., no?"

"No," I said. "It's a state on its own."

"Is that right?" the passenger said. "What do you think of that, Charlie?"

"Oh, I don't know," said the driver.

"You've got a long way to go, then, don't you?" the passenger asked me.

"Yes."

"You'll get there," the passenger said. "I'm betting on you. What about you, Charlie?"

"Oh, sure," said the driver.

"It'll be light in another couple of hours," the passenger said. "What do you think, Charlie? How long to Cheyenne?"

"Oh, another couple of hours," said the driver.

"Nice town," said the passenger. "We'll get some breakfast. We'll drop you. We'll drop you at the station in Cheyenne. We'll even slip you your fare. How about that, Charlie? Can we go that far for this young fellow, do you think?"

"Oh sure," said the driver.

"You'll be on your way," said the passenger. "Hell, you already are. I'm going to give you a piece of advice."

"What's that?"

"You're on your way," he said. "You're practically gone. Don't come back. Go to—where, did you say?"

"Vermont."

"Vermont. Stay there. You're out, so be out. Whatever it was down there, it's over. You've left it. Keep it that way. Don't come back through here."

"That's a promise," I said.

"Don't come back. Don't try, not even part of the way," the big passenger said. "My advice."

"Cross my heart," I said.

4

August 31, 1921. Warm. Temp. 12M 79. To Mtn. Fair nigt. S.B. K. Brige. Her perfum. Her ribon

"What do you really know about Claude Littlejohn, Noon?" Amanda asked me.

"Really know?" I said. "Nothing."

"You think you would have liked him?"

"I don't know."

"You think he would have liked you?" Amanda asked.

"No."

"You've got that right," said Amanda. "Claude was a freak. He lived up here all alone. The kids were scared of him."

"Kids are scared of a lot of things," I said.

"We used to spy on him," Amanda went on. "You'd see him sitting out in his yard, just sitting. If he saw you, he'd wave his arms, curse, chase you off."

"He was probably drunk," I said.

"He probably was," said Amanda.

"I thought you were supposed to be his friend," I said. "You and your brother. You visited him, you told me."

"Because my father made us," said Amanda. "We wanted no part of Claude. We thought this house was haunted. All the kids did. We thought if he caught us up here, Claude would—I don't know—eat us, kill us. The boys used to dare each other to come up here on Halloween night and play tricks. Denny and the other boys. My brother."

"You, too?"

"No," said Amanda. "My brother. My father licked him for it. My father wanted us to feel sorry for Claude. He wanted us to respect him. He liked Claude. But Denny and my brother and the others would come up here on Halloween and knock Claude's outhouse over, put it in the road, paint it yellow, nail the door closed—anything they could think of."

"What did Littlejohn do?"

"Nothing," said Amanda. "He'd put the outhouse back up—or maybe he wouldn't. Maybe he'd do without an outhouse. My dad said that, you know, sanitation wasn't a priority with Claude."

"Littlejohn was a kind of troll," I said. "What makes a man a troll?"

"I don't know, Noon," said Amanda. "What do you think?"

"Ugliness," I said.

"What else?" asked Amanda.

"Too much of himself," I said.

"And what makes that?" Amanda asked.

"Bad luck."

Amanda shook her head.

"You don't think so?" I said. "What, then?"

"It's a choice, Noon, is what I think," Amanda said. "A man's a troll, it's because he wants to be."

What was Mountain Fair?

Mountain Fair? Mountain Fair was quite a show—used to be anyhow.

Livestock exhibits, preserves, baked goods, ring tosses, Amanda says. That kind of thing?

Well, yes, there were all those things at Mountain Fair. In Manda's time, there wasn't much else. Before, though, there was.

What?

Use your imagination, son. You know: racing, gambling, dice games; drinking; any amount of fighting; freak shows, tit shows, crotch shows. You could see about anything you could think up at Mountain Fair in the old days.

Was there a bridge of some kind? The K. Bridge?

Oh, the Kissing Bridge? Sure. The Kissing Bridge. They set it up with two-by-fours and canvas painted to look like one of the old covered timber bridges. Maybe seventy-five feet long. They'd just put it up there on the ground; it didn't go over anything. It was like a ride, you see, like a Tunnel of Love. Tractor at the far end, or a power winch. Cable running through the bridge to a car, other end, like a one-seat wagon. You and your girl bought a ticket, climbed into the car, they pulled you through the bridge. Dark in there. Private. You and your girl could kind of get all over each other in there. If you wanted to, that is. Nickel a time.

It doesn't sound like much.

No. Well, but suppose you wanted to, you could always pass the ticket man some extra fare—say a quarter, he'd slow that cable right down.

You and your girl would have time to do some work, now. For a buck, you could stay in the bridge long enough to get yourself triplets.

I see.

Oh, yes, Mountain Fair was quite a show. Back before my time, I guess, it was even worse. The fights were worse. My day, Mountain Fair was mostly for courting, you know, but in the old days, men were cut at Mountain Fair. Men were shot. They said. Course, they always say that, don't they, son?

Say what?

Say how much worse a thing used to be. How much better. Maybe it's so. There's never any way to know for sure.

No.

It's funny how you know less, not more. It don't seem right. It's like that story about the old fellow. They asked him, "What do you know for sure?" You heard that one, I guess?

Yes, that one, too.

Sure, you have. They asked him, "What do you know for sure?" And he said, "Not a goddamned thing." Well, but Mountain Fair was something. The state police and the sheriff didn't even try, at Mountain Fair. They brought in extra deputies, made like a perimeter around the fairground, put three or four patrol cars at the entrance, and just let her rip till it was over and they could get in there with the bucket and the mop.

Amanda hated her father's indifference to his end. She hated his strength, if strength is what it was, his high spirits. Her father's illness was always with Amanda; it grew inside her as it grew inside him, like another tumor, like a baby. It was always there. It was always getting bigger.

In the middle of the night, I would wake, to find she had left the bed. She'd be sitting alone in the kitchen or outside on the step. She couldn't sleep, she said. She was restless. After a while, she would come back to bed, but then she'd turn on her side and lie without sleeping. So we two would lie side by side, touching at the hip, at the shoulder, that close, and as far apart as a couple of constellations far out in the universe: the Twins, the Friends, the Lovers.

"I wish he'd quit pretending it's no big deal, what's happening to him," she said.

"He's trying to make it easier," I said.

"Easier for who?" Amanda asked.

"It's his way," I said.

"It's selfishness," said Amanda. "It's hardness. His way? I know his way as well as you do, Noon. I went clear to California, didn't I? I put the whole country between me and his way. But I didn't expect this. This is not what I expected."

"What did you expect?"

"Not this," said Amanda. "I don't know, but not this. See, Noon, if he's gone, really gone, not around, never going to be around—then that's a whole new game for me, you know? I don't know if I know how to play that game. I don't know if I know the rules. I don't know if I know where the field is."

"Sure you do," I said. "It's the same field you have now, the same rules you have now. You have to get up, go to work, come home. Eat. Sleep. You can do it. You're doing it now."

"It sounds like Claude," said Amanda.

"I know."

"You're wrong about him, Noon," said Amanda. "You always have been. He was no hero. You think he's simpler, tougher, clearer. Not like us, you think. We get all tangled up in each other, get complicated, make each other crazy. You think he doesn't do that."

"Who are we talking about, here?" I asked Amanda.

September 1, 1921. Holds warm. Temp. 12M 81. Mtn. Fair gone. Red leaves

Yes, Mountain Fair. Everybody loved Mountain Fair. I recall one year somebody came up with the idea of having two Mountain Fairs, one spring, one fall. Everybody had such a great time, why have it only once a year? It didn't fly, though. Town Meeting voted it right down.

Why?

Too much fun.

"And so what happened to this girl, I wonder, Noon?" Amanda asked me. "Claude's schoolteacher girl from Mountain Fair. She and Claude, did they live happily ever after?"

"No."

"Didn't they?" said Amanda. "Why aren't I surprised? What happened?"

"She went away."

"Did she?" said Amanda.

"That's right. She went away and left him here."

"Did she?" said Amanda.

23. Blood Sport

Deer season. In November, in the low, gray and blue days, the hunters leave their trucks beside the road, load their guns, and step off into the woods. They find their spot and sit and wait for the deer to come picking their way along the old stone walls, putting down their little feet so carefully, like a class of ballet dancers learning to walk on their toes. The gunshot makes them scatter—all but one. It wasn't my sport. I didn't hate deer hunting, but I left it to others; it was harder work than I wanted. I could as easily have shot a child.

The white-tailed deer was the sovereign game on Bible Hill, but it was by no means the sole. We hunted black bear, as well, and squirrel, rabbit, coon, woodchuck, porcupine, partridge, turkey, woodcock, ducks, geese. We'd have hunted elephants and tigers if we'd had any; we'd have hunted dinosaurs.

It wasn't my sport, but one year I thought, Why not give it a try? I let the deer alone. With the shotgun I inherited when Calabrese went away, I set up in the fall as a bird hunter. On Bible Hill, we didn't fool much with gundogs and retrievers: You were on your own. You walked down a logging road in the woods, your piece held alertly at port arms, until you started a partridge. Mostly, you never saw them; they flushed from the side and racketed off into the thickets, but sometimes a partridge flew across the road ahead of you, or ran across. Others flew only a short distance into the woods and landed well within sight on low tree branches, swaying and looking back at you. Then you had a shot, but still it wasn't easy. Calabrese's shotgun put me right back on my heels when it went off, and its noise made me deaf. I burned up a hundred or more of the big red shells it fired, at three bucks for twenty, and I cut down a couple of acres of brush before I killed at last.

The partridge scurried across the path fifty feet in front of me, then took off and flew back across the path to land in a little fir. I threw up the gun and fired. I saw the partridge's feathers fluff, saw it thrown backward out of its tree and into the path. By the time I got to it, it was trying to get into the woods again, flopping and flapping on the ground but making no progress, because only one of its wings worked. The poor thing was scuffling around in a circle among the fallen leaves, like a crazy man trying to row a boat with one oar. I killed it with the gun stock. Having shot the bird, I finished by beating it to death.

So I took early retirement as a hunter. Hunting, I decided, is fun just as long as you fail.

There you are, son.

Here I am. Can I get anything for you?

No, son. Thanks. I'm not hitting on all six today, I guess.

Are you in any pain?

No, no. Nothing like that. I'm okay, that way. It's the time of the year. I don't like this time of the year.

The fall?

Deer season.

August 1, 1898. Fair. Temp. 12M 71. W. Blake says saw deer in orchard. Buck deer, he says

In Littlejohn's youth, there weren't any deer on Bible Hill, or anyway there were few. The landscape in those days—pasture, mowing, plow land, with small woodlots widely separated—made poor deer range. Nevertheless, Littlejohn and his neighbors were hunters, as their hearts beat and they drew breath; you don't stop being a hunter just because there's no game. On the contrary: Any deer that showed its white and lively hind quarters on Bible Hill in the old days drew a storm of shot and shell worthy of Passchendaele. And so the deer, already scarce, became scarcer.

Then the last hill farmers, Littlejohn's generation, sold up, and their places returned to forest, becoming in the process exactly the kind of small hardwood brush that deer were made to inhabit. The deer came back. They found a whole state's worth of new forage and cover. They multiplied. Today, deer are as common, are more common on Bible Hill than cats and dogs.

Yes, the deer multiply, but, curiously, the hunters do not. Every year, there are fewer hunters on Bible Hill. When there were no deer, everybody was a deer hunter; now there are a million deer, and the hunters dwindle. Not that deer hunting is obsolete—not at all. Bible Hill isn't hunting country the way it once was, perhaps, but neither is it any kind of sanctuary. Deer season remains a time of the year with a purpose, a time when you put away childish things.

I used to like it, this time of the year. It was the best time of the year, I thought. You get up early, get out in the woods. It's cold; it's quiet. Maybe there's some snow. There's nothing like it, deer season. I loved it. I did. You know what happened, with Win, don't you, son?

Yes.

I thought so. You live around here any length of time, you hear about it. You might not hear about anything else, but you hear about that.

Yes.

Best time of the year. The time you feel most alive. First deer I ever shot, it was up on the ridge behind your place. I can take you to the spot. I saw him and he was running and I shot him running. I was thirteen.

On Bible Hill, we hunted deer, bear, varmints, fowl. We hunted them with whatever weapon might do the job: rifles, shotguns, handguns, muskets, revolvers, crossbows, longbows, slingshots—if you can point it and shoot it, there are hunters who favor it.

Of all the hunters, the truest, perhaps, the most rigorous, were the bow-and-arrow men. To kill a deer, a bear, a turkey with an arrow, you need a perfectly clear shot; you need to be close. And so the bow hunters hid from their quarry in a way other hunters did not. They put on camouflaged clothing, mottled in green and brown and black, and they lay in wait in the woods. So hidden were the bowmen, so still, you wondered whom, exactly, they were hunting.

One afternoon in November, I took a walk in the woods above Sheep Desert. There was a kind of trail you could follow over the top of the hill. It went through a woods of oak and beech, with here and there a pine or a big sugar maple, and you came to little openings full of dead brown ferns. I dawdled along, not paying much attention to the trail, listening to the noise my feet made among the dead leaves, listening to the racket the crows were putting up in the trees about the top of the rise.

"I don't want to scare you."

Another two steps and I would have walked into him, would have kissed him: a man, a bow hunter, standing close beside the trunk of a pine, in the shadow of its lower branches. He had on the pied green suit and held a bow covered by a canvas sleeve similarly colored, and his face was painted green and brown like an Indian's. He stayed in among the pine branches.

"I didn't want to scare you," the hunter said. "I've been watching you for ten minutes."

I took a second to get my legs back under me. I had almost sat right down on the ground when he spoke. "I never saw you," I said.

"Course you didn't," said the hunter. I thought I knew him from town. He was a cousin of the Tavistocks, I thought, but I couldn't be certain, with his face painted over the way it was.

"I've been up here since four A.M.," the hunter said. "There's a buck up here someplace with a set of horns like your granny's rocking chair. I'm waiting on him. I haven't seen him, but I will."

It seemed strange to be so far out in the woods, conversing with this apparition, but it seemed stranger to part from him casually and go my way, as on a street in town. I lingered.

"Have you seen anything else?" I asked the bow hunter.

"Seen you."

August 4, 1898. Temp. 6 a.m. 58. Rain a.m. then fair. Saw deer long mowing looked prety big. Same one was at Blakes?

HOW THEY DO THINGS: PART I

Three boys from the streets, thieves, had been taken to the police station at La Palina. Hitchcock was going there to see them. He wanted me to come, too.

"This will interest you, Mark," Hitchcock said. "It will give you a sense of how they do things down here. Come along."

He hurried down the stairs. I followed him. When we reached the street, I saw Hitchcock meant to drive to the police station.

"It's right around the corner," I said. "Let's walk."

"We haven't time," said Hitchcock.

Win liked it too, right off. From the time he could figure out what was going on, he wanted to go along. He'd go out with Errol and me. Seven, eight years old, he'd sit out there with me, sit for four hours, five hours, in the rain. He wouldn't fidget, either, like you'd expect a kid to do. Sit there like an Indian, Win would.

They were set up in the little closed yard behind the police station, an area the size of half a tennis court: a masonry wall all around, nine or ten feet tall, with wire along the top; a row of motor scooters parked; the ground paved with brown gravel. Hitchcock and I came out the rear door of the station. There were nine men waiting, and at the end of the yard, under the wall, the three boys, seated on chairs, common kitchen chairs made of metal, with plastic seats.

I got him a rifle when he was eleven. Before that, it's no good—they think it's a toy. I got him a thirty-thirty, a little too big of a rifle for a boy, so he'd know it was something serious when he let it off.

A deer rifle.

That's right. I didn't let him go out alone. He went with me or with Errol and me, both. Young as he was, he took it seriously. He was careful; he wouldn't just shoot. The year before the last year, he took a shot for the first time, but he missed. He didn't care; it was just being out there like that, at that time of the year. He loved it.

He loved being out there with you.

It was the whole thing. He loved it, the way you do when you're a kid and you can really love it. Later, it ain't the same, is it? It's always good, but it ain't the same.

No.

Win and I set out before light. There had been maybe an inch of snow, and we were going up the beech woods there on Round Mountain, above where the road quits. You know where I mean?

I know the place.

The men waiting in the courtyard made a group. Five of them were in army uniform. They stood between Hitchcock and me and the three on chairs. Hitchcock went around to the side of the group. Lieutenant Hector was there. He nodded at Hitchcock. Hitchcock and I went over to stand near the wall where the scooters were parked. We were between the group of army officers and the three boys. The boys sat facing the wall of the courtyard, with their backs to us. Nobody was with them. Nobody was talking to them or otherwise paying any attention to them. The boys were tied to their chairs with clothesline.

December 1, 1898. Snow a.m. then clear. Temp. 12M 29. To Blakes to see deer he shot. Buck deer. Shot it out of orchard. Crowd to see it. 8 points. 227 lb.

No, the deer hunting isn't what it was. The hunters are different. The deer are different. They're diminished. In Littlejohn's time, you might have seen a deer every two or three years. If you were a hunter, you might have killed one six or eight times in your life. But the deer you so rarely saw weighed two hundred pounds, more. They were the size of horses.

Today, the deer overrun the woods. You don't have to hunt them: You hit them with your car. They have eaten up the woods; they're starving. They don't grow. Today, the hunters are bringing in deer that weigh sixty-five pounds, seventy pounds. They bring in deer the size of a German shepherd. These deer aren't juveniles, either. They're pygmies.

There are other differences between hunting today and the old hunting. In Littlejohn's time, deer hunting was a sport. You shot at bucks only, never does. There might have been life commandments that you could ignore, but not that one, not the buck rule. Partly, the buck rule had a scientific basis. Where deer were few, females had to be spared to reproduce. But mostly, I have always believed, the buck rule was a cracked analogue of antique chivalry: You were to treat women well; you were to treat women with courtesy. On no account were you to shoot them.

Today, both the science and the chivalry of deer season are quite obsolete. Deer hunting is now a means of population control on a badly overcrowded species. Deer season is a time for herd management. Does are therefore open game; in fact, from the game-management point of view, they are the preferred game. Nor do we any longer spare does out of a sense of right conduct. It is true that on Bible Hill, even today, you can't shoot women, but the analogy to deer hunting has evidently lost most of its force.

We left the car alongside the road about first light. My idea was that we'd have enough light to see to walk up to the beech woods and get there about when the deer were bedding down. Maybe we'd find a good line of tracks in the snow on the way up there, you see.

Yes.

We did. About half an hour into the woods, we found a big track going our way—not real big, but a good deer, and a buck, because we also saw piss tracks. We got to the beeches, and the tracks went right on in there. I believed the deer would be in the beeches, bedded down, because of the way the land lay there, and because of the way the little beech trees keep their leaves into winter, they make a lot of cover.

One of the boys was older, about twelve. He kept trying to turn his head to see behind him. The other two were nine or ten. They sat still and looked down at their laps. Their chairs were placed a couple of feet apart. Hitchcock and I were ten feet behind them and to their right.

We got into the beeches, and the tracks quit on us; there wasn't enough snow down on the ground in there for tracking. So my idea was that Win would take his stand where we were, looking ahead into the beeches, and I'd swing out to the left and work around the edge of the beeches, not taking much care about how I went, so as to put the deer up out of his bed and push him back to Win. So Win would have a shot, you see?

Yes.

There was a stone wall ran through the woods there. We put Win behind it, under a big beech. He was to wait there for the deer to be drove to him, or for me to come calling to him. He wasn't to move, not for nothing. That's how you do it. That's how we'd done it before, more than once. We'd done it in that same woods, maybe under that same tree. We left Win there and I set out by the left.

HOW THEY DO THINGS: PART II

Lieutenant Hector left the group of officers and started down the courtyard toward the prisoners. His black boots, crunched on the gravel as he walked.

. . .

I had the wall off on my right, I guess a hundred feet off, with the beech leaves hanging everywhere between—that tan color they have, you couldn't much see for distance. I went along; by now, the sun was up, all the snow was gone, and I was making a good deal of noise amongst the leaves as I went, to push the deer back to Win, you see?

Yes.

Hitchcock leaned toward me. He spoke quietly.

"Listen, Mark," he said. "It's important you keep your feet. We don't want you going weak in the knees. Do you understand?"

I didn't answer him.

"If you feel faint," Hitchcock said, "just sit on one of the bikes. Do you understand? Or lean against the wall. But stay on your feet. Stay on your feet and keep quiet."

I had about got through the beeches—they were thinning out—when I looked over and saw our deer. I saw him. I saw his head and his neck and his foreshoulder, and I saw his horns, hard and clean, six points. He was, I don't know, a hundred feet away, on the other side of the wall, down a kind of alley between the trees, where you could see through. I saw him. He was not going back Win's way; he was out in front of me, heading away, going along the stone wall in my same direction. Win wasn't going to get a shot at him, but I had one.

Yes.

Lieutenant Hector approached the row of prisoners in their chains. He stopped a couple of feet behind the boy on the left. He wore a sidearm in a holster on his belt on his left hip. Lieutenant Hector unfastened the flap on the holster and drew out the pistol with his right hand. He raised the pistol over his head and pointed it at the sky. He brought his left hand up to the pistol and cocked it—a double snap.

I put off my safety and I braced my barrel against a tree and I fired. I put the bead on his neck and I fired. But I knew the same time I pulled the trigger that he wasn't right. Something about him was not right. But I didn't know what it was. Yes, I did.

Lieutenant Hector lowered the pistol and held it about six inches from the back of the boy's head. He fired, one time. The pistol was a big and heavy one, and in the courtyard the shot was very loud. The boy jerked forward a little, but he was held against his chair by the clothesline. Lieutenant Hector took a step to his right and shot the second boy, then the third. The third was the older boy. He had been trying to turn in his chair, but now he looked ahead and down, like the others.

I walked over there. I didn't run. I got to the wall. Win was down on the other side, under the wall. Something had made him leave his stand and walk ahead along the wall. Maybe he saw the deer and went after it. He was not where he was supposed to be.

Win was lying on his side. He was lying under the wall in a pile of dead leaves. His eyes were open, but he wasn't moving anymore. There was blood everywhere: on the leaves, on the stones. Blood was coming out of his mouth, his nose, his ears. Then it stopped. I stood there and looked over the wall at Win.

. . .

Lieutenant Hector returned to the group of army officers. Somebody gave him a cigarette. Somebody else lit it for him. Nobody had much to say. The boys sat in their chairs; their heads and upper bodies sagged forward in their ropes. Their blood—not a great deal of it—had spattered on the brown gravel in front of them, as though someone had taken a paintbrush, dipped it, and flung the paint from it along the ground from left to right.

I don't remember much after that. It's like I went to sleep. I must have come down out of the woods and gone for help, but I don't remember doing it. I left Win up there. I couldn't have carried him all that way. Tubby Brackett and Errol went up and brought him out. I must have gone to find Edith and told her, but I don't remember it. Somebody must have gone for Manda—she'd have been in school. It might have been me. I don't remember doing it. Maybe somebody else did it.

"You held up very well, Mark," said Hitchcock. "Feel rocky, do you?"

Deer season. Every year, this time, it's with me. I wish it wasn't.

The body of the boy on the left slumped to its right and tipped over in its chair. It tipped over against the body of the boy in the middle, and the middle body tipped against the body on the right, and so the three fell sideways like a row of dominoes. Somebody laughed.

One thing, son, Mark: This will be the last time. Deer season next year, I'll be gone.

"What did they steal?" I asked Hitchcock.

"Food," Hitchcock said. "Let's go, shall we?"

December 2, 1898. Cold. Temp. 6 a.m. 18. With gun to Blakes orchard. No deer no traks

"We were doing state capitals," Amanda said. "Miss Drumheller had her map down. It pulled down like a window shade in front of the blackboard. The door opened and the principal looked in and he kind of beckoned to her. Miss Drumheller went out in the hall for a minute. Then she came back in and said, 'Amanda Applegate.'

"So I got up and went out in the hall, and the principal had my mom and Mrs. Brackett out there with him, Tubby's wife. I said, you know, hi, and she said, 'Hello, dear,' and looked at my mom. My mom didn't say anything. She was looking straight ahead, not at me. They took me down the hall and out the front door, and there was our car and Tubby standing by it and my father in the backseat in his red jacket. He and my brother had gotten up in the middle of the night to go hunting that morning early, but my brother wasn't with him now."

December 4, 1898. Cold. Temp. 6.a.m. 21. To Blakes. No deer

"When my brother died," Amanda once told me, "I was eleven. I didn't know what had happened. The truth is, I didn't really pay much attention. Does that sound bad?"

"You were eleven," I said.

"But then when my mom died," Amanda said, "I knew it. I knew it because of my dad. For him, it was like Win dying all over again. You see what I mean? I don't mean my mom's dying reminded him of Win's. I mean it was like Win had died a second time and my mom wasn't part of it—she was just not there. Do you see, Noon?"

"I'm not sure."

"And my dad went around . . . it was like he'd died, too, but they forgot to bury him. His life was over, too. He acted that way for a long time."

"He told me," I said.

"Even later," Amanda said, "after, when I was with him, it was like he wasn't with me, not all of him, not easily, not the way he was with you, say. It was like I always made him go away to the place where he went to miss my brother. And I wanted to say, you know, Hey, what about me? They're gone, but I'm not. I'm still here. I didn't die."

I didn't say anything.

"And so I wondered," Amanda went on. "What about my mother? Isn't she just as dead as Win? Don't we get to miss her, too? And I asked myself, If it had been me that died that way, and not my brother, would he have been so sad for so long? And I thought I knew the answer to that."

"You don't," I said.

"Don't I, Noon?" said Amanda. "Don't I know why he won't let them treat him now, why he just lets himself get sicker? It's because he'd rather be with my brother. He rather be dead and with Win than alive and with me. You know that's true."

I shook my head.

"You know it, Noon," said Amanda. "You know it because you're just like him."

"No, I'm not," I said.

"Sure you are," said Amanda. "You don't get it: You are, and that's the trouble. That's the trouble here."

November 26, 1914. Rain. Temp. 12M 44. To town. At store A. Usher with deer he shot. 207 lbs. Buck deer 6 points. Usher shot it on Round Mtn.

24. Departures

We are willing to see our sons emigrate, as to see our hives swarm. That is what they were made to do, and what the land wants and invites.

—Ralph Waldo Emerson, *"Boston"*

1

On Bible Hill, sooner or later, everybody went west. Well, not everybody. Amanda went west, to be sure, but some went east, Calabrese, for example (unless he lied). Some, like Usher, went nobody knew where. Some, like Miss Drumheller, went no place. And some went neither east nor west, but simply went, like Mr. Applegate.

Mr. Applegate died on an Indian Summer afternoon at the end of November: a bright, warm day, a day out of its season—a good day to go. Amanda had taken to bringing him his mail from the post office every day and spending the afternoon with him. *He and I get on okay as long as we keep it light*, Amanda had said; bringing the mail was a way of keeping it light. On the day I have now to tell of, I went along with Amanda to her father's. It was Saturday. I was working at Raymond's garage in Dead River that fall. Raymond gave me Saturday off.

Mr. Applegate had been feeling pretty well, he said, and when Amanda and I arrived at his place with his mail, we found him sitting out back on a lawn chair pulled into the sunny spot in front of his woodshed. Afternoons at that time of the year, the reluctant sun comes flat across the land and reaches through doorways and into sheds and barns and the like recesses that it doesn't penetrate in other seasons.

"There you are," said Amanda to her father. "What are you doing out here?"

"I'm working on my tan," said Mr. Applegate.

"That's good," Amanda said. "You could use some color, you know it?"

"Well," said her father, "I ain't sure for what, but it feels good. Does anybody but me want a beer?"

"I'll drink a beer with you," I said.

"I knew you wouldn't be behindhand, son," said Mr. Applegate. "What about your girlfriend here?"

"Sure," said Amanda.

At that point, I discovered we'd left Mr. Applegate's mail in the car. So I went around the house to get it, and Amanda went into the kitchen to get the beer. While she was in the kitchen, the telephone rang and Amanda answered it. I could hear her talking into the telephone. I got Mr. Applegate's mail out of our car, and as I shut the door, I looked across the valley and saw a hawk or other big bird sailing on the bright blue air above the Dead River. I watched it pass out of sight. As I started back around the house with the mail, I heard the crash of the breaking bottles on the stone path in the rear, where Amanda had dropped the beer, and I heard her cry out, "Noon!"

Over two hundred years, almost from its first settlement, the township has been shedding restless people to the west. Many of the children of the first settlers, and most of their grandchildren, moved on. They held to the north, for the most part, moving into western New York State and on to the Great Lakes. They were present at the creation of Michigan, Illinois, Wisconsin, and Iowa. They prospected for gold in California, for silver in Nevada. By all possible means, they went broke in every state and territory from the Ohio River to the Pacific.

Everywhere they went, they brought the names they had left behind. There is a little town in Michigan, not far from Lansing, called Vermontville; and you can drive through Ambrose, New York, in Niagara County, though it won't take you much longer than it would to drive through its Vermont namesake. Woodstock, Illinois, is an ex-Vermonters' town, I'll bet; and so is Grafton, Wisconsin; and Burlington, Iowa; and no doubt they would have a Bible Hill in Nebraska if they had hills in Nebraska.

Always the people left for a reason, they said: the lousy farming, the lousy weather, the no money, the nothing happening, the nothing to do. They left in search of opportunity, they said—but opportunity for what, exactly? No: Opportunity was no more than an excuse. In fact, they were restless, like Amanda. They simply didn't like feeling stuck, didn't like being held, even tenderly—just as a cat will lie in its place in perfect contentment until you take it lightly by the tail and gently hold it, when it will decide to move.

The people went west, and at their backs there quickly evolved the specific, unmistakable emblem, the epitome of Bible Hill: the abandoned farm. The fallen barns, the cellar holes, the scattered bricks, the machinery rusting in the corners of mowings gone to wild Christmas trees, the stone walls, stone piles, stone pens, stone foundations embowered in woods and thickets—they are the charmed remnants of a stark and frightening choice. For what kinds of choices do you get, mostly? Choices with soft edges. You can be a doctor or a lawyer, a scholar or a wage earner, a husband or a bachelor, rich or poor, idle or busy, happy or melancholy. These choices are nothing: You can and will move between and among them; you can decline to make them. But the choice of place is different. The choice to move on, you make once.

2

April 2, 1907. Rain a.m. Temp. 12M 48. To Lincolns aucton
April 5, 1907. Fair Temp. 6 a.m. 39. Robbin. Lincolns gone

Arthur Brackett had a registered letter for Calabrese, but Calabrese was not to be found. Tubby stopped at my place. He needed a signature.

"Carlo's not there?" I asked Tubby.

"Not yesterday, not today," said Tubby. "His mail's piling up, too."

"He must have left, then," I said.

"He's supposed to sign for this," Tubby said.

The letter was from a law firm in Philadelphia.

"I could sign for it, I guess," I said.

"I wouldn't," said Tubby.

"No," I said.

After Tubby drove off, I went up the road to Calabrese's. His truck was gone. His front door was open. I went in. If Calabrese had left for good, he hadn't taken much with him: Shelves and cupboards were full. On the table in the kitchen was an envelope with my name written on it.

TAKE WHAT EVER YOU NEED I WONT
NEED IT WONT BE BACK GOOD LUCK
C. C.

I looked around Calabrese's kitchen, a neat kitchen, with its supplies in place just so. What did I need of them? I took salt, coffee, soap. I took a windup kitchen timer, a kerosene lamp, another lamp. As I got ready to leave, I saw Calabrese's shotgun leaning against the wall behind the door, the same shotgun he had wanted me to fire to warn him of visitors looking for him. I took it, too. Everybody ought to have a shotgun, I thought.

On the way back to my place, I collected Calabrese's mail from his box on the road. Later, I took it down to the post office and turned it in. Tubby might have done that, but postal regulations were that he couldn't, he said. So I did it, and then Calabrese was really gone. If the post office thinks you're gone, you're gone.

"I understand your lady friend has decamped," said Miss Drumheller.

"Yes."

"Where to?"

"Ohio," I said. "She's going to stay with her cousins. She'll be back, she says."

"I doubt it," said Miss Drumheller. "Ohio . . . Sibyl came from Ohio, a town in Ohio. It had an odd name. I'll think of it. Her father was one of the big men there. He had the bank or the store—I don't remember which. Sibyl had her training at a normal school around there. I'll think of the name. Then she came east. I'll think of the name by-and-by."

"How did you know her?" I asked Miss Drumheller.

"Chillicothe," said Miss Drumheller. "She came from Chillicothe, Ohio."

"You were out there, too, then?" I asked.

"Never," said Miss Drumheller. "I knew Sibyl in Albany. We boarded in the same house in Albany. We both had our first teaching posts at schools in Albany, and we boarded in the same house. It was run by an Irishwoman. I'll think of her name. She was a widow. Irish, but very nice just the same. She catered to teachers. I'll think of her name."

"You haven't thought of the name of the school yet," I said.

"I will," said Miss Drumheller. "We lived there that first year. Then Sibyl took a job in Boston and I came up here. Nineteen nineteen. Mrs. Maugham. That was it. The same name as the author. It doesn't sound Irish, but she was. She was very nice, though, very strict. Sibyl didn't get on with her at all."

"Why not?"

"Sibyl could be—not wild. Stubborn. Not stubborn—impulsive—quixotic. She followed her heart, she said. I laughed at her. I told her she didn't know what she was talking about. Her children loved her and she loved them, but she was no teacher. She had no discipline. And, of course, she had no real education."

"Unlike you," I said.

Miss Drumheller looked at me. "That's right," she said. "Unlike me. The truth is, Sibyl was a fool in many ways. When she came up here from Boston for her summer visit the last time, she was engaged to a perfectly suitable young man who was at the Harvard Law School. A most promising young man. They were engaged, and then what does she do but fall into some ridiculous . . . intrigue, some . . . flirtation . . . with Claude Littlejohn."

"Flirtation?"

"Yes. That's all it was, at least for Sibyl. She led him on, is the truth. Oh, she didn't admit it. She insisted it was more. She made a fool of him and she made a fool of herself. She went with him to that horrible carnival they had here in those days, where no decent woman could be seen. She hung on his arm through the fair like any . . . factory girl . . . like any . . . tart. It was pathetic, but it was not out of character."

"Maybe she liked him," I said.

"I suppose she did," said Miss Drumheller. "What of it? Yes, she liked him. She talked about breaking off her engagement, giving up her post in Boston, and coming back up here to be with him."

"That doesn't sound like a flirtation to me," I said.

"A flirtation is all it ever was," said Miss Drumheller. "But when she pretended it was more, when she threatened to break with her young man in Boston, that was the . . . end—that was the . . . limit, for me."

"For you?"

"Yes. At last I sat her down. On that sofa. I sat her down and I talked to her. I talked to her in no uncertain terms. I tried to make her see that she could not simply throw over her fiancé and quit her school and . . . traipse—traipse up to the hills and into the—well, into the bed of some, bathless, drunken, illiterate, bankrupt—dirt farmer."

"He wasn't illiterate," I said.

"I beg your pardon?" said Miss Drumheller.

"He wasn't illiterate," I said. "I have the diary he wrote. He wasn't illiterate."

"Oh, spare me," said Miss Drumheller. "Very well. He wasn't illiterate. But for her, he was out of the question—impossible."

"Unsuitable," I said.

"*Unsuitable* doesn't begin to say it," said Miss Drumheller. "At last I told Sibyl that if she was going to continue to carry on with him, she would have to leave my house. 'If you want to go to him, then go,' I told her. 'Go ahead. Go today, this minute.' Well, even Sibyl wasn't that much of a fool. In any case, she left not long after to return to Boston."

"Married the Harvard Law School guy," I said.

"I believe so," said Miss Drumheller. "We didn't keep up. We didn't part on good terms, that summer."

"About the fair," I said.

"What fair?" asked Miss Drumheller.

"Mountain Fair," I said. "Where Littlejohn took your friend? Where she hung on his arm like a tart? Where no decent woman would be seen?"

"What about it?" Miss Drumheller said.

"How do you know she hung on him there?" I asked her. "Were you there, where no decent woman would go? Did you follow them there?"

"Lorain," said Miss Drumheller.

"What?"

"Lorain Central Normal School," said Miss Drumheller. "Where Sibyl trained. I told you I'd think of it, and I have."

3

October 25, 1933. Fair. Temp. 12M 60. V. Munro says patriges at Lincolns

October 26, 1933. Frost then mild. Temp. 12M 68. To town for shells

With everybody leaving for the west, Vermont more and more came to look like the Israel of America, exiling its sons and daughters to populate every part of the land, to the point where the home patch began to show a bit thin. In 1850, half the people then living who had been born in the state of Vermont were residents of other states, and for the town of Ambrose, the figure was closer to two-thirds. At the turn of the twentieth century, those ratios were essentially unchanged.

Even a superficial knowledge of our national past allows you confidently to plot the exodus from Vermont against the famous stations of American history. Beginning with the opening of the West via highway and canal around 1825, continuing through the experience of the Civil War, the coming of the railroads, the factories, and the industrial economy, and culminating in the rise of the great eastern cities and their suburbs into the twentieth century, every event, every theme in the country's story was a reason to leave places like Bible Hill, not to stay. People are not dumb. They know what is happening in their times; they feel it. For a hundred years and more, people in these parts had no choice but to conclude that if they would prosper—not only in their purses but in their larger lives—if they would take the full ride that their extraordinary nation held out to them, then they must join the diaspora. The alternative was to fail your own history, to live and die outside of it.

Still, grateful as they were to be away, they doubted from time to time, or at least those of the generation that actually put shoe leather to the road doubted. They wanted somehow to have both lives, if they could: the new life in the new land that they had sought, the life they were living, and the old life in the hills that they had left, the one they knew they might have lived had they stayed home. The exiles to the West, perhaps, couldn't quite bring themselves to choose between their lives. Hence the curious and short-lived institution of Old Home Week, for twenty or thirty years an annual event in towns like Ambrose, Vermont.

Old Home Week began in New Hampshire in 1899, but the occasion was quickly reproduced in the other New England states, for the idea plainly answered to the spirit of the time. During Old Home Week, men and women who had moved away from town were invited for a week in August to return to their former setting. They would stay with family or in lodgings, visit with old friends who had emigrated, with old friends who had not, join Old Home Week parades and pageants, drink lemonade and eat chicken dinners, listen to band concerts and lectures and speeches and recitations of the sentimental verses that were composed by the furlong for the occasion. They would attend church services, they would let on that, yes, they had done pretty well in Buffalo or Cleveland or Detroit (the ones who couldn't make that claim were not apt to come to Old Home Week, perhaps), they would have their pictures taken by a hired photographer, and they would leave town at the end of the week rested and restored by this brief immersion in their pasts, in their own lives as fondly imagined but never lived.

They would leave rested and restored, and they would leave having spent a certain amount of money, an aspect of Old Home Week by no means lost on its organizers in towns whose treasuries had gone west along with the emigrants. If those enterprising townsmen had done so well by departing, then let them bring something back, some gold from away for the benefit of their old neighbors, who, in ever leaner times, knew the name of every quarter and dime in circulation in their township. Old Home Week was an opportunity for lively commerce in rooms and meals, souvenirs, maple sugar, and cemetery plots, and it was the occasion for considerable lobbying by the town fathers of any prosperous returnee.

The first Old Home Week in the town of Ambrose was held in 1902. The occasion was an annual event for thirty-four years. At Old Home Week in 1905, it was announced that Pliny Addams, who had left town to go to war in 1862 and later set up in the Middle West, had donated twenty thousand dollars to build a library on the town green. Addams had settled in Chicago after the war, and there, it seemed, he had invented, or perfected, or anyway improved a kind of rivet that came to be widely used in steel construction, as, for example, in framing the new skyscrapers that were then being put up in cities all across the land. Pliny Addams was rich and he was old, and he remembered—or said he did—how in Ambrose in days now long past his boy's mind had thirsted after books and had drunk not, the town in his youth having no library. Pliny Addams would remedy that now, fifty years on, by the stroke of his pen.

The library was built that same year. It was dedicated at Old Home Week the following summer. Pliny Addams had sprung for a firm of architects from Boston, and the library was a handsome edifice of red brick, with marble facings that looked a little like a bank. The dedication had been planned as the climax of Old Home Week. A dais had been put up in front of the new library, speeches had been written and rehearsed, a band laid on, programs printed. Unfortunately, the event did not go off well, for when the cloth was ceremoniously removed from before the library's doors, it was found that the marble lintel above them had been inscribed.

ADAMS LIBRARY
1906

Yes, the benefactor's name had been misspelled. It was an easy mistake to have made. Nobody in the town had the least recollection of Pliny Addams, or his family, or their double *d*; the Addamses were a sparse and obscure lot, evidently, and anyway, why couldn't they spell their famous name the way everybody else did?

Certainly the town fathers regretted the error. They aimed to make the thing right. They offered to let Pliny Addams buy his library an edited tablet, but there they struck up against the meaning of the philanthropist's life as lived, rather than as revisited. Pliny Addams was damned if they'd see another cent of his. Screwing things up and then paying out good money to do them over was not the way he had made a fortune in Chicago, and as far as he was concerned, they could all go straight to hell. The town of Ambrose saw him no more. The Adams Library stands and thrives, however. There I have spent many a winter afternoon when my place was too cold to live in, and there this book, if it ever finds a publisher, will, I hope, repose unread forever.

Old Home Week declined as the century wore on and the exiles who had been its protagonists and victims aged and ceased to come back home (or came back for the last time, riding in the baggage car). By well before World War II, the institution was history. The last Old Home Week in Ambrose, Vermont, occurred in 1936. The children of Old Home Week participants didn't care to return to a place they had never known. Nor, in truth, was the institution ever built to last. In the end, Old Home Week was only a play: The old home is not your home, and the life you didn't live is not your life, however you try to make it be.

October 27, 1933. Rain then fair. Temp. 12M 63. With gun to Lincolns. Barn down and house roof off yard grown in. No mowings now. No patrige.

4

"You could come, too, you know, Noon," said Amanda.

"We've talked about that," I said. "I could come. You could not go."

"I can't not go," said Amanda.

"We've talked about that, too," I said.

Well, that was how it went for Amanda and me, the way it has to go, perhaps: You talk and talk about whatever is between you, and then you shut up for a while, and then you talk some more. Eventually, you run out of talk, and then whatever has been going to happen all along happens. In the end, I didn't fight Amanda; on the contrary, I bought her ticket. I watched her go. We Noons know how to part. And, in reality, what else could I do? Had Amanda been a princess in a fairy tale, I could have shut her in a tower, but she wasn't, and I didn't have a tower.

Parked outside the Weed on a warm autumn noon, a yellow Ferrari with New York plates, a little circle of boys admiring it, as boys might have admired, in other times, a prize hog. I mistrusted fancy cars. For a moment, I thought more seekers of Calabrese had arrived, too late, but no.

"Whose is this?" I asked the boys.

"Some guy," said one. "He's inside." The boy bent and looked in the passenger's window. "Cool," he said.

"Is he looking for Carlo?" I asked him.

"He didn't say so," the boy answered. "He asked about you."

I went ahead into the Weed. At the bar sat Goldhammer, ex-soldier of the revolution, ex-saboteur, ex-fugitive, last seen being frog-walked out of these same premises between a couple of U.S. marshals—how many years ago? It was Goldhammer all right, but it was Goldhammer augmented, Goldhammer plus impressive earnings. He was taller, grayer, and far more groomed, with a balding dome from which he pulled his hair back into a little ponytail. Soft shirt with broad blue stripes, soft gray flannel trousers, shiny black loafers, a gold wristwatch that might have represented my earnings for the past decade. Goldhammer had suffered a sea change into something rich and strange—or rich anyway. Rich for sure.

"Well, well," said Goldhammer, "if it isn't Robert Frost. I thought I'd find you still here."

"Here I am," I said. "I thought you were safely in jail."

"Two years," said Goldhammer.

"Pretty rough, I guess?"

"Not really," said Goldhammer. "There were two other guys from Bronx Science down the hall. We took computer courses. Bad food, though, you have no idea. Really terrible."

"Computer courses?"

"Yeah," said Goldhammer. "What about you? This all looks pretty much the same. You're still up on the hill?"

"Same place," I said.

"I never doubted it," Goldhammer said. "Is that cop still up there? The one from Philly?"

"He moved away," I said.

"I used to worry about him," said Goldhammer. "What about that girl, she worked here? Nice girl, a little heavy. You were screwing her. Amanda. Did you make an honest woman of her?"

"No," I said. "She left, too."

"What about her father? Applegate. Your pal. The village explainer. Don't tell me he left."

"He died," I said.

"Sorry about that," said Goldhammer. "When?"

"Seventy-seven," I said.

"My God," said Goldhammer. "They've all gone, haven't they?"

"No."

"Who's left?" Goldhammer asked.

"Everybody else," I said.

"And you," said Goldhammer.

"And me," I said. "So you're in the computer business now?"

"No," said Goldhammer. "Was. We had a little start-up, you know. In Palo Alto. We spun it off two years ago. I moved back to the Sagaponak place. I've got some downtime, I thought I'd drive up here, look the old neighborhood over. That's my ride out front, that Ferrari."

"I saw it," I said. "What are you doing, now?"

"Banking," said Goldhammer.

"What about the revolution?"

"What about it?" said Goldhammer. "It's still there. Look: I'm the same as I always was, I'm just doing a different thing."

"But you joined the middle class," I said.

"Never," said Goldhammer. "I joined the upper class."

September 8, 1945. Cool. Temp. 12M 53. Fair p.m. Red leaves

"She says she'll be back," I said.

"I doubt it," said Miss Drumheller. "They don't come back, once they go, not to stay. Why would they?"

"She came back once," I said. "She can come back again."

"Don't count on it," said Miss Drumheller. "Don't count on it, and don't be downhearted. There's always another pebble on the beach, you know."

I said nothing.

"No, really," Miss Drumheller went on. "You're not a bad-looking young man at all. You're reasonably intelligent, well-spoken. You're not a drunkard or a madman. If you'd only move out of that hovel and get a real job, you'd be a perfectly decent prospect for any girl—well, for any girl in a place like this."

"Thank you," I said.

Miss Drumheller was sincere, I knew. She liked me and wished me well, always. Of course she did. My romantic and sexual life has not been busy, I know; it has not been a tale of much color or adventure. But with women in their late seventies, women in their eighties, I have always been dangerous.

"No," said Miss Drumheller, "she's gone. You'll see. When are you leaving, I wonder?"

"I'm not," I said. "When are you?"

"I'm not, either," said Miss Drumheller.

August 9, 1907. Warm. Temp. 12M 81. W. Emerson stopd. Had place up hill went west 71. Did I rember. No. He hired N. Groom to drive him from vilage $5!

August 10, 1907. Temp. 6 a.m. 64. Rain p.m.

We buried Mr. Applegate at ten on Saturday morning, bright and early, so as to leave the church free for a wedding at one. The late-autumn morning fog had burned off, and in the sky a belated flight of geese passed high overhead toward the south. Their cries came down to us clearly and mingled with the words of the graveside service.

"Unto Almighty God we commend the soul of our brother departed, and we commit his body to the ground; earth to earth, ashes to ashes, dust to dust," said the minister.

Honk, honk, honk-honk, honk, said the geese.

Mr. Applegate had a pretty good turnout, maybe a hundred. They filled the front of the church, and after the service there, most of them drove the quarter mile to where the little hillside cemetery looked down at the back of the village. Fallen leaves brown and faded, dry, covered the ground thickly, and the people kicked and rustled through them going up to Mr. Applegate's grave and then coming back down when everything was over.

Amanda, Errol Burgoyne, and I were about the last to leave the cemetery. Coming down through the leaves, Amanda took my arm. She was composed, her face a little drawn, so you began to see what she might look like as an older woman. She was to leave town on Monday.

Amanda, Errol, and I went out the gate of the cemetery and stood by our cars. Errol loosened his tie. I loosened mine.

"Well," said Errol Burgoyne.

"Well," I said.

"Well," said Amanda.

TOWN OF AMBROSE, VERMONT, PATTERNS OF RESIDENCE AND EMIGRATION OVER EIGHTY YEARS

CENSUS	AMBROSE, VT. RESIDENT POPULATION	AMBROSE, VT.: NATIVE RESIDENT IN OTHER STATES*
1850	1,417	449
1870	1,113	683
1900	905	591
1930	662	392

**Old Home Weeks in a Hill Town*, compiled for the Ambrose, Vermont, Historical Society, 1949.

25. Biography

1

Let me introduce myself. With Mr. Applegate gone, and Amanda gone, and so many others gone, and having run out of local history (well, not entirely), I don't seem to have much choice. I find myself peeled right down to my socks: the last of the Noons.

Royalty, ancient royalty, that's what the Noons are—or the Noones, Nunns, Newns: They're all the same bunch. Descended from Scottish kings, as the world knows, but descended, sadly, rather a long way, to the point of having been forcibly removed from their Highland hovels by the English Tudors in the time of Shakespeare and settled in other, equally mean hovels in Ulster, where they were to replace the dispossessed and troublesome Irish. It was a harsh deal for the Irish, an English deal, and a not much better one for their successors, few of whom prospered in the new old country. Nevertheless, my people seem to have stuck it out in the County Down, or Antrim, or Tyrone, or wherever you please, for a good two hundred years. We Noons are slow learners.

Sometime before the American Revolution, a Noon crossed to

Virginia, probably as an indentured servant, like the rest of the inheritors of the Scottish kings. Succeeding Noons spread west by north, leaving—or not leaving—paradoxical traces, obscure but pointed. In the northern Adirondacks, for example, not far from Lake Placid, there is a middling peak called Noonmark Mountain (3,556 feet). I happened on it not long ago in an article in the *National Geographic.* It gave me a turn, I can tell you. That's a funny name, I said, for a mountain. By the map, Noonmark looked like about a three-hour shot from Bible Hill. I thought I'd drive right over. Then I thought I wouldn't.

My own line of Noons emerges from the primal swamp of genealogy in the person of Francis Noon, a saddle maker in Greene County, Pennsylvania, my great-great-great-grand-father, born in 1799. Over the next century, his offspring apparently made Greene County too hot to hold them, probably not much of a feat. In any case, the Noons of that ilk wound up in Bay City, Michigan, where my father was born in 1911, the same year as Mr. Applegate.

You have, therefore, good, hardy, dead-center middle-class stock aspiring fitfully to lower-upper-middle: an honest, useful family unadorned by famous names (always excepting the Scottish kings). My mother's family bore the brighter arms. She was an Austin from Illinois and supposed to be related to the Grants. Mine were strong Union people on both sides, undoubtedly. There was a tradition in the family that one of my mother's great-uncles was the youngest enlisted man in the Union army. He joined up at thirteen. We Noons know how to answer when the trumpet sounds.

October 31, 1959. Fair. Temp. 12M 51. Boys put privvy over last night

I wondered more than once whether Littlejohn was my ghost or I was his; whether I was living his life over again or he had lived mine already. A couple of times every year, and invariably at Halloween, I would find my mailbox knocked over, my trash cans emptied across the yard and hoisted up into the trees, the trees themselves swagged and swooped with toilet paper. I thought I knew who did it: the Scotts' boy from over on the way to Dead River and two or three of his delinquent pals. I'd see them walking along the road around dusk as I drove home from work, and I'd know I was in for some witty damage that night; those boys never by any chance went anywhere on foot unless they were bent on vandalism. To see them abroad out of an automobile meant one thing.

"Don't they come to your house?" I asked Miss Drumheller.

"Not anymore," she said. "One year, they knocked my mailbox down. I was at the Scotts' front door before eight the next morning. I had a state police trooper with me. I haven't had any trouble since. Neither would you, if you'd do what I did."

"I don't really know it's Kevin Scott, though," I said. "I haven't caught him at anything."

"Neither had I," said Miss Drumheller. "I didn't have to. I called the state police anyway. The word got out. You should do the same, next time."

"I don't know," I said. "Kevin seems like a nice-enough kid, for the most part. He works at Jordan's, weekends and summers."

"I know he does," said Miss Drumheller. "What of it? He's a vile, poisonous little moron. You aren't doing him any favor by ignoring this, you know."

"I'd feel like a fool calling in the police for something like that," I said.

"You're a fool if you don't," said Miss Drumheller.

Well, maybe she was right, but I let it go. I allowed the children, the grandchildren of Littlejohn's tormentors to do their damndest—I'd seen worse in my time, hadn't I? In fact, I was in some ways comforted by the shadow Littlejohn's life threw upon my own. And if, after Amanda took off I found my thoughts began to stick on the parallel between Littlejohn and me more than seemed healthy, I'd drive down to the Weed, order a beer, and watch the TV for a couple of hours. I always felt better for it. TV belonged to my life, not Littlejohn's.

November 1, 1959. Cold. Temp. 6 a.m. 29. Privvy over agen sick of this

I am on Bible Hill today because many years ago in the late fall, Hugo Usher went up into the woods on Round Mountain and was never seen again. He vanished. In time, he was given up for dead. His will was read, and in it was found, a little to the probate court's surprise, no doubt—my name. I am Usher's legatee.

I am Usher's legatee, though I never knew him, never saw him. He disappeared some years before I had ever heard of Bible Hill. The day Usher vanished on Round Mountain was a Friday. It was quite a day in this town, quite a day, as it was elsewhere. Whoever you are, wherever, if you were alive and past infancy on that day, you remember where you were and what you were doing, and you remember with a clarity and detail quite unlike your other memories of that many years ago. The twenty-second of November 1963. It has become an oddly luminous day. Not every generation gets to have such days, perhaps, and perhaps generations lacking them are fortunate, for these brightly lit days are days history has stolen from us. They are never good days.

Mr. Applegate told me about that day more than once. It is the nature of such days to be recounted, as if by telling them over and over, we try to reclaim them for our own lives and take them back from history.

Usher, that morning, was to have met with the town selectmen and the road commissioner at a little timber bridge on his property, a bridge that he claimed the road crew's heavy trucks had damaged. Mr. Applegate was a selectman at the time. He waited with the others at Usher's bridge. Usher didn't turn up. The others went to his house. No one was there, and Usher's truck was gone. The selectmen and the commissioner gave it up, and Mr. Applegate returned to his office. On the way, he stopped at the post office, and there he met Arthur Brackett, who said he'd seen Usher's truck parked at the end of the old road up Round Mountain. Was he hunting?

Mr. Applegate didn't like it. He went on to his office, called Errol Burgoyne, explained how Usher's truck was up in the woods, no sign of Usher. Errol didn't like it, either.

By now, it's noon. Mr. Applegate and Errol Burgoyne decide to have lunch, try to get a little more work done, then drive up Round Mountain. Suppose Usher's truck is still there—they'll see if they can't raise him, beep his horn, shout out his name, call him out of the woods. They live at opposite ends of the township, Errol and Mr. Applegate, so they determine they'll drive to Round Mountain separately and meet at Usher's truck about two o'clock, supposing Usher hasn't turned up by then.

Mr. Applegate gets there first, right at two. He finds Usher's truck, pulled over into the brush. He parks behind it, walks down the rutted, abandoned road ahead, walks into the woods. He doesn't shout out Usher's name. He doesn't beep his horn. He doesn't want to hear the noise. Not more than half a mile from this spot, on another day in November, another boy died in a loud noise. It has cost Mr. Applegate to come out here today. He doesn't make a sound. And, in any case, he knows calling would be useless. Usher wouldn't hear him calling. Mr. Applegate understands he won't find Usher on Round Mountain: it's too big, it's too wild, it's too dark. If Usher is up there, he's gone.

Mr. Applegate turned and walked back out of the woods, toward the vehicles. He found Errol Burgoyne's Buick pulled up behind his truck and Errol sitting in it. Why was he just sitting there? Mr. Applegate couldn't understand why Errol hadn't left his car. Errol sits in it with the engine running and the radio on. He was listening to the radio.

2

November 2, 1959. Rain. Temp. 12M 45. Sat up til 1 a.m.
No boys. Privvy ok. They mean no harm but why

I have a picture. It's a small photograph, black and white, three by five inches, with a deckle-edged border, the kind of photo you took years ago with a two-dollar Kodak camera. It shows a man in a white uniform holding a new baby wrapped in a blanket. Behind them, a long, low building with little porches or stoops at intervals receding in perspective. The man is smiling at the camera, but you can't tell what he looks like because his eyes are shaded by his hat, an officer's peaked cap. The baby looks like a baby. On the back of the photo, in soft pencil, is written "Mark & Dad/L.B. Jan. 8, 1945." The photo was taken in Long Beach, then a navy town twenty miles down the coast from Los Angeles.

The officer in the picture is my father, Lt. (jg) Trevor Noon, USN; the baby is I. So at least I have always believed, though for no reason other than maternal testimony. How do you know that man's your daddy? Because your mama told you so. There was no one else to tell me, for I had no brothers or sisters, no grandparents within hail at the time, and, presently, no father. On the same day that picture was made, my father shipped out from Long Beach to the Pacific, where he died. I am a war orphan, the real thing—or half a one, anyway, which is close enough.

My father's vessel was the tender *Sheldon P. Jones*. I don't know who Jones was. The *Jones* was not a fighting ship. It was a stores and supplies carrier, and it served from time to time as a hospital ship. In late 1944 and early '45, it plied the seas among the Pacific islands where the war went on, strategic islands, hideous little islands that would seem to have soaked up so much blood so quickly, you wonder they didn't dissolve like sugar cubes and turn the ocean pink.

My father was far from being a navy man by career. He was a sports reporter on the *Detroit Free Press*. He joined the navy late in 1942, and because he was married, comparatively old (thirty-one), and had a college education, he was trained as an officer, commissioned, and sent to California to join his ship. So we all three went out: Lieutenant (jg) Noon; Penelope A. Noon, his wife; and myself (*in utero*). My father joined the crew of the *Sheldon P. Jones,* then being refitted and prepared for sea. We lived in married officers' housing on the base at Long Beach, where I was born in January 1945. Three months later, my father was killed. Not in action: He went overboard during a storm at sea. My mother took me back east to live with her parents in Chicago.

Stayed behind/Gone before read Littlejohn's cryptic epitaph in the Bible Hill cemetery; nobody knew why. It was one of the small mysteries of the neighborhood's past—the inscription, not the stone. There was no mystery about the stone. The stone had been placed by charity. Littlejohn had died penniless: No stone was coming from him. None was wanted.

"Claude?" Mr. Applegate told me once. "Claude? Hell, Claude had nothing to do with it. You know what one of those granite markers costs? Claude didn't have a dime. Not that he cared. 'Stone?' said Claude. 'What for? Time comes, just put me over the bank, see? Just take me to the dump.' Claude wasn't what you'd call sentimental on the score of memorials."

"So where did his stone come from?" I asked Mr. Applegate.

"Us. Errol, Hugo Usher, Tubby, me, Tris Rand, Bob Gorsuch, a couple of others. It didn't seem right to us Claude shouldn't have any stone at all. He'd been up here, you know, all our lives. He was one of the landmarks, you might say. So we chipped in on a stone for him. God, it cost like fury. Something like three hundred bucks for that little slab. From a place in Brattleboro. Those guys are on to a good thing, gravestones, you know it? We explained to them it was for a pauper, that we'd have to raise the money among ourselves. Think they cared? No sir. Cash up front."

"Did Miss Drumheller contribute?" I asked him.

"She did. She pissed and moaned about how she had no use at all for Claude, never had had, and she couldn't see why she should help pay for his marker, but in the end, she was in it, yes."

"I bet she had the inscription carved, too," I said.

"I bet she didn't," said Mr. Applegate. "She says not."

"Who, then?"

"I can't tell you, son," said Mr. Applegate. "All I know is, one day in the spring, I don't know, quite a few years after Claude died, I happened to be driving up there—fact is, I was going out to meet the surveyor to draw a map of your place so we could break it out of Hugo's estate. Well, I'm passing the cemetery up there, and there's a truck pulled over and somebody in among the markers doing—you couldn't tell what he was doing—something with a power tool that made just a hell of a screech.

"So I stop and go in there, and here's a guy down working on Claude's marker, old guy I never saw before in my life, wearing an apron, got his tools all laid out on the grass, some kind of electric drill or cutter, ran it off a generator on his truck. He sees me, turns off his cutter. I ask him what in the world he thinks he's doing, but he don't understand. He don't hear me. He's deaf as a stump from using that cutter all day—really, the racket it made was something. I finally get him to understand I'm inquiring as to what the hell he's about, fooling with that stone, and he shows me a work order from the same company in Brattleboro, the monument company, for having these and so words cut into this and such stone in the old Bible Hill cemetery, town of Ambrose—and that's all he knows.

"I called the shop," Mr. Applegate went on. "They said, yes, somebody came in, ordered the work, paid cash. Who was it? How should they know? Paid cash, didn't he? No name on the order. Man or woman? Old or young? They didn't know. It seems whoever I was talking to wasn't who took the order; whoever took the order was unavailable. So that's it."

"I still bet on Miss Drumheller," I said.

3

From his post of duty on the *Sheldon P. Jones,* my father wrote eleven fat letters to my mother in Long Beach. These letters were eventually lost, but when I was a boy around fifteen, sixteen, I read and reread them. My father, in peacetime, was, as I have explained, a sports reporter, and like every other sports reporter—of that generation at least—he figured he had a touch of the poet, a tart, sardonic touch. The war he described in his letters was no momentous clash of nations in arms, no epic, but a vast comedy of nonsense, boredom, and futility. That was not entirely accurate, perhaps. Although it wasn't a warship, the *Jones* was close enough to several of the Pacific battles to be in harm's way, but of those episodes, my father had nothing to say. Nor were the lurid Pacific sunsets much on his mind, nor the easeful Pacific islands. Instead, he mocked his service: an endless ferrying of toilet paper, toothpaste, hemorrhoidal suppositories, and prophylactics from Honolulu to Saipan.

He wrote about his shipmates, as well, in particular the other junior officer on the *Jones,* a man a little younger than he, a congenial man: Lt. (jg) John Hugo Usher, of Ambrose, Vermont.

Usher and my father hit it off. They were united by what they saw as the imbecility of the *Jones*'s captain and executive officer (whom my father referred to in his letters as "Gertrude" and "Alice," and also by their half-admiring superiority toward its crew, whom they affected to regard as something like wicked children or a lazy, life-loving native population. The Japanese enemy hardly figured. Days were long, nights were hot, and that is a big, big ocean. My father called Usher "The Farmer," or "The Green Mountain Boy," or "Mr. Coolidge." He had a poor picture of New England geography, it seems (in this, I have found, he was like a good many people from his part of the country), for he evidently thought Usher's place in Vermont was quite near the seacoast; he wrote as though Usher lived on lobster and codfish, as though Vermont were a department of Massachusetts or Maine. Maybe Usher led my father astray there, or maybe Usher's New England identity and my father's midwestern obliviousness of its implications were a joke between them, part of their companionship in the long watches on the *Jones.* Or maybe my father knew his map perfectly well and was entertaining my mother with his account of Usher's provenance. I can't say how my father's humor might have gone, for, of course, I never knew him.

Usher was a strange character, in my father's telling, contradictory: a gentleman farmer who didn't farm and was nobody's idea of a gentleman. He was a hardheaded man, a dangerous man in a stud game; but also a man of passion, a kind of romantic, a believer. Usher was physical, a man who could go off half-cocked, a drinking man who, drunk, was willing to fight, unlike my father, who, as drunk as Usher, would talk any kettle down off its boil. (Strong genetic material there: We Noons are born in striped pants.)

Usher was glad of the war, my father wrote. He had been bored with his life at home, where he was in the shadow of a massive father who was very much a local figure. He'd tried college, quit; he'd traveled; he'd tried New York; he'd come home. The day after the Japanese attacked Pearl Harbor, the Farmer was down at the recruiting station when the doors opened. He didn't expect to survive the war, he said, though it remained a question how he was going to find a satisfactory death ferrying toothpaste and the rest of it from Honolulu to Saipan. In the end, Usher didn't find one, but his shipmate did. My father was lost off the *Sheldon P. Jones* on April Fools' Day 1945 somewhere east of Guam, one of the Mariana Islands.

Those are the deepest seas on earth. Full fathom five doesn't begin to say it.

As far as I know, Usher never made any effort after my father's death, or after the war, to communicate with my mother. Living, he had no presence for us except in the small bundle of my father's wartime letters. Evidently, Usher, bored or not, went home and took up his life in Ambrose, and by-and-by, the navy and the *Jones* got to be a long time ago, and so did his comrade, the fast-talking and profane (I'm guessing) Lieutenant (jg) Noon. Maybe Usher had forgotten him, or maybe it was in the nature of another joke, a posthumous one, between them that he put in his will a kicker, a bequest to the widow and survivors of his midwestern shipmate—more than a bequest, a mortmain, an entail, a legacy of land, Green Mountain land, with not a lobster or a cod in sight.

April 10, 1960. Warm. Temp. 12M 67. Shad Blow. O. Applegate here p.m. Says Lambs barn burned last night. Nothing left. Told him how I worked for Lamb haying when 10 lived in barn. 1888

By the time I'm old, I often think, some quantity of my sweat will have soaked into every square foot of ground in this township. Already, there is scarcely a house where I haven't helped my betters carpenter, paint, paper, mason, plumb, or wire; scarcely an acre where I haven't bent to mow, cultivate, weed, chop, or dig. One thing about having low and lousy jobs: You don't have one only; you have a whole string. Another thing about it: You get around the neighborhood.

Ten years ago, the tail end of Hurricane Hugo came over these parts and tore half the roof slates off Mackenzie's big barn at the Four Corners. Imagine the big slates, each one the size of a doormat and weighing five or six pounds, lifting off irresistibly from the barn in that wind and flying away, as crows leave a field: one, then three, then the whole flock.

Mackenzie hired Junior Tavistock to come over, chase down whatever slates could be found unbroken, bring new ones, and put them up. Junior Tavistock hired me to help. Not till Junior and I had the ladders set and were up on the roof did I remember I'd been up there before, in the same place, with Junior's brother Milo, when Mackenzie's slates had been blown away by Hurricane Camille. Twenty years had passed. Now I was there again. How many more times in my life would I find myself astride Mackenzie's barn's roof beam? Not many. Once, before my end? Twice? Never? These moments make your life go fast. They make your life seem so short.

"Are you waiting on me?" asked Junior, "or am I waiting on you? I don't want to be up here all day, you know."

Littlejohn worked his own place, mostly, I guess, but as he never made much out of it, he, too, had to hire himself all over town doing this and that. Once again, as I ditched and delved my way around Ambrose, I was following in his footsteps. Mr. Applegate said Littlejohn had known the town the way he knew his kitchen table and seemed to have total recall for its people, properties, buildings, incidents—even its animals.

"I'd go up to Claude's, the last few years he was alive," Mr. Applegate told me. "By that time, he wasn't getting around too well; he was living mainly in the downstairs. I'd go up there and see him, oh, every week or so. I took Win and Manda with me, when I could get a rope on them. I don't mind telling you I'd generally bring a six-pack or a bottle of something along, too, and I don't mind telling you I'd help Claude dispose of it.

"Claude was like an encyclopedia of this town," Mr. Applegate went on, "but he had what you might call gaps. For instance, he had no idea who our representative to the state legislature was; he didn't know who the congressmen were, or the governor, or even the president. But if I'd mention that, say, I had so-and-so's place listed for sale, Claude would say how in 1895 so-and-so's grandfather had had a trotting horse named Ethan Allen, who won second prize at Mountain Fair. He was a bay; and he had a white blaze. That kind of thing. It was something, what he could recall, going back sixty, seventy years."

Mr. Applegate reflected. "Of course," he said, "you didn't know if any of it was so. Nobody was going to get up and say, no, Claude remembered wrong. Nobody who might have was left. You didn't know. He might have made it all up."

"Did he ever talk about his lady friend, Sibyl?" I asked Mr. Applegate.

"Who?" asked Mr. Applegate.

"I hope you don't think it was I," said Miss Drumheller.

"It had occurred to me," I said.

"Disabuse yourself," she said. "I live on my pension and Social Security. I don't make a habit of charity, especially not to benefit the so-called disadvantaged, most especially not the disadvantaged dead. I prefer eating."

"Who, then?"

"Well," said Miss Drumheller, "I suppose Sibyl would be the logical one. Claude Littlejohn was her connection, her interest—her story, if you like. But I don't believe it. I don't see how Sibyl could have known of Littlejohn's death without my having told her, and I didn't. I hadn't been in touch with her for years. I'm not even sure Sibyl was still living. My guess is your friend Orlando Applegate had the stone carved that way."

"Why?"

"He liked Littlejohn. Visited him, drove him around, helped him—well, hardly helped: got drunk with him, to be accurate. He acted as though he thought Claude Littlejohn was some kind of great man. Especially after his son's death, he spent a good deal of time with Littlejohn. Orlando was probably the only friend Claude Littlejohn ever had. Sad, in a way."

"I don't know," I said. "The lines on the stone: *Stayed behind/Gone before*? That doesn't sound to me as though Mr. Applegate had thought it up. It's an interesting business, isn't it? Epitaphs. The summing up. The expressing of a whole life. Can it be done? You, for example: What shall we carve on your stone?"

"Nothing," said Miss Drumheller. "I won't be needing one. I don't intend to die. I never have. I expect to continue much as I am. It's more likely I'll be making arrangements for you, young man. Not for many years, of course. Or so one can hope. But when the time comes, what will you have for an epitaph? Have you considered?"

"I have," I said. "I want that old one. You know it: *If you seek his monument, look about you.*"

"My," said Miss Drumheller. "Very grand. And let me see: five, six, seven—no, eight words. That one is going to cost you."

One of our authors today writes somewhere that he took up religion to give himself a place to go on Sunday morning, when the post office is closed. You're a fool to live for the mail, but he did; every writer does, and I did, too. I waited for letters from Amanda, and I got some. She found she didn't get on with her cousins in Chillicothe. She moved on. Cleveland saw Amanda, and Dayton. From Dayton, she wrote that she had found work tending bar, once again, but at a place a bit higher up the bean stalk than the Weed I gathered. I didn't like that. Everybody falls in love with his barmaid; it's like the psychoanalytic transference. It happened to me. It could happen to some boy wonder in Ohio, to many boy wonders. Evidently, it didn't. Amanda kept moving. She tried Indianapolis, then Milwaukee, then St. Paul. She gave no sign of considering a return home, but neither did she settle. Amanda signed her letters with love. I tried to interpret that little word. I held it up to the light and inspected it from different sides. I didn't get far.

I also heard from Calabrese—once. Not from Italy, where he'd said he was escaping to; Calabrese had gone home. A postcard: Independence Hall, Philadelphia—the famous belfry, the famous red-brick front. On the other side, a short message:

> Greetings from City of Brotherly Love. Back on the force. Three years to pension. Why fight it? Have a little apt. in Upper Darby. NO DOGS ALLOWED (ha, ha!). Couch for you anytime. Come on down.
>
> C. C.

His place on Bible Hill remained unsold. Nobody wanted twenty acres with a crudely fixed-up sugarhouse, no well, no electricity, at the end of a bad road. Calabrese's cabin stood empty. The Scott boy and his friends worked on it. They kicked down the door. They broke the windows. They pissed in the kitchen. Once they evidently tried to build a campfire in the middle of the floor, but it went out before the place burned down. When aerosol cans of paint became fashionable among the young, they wrote on Calabrese's front door:

FUCK YOU BOB.

No water, no electric, bad road, a certain odor, and wall art like that do not give your real estate a favorable position for sale. As Mr. Applegate used to say, a place like that, you need to wait for the right buyer. The right buyer will come along if you wait. It may not always be so, but in the case of Calabrese's property, he was right. A couple of years ago, I bought the place myself for the unpaid taxes.

4

We come to childhood and youth, unfortunately. We will not linger. It's a dim stretch, mere business, nothing we haven't seen before in other lives, in our own lives—a good spot to slip out for a smoke and some popcorn.

My widowed mother, Penelope, brought me back east and moved in with with her parents in Chicago. There was little money. My mother had to support us. She took a job as a secretary in the offices of a law firm in the Loop. When I was six, she married one of her lawyers, a nice guy, a graduate of Princeton, a fly fisherman, Bill Templeton, my stepfather. Bill must be near eighty today. He lives in Arizona. I hear from him at Christmas. My mother died when she and Bill had been married almost twenty years. She had cancer.

I went to grade school and high school in Chicago, a big town, a good town, but a town I'm afraid I never really got. I came out alive, however, and with high school, you shouldn't ask for more.

I went on to the University of Michigan, in Ann Arbor, my late father's school, an extraordinary place at the time, not Mr. Jefferson's academical village, but something like it—a kind of academic Babylon. Imagine the famous floating island of scholars, scientists, and philosophers in *Gulliver's Travels,* but imagine it with a football team, a couple of dozen fraternities going full bore seven days a week, and draft beer at ten cents.

I bloomed in Ann Arbor, but I bloomed unseen. Through its streets and lecture halls, for four years, I moved purposeful but unremarked, like a secret agent. The world knew me not, for in Ann Arbor I found at last my talisman, my magic sword: *The Norton Anthology of English Literature.* Know it backward and forward, I thought, and you'll know—what, exactly? Hard to say, but I packed the *Norton Anthology* with me when I moved on, and I pack it yet. We Noons learn slowly, but we learn for good.

I'd go in for the scholar's life, I thought: the master of arts, the doctor of philosophy, the fellowships, and the rest. Lousy pay, but easy work, plenty of time off, they won't draft you, and you'll have *The Norton Anthology* always by your side. It looked good. It wasn't. I found very quickly that in the university as it was professionally constituted, I had walked into the wrong bar. They hustled me into the men's room, knocked me out, took my wallet, and pitched me unconscious into the alley. I awoke in another country, another hemisphere, opened my eyes on the Southern Cross. I aimed to be hard to find, down there, and I was—hard to find, but not too hard for Mr. Applegate, who, as I have related, reached me on the telephone:

Is that Noon? Mark Noon?

Yes.

There you are, son. You are a hard young fella to get ahold of, you know that?

So the circle, if it was a circle, closed.

. . .

An article in the news recently tells of an ancient tortoise living on the island of Pinta, one of the Galápagos. There is a photo of the thing: It's the size and probably more than the weight of a large barrel stove, with awkward legs like tree trunks, a corded neck, and a sleepy, irritable eye, much clouded by age, that might belong to a veteran of World War I. The tortoise is a male. Nobody knows how old it is. It was found twenty-five years ago and is the only tortoise of its kind on the island; it is, therefore, the last representative of its particular subspecies in existence.

A group of scientists from Yale have taken the tortoise in hand. They aim to find a mate for it so it can reproduce and its race be saved from extinction. But the tortoise won't cooperate. Yale flies in female tortoises from all over the Galápagos, from all over the equatorial Pacific, females in no visible way unlike the solitary bachelor on Pinta. He ignores them. For twenty-five years, he's been celibate, and yet, when a suitable female is proposed, he prefers not to.

I know exactly how he feels: He's going down the road alone, and, no, he doesn't like it, but he's choosy. He's waiting for the right girl, the right curve of shell and touch of leather flesh, the right mole beside the collarbone—if tortoises have collarbones, if they have moles. He won't be hurried. He knows what he wants. He can wait till it's right. And if he has to wait, alone on his island, for another twenty-five years, for another hundred years, well, time is what he has. Time is all he has. If you ask him, he'll sing you his song. It's an old one from the Motor City. It's not in *The Norton Anthology of English Literature,* but it should be. Listen, Amanda, it goes like this: *You can't hurry love.*

June 2, 1961. Fair. Fair. Temp 12M 72. Lilac. Swallows. Swallow got stuck in attic. Went up to let it out. Looked in trunk found S.B ribon. It still smells of her

Well, the years come and the years go and things change. They go forward, but they don't go back. Though regret is vain and missing things is futile, still I remember my friend Mr. Applegate, my native guide, my savage tutor, half man, half beast, who showed me that I need no longer be a visitor in my own life.

26. Mr. Usher Enters Heaven

Usher arrived in the capital in the early morning. He came on the ferry that crossed the strait from the big island. Nobody met him. He stepped down onto the quay and looked around him: ragged palms; white buildings, deep galleries; the great brown church, before it the statue of the Liberator; in the distance, the dry mountains.

What a hole, thought Usher. What a place to end up.

He observed that the statue of the Liberator was hung with a black pall, and its base was strewn with flowers, ribbons, bits of colored paper. The whole world was in mourning for the fallen leader far to the north. The capital, an insignificant port of an insignificant coast where bananas changed ownership, was in mourning for him, too. Usher found a hotel on the square. The windows looking onto the plaza were decorated with pictures of the martyred president.

"What do they care?" asked Usher.

"Oh, he was very popular down here," said Hitchcock. "Not sure why, really. They hate gringos, as a rule. They hate me. They'll hate you. One gets used to it."

"You?" asked Hitchcock. "You're in charge here?"

"Actually, yes," said Hitchcock.

"You're a kid," said Usher. "How long have you been here?"

"Quite a long time, in fact," said Hitchcock. "It's not a post where the rota turns over very quickly. Quiet place, really. It's a poor country."

"It's a hellhole," said Usher. "What do you do all day?"

"I'm in the nature of an instructor, if you like, a mentor. For new people," said Hitchcock.

"A mentor?" Usher said. He was beginning to enjoy himself. "Do I look to you like someone who needs a mentor?"

"Everybody needs a mentor," said Hitchcock.

"In hell," said Usher.

"Oh, dear," said Hitchcock. "Well, of course, you'll have a good deal of latitude, of discretion. You acclimate. You sort of take the place in through your skin. Like a frog, if you understand me."

"Perfectly," said Usher. "I understand you perfectly, old sport."

"You'll take it in—or you won't," said Hitchcock. "There are those who never do."

"You're talking about that kid," said Usher. "That kid couldn't find his ass with both hands."

"You're not far wrong, I'm afraid," said Hitchcock. "I'm reminded of the time he spent the quarter's budget on some kind of meaningless World War Two surplus. I'm still hearing about that."

"A goddamned fool," said Usher. "His father was another."

"What about a drink?" Hitchcock suggested.

Usher and Hitchcock sat on the long veranda at Hitchcock's club. Soon it would be Usher's club, too. In reality, it already was. Their feet were up on the railing. They watched the shadows of the headland advance across the harbor, across the town. They watched the lights come on. They were drinking rum.

"What is this filthy stuff?" Usher asked.

"Wine of the country," said Hitchcock. "One gets used to it."

"You said that before," said Usher.

"Did I?" Hitchcock asked. "I suppose I did. Well, it's so."

Hitchcock was thoughtful. The rum was moving in on him; it was moving in on them both, just as the night moved toward them over the water, over the town.

"It's a terrible thing," said Hitchcock. "It's almost unbelievable, really, isn't it? Who imagined, in this day and age, that someone could simply get a rifle and sit in a window and shoot down the president? Who could have imagined that?"

"Who imagined anything else?" said Usher. The rum made him silent. "And who cares?" he asked. "One less Democrat."

"Oh, really now," said Hitchcock. "What about another drink?"

"That kid?" Usher asked.

"Yes?"

"What happened to him, in the end?"

"What happened to him? Surely you'd know. He's up your way, isn't he? Some little town up there?"

"Oh."

"Good luck to him, I say," Hitchcock concluded. "Better him than me. He than I. Another drink, did you say? By all means."

"Good luck to him," said Usher. But he thought, What a place to end up. What a long way from home.